Ginny left a l bread on the table for Kathleen and ambled outside with the laundry basket. Handling the steaming wet clothing today was a loathsome chore, and she moved sluggishly. The job routinely took an hour. But this hellish morning, the effort commanded twice the time. Laying the clothing to dry usually evoked a feeling of satisfaction. Yet, with temperatures nearing one hundred degrees, completion of the task elicited little comfort. She gripped the cauldron and tipped the soapy water to smother the fire.

A braying bear cub sprinted past the barn.

Close behind, a second cub and its mother followed, undistinguishable against the sky, now as black as their eyes, snouts, and fur.

The cauldron fell from her hands and thudded to the dehydrated earth, sounding an eerie moan as it rolled into the ebbing fire.

"Kathleen," Ginny howled.

Her words were broken apart by the strength of the wind whipping her skirts and blowing the laundry off the maple limbs. "Kathleen," she screamed. She lifted her skirt and tripped across debris dumped by cyclonic winds. "Kathleen." Ginny's shriek vied with the wind's cacophony.

Praise for Carol Nickles

"Like its heroine, seamstress Ginny Dahlke, THUMB FIRE DESIRE deftly pulls together threads of Michigan's history, Native and immigrant cultures, and natural beauty. Meticulous research, poetic passages, and touches of humor enhance this engaging story."

~Nan Sanders Pokerwinski, memoir author

~*~

"Having been raised attending St. Mary's Church in Parisville, Michigan, I "recognized" the community and the families with great fondness and worried about who would survive the great 1881 fire."

~Anita Gliniecki, President Emeritus, Housatonic Community College

~*~

"A compelling, nail-biting read of life of the very first Polish settlers in Michigan's Thumb."

~Roger Laske, Polish Genealogical Society of Michigan Board Member

~*~

"Nickles's story, following the Civil War, is full of things plain and rich: love and work, fire and disaster, the author's forebears, black kid shoes from Bloomingdale's Department Store on the Lower East Side of New York and a genuine Chesapeake Bay Ducking Dog. Nickles joins the Midwestern women writers—Angela Flournoy, Lorrie Moore, Ling Ma—who remember and recreate the life and loss of that time."

~John Crowley, fantasy, science and historical author

Thumb Fire Desire

by

Carol Nickles

Thumb Fire Desire

Cover Art by *Diana Carlile*

The Wild Rose Press, Inc.
PO Box 708
Adams Basin, NY 14410-0708
Visit us at www.thewildrosepress.com

Publishing History
First Edition, 2022
Trade Paperback ISBN 978-1-5092-4198-9
Digital ISBN 978-1-5092-4199-6

Published in the United States of America

Dedication

Virginia is the name of the heroine in this story.
In my life, there have been two women with
the same first name who are heroines:
Virginia Dahlke Nickles, my mother-in-law,
who modeled inclusive curiosity and acceptance,
and Virginia Brungard Fitzgerald,
who mentored me through doubts and droughts and
celebrated the bounties of perseverance and creativity.

~

And to my artist mother, Marjorie Sheridan Andreae,
who read to me.

Prologue

To chronicle a story with a Michigan setting, Michiganders hold their left hand aloft, palm facing outward, thumb on the right. Any locale in the Lower Peninsula can be illustrated by emphasizing fingertips, knuckles, the back of the hand, or, as in the case of this story, by stretching out the thumb. On a map, Michigan's thumb is an extended peninsula that juts northward into Lake Huron, one of the largest of the Great Lakes.

On September 5, 1881, a series of fires whipped together by a cyclonic north wind annihilated the tract of land embodied by the thumbnail. More than two thousand square miles burned in the conflagration known as the Great Thumb Fire of 1881, the state's most significant natural disaster. Two hundred eighty-two people died. Eleven villages and one thousand one hundred and forty-seven pioneer homes were heavily damaged or destroyed. Countless livestock, forest mammals, fish, and fauna succumbed to this unimpeded tragedy.

To tell a tale of the beginning of the American Red Cross, historians raise their left hands. They say this region, indicating the thumbnail, witnessed the first national relief effort of the organization founded by Clara Barton in response to the Great Thumb Fire of 1881.

To tell a tale of their United States beginnings, Americans of Polish descent also use their left hand to disclose their story. Parisville, Michigan, in the middle of the thumb, is one of the earliest Polish American settlements, established in the 1850s.

To tell the story of textile manufacturing in the state of Michigan, business historians point to Yale, Michigan—formerly known as Brockway Centre, in Michigan's thumb, forty-seven miles directly south of Parisville. On the banks of Mill Creek, the state's longest-lasting full-production woolen mill existed from 1881 to 1963, founded by a German immigrant, Charles Andreae.

To tell the tale of their peoples, the Anishinaabe Three Fires Confederacy of Ojibway, Odawa, and Potawatomi raise their left hands. They respectfully point to the thumb to show the location of Ezhibiigaadek Asin, a forty-foot-long, twenty-foot-wide sandstone marked with one hundred three etchings. Ezhibiigaadek Asin has great spiritual significance to the indigenous peoples of Michigan. They see the carved symbols as teachings from Gichi-manidoo, their creator.

Though known for centuries through the oral history of Michigan's native peoples, this great rock was concealed by layers of overgrown foliage until the Great Thumb Fire of 1881. This rock is as relevant to the Anishinaabe people today as it was hundreds of years ago and has the recognition of encompassing the only known petroglyphs in the state. Located at 8251 Germania Road, Cass City in Greenleaf Township, this narrative sandstone resides in the two hundred forty acre Sanilac Petroglyphs Historic State Park and is on the National Register of Historic Places.

A hand, a rock, a cross, a fire, and a woolen fleece all endure as significant symbols that merge in this history of Michigan's thumb.

Chapter 1

Michigan's Thumb, April 1881

Ginny Dahlke squeezed the cap rail of the mahogany bench ahead of her. Vibrations from the train braking rocked her shoulders forward and then back. Reaching under her seat on the Port Huron and Northwestern train, she spread her trembling fingers, registering the wicker basket's spiny texture, the coarse woolen cover, and the rhythmic rise and fall between basket and blanket. Ginny retracted her hand, leaned back, and sighed. They would be home free at the next stop.

Train doors opened, ushering in locomotive smoke, chill air, eye-shuttering sunshine, and onboarding passengers. A wrought iron birdcage—with a pair of girl's high-topped boots below it, and a pair of small-gloved hands grasping it—led the parade squeezing through the northbound train's narrow aisleway. Trapped in their enclosure, two golden finches darted, flinging seed from tin trays and jingling the bell dangling from a basilica-shaped dome top. Their black-tipped wings and waxy orange feet created an aviary kaleidoscope. Their exaggerated chittering disrupted dozing passengers' dreams.

Ginny stiffened her spine against the wooden seat, wishing the bowed bench would fuse her a new backbone. Warmth drained from her body. Providence had been hers since she boarded in Dansville, New York, but Ginny's luck ended as a chorded whistle blew, signaling the train's departure from the station in Croswell, Michigan.

The imprisoned finches advanced.

Jesus, Mary, Joseph, and St. Anthony, please keep our secret safe. Ginny thrust her hands under her seat.

Chessie barked. Not once, not twice, but three times.

She snatched the puppy from the basket at her feet. "Chessie." She clamped his jaws and nestled him to her lamb's wool cape. His baby heartbeat thrummed against her neck. But her attempts to avert exposure were too late.

"Conductor."

A shrill voice rent the air.

A slack-jawed fur-collared woman, backing the pigtailed birdcage transporter, wobbled sideways and jabbed a finger toward Ginny.

"Ma'am," a Port Huron and Northwestern official responded, doffing his peaked cap.

"There's trouble. Take care of it. Now."

Acid bile spewed in Ginny's throat. She gagged. Outside her window, an infinite backdrop of leafing maples, oaks, hemlocks, poplars, and papery birches fronted massive conifers so thick she'd never find her way through. How many miles might she be walking to Parisville, Michigan?

"Sir, if it's a question of an additional fare, I will pay." A man rose from a seat at the front of the train.

He resembled the soapstone carving that weathered in Auntie Valentine's garden. But instead of moss, white whiskers masked this man's face. The quirky smile, however, was the same. With all his bulk, the statue lookalike stepped into the aisleway, blocking the conductor's forward movements and every neck-stretching passenger's view.

"Young woman," the man called to Ginny, "Where are you departing?"

"Adam's Corner." Ginny's throat cinched, allowing only a tiny squeak.

The large man pawed at his ear, raised his eyebrows, lifted his bristly chin, and lingered to the visible disdain of cargo-laden passengers.

Ginny cleared her throat and tried again, but the chaos surrounding her, the juddering of water pouring into the train's tender, the hiss of steam, children mimicking finch calls, and a stowaway puppy whimpering in protest to her tight hold shrunk her voice.

"I think she said, 'Adam's Corner,' sir."

The voice, delivered in elocution reflecting private east coast schools and a home that modeled proper pronunciation, came from one of the head-to-toe garbed-in-black Catholic nuns sitting in the row ahead. Ginny ventured a look at the stalwart man commandeering the aisle. He had eyes that held the quality of kindness she left behind in the Lady's Circle with whom she ripped and rolled cotton strips, fashioning bandages every Wednesday afternoon at St. Paul's Lutheran Church.

Extracting a fob watch from a back pocket, the man examined the timepiece's crystal face. He turned to the waiting train official. "Sir, we arrive in Adam's Corner in under an hour. Surely, we can all bear the presence of this innocent puppy until then." Fumbling in a coverall pocket, the man extracted a silver dollar and flipped it palm up in his hand.

Seizing the coin, the conductor snorted and withdrew.

The fur-collared tattletale pressed her lips together and prodded the little girl and the birdcage toward the train's front.

Three short whistles blew.

The train lurched forward.

A cracking noise sounded as Ginny's benefactor dropped onto a bench opposite her. He emanated a musty scent, harkening a related memory of the grotto where Auntie Valentine displayed her statuary. Ginny wrinkled her nose.

Dragging a handkerchief from his sleeve, the man wiped his forehead.

Wetted by perspiration, the cross-stitched words *Love You, Darling* stuck across his flushed face like a layer of plaster of paris. Ginny giggled.

The man folded his arms atop his imposing paunch and sniffed the air. "My name is Martin. Martin Oberski. What's your name?"

"Ginny Dahlke." She exhaled a lungful of bated breath. "I can't thank you enough, Mr. Oberski. Once we reach Adam's Corner, I'll have my brother Joseph repay you. Chessie is a present for him. And Chessie is a genuine Chesapeake Bay Ducking Dog."

"You don't say?" Martin leaned forward, scratching his beard. "And Joseph Dahlke is your brother?"

Ginny nodded.

"I know Joseph," Martin continued. He arched his

furry eyebrows. "Fine young man. My, my, this is the hunting breed I've heard so much about." He reached across the passageway.

Ginny placed the fidgeting puppy into his hands.

Chessie licked Martin's beard, nipped his fingers, and sprawled across his lap, inviting a belly rub.

Martin complied with the enthusiasm of an eight-year-old pet-deprived child. Ginny bent and shook her head.

The puppy shut his eyes and lolled his tongue, all wriggling and jiggling born away by their first Parisville friend's attention.

"Look at this thick coat. The fur is certain to protect him from the cold. Maybe I appear to be just a well-fed farmer." Martin shifted his gaze to Ginny. "But I also like to read, you know, stay on top of the news. I recently saw a letter to the editor in one of my farm magazines. This guy watched a Chesapeake Bay Ducking Dog crack through the ice over the Susquehanna River. He wrote to say what good swimmers this breed is. And here you are, getting your tummy tickled. He twisted Chessie to speak to his face. "Imagine that. Well, little fella, you are perfectly suited to Michigan. Just wait 'til you jump in Lake Huron."

With Chessie settled, Ginny opened her valise and pulled out a book. She set it on her lap and let the pages fall open. She fingered the bookmark holding her place. *Dear Wallace, will I ever see you again*? Wallace, with eyes the color of flax as it flowered and lashes as thick as the Persian lamb jacket hanging on a padded hanger in Mother's lavender-scented closet, had once made exact eye contact with her. Ginny took a breath, lifting her shoulders. She closed her eyes. Wallace hadn't gifted her with the bookmark, but the association was close.

His mother signed his name, next to Clara Barton's, and other members of the Dansville Relief Society, in the copy of *The Adventures of Tom Sawyer*, they gifted Ginny as a going-away remembrance.

"Adam's Corner, Adam's Corner, Michigan, three minutes," the conductor shouted, grabbing alternate seatbacks on his route to the next car.

Ginny closed the book, stowed it in her valise, and righted her hat.

"I'll carry him off the train for you, Ginny," Martin shouted over the three long whistle blasts signaling the train's arrival.

The train slowed, and Ginny froze, scanning the people poised on the platform—ladies garbed in somber skirts and cloaks with disappointedly nondescript bonnets, men homogenous in their appearance of faded overalls, dog-eared boots, and denim shirts. She fiddled with her hat, stroking the royal blue ribbon tied in a bow on her face's right side. The bonnet was her masterwork and garnered high praise from her mentor, Irene Sheridan. It complemented the shirtwaist dress she wore, cut from plaid taffeta, and fashioned in a style to maximize her trivial curves with princess seaming in the bodice and a bustle riding high in the back.

She flexed her feet and hummed. The black kid shoes she wore were a present from Mrs. Sheridan and purchased at Bloomingdale's Department Store in the Lower East Side of New York City. They were the most extravagant items Ginny owned, and she worked diligently at keeping the scuff marks to a minimum and the black grosgrain toe bows crisp. A niggling question returned, and her chest-squeezing respiration resumed. *How will I know Joseph?* A dozen years had passed since he left home, slamming the door so forcefully two screws popped from the casing and wedged in her slippers.

"Final call. Final call. Adam's Corner. Adam's Corner, Michigan," the conductor shouted.

Ginny stood, balanced her valise and a bundle of blankets, and stepped into the aisle, allowing the nuns to queue first.

Martin followed, with Ginny's basket looped over his arm and a squirming Chessie tucked against his side.

With her heart fisted in her throat, Ginny tottered forward, her anticipated first vision of Adam's Corner was blocked by the opaque habits worn by the women exiting ahead of her.

"Watch your step. Watch your step, please," the steward beckoned from his place on the platform, offering his arm to leave-taking passengers.

Ginny stepped down. The heel of her kid leather pump caught in the juncture of the aisle floor and the train ladder's top step. The blankets in her arms dropped onto the backs of the descending nuns. Her valise—weighted with a treasured book collection, conveyed from her father's study, and two pounds of beef jerky wrapped in butcher's paper—whacked the starched veil of the woman who spoke on her behalf.

The target's knees buckled. The nun tumbled face down on the back of her traveling sister.

Ginny toppled next. Mark Twain's bestseller, the Dahlke family Bible, and a cracked leather-bound copy of *Aesop's Fables* fluttered open and sailed into the congregation of the fallen.

From behind them, platform-roosting farmers rushed to retrieve the books, the butcher paper, and the integrity of three ladies.

A man resembling her father's daguerreotype tugged Ginny by the shoulders and plucked her from the rubble. She clasped his neck and crushed her bonnet against his cheek. "Joseph," she whispered, kissing a prickly cheek and whiffing aromatic cedar. She sneezed.

"Ginny, so glad you made it safely, even though the very last step of the journey is a sure-as-hell chance you're going to Purgatory." Her brother laughed, claiming her. "I mean, Ginny, you almost killed some nuns—nuns, for God's sake," he whispered as he tipped his hat to the black-and-white-clad women scurrying to a waiting wagon.

She pressed the palm of one hand on her forehead and ventured a glance at her brother. Both her mother and her father were there: Mother's jade eyes, veined in gold and rimmed in eyelashes so lengthy they often stuck to the inside of her spectacles, Father's hair, thick as hay, and his voice, thick as old Poland, discarding the *th* sound and pronouncing *though* as *dough* and the article *the* as *ad*—"even dough da very last step."

He hugged her so tightly the rise and fall of his chest resonated on her breast.

She wiped a tear from her cheek and fell into step with him.

"You're all grown. What happened to my chubby little sister?"

Ginny snorted and swatted him.

"Nice hat, though." He held her at arm's length,

taking a second look.

She leaned into him. Radiant sun surges, blurring her vision, dimmed in comparison to the bursts of joy filling her heart. She was no longer alone, and her brother would ensure she wouldn't starve.

"Well, lookee here." Martin Oberski gripped Chessie with one arm and the puppy-stowing basket with the other.

"Martin, you old coot. What are you dragging home this time? Does Marta have any idea?" Joseph shook his head.

"This is an honest-to-goodness Chesapeake Bay Ducking Dog, and he just so happens to belong to you." Martin thrust the curly furred puppy into Joseph's arms. "Your sister risked guaranteed passage to bring this fellow, Joseph. You are a lucky man."

"What the hellfire?" Joseph grappled with the squirming puppy, squatted, and set Chessie on the ground.

The puppy ran in figure eights, trotted to a hitching post, lifted his right leg, and peed, spattering the conductor on his spit-shiny striding-to-the-depot boots.

"Chessie." Ginny crouched on one knee and slapped the other.

A burly, thick-necked man with hair sprouting from his open denim collar and his oversized ears shook his head and laughed.

The laugh wasn't friendly or good-natured. His laugh rang with the crudeness associated with knuckleheads, riff-raffs, and manhood's lowest dregs. From her kneeling position, Ginny pursed her lips and cast the man a stink stare.

Uninvited, the riff-raff approached, leaned over,

and scratched Chessie's head.

"Nice boot polishing, fella." He stepped back and tucked his thumbs into his body-hugging jeans' waistband.

Ginny scowled, gathered Chessie in her arms, struggled to rise with no offer of assistance from one of the lowest dregs of manhood, and turned to Joseph.

"What a fine gift, sister." Joseph braced his feet and scooped the puppy from Ginny's stock-still grip. "So, it's Chessie, is it?" He flipped the puppy on his back and rubbed his belly.

The stuffed-into-his-jeans buffoon sauntered over to Joseph and fawned over the puppy she had protected from stiff-faced conductors and fur-collared privilege. Ginny straightened, clenching her hands into fists. This uncouth stranger threatened to spoil the moment when Joseph recognized what a loving sister she was.

"Fine name, don't you think?" Martin leaned heavily on one hip and scratched his head. "Short for training. Well, good luck, fellas, and nice to meet you, Ginny. See you in church, yah? Oh, and Peter, Bette will be expecting you to join us for dinner." Martin pushed his hat low on his head and hurried to the pile of parcels forming at the end of the track.

Joseph and the stranger exchanged a grin.

"That old man collects trinkets like a Polish woman collects recipes." Joseph laughed and shook his head.

"Mr. Oberski, please wait. I owe you a dollar," Ginny called.

Martin shuffled away, advancing his globe of a silhouette backlit by unchecked sunshine.

Ginny fashioned a bullhorn with her hands. "Mr.

Oberski, wait."

Martin raised a hand and affected a dismissive wave.

"Hey, Ginny." Joseph drew her close and turned her toward the stranger. "This is Peter Nickles. Like me, he's just a crazy Parisville Pole. We combined a trip to pick you up with a trip to purchase seed. C'mon."

Doesn't the character of his friends judge a man? What else don't I know about you, Brother? Ginny pursed her lips, scrunched her eyes, and took a deep breath.

She followed Joseph to a wagon brimming with quarter-cut potato pieces, parked parallel to a storefront with the title *Adams Corner General Store* emblazoned in red and outlined in gold paint on the window. The gilded lettering appeared mawkishly out of place with the rough-sawn storefronts lining Main Street.

A man sporting a sparse beard and a leather apron tied twice around his skinny frame motioned to a crew advancing toward the store. All four grunted from their guts and shuffled with their feet as they lugged a boxed crate. A *Montgomery Ward* stamp marked one of the slats.

"Another sure sign of seed planting time—plows arriving." Joseph rolled his shoulders and scratched Chessie's ears.

Peter jumped on the wagon box and fashioned a squared-out section among the sprouting potato wedges.

Joseph handed Chessie to Ginny, and the two men arranged Ginny's trunk, valise, and basket within the square, creating a make-do puppy pen. Chessie yawned, shut his eyes, and once Joseph set him in the improvised cell, he curled up next to Ginny's luggage and fell asleep.

"We'll all have to squash together on the board seat." Joseph set one hand on the side of the wagon, jumped, and landed next to his sister. "First, Ginny, we gotta get you up there."

Peter hopped onto the front of the wagon and held out his hand.

Joseph locked his fingers together, creating a makeshift step.

Ginny wrapped her left arm around Joseph's neck, placed her right foot in his linked finger step, hopped with her left foot, and prayed for grace. With Peter tugging and Joseph boosting, she catapulted into the wagon.

Peter seized her shoulders, righted her stance, and guided her to the middle of the seat, with all the intimacy of arranging a burlap bag ballooned with rutabagas.

Ginny stiffened. She squeezed her eyes shut, her lips together, her elbows to her waist, her thighs together, and her crisp-bowed shoes to the wooden planks below her feet.

Joseph fronted the team and jumped aboard on the driver's side. "Think we'll try taking Purdy Road to Parisville Road and then over to Helena this time. That east stretch of Helena was swampy, and we've got more weight now."

Peter nodded, reached back into the wagon, pulled out a felted hat, and set it on his lap.

The hat was classic Fedora style. The pinch on the crown was diamond-shaped. An embroidered leather band circled the bottom of the crown. The stitching was eye-catching and ornamented by rainbow-hued glass beads, alabaster-lined clamshells, and gray-and-white-striped mollusk husks. The craftsmanship was every bit as lovely as the handiwork she witnessed peering over the shoulders of the nuns as they swayed along the miles of train rail.

Peter held the rim with all ten of his fingers, gripping and releasing and turning it full circle.

He stroked the beadwork using a whisper of his fingertips. The corners of his lips rose as if the hat held love letters addressed *dearest darling* in its bowl. Ginny scowled. *What an oaf, treating his hat with more regard than the lady seated next to him.*

Peter positioned the hat low to his ears' rims.

"Ho, Buster. Ho, Blue." Joseph flipped the reins.

The wagon jolted forward. Potato pieces lifted as a league of marauding grasshoppers. It was dandelion season, and the plants were ubiquitous. Bees lit from one yellow globe to the next. A crimson cardinal soared between tree limbs and hopped along Purdy Road, pausing to stretch a worm from the earth. She craned her neck and drew a deep breath. In his last letter, Joseph had promised her a clean start in a countryside rife with promise and unfettered with what he referred to as "city stink."

Unlike Dansville, New York, the air was fresh in this landscape ten miles inland from Lake Huron's west shore. The scents were piney, grassy, and sweet clover. They were the smells of life beginning anew and a brother's assurance. She filled her lungs. The path was paved with rocks and pitted with holes, and Ginny jostled between her brother and Peter, her thighs bumping against the men.

The men's distinctions were clear. Joseph sported a precision haircut, lacked facial stubble, and smelled of Ivory soap. On the other side, Peter settled for self-inflicted grooming and smelled like the back end of a cow. She wrinkled her nose and turned her face toward her brother.

Joseph angled a sideways gaze. "Comin' up on Helena Road, Sister. Lots of rye and alfalfa fields."

The sun disappeared by an unbroken track of towering hemlocks and cedars.

Shivering, Ginny pulled her cape tighter.

On the edge of the board seat, Peter shifted his backside and craned his neck. "Getting close. Once you see the oak right-angled like a goal post, get ready to turn."

"I know this, Peter. How many times have I been here?" Joseph pulled the slack in the reins and tugged with his right hand. "Gee."

Buster and Blue swung right.

Ginny fell across Peter's lap.

"Not you, girl. That was meant for the horses." Peter shoved her upright.

Ginny bit her lip and gripped the seat, capturing the space made vacant by Peter's left hand. The narrow path to his homestead was undetectable to the road and lined with a motley collection of scrub pines, adolescent black gum, budding dogwood, and mongrel bushes. An undulating meadow of thick grasses spread from the sandy border on the east side of the drive. Bluebirds soared over a plowed field. Ahead was a multi-windowed chicken coop, a barn with a paddock, and a sandy-colored horse bounding and bugling as they approached. Peter's cabin faced south, and the windows framing the door blazed with a solar radiance. Dungarees and union suits dangled from a clothesline bereft of women's pantaloons, skirts, and blouses. A single, pruned rosebush flanked the path to the front doorway in which no wife appeared to welcome him home.

Flicking the reins, Joseph directed Buster and Blue to the left side of a wagon parked outside Peter's barn and adjacent to a water trough. "Whoa."

Peter jumped off, threw open the barn door, and disappeared inside.

Joseph reached for the puppy and lowered him to the ground.

Chessie ran after Peter, and in his wake, chickens squawked and cows lowed.

Ears flat to their heads, a calico cat and a sleek, black kitten darted from the barn.

Barking and yipping, Chessie scampered behind.

Joseph tethered the team and removed their bits, allowing them to drink.

Peter emerged with two shovels and tossed one to Joseph. Both men sprang back on Joseph's wagon and dipped their tools into the pile of seed potatoes.

"Best move, Ginny," Joseph called.

Potato chunks rained behind her. She scrambled down, grimacing as blood circulation flowed, reactivating her dormant feet. Exercising long strides, she followed Chessie's zigzagging lead. Wallace-eye-color blue embraced a landscape transitioning from winter drudgery to spring flourishing. Clouds, virginal in their whiteness and sinuous in their contour, drifted above. Her breath caught in her throat. She extended an arm and twisted her fingers. Wallace's fingers were long and burnished with dark hair. If only he were standing next to her in this field, entwining his fingers with hers.

Chessie raced, his nose aimed into the breeze. His carriage proved sturdy.

His tail sliced the meadow, and Ginny imagined a homesteader wielding a scythe.

Chessie skidded to a halt and barked.

A pheasant rose from the undergrowth, flailed its glossy wings, and shrilled its two-note call.

Ginny gyrated and raised a hand over her eyes as the bird skimmed the grasses. The wagon came into her vision.

Joseph and Peter, their shovels stalled, stood atop Joseph's wagon.

Peter pointed to the pheasant, flying hell-bent across the field.

Nearby, Joseph tossed his hat in the air.

Peter's shoulder butted him.

Their guffaws and adolescent wrestling resonated in Ginny's heart. She had done the right thing.

Joseph formed a megaphone with his hands, "Good Dog, Chessie." He tossed his shovel to Peter and motioned to Ginny with a come-hither swipe. "Finally, on our way home, Sister."

She picked up her skirts and walked gingerly over the muddy field.

Chessie bounced alongside.

Both men hopped off the wagon and repeated the motions of foisting Ginny into the wagon.

The good dog ran to Peter, jumped on his thigh, and received an open-handed head patting.

"This guy goes, too." Peter held Chessie in the crook of his elbow and scratched the puppy's ears. "Go to your missus." He dumped the proven bird detector into Ginny's lap.

Chessie wriggled loose.

In the ensuing tussle, Ginny head-butted Peter's chest.

Peter fumbled his hands in the folds of Ginny's skirt.

She jerked upright. Blood rushed to her cheeks.

"I hope you're not always going to be this much trouble," Joseph mumbled as he intervened. He stowed the puppy in the wagon, hoisted himself onto the board seat, and took up the reins. "See you Sunday."

The wagon rolled forward, and Ginny snuck a look behind her.

Peter stood in the flattened grass. He straightened his shoulders, crossed his arms, and stared ahead with a narrowed gaze.

She swiveled her head so fast her bonnet slid to the middle of her back. The attached ribbons choked her. She untied them and placed the bonnet in her lap. "Joseph, I'm curious. Is that guy a friend?" Ginny tightened her grip on the seat.

He sighed and tugged his hat. "Aw, he's a decent guy. Peter's a widower and seems content to live alone. That doesn't sit well with the good women of Parisville." Joseph snickered. "Every marriageable woman flaunts herself, and every married woman tries to match him up or dotes on him like he's a lost boy." Joseph shook his head, peered from under the brim of his hat, and smirked.

"Heck, they all know he's got a weakness for

sweets. Every Sunday, he leaves St. Mary's Church with cinnamon rolls, chocolate cake, and prune cookies that all get stuffed into his saddlebags. You'll see him from time to time since we trade tasks, like shearing and threshing and seed potato shoveling. And I'm no dummy, Sister." Joseph lifted the reins and let them fall lightly. "I aim for task trading on a Monday. Sunday sweets are still in Peter's larder."

Ginny punched his shoulder.

Joseph slapped both hands on his thighs, shook his head, and let out a thunderous whoop.

Ginny slid forward, her knees grazing the almost-nonexistent barrier between her and the ground. "Joseph?"

He whooped again. "Sister, I can't believe Kathleen married me. Just wait 'til you meet her. I wish I had words to describe how pretty she is, but you'll soon see for yourself. She's not much of a housekeeper, though, Ginny."

Just how bad of a housekeeper could she be?

Chapter 2

Unlike Peter's sequestered property, Joseph's house, barn, chicken coop, and outhouse were visible to Parisville Road traffic. Wan sunlight filtered through an ashen skycap. Gloomy crows darted, interjecting their jarring calls. Ginny quivered.

The team slowed, and Chessie clambered from the wagon.

The front door opened.

Ginny clasped her hands. *My sister, my sister. She's so fine and so elegant. We'll be friends, twisting flower wreaths together, reading Tennyson sonnets to each other, and cooking* pierogis *for picnics.* Kathleen could be stepping out on the parquet floor of Bloomingdales lined with Chippendale chairs as she sashayed, modeling the spring collection. But pecking chickens, not fashion reporters with notepads, formed the aisle as Kathleen stepped from the porch.

Chessie scampered close and leaped on her skirt, leaving muddy prints in his wake.

"Oh no, Chessie." Ginny pressed a fist to her mouth and squeezed shut her eyes.

Kathleen screamed, her eyes bugging, her graceful gliding dissolving into clumsy scuttling. "What is this dog doing here? Make it go away." She stepped backward, turning from Chessie's frenzied jumping.

Joseph released the reins and vaulted from the

wagon. "Whoa, boy." He dove after the puppy and trapped him in his arms. "Honey, this is Ginny."

Ginny inched her way from the buckboard and walked to the porch. "Kathleen."

"You didn't bring that dog, did you?" Kathleen curled her lips and clenched her teeth. Air huffed in and out her nose at a suffocating speed. "You didn't even ask," Kathleen yelled.

Ginny slumped her shoulders. She removed the millinery marvel from her head and rotated it in her hands. Kathleen's skin was parasol-protected creamy. Her figure boasted gentle curves above and below her corseted waist. But Ginny noted more—a face comprised of harsh lines, cheerless eyes, and lips pinched in position to snarl. And her sister-in-law smelled like a rabbit corpse. Ginny moved a hand to cover her nose.

"Now, honey, this puppy is a real good retriever." Joseph gazed at his pretty wife. "You should have seen him today. He flushed a pheasant out at Peter's place. If I'd had my rifle ready, I'd be bringing you some beautiful feathers for something fancy," Joseph cajoled, stepping toward her slowly. "Maybe even a new hat. How smart would pheasant feathers look against your adorable chin?"

Kathleen edged close to her husband. "As long as he never-ever, never-ever jumps on me again."

Stepping slowly toward her, Joseph patted Kathleen's bustled backside. "I promise."

She jumped and squealed.

Ginny looked away. *Joseph is a married man, not just my big brother. I'm an interloper here.*

Kathleen turned to face the house, stretched her

spine, stepped through the doorway, and slammed the door.

Joseph sighed. He tapped his fingers over his mouth, gazed heavenward, and shook his head. He started down the steps, stopped, and retraced his steps. Laying his fingertips on the door, he paused and pushed on it. He ushered Ginny inside. "Kathleen, Kathleen, honey, Ruta Pawlowski left a pot of squirrel stew in the springhouse to welcome Ginny. Once I get the team taken care of, I'll get supper ready. Ruta also sent applesauce and a spice cake."

Ginny clenched the handle of her valise and blinked her eyes. Filth shrouded the lath-and-plaster walls, the pine trusses, and the puncheon floor of Joseph's frontier home. Tin plates caked with congealed food remnants lay abandoned on a hand-hewn table. Four chairs of similar construction appeared to have never had an acquaintance with a dust rag. The table and chairs rested within four feet of the hearth, mortared with mud, fashioned of fieldstones, and forsaken with soot. Ginny gasped and brought her hand to her nose.

Joseph squeezed her shoulder and led her back outside. "Let's get your luggage, and after I fashion a pen for Chessie, take care of the team, and gather up some supper, you and I can go in together, okay?"

"Yes." Tears leaked down her face and plopped, dousing the black-and-blue squares in her plaid gown. She crossed her arms over her chest and rubbed her upper arms. Her heart froze in her chest, and then fractured like ice splitting on a wintry New York river.

"*Myszka.*" Joseph draped an arm over her shoulders. "She'll come round."

Ginny raised a hand and wiped her cheeks. "I haven't been called mouse in a long time, Brother. That's a sweet memory. Thank you." She tucked her head and sighed. *If I were a mouse, I bet Kathleen would brandish me with a broom.*

****

Supper was a stilted affair. Even though the applesauce was pureed to blandness and wholly milled of seeds, and the squirrel stew laced with sorrel was strained sufficient enough to be spooned to a baby, Ginny gagged on her first Parisville meal.

Joseph and Kathleen heaped their plates, chewed with gusto, and avoided any mention of Ginny's arrival.

"Ginny's good at laundry, I'll bet." Joseph brought his forearm to his face and wiped his mouth on his sleeve.

Kathleen stalled her right hand, poised with a fork piercing pulled squirrel.

"Oh, yes, I am good at removing stains." Ginny inhaled quickly, slowing her words from a canter to a walk. "And Mother taught me how to iron ruffles, pleats, tucks, and buttonhole plackets."

"Well, you can prove that tomorrow." Kathleen snorted. "Joseph butchered a hog, and those overalls are rank with offal. You'll find them in the barn. If you're working on stains, you might as well take the shirt off your brother's back. The one you are wearing." She glared at her husband, aiming her anger at the sleeve he used as a napkin.

The could-be Bloomingdale model concluded her outburst by opening her mouth and shoving in the unwavering fork.

Kathleen stood and backed away from the table.

"I'm going to our bedroom now. I want to finish the dime novel Mother sent me."

"Oh, what are you reading?" Ginny willed her voice to sound girlfriend conversational.

Kathleen stiffened, curved her neck, and scowled. "*Brownie's Triumph* by Mrs. Georgie Sheldon."

"I love her stories. I followed them in the…"

The curtained doorway swished and concealed Joseph and Kathleen's bed.

"*New York Weekly*," Ginny murmured.

Joseph walked to the sink and scraped leftover applesauce into a crock.

The fork scraped across the pottery, and Ginny grimaced. She stacked their dinner plates and joined him.

Joseph bumped her shoulder with his.

She leaned into him.

"I will finish, Sister. Why don't you go look around?"

Perhaps it was the fading light, or maybe it was the culmination of a day that required exercising back and shoulder muscles, initiating introductions, and navigating female personalities' treacherous terrain. Her brother's voice had faded from boisterous to mumble.

Her heart dropped. She squeezed his hand. "I think I will go for a little walk, Joseph. Thank you for taking me in. I will do my best to make your life and Kathleen's better," she whispered.

He offered a faint smile. "Don't wander far. You're not in the city."

The sun wavered low in the sky and withdrew its warmth. A chill, lingering from winter's ministrations,

26

seeped through her thin-soled shoes as she stepped through the yard, lifting her skirt. A pungent smell surfaced as she rounded the barn and brushed through a thicket of ground cover. Long-stemmed, pointy-leaved plants lay strewn helter-skelter atop clumps of churned earth. She bent to investigate and held one aloft. A translucent bulb punctuated it like the ball on an exclamation point. *Onions.*

"Baa…"

A bear cub charged, a mouthful of the pointy leaves dangling from its jaws. Gaining ground, a mother bear bellowed, saliva swinging from her jowls.

Ginny tossed the onion and ran, stumbled, and fell facedown. *Jesus, Mary, Joseph, save me. Jesus, Mary, Joseph.* She remained prostrate, mud wadding her nose, as the ground about her recorded the footfalls of the cinnamon-hued baby and the wobbly mama lumbering past. Ginny rolled on her side, bent her knees, put her weight on one palm, and hoisted herself upright. As she stood, her foot struck a flat-faced rectangular stone.

Someone had dug a hole and fit the rock level with the soil. A crudely etched cross marked its face. Rubbery blue-green creeping juniper needles trailed across it.

Ginny knelt and ran her fingers over the surface, clearing dirt from the etched gullies. She leaned on her haunches and hung her head.

Tree frogs, obscured by nightfall, trilled their high-pitched babble as she returned to the cabin. Joseph had joined Kathleen in the bedroom, and a sheet now hung in the front room. Ginny's valise, trunk, and a folding cot were behind it. A pair of cracked boots, elephantine enough to be Joseph's castoffs, lay under the cot, the shoelaces splayed, the tongues lolling. Ginny slipped off her New York shoes, used the hem of her skirt to dust off the toes and the heels, opened the trunk, and stowed them inside. Her brother's discards were more suited for scraping hog guts from coveralls. A doubt surfaced and left her mouth dry, her breathing ragged. *Will I survive*?

Chapter 3

What kind of girl spent her last dollars on a genuine Chesapeake Bay Ducking Dog as a gift for her brother and defied conductors across interstate travel to bring it to him?

This question bamboozled Peter all day—from the moment he took in the tearful reunion of his friend and his friend's sister to the current moment of his nocturnal check around his barn. Most nights, after he made the rounds, he slunk to his bed, dropping anchor into a vast sea devoid of dreams.

But tonight, he dallied. Barn bedtimes once were his favorite time of day. Franny waited, hurrying through her inside day-ending tasks, measuring a cup of dried navy beans and two cups of water into a pot, scrubbing the mud clinging to the beets to be canned the next day, filling the teakettle, and flinging soapy dishwater onto the rose bush outside the front door. She lit a kerosene lamp and placed it in the center of a starched lace doily that sat atop a circular rosewood table fronting the window with a view of the barn. Franny crocheted the pineapple motif in three-ply cotton thread. The filigree work extended bumpily into a compass shape. During their six-month betrothal, she worked on it, eagerly sharing her progress each time he visited during those long days of anticipation.

The night sky gleamed penetratingly clear.

His sow laid pregnant and slumbering, her snout quivering. Her semiconscious grunts tainted the stillness. Piglets were coming soon. Peter shuddered, intimately aware of the risks ahead. Never again would he underestimate the treacherousness of the biological sequence of pregnancy to birth.

He pushed the barn door, and Star whickered a hello. Her namesake marking shone in the arc of the light he held aloft. An owl roosting in the rafters screeched. The wise bird needn't foray far for his midnight breakfast. Barn mice rustled through the haymow above and the hay carpet below.

Joseph hadn't divulged much about his sister. All he had told Peter was Ginny had no resources of her own. Their father's money dissolved in card play and skiddy palms of shysters touting knickknacks, bric-a-bracs, and too-good-to-be-true, get-rich-quick schemes. Ginny's future relied on her brother. And Joseph eluded Kathleen fretted about the situation.

Satisfied that the barn and its occupants were snug for the night, he closed the door and turned toward the house. No lighted kerosene lamp beckoned him. The pineapple-patterned doily, along with a pitifully sparse collection of women's clothing, lay tucked in a tin-trimmed trunk obscured in a dark corner of the barn. Franny deserved so much more. That trunk should be full of lady's niceties and jewels worth a king's ransom. Diffuse moonlight guided him to the cabin door. Familiarity steered him to the bed he stayed on one side of still.

She came to him. In sleepy wonder, he sensed his heart swelling. His chest expanded, busting loose suffocating shackles of heartache. She pranced barefoot, and Lord, she was naked. She glided on tiptoe, her satiny tresses swinging free, alternately baring her breasts and camouflaging them. She threw open the cellar door and disappeared.

Peter leaned over the stairway, starstruck and mute, his heart hammering.

Franny disappeared into the dark cave.

Crash-Crash-Crash.

Peter stretched his boot and fanned the toe along the floor, feeling his way down the stairs. A light, glittering and red-hot, impaled his eyes and suspended his steps.

Crash-Crash-Crash.

Glass shards bit his face and fell into his breast pocket.

"Tomatoes," she screamed.

Crash.

"Beets," she hollered. "I hate beets. Red, they stained my fingers red."

Crash.

"Sauerkraut, yuck. Caraway seeds scattering everywhere. I hate sauerkraut, but Peter, Peter craves it, and so do maggots."

Crash-Crash-Crash.

Peter awoke. Moonlight pricked his forehead. A ring of sweat wet the collar of his nightshirt, and below the garment's pocket, his chest stung. In all the time they had been together, Franny had never uttered a nasty word. Why was she mean now? What was she trying to tell him? Sheets and blanket cocooned him to inertia and the steel clamp of reinvigorated grief.

Chapter 4

Today was Easter, the holiest of holidays in the Polish culture. Snow fell overnight, discouraging spring's first buds and the donning of straw bonnets, so Ginny chose structured pink faille with grosgrain ribbons. Several days had passed since she arrived in Parisville, and she had come to view the Michigan spring season as fickle as a princess with an abundant choice of suitors—beloved in warmth one day but iced out in disfavor the next. She had yet to meet anyone besides *Forest and Stream* subscriber Martin Oberski, her snippy sister-in-law, and the crude, lion-maned friend of her brother's—Peter Nickles. The prospect of attending church and making new acquaintances put a dance in her steps and an urge to hurry through the morning household tasks.

Joseph brought the wagon, with Buster and Blue harnessed to it, to the front door. He jumped down and assisted each lady into the wagon.

Ginny sat behind Joseph and Kathleen in the wagon bed. In her lap, she held a basket cinched in an oilcloth containing a traditional Polish cake shaped like a lamb—to signify a risen Christ. She spent the better part of the day before, Holy Saturday, preparing the pastry to share with their closest neighbors, the Pawlowski family. But first, she would attend her inaugural visit to St. Mary's Catholic Church in

Parisville.

Joseph grabbed the reins, manipulating them to slap the backs of Buster and Blue.

The horses stepped off. *Clip-Clop. Clip-Clop. Clip-Clop.*

St. Mary's Church steeple, a shape as intricate as a German *scherenschnitte*, popped against a gray sky. The steady beats of Buster and Blue's iron shoes sounded as they plodded along Parisville Road. A raindrop landed on Ginny's forehead, and wet missiles blitzed her bonnet. A drizzle enveloped them, and Ginny stretched her cape over her head and the cake in her lap.

"Tarps are back there, Ginny. Could you pass one?" Joseph turned his head.

Ginny pulled crackling canvasses from the hay and handed one to Joseph.

A chorus of "You whos" sounded.

"Oh, there's the Pawlowskis, and behind them, the Oberskis. And there's the Urdzela family. Oh, my goodness, how many children are in that family?" Kathleen pointed toward a wagon.

Ginny followed Kathleen's direction. The wagon bed brimmed with towheads bobbing atop legs and arms sticking from britches and shirts, and dresses and bonnets, garbed like garden scarecrows in hand-me-downs.

"Tsk, tsk." Kathleen draped an oilcloth over her head and bunched it to her chin.

Wagons filled with men, reins in their hands, with taciturn women next to them, and with rambunctious children behind them, arrived from all directions. The men concentrated on parking their teams at the rows of hitching posts north of the church building among the crowd of churchgoers, while the women called out greetings to each other and hollered at the expanding swarm of children.

One by one and in pairs, the Urdzela children jumped from their wagon or were pushed by a sibling. A torrent of rain descended.

"Oskar, Oskar, come and save me. Rain is falling on my head and hurting my hair," the tiniest Urdzela toddler cried.

A gangly boy wearing a pair of pants ending in a length to withstand wetting in an apocalyptic flood stopped running with the pack of Urdzela children. He backtracked to the wagon, swooping his arms.

"Oskar, Oskar." The child held her arms wide.

"I'm saving the princess from the monster raindrops." Oskar grabbed the little girl around her pinafore waistband and swung her to the ground. The pinafore bow inflated like butterfly wings in an updraft. The child squealed, and holding hands, the older brother and sister sloshed through puddles, splashing polka-dot mud spots on their legs, running to catch up with the others.

A church bell rang.

An organ pealed.

Horses shied and required settling.

People streamed through wide church doors, where a priest stood shaking hands, clasping shoulders, and pinching cheeks.

Father acknowledged his parishioners with surnames unfamiliar to Ginny: Slawik, Worchok, Ciechanowksi, Susalla, Smielewski, Polk. "Ah, Peter Nickles, good morning," Father boomed.

Picking her way to the church entrance, Ginny craned her neck. Her breath caught like a cheek in the hands of a Polish priest. Peter's beard was trimmed, and his hair tamed—all but for a cowlick at the crown of his head, that despite being drowned like the rest of the incoming heads, stood straight and undeterred.

An elderly lady clung to his right arm. She stooped rather than stood, her head nearly parallel to the floor. She moved her lips in a gumming motion over a toothless jaw, leaving a gap between her furry chin and the worn-thin ribbon tied beneath it.

The priest bowed to stroke her cheek and spoke into her ear.

The pair took seats at the back of the church.

Kathleen moved forward in the queue. She bowed her head as she faced the priest.

Ginny followed.

Joseph stepped beside her. "Father Graca, allow me to introduce you to my sister, Ginny Dahlke. She lives with us now." Joseph squeezed the back of her neck.

From beneath his three-wing biretta, Father beamed.

Ginny traipsed behind Joseph and Kathleen and passed several rows of parishioners before Joseph stopped and ushered his wife and sister into a line of chairs.

Jars with woodland flowers, including bell-shaped lilies of the valley, purple violets, and yellow-green, fluted jack-in-the-pulpit adorned the altar. Encouraged by their mothers, children approached the front of the church and tucked *pysanki*—colorfully decorated eggs—into the altar arrangements. Cool breezes sailing west from Lake Huron blew through the little church's windows, carrying the scent of awakening earth and mustering the lemony perfume of the petite altar-adorning lilies, filling the lungs and feeding the spirits of the winter-weary pioneers.

From his seat facing the congregation, Father Graca rose and scanned the church.

He stepped to the shortest pulpit Ginny had ever seen.

Mothers shushed their children.

Fathers meted sharp looks to their offspring.

With palms together and hands held upright in the center of his chest, Father paused. He moved his hands in an expansive position and greeted them good morning in their native tongue.

"*Dzien Dobry*," the parishioners replied.

He possessed a robust voice for such a small-featured man. Maybe it had something to do with his nose. God had not spared any flesh creating the proboscis of Father Graca. Ginny bent her head and made the sign of the cross. *Jesus, Mary, Joseph, I could be struck dead for less than making fun of a priest's nose.*

"Christ has risen. We begin anew. Is that not right, neighbors?" Father twined his fingers together and rested them on his belly. "We welcome sisters of the Felician order." He lifted a hand toward two women, who were distinct in black dresses and veils.

Ginny swiveled at the waist, turned, and gasped. A purple bump abutted the buckram wimple on the right side of the slimmer nun's face. Ginny scrunched her shoulders. Heat clawed her neck.

"We praise God for their teaching skills, their mission work, and for their safe travels," Father continued.

A few seats away, two matrons nodded in unison. The wall-eyed spectacle-wearer arched her neck and pointed her nose toward Ginny. The matrons pursed their lips in a silent "ahem."

Ginny closed her eyes. She was surrounded by pious women, a big beaked mouthpiece of God, a bruised bride of Christ, and if that wasn't shame inflaming enough, a big brother with a keen memory.

Joseph dug an elbow in Ginny's side. "And praise God. They still live."

Ginny stared straight ahead. Her face flared anew, igniting heat spots in the apple of her cheeks. She snuck a glare at Joseph and covered her face.

"And we welcome a new member today," Father said. "Virginia Dahlke. Joseph Dahlke's sister. Please make her welcome in her new parish."

Fellow parishioners turned their heads and twisted in their seats. A rustling noise filled the church and boomed in Ginny's ears. Unprepared for scrutiny from seemingly the entire congregation, Ginny dropped her hands to her lap and feigned a smile, feeling the flush in her cheeks and the plummeting of her heart, imagining the sight of her bonnet as it lay soaking wet and deflated on her head.

Following two verses of "Take My Life and Let It Be" and the closing snap of hymnals, people donned makeshift covers and dashed to their wagons.

On the way to the Pawlowskis', the rain lessened.

"Joseph, remind me again about the family I'm meeting." Ginny leaned forward.

"Sure, Sister. Happy to oblige. The Pawlowski family descends from the first Polish Catholic immigrants who came here in the 1850s. Henryk can tell you about every crop grown in Parisville. Watch out. He's a teaser. Some people call Ruta nosey. I bet she knows the birthday of every person in St. Mary's Parish. And she loves to pinch cheeks." Joseph chuckled. "Ruta is looking forward to meeting you, by the way. She said so when she invited us for Easter dinner."

Ginny rose to her knees. "Let me try this again. Henryk is the father. Ruta is the mother. Nadia is the daughter, and Dawid is the son. Did I remember right?"

"Yah, good sister. You always had an exceptional memory." Joseph turned and nodded.

. The hostess greeted them at the door of their modern clapboard house. "Joseph, Kathleen." She shook each of their hands with vigorous pumps. "And this," she said, "must be Ginny." Ruta pulled Ginny into an embrace.

The older woman was plump as a Halloween jack-o'-lantern and rallied a field hand's strength. Ginny returned the welcome by planting a kiss on the older woman's apple-round cheek, inhaling a bouquet of garlic permeating Ruta's skin and russet-tinted hair.

"*Kochanie*, sweetheart." Ruta pinched Ginny's cheek.

"Come, let me introduce you." She ushered the Dahlkes into a parlor.

A braided wool rug spread across the floor, anchoring an over-stuffed sofa and two rosewood chairs with matching ottomans, two glass-topped tables, and an assortment of ladder-backed chairs. Potted ferns graced elaborately carved side tables flanking either side of an enormous picture window, with a southward view that collected not only the warmth of the emerging sun but also framed a vista of newly broken fields prepared for planting. A painting of Our Lady of Czestochowa, the Black Madonna, hung above a narrow, marble-topped table. Molten tea candles, splayed in short glasses, rested below, awaiting the spark of flint to pay homage to the Polish Catholics' patroness. The combined features of the lady—the pointy, aquiline nose, the sullen eyes, and the stiff posture—harkened the sensation of Kathleen glaring. Ginny shuddered.

A short man resembling cartoons of French dictator Napoleon Bonaparte rose from the sofa and extended his hand. Ginny offered hers, and he clamped it with the pressure of an iron exerted on a resistant cotton wrinkle. His smile originated and ended with dimples boring deep into his boyish face. Most notable were the double-wide suspenders against his double-wide shoulders—no trace of epaulets.

"This is my husband, Henryk. We've been married twenty-two years, and he still makes my heart go whoopa." Ruta draped an arm around Henryk's neck and pulled him until he inclined his head and kissed her cheek.

"I've kept her because she's such a good cook. Wait 'til you try her *biala kielbasa*. Anything with horseradish, yah? It makes you hale and hearty." Henryk beat his chest, plucked his suspenders, and laughed. "How soon until dinner, Mama?"

"We're waiting until everyone gets here." Ruta lifted to her toes and looked past him to the window.

"I think I'll drag Joseph here to the barn and let you women talk. We'll come for dinner once Peter arrives." Henryk grabbed Joseph's arm.

Ginny shifted her gaze to the vista beyond the picture window. *Did Henryk mean the same dour-faced Peter who shoved her upright on the buckboard? Did Henryk mean the same slicked dandy, with an undeterred cowlick she saw in church?*

"Dawid, come along, son," Henryk hollered up the stairs leading to the top of the house.

"Yah, you men go to the barn." Ruta flicked her arms in a shooing gesture and strode to a doorway. "We women, we'll get the dinner on, isn't that right, Nadia?" Ruta yelled into the air.

"Sure, Mama."

A lyric soprano voice preceded the appearance of a petite brunette with enviable eyelashes and a physique that duplicated Henryk's. Her posture was pattern-fitting perfect. Ginny sighed. Cutting a pattern to fit her own figure required extending the lengths of the sleeves, back waist, and shoulders.

Ruta entwined her fingers into one of the young woman's hands. She guided her toward Ginny. "This is my daughter, Nadia. She is newly engaged."

Nadia blushed.

Ruta kissed her daughter's forehead.

"Hello and congratulations." Ginny smiled.

"So glad you are here, Ginny. It's wonderful to have another young woman in the community. Now you ladies sit and relax. I'll keep watch over the oven." Nadia scurried to the kitchen.

"Come, come," Ruta pointed to the seat closest to the Black Madonna. "Ginny, Joseph told me you have millinery skills." She sank into one of the overstuffed chairs.

Ginny's heart lifted. "Yes, I spent two years employed with Mrs. Sheridan, a shop owner in Dansville, New York, where I lived with my parents. Mrs. Sheridan is a highly sought-after milliner and seamstress, and I was fortunate to work with her."

"Well, that's welcome news. I'd like to employ you to make the headpieces for Nadia's wedding. It will be a grand affair, no matter what Henryk, the old pinchpenny, has to say. It's my only daughter's wedding, and she's marrying a successful young lawyer, Tad Sterling."

Ruta leaned forward. The overstuffed chair emitted a wheezy sound. "Cake with real Belgian chocolate from my grandmother's recipe. Horses curried and combed, brushed and braided, and beribboned. Carriage wheels wrapped with colored streamers. And the veil— oh, the veil must be thick with beads. You do fancy work, don't you, Ginny? I can cook, but I'm all thumbs and knots when it comes to needles and threads." Ending with this affirmation, Ruta curled her hands on her chair's seat, leaned closer to Ginny, and stared.

Ginny cleared her throat. "I believe I can do what you want, Mrs. Pawlowski. I will ask Joseph for permission since I am indebted to his household's needs."

"Oh, I understand." Ruta continued to stare. She furrowed her brows.

"But surely, he will consider how grand this event will be, and of course, you, Joseph, and Kathleen are invited, as well. And please, dear, call me Ruta."

Ginny nodded. Tension emptied from her shoulders and her hands.

"I'm thrilled we have such a talented needle artist

in our midst. And I insist on paying you."

Ruta's compliment and the pledge of compensation buoyed Ginny's heart.

"So, you invited Peter Nickles to dinner." Kathleen shifted in her chair and coiled a lock of hair around a finger. "Such a captivating man, that one."

"Peter Nickles…Oh ho, now there is a dyed-in-the-wool bachelor if ever I saw one." Ruta rose and peered out the front window again.

"How many Parisville girls have tried to catch his eye?" Kathleen snickered.

"Oh, ladies, not only Parisville." Nadia stretched her hands against the door frame separating the parlor from the kitchen. "Matrimonial interest in Peter far exceeds our little town. Remember those sisters who came all the way from Minden City one Sunday? They pretended interest in hearing Father Graca's sermon, but they kept asking everyone did they know a farmer named Peter Nickles."

"And what about Bette Oberski?" Kathleen wagged her head.

"Oh, yah, now she is one love-struck girl." Nadia stepped fully into the parlor, wiping her hands on a dishtowel hanging from her waist.

"You have to admit." Ruta grinned. "Peter has to be a wily old wolf, considering all the ways Bette has tried to trap him, and he's still free to roam, staying low to the ground. I know Martin and Marta Oberski would bless that arrangement. Bette comes with a huge dowry, being the only child to inherit that big farm."

"Not to mention, Bette has big…" Nadia glanced at her mother.

"Bosoms." Ruta cupped her hands over her

generous breasts.

Both Nadia and Kathleen laughed.

Ginny covered her mouth with her hands and bent her head to her lap. The ladies in the Dansville Relief Society would be shocked. The earthiness of this new circle of ladies was more entertaining.

The front door creaked open.

Shuffling sounds broadcast over the threshold.

"Oh, here he comes now. Shhh..." Ruta giggled.

Peter lumbered into the parlor, escorting the old lady he accompanied in church.

"Josephine, *kochanie*, here is your chair, by the fire." Ruta took over from Peter.

The old woman inched her diminutive frame to the offered seat and screwed her eyes shut as she settled herself.

Ruta tucked a garter-stitched afghan around her and kissed the pink-and-white seam in Josephine's balding head.

"Thank you, Ruta." The old lady wheezed and brought a handkerchief to her mouth. She coughed. "This must be Ginny. Peter told me the story of Joseph's new puppy. What a sweet thing for you to do, and what a challenge that must have been."

A spring bud of happiness, coaxed by Josephine's sentiment, infused Ginny's heart.

"Ginny, meet Josephine Pyonk. Josephine knows everyone in Parisville. And everyone knows her. She is responsible for pretty near all the babies birthed in St. Mary's Parish."

Josephine chuckled. She wagged a gnarled hand. "Pshaw."

"Nice haircut, Peter," Ruta said. "My, my, looks

like you actually paid a barber. Anyone you trying to impress?" She jumped her eyebrow-arching gaze from Kathleen to Nadia to Ginny.

"Bette cut it while I was there for dinner." He shrugged.

Ginny bit her lip. *Bette Oberski, with her big farm, big dowry, big bosoms, no big brother to be beholden to, and best barber skills could beguile a bachelor like Peter Nickles.*

The other menfolk entered via the back door through the kitchen. Joseph, Dawid, and Peter followed Henryk's example of removing boots and leaving them by the backstep.

Ginny stiffened. She had not removed her shoes. *Was this the custom here?* She held her breath, bit her lip, and transferred her gaze from Ruta's feet to Nadia's feet to Kathleen's feet. All the ladies wore shoes. Ginny sighed.

From the top of Peter's neatly parted hair to the hem of what appeared to be fresh off the clothesline denim jeans, Peter appeared a country gentleman. His socks, however, exposed another identity. The holes in the heels confirmed Ruta's, Nadia's, and Kathleen's opinions that Peter remained content with the single life. If that was the case, he could benefit from knowing how to use a darning egg, needle, and thread.

"Let's all sit. Dinner is waiting." Ruta took Josephine by the hand, led her to the table, and seated her on one side of the end closest to the parlor. Ruta sat at the end, kitty-corner from Josephine.

Henryk sat at the opposite end, facing his wife.

Joseph and Kathleen sat side by side.

Nadia sat across from her teenage brother Dawid.

Peter pulled one of the remaining chairs and rested his squared-off fingertips on the top rung. He sought Ginny's gaze and nodded.

A fluttery lightness floated through her, and the soft scent of cedar diffusing from Peter's shirt swirled about her. She smoothed her navy skirt and eased into the vacant chair.

With one hand, Peter pulled the only chair left, crouched, and sat to her right.

Josephine, Ruta, and Nadia exchanged smirks.

Kathleen held her aquiline nose as rigidly as the Black Madonna's.

"Let us bow our heads." The dimples in Henryk's cheeks sank toward his chest. "Lord, Father, thank you for the Resurrection, which we celebrate today. Thank you for softening our fields with your gentle rain and filling our table with the fruits of those fields and for those who prepared it. Thank you for gracing our home with these wonderful neighbors. *Gosc w Dom, Gog w Dom.* Guest in the home is God in the home."

"Please slice the Easter bread, dear." Ruta stood from the opposite end of the table and moved next to her husband. She placed a knife in Henryk's palm.

He made the sign of the cross over the loaf, cut a cross shape in the top, broke off a piece, and handed it to her.

Ruta fumbled the bread, and it dropped to the floor. She dove after it, scarcely avoiding bashing Dawid's head and, with an exaggerated motion, kissed the rescued morsel.

Joseph tipped his chair, balanced on the back legs, and gut laughed. "See, see." He jabbed a finger toward Ruta. "Another silly custom of the Poles. Italians drop bread, and they don't kiss it." His chair clunked forward, and he slammed the table. "Germans, have you ever seen a German kiss a piece of bread?" He threw his hands in the air and laughed. "*Nein*. Irish? Heck, no. Well, they might kiss a potato." He drummed his fingers on the table. "But not bread fallen on the floor. No, we Poles, we crazy Poles, are the only bread kissers in the lot."

Henryk snapped his suspenders. "Hah. I always say, 'kiss it and make it better.' "

"If there had been no kissing, there would be no work for me." Josephine's tiny voice wavered, and her chin vibrated.

"Surely, Joseph, you don't object to Poles *kissing*, do you?" Ruta teased.

Everyone laughed.

Everyone except the two Dahlke women.

It was the briefest of looks, but Ginny caught a message of concern Ruta leveled at Kathleen.

"Well, what about you, Peter? Do you object to Poles kissing?" Joseph made a fist and bounced it off his lips.

Choking, gasping, and giggling, Nadia set her glass on the table and dabbed her napkin over her eyes.

Josephine, Dawid, and Henryk continued slurping and shoveling.

Ginny stared at the gold leaf scroll rimming her dinner plate.

"No, Joseph, I do not object to kissing." Peter leaned both elbows on the table, twined his fingers together, and cradled his chin into his knuckles.

With no more provocation than that, Ginny's temperature rose.

Peter stretched his legs, and his stockinged feet grazed against her calf.

In her mind's eye, she saw the heels of his bare feet so innocently displayed when he removed his shoes. A private part of his body touched her. *Jesus, Mary, Joseph.* Heat ascended her neck and spread to her face. *How many women had he kissed?* From the Pawlowski women's accounts, Peter had ample opportunity to kiss any willing girl in Michigan's thumb. Ginny ventured a sideways look at him. His unswerving gaze bore through her. She wrapped her arms tight across her chest, defending her imagined bareness.

"Ginny, I said, please pass the *kapusta zasmazana.*" Kathleen furrowed her brow.

"Of course. Pardon me." Ginny's hand shook as she lifted the bowl laden with pan-fried sauerkraut and fried onions. She passed the vegetables across the table to Kathleen.

Ruta leaned over and cut the meat on Josephine's plate.

The old lady lifted a piece to her mouth and gummed it. "The pork is so tender. How did you fix it?" Josephine flexed her fingers on the table.

"Ruta's got a giant cleaver." Henryk curled his fingers into a fist and made a battering motion.

His wife rolled her eyes and shook her finger.

Through the meal's duration, Ginny nodded at her hosts' descriptions of the first wobbly ventures of a new colt, frowned at their concerns for acquiring healthy livestock, and feigned interest in their predictions for crop yields. She tucked her feet to the floor, her forearms to the fringed edges of her placemat, and focused on the violets painted on a chipped teapot to avoid further connection with the man sitting beside her.

The sun hit high on the picture window in the parlor.

Ginny squinted her eyes in the wavy reflection.

As her flaccid chest rose and fell, Josephine snored softly next to Ruta.

Dawid squirmed in his seat. "Mama, may I be excused?"

"Yes, Son." Ruta blew him a kiss.

Peter rose from the table, walked over to Josephine, and rubbed her shoulder.

She flailed her arms and snorted.

"Time to go." Peter clamped his hands on the back of Josephine's chair and dragged the chair with the retired midwife from the table.

"I am happy to help with cleanup," Ginny offered.

Ruta flapped a hand. "No need to keep your brother waiting. He has stock to care for, too. Nadia and I will have the kitchen back to order in no time. I'm so glad you will help me prepare for Nadia's wedding."

Ginny crossed her fingers and held them up.

Ruta embraced Ginny and whispered, "You're not a piece of bread dropped on the floor, but I'll kiss you anyway. It's okay if you dream of kisses and that old bachelor Peter tonight. I saw him looking at you like you were a lump of sugar. Maybe you are the one to change his ways." She kissed Ginny on the cheek and turned her toward the door.

Despite it being the conclusion to the holiest day in the Polish calendar, Ginny left the Pawlowski farm feeling anything but holy.

Chapter 5

From her precarious position teetering on a spindly ladder, Ginny smiled. Today, the first Monday after Easter was known as *Smigus Dyngus*—or Wet Monday—in Polish culture. Long-held pagan fertility rituals had distilled through the years to a silly custom of pouring water on each other. *Just as ridiculous as the Polish custom of kissing bread. What did farmer Peter think of the tradition of water play?* Ginny snorted. "Kathleen, could you toss me the rag? It fell. Kathleen? Kathleen?"

"Oh, my goodness, what's the rush? I just got comfortable."

"Never mind." Ginny descended the ladder. She clenched her teeth.

Kathleen sat no more than six feet from the ladder's bottom rung.

Harumphing, Ginny stooped to recover the rag, flicked an evicted spider off her wrist, climbed the ladder, and resumed her top-to-bottom, spring- cleaning regimen.

Out the window, the sky roiled and thickened. The wind scattered twigs, thatched hay, and the hair Ginny shook from her brush this morning—all perfect nesting materials. A pregnant robin, her typical call a series of ten cheery, repeated syllables, protested with abbreviated anxious tweets. The bleak vista signaled another day inside, cooped up with Kathleen. Ginny gripped the ladder with her right hand and lashed out with misplaced anger at the spider trail defying her reach. The ladder shifted, and Ginny scurried down. Keeping her demeanor civil regarding Kathleen's hapless homemaking skills remained no easy task. Time and time again, during her daily dusting, sweeping, and putting things in order, Ginny came across Kathleen preening in front of a mirror or a window, shaping and reshaping her dark tresses into coils, braids, rolls, and many variations thereof.

Kathleen liked to practice her letters, scratching and swirling elaborate swags on any paper she could find.

One night after Joseph and Kathleen retired, Ginny knelt and withdrew her treasured copy of *The Adventures of Tom Sawyer* from under her bed. Inside the flyleaf, black-ink drawings of fanciful bonnets obliterated the sweet sentiments penned by the ladies who gifted her with this book. And worse. Ginny's stomach knotted.

Had Kathleen noticed the bookmark with Wallace's forged signature? Since the bookmark now lay crosswise in the back of the book, instead of vertically tucked in the middle of chapter five, Kathleen must have. *What would Kathleen do with the knowledge of Wallace?* A swarm of nausea thickened in Ginny's throat.

Kathleen spent her days doodling and hair coiling, but her pet activity was gossiping. She chin-wagged about neighbors, each parishioner of St. Mary's Church, people who died, and people she never met. No one stayed immune to the insulting comments conjured by

Kathleen's blabbermouthing.

"That Sister Vincentine, thank God she heard the call of Christ to be his wife. With that hairy lip, mushroom nose, and cracker-barrel shape, she wouldn't have much luck hearing a marriage proposal from a real man. That Casimir Urdzela, does he know how to do anything but get his wife with child? And his hands are always ringed in dirt. Good Lord, does he bring food to his face that way? I daresay most people are happy with our new president. But he wouldn't even be considered if Ulysses S. Grant stayed in the running."

Kathleen's comparisons were prickly as nettles and worked their way into Ginny's psyche. Today was no different. Ginny collected the ladder to put it back in the barn.

"I don't have much hope for you in the way of finding a husband." She sashayed to the mirror hung inside the front door.

From across the room, the actions of Kathleen practicing pouting expressions and ogling herself reflected within Ginny's range of vision. She balled a rag between her hands. A sticky spider web transferred to her thumb. *Ew.*

"Joseph and I have discussed your future at length. We both think to secure you in a life beyond staying with us will be difficult." She turned to face Ginny and tapped her foot. Her brows pinched in a *V*.

Ginny rolled her lips and pressed them together. If she opened her mouth, slivers of her heart would jettison to Kathleen's feet.

"I mean, you're more rugged than refined, and you lack charm or wiles to attract a man." She curled her fingers and buffed the fingernails against her skirt. "I'm going to nap." She stretched, yawned, and tucked a wispy lock of hair behind her ear. "Oh, for dinner, how about *golumpki*? And some thick slabs of rye bread that Ruta sent home with Joseph. Check our supply of butter. Maybe you need to make some."

Make some? Why does she assume I can make some? Ginny puffed her cheeks. *I can figure this out.*

"Cream and butter churn are in the springhouse. Follow the trail beyond the chicken coop. It goes straight uphill. Joseph made the springhouse himself and put a strong latch on the door. You might need a pry bar. One's in the barn."

On her way, Ginny slouched past a cabin window. She studied her likeness and took an appraisal—sullen eyes, barely noticeable brows, conspicuous shoulders, and very unfeminine hands, large enough to palm Mason jar canning lids. Kathleen's depreciations gave voice to the one fear Ginny harbored—the fear she would be spending the rest of her life tied to her older brother and his mean-spirited wife.

The barn was warm and welcome.

Ginny shook her head, loosening rain spit and bits of hay from her hair, and returned the ladder to its wall pegs outside the tack room. A horse blanket lay across a workbench. She picked it up, tossed it over her head, grabbed two corners, and cinched it to her throat. The comforting odor of horse filled her nose. "Thanks, Buster. Thanks, Blue." Her voice boomed in her ears and infringed on the soft shushing of slumbering livestock and rain brushing the roof.

A somnolent whinny resonated.

She tiptoed out of the barn, rounded the chicken coop, and embarked on an uphill ascent, acknowledging her calf muscles' resistance and the shallowness of her lungs. More than fifty yards from the low-hanging chicken coop door and built into the side of the hill stood a structure of notched field stones, more than six feet tall, straddling a stream.

A wooden latch secured a rough timber door. She edged the fastener with one finger. It skimmed effortlessly and rotated in a semicircle. With a sigh of relief, Ginny shoved the door. It didn't budge. *Ah, the pry bar.* She searched the ground and grabbed a thick limb. She sampled its tenacity by holding it against her knee and pulling both ends as if she were rowing a boat.

Crack.

She cast it aside and chose another.

Crack.

Then another.

Groaning, she braced her feet on the wooden beam fronting the stone structure and heaved against the solid door. It gave way—giving credence to Kathleen's assessment that she acted more rugged than refined. Inside, she stood to her full height and blinked. Cold blighted her nose and stiffened her fingers. The interior smelled of quarantined earth cracked open and felt as dank as the coroner's laboratory she'd been obligated to call on in Dansville, New York. She shivered. A limestone-mortared channel, a foot high and a foot wide, bordered the north wall floor. A steady stream of winter thaw funneled through the passage and dropped to the gulley below. Its musicality hit granular notes as water splatted against embedded rocks, their crowns above water, and rested in smooth babbles as it flowed across leveled topography.

She shuffled along the stone floor and kept one

hand outstretched to maintain her balance. Joseph's cast-off boots prevented a one-inch water stratum from sousing her feet.

Above the water aisle, warped shelves lined with an assortment of crocks framed the structure. She selected a pot and dusted the top with her sleeve. Holding it at arm's length, she sprung the wire holding it closed. *Empty*. She cracked the next one open. *Empty*. She flipped the following top. Malodorous sulfur fumes escaped, and stink coated her lips. She gagged. She shook the crock upside down. Eggshells scattered onto the floor. Ginny waded to the channel, bent low, and scooped water to her lips.

A steady flow of spring water spilled through the man-made canal. Milk-filled glass jars, cordoned in a wire rack, knocked against each other. A cheery tinkling sound resulted. Tucking the churn under one arm and the wire basket loaded with jars of cream under the other, she stepped outside, slammed the door, and latched it. But before she returned to the cabin, she followed the trail to the cross-etched stone. Today the stone harkened a fleet of saffron-winged butterflies and a unit of marching ants. She opened her clenched hand and placed three, small, rimmed-in-limestone rocks atop the marker. Peace flooded her heart, yet she knew not why.

****

"Whew." Joseph waved the air. "Mother's *golumpki* sure does taste good. But geez, the smell." He continued his futile attempt to exorcise boiled cabbage fumes. Foregoing that, he took up his fork shoveling, punctuated with intermittent murmurs.

Ginny giggled. Joseph's sounds came across as

ten-note robin happiness. She pushed her chair from the table, rose, walked across the room to a west window, and opened it. "That should help." She flapped a hand and returned to her place at the table.

Kathleen sat posture perfect, fingering the upright ruffles gracing her neck.

The *golumpki's* cabbage leaf wrappers were cooked to translucence and encased bumpy lamb and rice filling. Nonetheless, the cabbage cover required noshing over normal chewing. Neither the noshing nor the stink deterred Joseph or Kathleen from filling their plates with a second helping.

"Good job on the stonework of the springhouse, Brother. Maybe we should use that building to full potential. And the root cellar, too."

Joseph tilted his head and folded his arms in front of his empty dinner plate.

"I mean, the building is empty except for cream. What about other foodstuffs and medicines in our larder?"

"Like what?" Joseph arched his eyebrows.

"Like fish. We are close to creeks, rivers, and even an ocean-size lake. We should have herbs for poultices and ointments on hand, you know, for ailments like stomachaches, coughs, fevers, skin rashes, constipation, diarrhea, and women's monthlies."

Joseph squeezed his eyes and shook his head. He lifted a stiff hand and jabbed the air.

Kathleen snickered. "While you're at it, snoring cures would be welcome."

"What do you know about preparing fish and choosing herbs, Sister?"

Ginny frowned. "Well, I admit I have no

55

experience in either, but maybe someone could teach me?"

"Hmmm." Joseph drummed the table with his fingertips. "I do know someone, Nokomis Wilkowski. She is an Odawa woman who married Chet Wilkowski. Well, now she is his widow. She and her boys live on the west side of Elm Creek, close to the old lumber camp. Nokee knows how to survive in any element. She has filled in as midwife, doctor, and even as a veterinarian. Yes, I think Nokee is the one to teach you what you want to know."

"I would like that, Brother." Ginny straightened her fingers in a familiar gesture of offering a prayer of thanks. Later, as she drifted to sleep, she tried to dismiss Kathleen's needling. *Learning from Nokee will be a good excuse for leaving this house, if only for a short time. Maybe knowing how to cull medicines from the woods and making good use of the perch, bass, and whitefish swimming in creek beds, sand-bottomed rivers, and Lake Huron will make me more appealing as a wife, perhaps even prompting a man to overlook my bony shoulders and big hands. Even if these skills are never used in marriage, I will become a more resourceful person and able to survive on my own.*

A droning noise arose. Ginny swatted the air. A lone mosquito whirled, threatening a prickly bite. She bolted upright. *The woods are full of these bloodsuckers. Maybe I'm biting off more than I can chew.*

Chapter 6

Today the predawn late April morning was finally warm enough to do without lighting a fire in the hearth, and Ginny enjoyed that simple freedom as she poured Joseph a cup of coffee.

"Ginny, I saw Nokee Wilkowski last week. I mentioned you wanted to learn food preservation ways. She said to send you over on the next sunny day, and here it is. Would you like to go today?" Joseph placed a covered pail by the separator and pointed his chin toward the window.

Sunshine separated from the horizon like cream rising from milk. "I would." Ginny handed the mug to Joseph. She inclined closer, savoring the fecund scent of Mrs. Mulligan that perfumed his face.

Kathleen fended off immediate post-barn embraces from Joseph, complaining of the odor, but Ginny found it as aromatic and comforting as a woolen scarf plucked from a cedar chest. The family's favorite bovine's name paid homage to Joseph's first landlady.

"Always in everybody's business and broad as a Dutch barn," Joseph said the first day Ginny toured the outbuildings.

Mrs. Mulligan, meddling in her eye-popping and sarcastic in her baritone-pitched lowing, produced sweet, creamy milk every day.

"Best way to get to Nokee's is by boat." Joseph gripped the mug and hooked a chair leg with a booted foot. Pulling the furniture piece from under the table, he took a seat, all without spilling a single drop of Mrs. Mulligan's contribution to his morning brew. "You can row up Elm Creek. Water's high now, so you should navigate just fine. Nokee's youngest son, Lerk, will be on the lookout, and he'll help you stow the boat. After I eat my breakfast, I'll get Buster hitched, and we'll be off."

Ginny hummed polka beats as she washed, rinsed, and dried the bucket and the funnel. She scooped a serving of oatmeal into a bowl, added a spoonful of Ruta's gifted raspberry jam, and covered the bowl with a cotton tea towel. Maybe her efforts to keep Kathleen's breakfast warm would reap appreciation. She grabbed her hand-me-down boots and ran out the door.

Dew burned off the tips of pink-tinged clover and perfumed the air with delicate *eau de toilette* scents.

"Here's a thank-you offering for Nokee." Joseph handed a brown paper parcel to Ginny, offered his hand, and hauled her behind him on Buster's wiry-haired back. "You might want to use this for a seat cushion on our ride." He chuckled. "It's downy wool."

Ruts, dips, and gullies pocked the terrain, and Ginny's backside rocked and tilted with every elevation change. "Thanks for Nokee's gift, Brother. I'm glad you thought to send wool and not a pitchfork!"

Joseph laughed.

The lightweight boat roped to the saddle's cantle bounced and bucked behind them.

Chessie ran ahead, chasing grasshoppers and ferreting squirrels.

"Ginny," Joseph called over his back. "Watch for landmarks since you'll be traveling back this way on your own—like those white pines—they're probably one-hundred feet tall and damn lucky to escape the axe of the lumber companies."

She tightened her hold on Joseph's middle, stretched her neck backward, and admired the unchosen. Layers upon layers of limbs were frilled in blousy green needles and decked in heaven-bound columns. Ginny pressed her cheek against his back. Her head bumped in tandem with Joseph's bobbing movements, and her heart pulsated in a mollified rhythm.

As they neared the creek, Buster slowed. With each advancing step, his hooves sank.

"Better get off here before Buster breaks a leg."

Ginny slid off the horse's back and helped Joseph drag the rowboat to the water's edge. Grasping each of the gunwales, she crouched and stepped into the boat. She steadied herself, sat on the narrow seat, and wrapped her fingers around the oar handles.

Bracing his feet on the shore, Joseph pushed the stern and stepped deep into the water.

The boat moved away from the shallow edge, which afforded Ginny ample depth to manipulate the oars without sticking them in the creek bed.

"I forgot to ask. Do you remember how to row a boat?" Joseph stood with his hands on his hips. His pants were dark from the wetting.

Ginny laughed. "Of course. Who could forget those summers at Auntie Valentine's lake?"

"Hmm…" Joseph grinned. "I remember dunking you a time or two. Are you sure you know how to handle a boat?"

"Watch me, Brother." She leaned so far back off the seat her butt lifted. Twisting the handles so the blades were perpendicular to the water's surface, she cocked her elbows parallel to the bottom of the boat and thrust her arms straight forward.

The boat glided past Joseph.

Joseph splashed water and laughed.

The exchange buoyed her heart, making it float like a thin-skinned canoe. "Hey, boy, want to go with me?" she called to Chessie.

The retriever ceased his sprinting back and forth and barking at the shoreline. He vaulted into the boat and claimed a seat in the bow.

Ginny grinned. Chessie's confidence mirrored the pomp of a king reigning over his turf.

Joseph squinted. "Well, off with you then. Mind your manners, Chessie. Ginny, get your bearings. Come back to this same spot, pull the boat on shore, and secure it with a rock. Sorry, Sister, you'll be walking home once you stow the boat. When you get home, Buster and I will retrieve this sturdy little tub."

"I know. Look for the hundred-foot-tall pines, right? Besides, Brother, I think I could walk a hundred miles today." She leaned back and heaved on the oars.

Joseph shook his head, waded to shore, and waved with one hand.

On days like this, she wished she could paint as well as she sewed. She imagined selecting brushes and colors to capture the scene to be enjoyed forever. Today she'd need a range of blues from baby to cobalt, a mixture of Mother Nature's greens and yellows, and the tenderest of whites. Infant blue heralded the edge of the sky that met the sagest of greens. Tufts of grasses, waving antique emerald, budding citrine, and age-old amber hues sprung from the beds bordering Elm Creek.

The water appeared clear to the silt bottom, where bumps of rock and clumps of reeds rooted and waved skyward in the current. Water bugs skated the surface, and luminescent minnows raced below it. Everything seemed so fresh and so removed from the squalor Ginny had yet to expunge from Joseph's cabin that she gulped the air and gazed deep into the crystalline beauty of the sparkling creek.

Rowing warmed her arms and upper chest. She excised reflections of harpy Kathleen, Chessie's unbroken habit of peeing on boots, and farmer Peter's fluctuating attention. She directed her thoughts into the abyss of the splash-and-dip rhythm of the oars. A southerly breeze lifted wisps of hair from her temples and polished every part of her exposed skin. She pulled her bonnet to her shoulders and felt the glory of the sun shining on her face. She'd regret the freckles later and Kathleen's criticism of them, but the sensation was heady.

Oh, to be a man and a spectator only, regarding parlors and stoves and hanging wash. The freedom of strolling through the woods, swinging an axe, and rowing a boat felt so much more appealing. According to Kathleen, though, acting like a man resulted in not catching a man. Perhaps she was right. Men such as Wallace might prefer women who poured tea with delicate fingers and executed fanciful scrolls on the flyleaves of best-selling novels. Again, Ginny tallied her shortcomings. She presented more sinewy than soft—more apt with spring house doors and rowboats than with fountain pens and potted ferns. She lacked what Kathleen referred to as feminine wiles. "Well, at least I have you for company, Chessie."

The puppy turned and replied with a single yip.

The stand of aspen, distinctive in their saw-tooth-edged leaves Joseph had described, came into sight. She let the right oar drag while she pumped hard on the left. The boat pointed toward shore, and Ginny rowed toward the creek bank.

Chessie barked and ran in tight curlicues.

Ginny slapped the sides of the boat. "Go!"

The puppy plunged into the water, swimming with his webbed feet, alerting everyone in earshot of their arrival.

"Miss Ginny?" An ebony-haired boy appeared at the water's edge.

He could be a praying mantis, his brown skin and muted clothing blended so modestly into the thicket of trees he stepped from. Ginny let the oars idle and turned from her waist to face the shore. She raised her right hand to shield her eyes. "Lerk?"

"Yah."

"I'm here to see your mother."

"Yah, she told me to watch for you." The boy waded into the creek and pulled the boat onto shore, the hull grating on sand and pebbles.

Ginny stowed the oars inside the boat, tucked the bag of wool under an arm, grabbed the gunwales, and stepped onto land.

Lerk lugged a large stone and put it in the bow.

Sloughing creek water, Chessie sped between them.

The boy jumped, wiped his face, and chuckled.

Ginny smiled. The boy's laughter sounded part crow cackling and part cricket caroling.

"Is he yours?" Lerk knelt on the shore, petted Chessie's head, and stroked his curly ears.

"He's Joseph's dog. I brought him all the way from New York. Joseph wants to train him to retrieve ducks and pheasants."

"Really?" Lerk took the curly-haired dog's face in his hands and gazed into his eyes. "Gee. I can tell he's real smart. And look how handsome he walks." The boy whistled.

Chessie pounced on Lerk and licked his face and hands and conducted a thorough sniffing of the boy's fishing net.

"I think Chessie likes you."

Sparks ignited in the boy's flint-black eyes.

"C'mon then, Chessie." The boy ruffled the dog's fur.

The puppy tagged Lerk's heels.

Ginny followed them and slogged her way up a sandy path.

"I'll take Chessie with me, okay, Miss Ginny?" The boy flung a piece of driftwood.

Kicking a stream of sand in his wake, the puppy bounded after the water-smoothed plaything.

The aroma of fresh-baked bread reached Ginny's nose as she approached the solid oak door of a faded log cabin. It smelled like the threshold of heaven. She knocked.

"Yah, come in." A woman's voice beckoned. Flour coated Nokee from her handsome brown face to her muscled hands. "Joseph's sister?

The woman's expression appeared as a soft smirk

with the concentration of a fortune-teller. "Yah, I am Joseph's sister, Ginny. I brought some wool from Joseph. It's from last year's shearing, and it's washed and scoured."

Nokee took the bag from Ginny's hand. "Thank you. Joseph told me you would like to learn survival secrets." She walked to a dust-covered counter and plied her hands into a mass resembling river rock.

"That's the idea. I'd like to learn how to dry fish and what plants to use for making medicines. And before I forget, Joseph wants to know if your sons would like to go squirrel hunting in the morning."

"I'm sure both boys will want to go. Now, sit and pour yourself a cup of tea."

Ginny sat on the proffered seat. Sheaves of dried sage, rosemary, marjoram, thyme, and lavender hung from the rafters. Frypans hung above, and cylinders fashioned of rawhide, hair yet clinging, sat upon a mantel framing the hearth's top.

Bustling around the stove, Nokee oiled bread pans and folded dough into them. She placed a cotton feedbag over the lot and put them on a sideboard. "I'll join you while the bread is rising." She poured herself a cup of tea and sat across from Ginny. Looking up from her cup and craning her neck, Nokee stretched a hand and moved two woven baskets within her reach. She slid her hand in one and extracted a pile of one-half inch, cornucopia-shaped, gray-and-white, spiral-striped shells. She spread them on the table. "I like to keep my hands busy." She turned from her midriff and lifted a bead loom from the floor. A three-inch-wide work featuring tiny glass beads formed a chevron pattern.

Ginny gulped. "I've seen your work before."

Nokee stilled her hands. She cocked her eyebrows. "Where?"

"On a hat." Ginny bit her lip. Nokee's welcoming smile dropped like a stone onto the silt bottom of Elm Creek.

Nokee slid her fingers into a basket, culled two shells, and twirled them on the table.

Ginny lowered her head and closed her eyes. The sluggish rotations made a soft, shushing sound. The shells were like the errant screws, falling into and entrapped in her hand-knit slippers. Years ago, as Joseph fled, taking comedic relief and companionship and leaving residual anger, reproach, and ugly silence, Ginny defiantly withheld the screws.

Father had cursed away the day crawling on his knees looking for the hardware.

Ginny should have felt guilt then. She didn't like the feel of it now. She had no right to daydream of Peter. If Nokee provided solace for him, shouldn't she be happy for them? Both Peter and Nokee, like she, had been victims of life's grief doling. She lifted her head, splayed her hands on her teacup, and took a sip. A delicate scent wafted, soothing, enchanting, like what she'd expect brushing the cover from a secret garden. She lifted her chin. "What's in the tea?"

"Lavender."

"Lavender? I never put it in tea before."

"It smells good and relaxes folks." Nokee brought her cup to her lips and swallowed.

"I'm here to work, Nokee. You will find me a willing student." Acquiescence, she could testify, allowed a polite channel for hiding anxiety. Without intending to, she backed Nokee into a triangle.

Nokee lifted one of the shells and dropped it in her apron pocket. She walked to the east window over the sink and leaned out. "Lerk? Lerk, we're waiting for the fish."

A ginger-colored cat purred against Nokee's muscular calf.

A spider dropped from the ceiling and dangled on its self-emitted lifeline.

A fly adorned in gossamer wings droned its obnoxious buzz in the corner of a loose-fitting glass pane.

Whump. Flour motes burst about Ginny, and the smell of dank earth assaulted her nose. A pile of glossy fish lay on the table shadowed by the long handle of a fishnet. She flinched and put a hand to her chest. "Oh, my goodness, you gave me a fright. I didn't even hear you come in."

Nokee laughed. "Yah, he is a quiet one. Not like you Poles, who could pop the dead from tombstones with all your hollering about."

"Some Poles they chase away the fish." Lerk backed from the fish-topped table, empty net in hand.

Nokee and son shared the smitten grin of an inside joke.

Ginny chuckled and brought her hands to her face. The tension squeezing her temples like a narrow hat on a fat head eased.

"Lerk, start the fire."

The ginger cat leaped onto the net and rubbed her nose against the worn roping.

"Scat." The boy shooed her out the door. "Mama, watch her. She's hungry for fish."

Nokee hurried to secure the table. "Now we get

busy." She dusted off and rerolled faded, cotton sleeves revealing corded arms edged in silky hairs. Her center-parted hair was tied in two waist-length hanks and shined in the afternoon sun. She pulled two canvas aprons from a peg and offered one.

Ginny slipped the apron over her head, crisscrossed the ties and secured a bow.

Nokee withdrew two knives from a drawer and set them on the table. "First, coat your hands in salt." She motioned to a bowl on the table. "Now, pick up the fish. This one is a nice small-mouth bass, real good eating." Nokee licked her lips. "Take the knife and run it down the fish's belly, like this. Leave the head and tail. It makes cutting the belly easier." Nokee wielded the knife and sliced into the greenish scales. She splayed the fish and, using the blade's flat side, swept the entrails into a pail below the table. "Now, you try."

"It's so slippery." Ginny tightened her grip on both sides of an eight-inch-long fish. The carcass skidded from her hands and flopped on the table.

The transfer juddered the motionless eyes and the rubbery tail.

"Try more salt on your hands. But, first, wet your hands in the pail of water."

Ginny followed Nokee's instructions. Coarse salt studded her hands and tickled the sensitive palms and finger pads.

"Stick deep, but not too deep if you want to preserve the whole fillet."

Dragging the tip of the knife from the juncture of the fish's head to the rest of the body, Ginny encountered a halting resistance at the area marked by a fin.

"Pull faster," Nokee said.

Pressing harder, gripping tighter, and slashing with the quickness of a determined fencer, Ginny succeeded in completing the dissecting slice. She placed her thumbs on either side of the splintered fish, cleared out the guts, and held it aloft. "One down, four hundred and forty-nine to go for the long, hard winter of 1882." Ginny sighed.

Nokee offered a half-smile and a shoulder shrug.

"Before I came to Michigan, Nokee, the only time I used a knife, I spread store-bought butter on my bakery bread. Here you must grow the grain to feed the cow. Then you milk the cow and churn the milk to make the butter. It's time-consuming, but I've learned good things come at the end." Ginny wagged the knife and sliced the air.

Ginny and Nokee spent the afternoon gutting the string of fish Lerk culled from the creek. Ginny learned Nokee had an older widowed brother who lived along the Cass River.

"I like my boys to spend time with Thomas. From Thomas, my sons know the teachings of Gichi-manidoo, our Creator. Thomas passes most of his days fishing. He tells me the Cass River is where he most feels the spirit of our people. We know that sensation as blood memory—a feeling that connects us with our past, our language, and our customs. Thomas teaches the boys how to fish and hunt, and I suspect Thomas influenced Lerk in his ability to sneak up on someone." Her lips turned in a smile that started at the flat horizon of her mouth and emoted into a soft snicker. "Now for the second part." Nokee carried the basket of eviscerated fish to the backyard.

Lerk tended a fire.

Nokee positioned pine boughs atop the glowing pile.

Conifer seeds cracked and hissed, breaking open a pleasant, woodsy odor. "Once the fish is smoked, we put it in a fry pan, go back to the fire, and fry the fish to make sure it is dry as sand. Then you will see how easy it is to pick out the bones."

"Oh, that is wonderful. The worst part of eating fish is having a bone stick in your throat." Ginny ran a hand down her neck, from chin to collar bone.

After the fish was fried and deboned, Nokee broke the fish into pieces and placed it in crocks.

"Nokee, thank you for teaching me."

"When you get back, put those crocks in your root cellar. The best way to prepare dried fish is to put it in a pot of boiling water with a few vegetables like onions, squash, or beans. This food has kept my people alive during many starving winters. Now, let's rub a bit of lavender on our fishy hands. Ach, that smell. You come back, and we will gather forest medicines."

Ginny rolled the plant between her hands. Dry purple pips broke and spread their sweet scent. "Nokee, you have already shown me two new uses for lavender. And yah, I'll be back."

"Ginny, don't forget this." Nokee handed her a packet.

Scrunching her nose, she reached for the offering.

Nokee laughed. "It's fish guts. Bury them in your garden. Wait 'til you see how your plants grow. Better keep that away from Chessie, though. He will want to roll in it, and there goes your pleasant boat ride home."

Ginny held the containers in the bend of an elbow.

"I'll transfer the fish to some of our crocks and return yours on my next visit." She smirked. Guilt and fish entrails could be buried and decompose—the latter to benefit beets, onions, potatoes, and tomatoes. Burying the former would nurture the friendship growing between an Odawa woman and a lowly ranked, much-to-learn pioneer woman.

Nokee and Lerk walked Ginny and Chessie to the shore.

The boy knelt to pet the head of the dog.

The dog returned the affection with wet licks.

The women—one with large hands and humbled heart, the other with small hands offering fish guts—looked at their feet.

Monet, Gauguin, and Winslow Homer would have pledged their plein air easels for a crack at the scene. But the scene sticking in Ginny's mind on her return home was Peter, brushing his rough hands over an embroidered hatband. She couldn't decipher all it entailed, but this she knew—a bond existed between Peter and Nokee that surpassed any of the dime novel love stories authored by Mrs. Georgie Sheldon.

Chapter 7

Clackety-clack. Clackety-clack.

Star whickered and knocked her nostrils against the tin pail hanging in her stall. A shaft of sunlight filtered through the hay stored above and glinted on the swinging bucket.

The glare blazed Peter's eyes. The incessant clattering rang in his ears.

"Moo…"

"Aw geez, Gertrude, sorry." Peter eased his grip on the cow's teat. He shuffled his backside on the milking stool and fell backward.

Clackety-clack. Clackety-clack.

"Damn it, Star…"

Clackety-clack. Clackety-clack.

"You're not helping, you know." He crouched and aimed his backside for the stool. He grasped Gertrude's warm udder.

Franny had appeared in his dreams again. *"Damn you, Peter Nickles, stop acting like a half-assed jackass." She snarled. Her gaunt face angled in angry lines. She pitched swollen, thorn-studded chestnuts, startling him in her accelerated rage and her perfect aim.*

He ducked and cowered, throwing his arms over his head and face. He had awoken foggy, confused, heartsick, and full of questions that matched no earthly answers.

But the mortal gravity pulling his horse and inciting him this winter-released morning, he understood. Spring pulled Peter in two directions—the spring that required feverish farm work and the spring that bit his ass with the notorious gravity that affected every mammal—Star included. The fever pounded in his soul. The craze meshed with the sounds of clacking and swearing, the salty taste of blood as he bit his lip in indecision, and the itch of curiosity as it entranced him into looking again and again at the waiting saddle. The fever festered and burst. He stood, kicked the milking stool out of Gertrude's stall, and strode straight to the springhouse with the pail in his hand.

He poured milk from the pail into a line of glass bottles, capped them, and set them in the floor's damp channel. In his hurry, two bottles fell against each other.

Clank.

He righted them. Stumps needed burning on the north field. Warping boards on the coop needed tacking. Pigsty needed shade for mama-to-be. He should stay right there and stick to the tasks.

A flash of fur bounced over his boot.

He jumped.

The end of the creature's tail disappeared into a hole ample for a battalion of rats to enter. *Ah,* he needed mortar. Taraksi's General Store in Forestville stocked mortar. He ran to the barn, ran before he changed his mind, pulled the tack from the wall opposite Star, and readied her for a trip.

She tossed her mane and swished her tail while Peter hooked her to the wagon.

Planting his hindquarters on the board seat with a

few silver dollars banked in his pocket and Bette Oberski's baked apple fritters tucked in his saddlebags, he slapped the reins.

Star neighed.

Forestville, located thirteen miles east on Lake Huron's shore featured a dock for incoming and outgoing marine commerce. Today the dock buzzed with the arrival of the *M.D. Ward*, which had sailed north from Port Huron. Fishing boats moored close. Their decks sustained harried fishermen scooping nets of flopping fish into smaller deck-bound boats. The fishermen's hailing cries rang with urgency to get their product on the *M.D.* return trip.

Fish stink swirled and filled Peter's lungs.

Farmers-turned-stevedores grunted and staggered as they transferred crates.

Peter sidestepped the dock traffic, stood tall on the balls of his feet, and gazed over the scene.

"I hope that scythe I ordered from Montgomery Ward is here," exclaimed one onlooker.

"Doc Murphy's been waitin' on a shipment of Mrs. Winslow's Soothing Syrup," carped another.

"Looks like most everything has seagull poop on it," a bearded passerby joked.

"Anybody expecting a cannon from Dansville, New York?" groaned a mover.

Peter stopped. *Dansville, New York, that sounded gosh darn familiar. That's it—Joseph and Ginny Dahlke's hometown. A cannon?* He sidled up to the box. Hand-painted letters spelled out the addressee and address. *Miss Virginia Dahlke, Parisville, Michigan.* "Here, here, I'll sign for that package." Peter stepped forward, stretching a hand to intercept the pencil hanging on the cannon guesser's ear. "What makes you think it's a cannon?"

"Well, it weighs real heavy. Are you goin' that way, mister?"

"Yes. I know her brother."

"Where do you want it?"

"My horse and wagon are parked on the north side of Taraski's store." Peter stooped to grab an end of the crate.

The two men wrestled the box to the back of Peter's wagon.

Peter strapped the crate in the bed of the wagon. He reached in his pocket and pulled out a quarter. "Hey," he called to the dockhand as he flicked the coin through the air.

The man caught the recompence and gripped it in his palm.

Peter hurried into Taraski's store, grabbed a twenty-pound bag of mortar, paid Tom, hefted the bag, returned to Star, and set the mortar next to the crate. The excuse for visiting the Dahlke homestead struck a chord inside him. *What was in it?*

Curiosity just about did him in. The crate bore a stamp of *Handle With Care*, so it had to be something substantial but potentially breakable. *Who was it from?* Ginny had no remaining family in Dansville. *Was it a gift from someone sweet on her?* This thought took root and twanged in the back of his mind.

****

Chessie darted from beneath the front porch, barking an arrival.

Peter guided the wagon close to the Dahlke front door. "Delivery for Miss Virginia Dahlke, all the way from Dansville, New York."

Kathleen appeared on the inside of a windowpane—her long nose pressed against the glass.

Ginny burst through the front door, dragging a cast iron frying pan.

Stumbling behind her, Kathleen raked her hair into a knot atop her head.

Peter pulled an envelope from the top of the box, jogged up the porch steps, and brandished it like a printed poster advertising a farm auction. His hand brushed Ginny's.

She dropped the frying pan—barely missing his foot.

He jumped and held up his hands in a motion of *I give up*.

Ginny laughed, tucked the envelope in her apron pocket, and put her hands over her face.

Sliding both hands on his thighs, Peter burst into guffaws. "Is this how you greet a gift deliverer?" Her responding giggle caused his chest to expand.

Ginny extracted the envelope and edged a fingernail under the seal.

Chessie pranced on the porch between Peter, Kathleen, and Ginny. He jumped on Ginny's skirt, smelled her hands, and flaunted as much interest in the letter as the three humans.

She scratched Chessie's head, held the message, and indulged the puppy in his sniffing.

"Oh, you're taking too long." Kathleen grabbed the letter, tore the envelope's end, and pulled out a crisply folded, onion-skin stationery. She thrust it at Ginny. "Here. Read it."

Ginny bit her lower lip. The light paper trembled

between her fingers.

Peter shifted his weight and tarried. Ginny's gaze tracked like Star, swishing back and forth, feed pail, tack wall, feed pail, tack wall. Peter snorted.

"It's a sewing machine." She squealed, leaped from the porch, and sprinted to the wagon.

"A sewing machine." Kathleen lifted her skirts and ran after Ginny.

"Whoa, ladies." Peter sped past the women and clambered on the wagon. He stood atop, looking down at the two wide-eyed women. "Well, here you go then." He feigned a wild toss with an imaginary crate.

"Stop." A strangled cry escaped Ginny's throat.

Peter put his hands on his hips and laughed.

"Don't even tease me, Mr. Peter Nickles. That's my new, very own sewing machine." Ginny grabbed the frying pan, held it high over her head, and glared.

"Be careful, Peter."

Peter gritted his teeth. Kathleen's voice reminded him of a crow's caw. "Ladies, ladies, I will treat this package as if it were a new gun and a year's worth of ammunition."

"Wait, wait. I'll grab boards. We can put the crate on the boards and slide it to the ground." Ginny turned and ran toward the barn.

Gosh, that girl is handy. She's got a knack for problem-solving. And there's Kathleen, looking like she spent the morning solving a crossword puzzle, her blouse and skirt without a smudge or a wrinkle.

Ginny rolled her sleeves beyond her elbows and mussed her hair as she ran in her bare feet. She returned carrying two, one-foot-wide boards and shoved them toward him.

He leaned over, gripped the ends, and placed them at the edge of the wagon. He attached ropes to the crate and slid it down the boards to Ginny. From a wooden toolbox in the back of the wagon, he extracted a hammer and jumped to the ground. He poked the claw side of the tool under the top slat and yanked. Wood splitting noise mixed with feminine shrieks.

Neatly folded fabrics topped the contents.

"Muslin," Ginny cried. "Cambric," she crooned. She stroked a cloth with little white flowers. She plucked another folded fabric. "Silk...Oh, my, it's rustling. Hear that, Peter?"

He heard her. She swooned—over silk. She pronounced the word with all the reverence of Father Graca praying Our Lady of Czestochowa.

"Who sent all this?" Kathleen pushed her way between Ginny and Peter.

"Mrs. Sheridan, my mentor. She sent fabrics and buttons." Ginny's voice rose as she dug farther through the box. "And ribbons."

Peter shrugged. *The woman rummaged through the materials as excitedly as a hen scratching worms in the yard following a rainstorm.*

"Oh, my goodness. I thought perhaps it might be from Wallace," Kathleen drawled.

Who the hell was Wallace?

Ginny jerked her head and gazed at Kathleen. The color drained from Ginny's face. She drew in a deep breath and tightened her grip on a rectangular tin she lifted from the crate.

Who the hell was this Wallace, and what's in the shiny box? Peter stepped forward and scanned the inscription on the side of the container. *Huntley and*

Palmer's Superior Reading Biscuits. His mouth watered.

Kathleen squealed and ran her fingers over the filigree letters and the bright logo with rear-standing lions, a chained unicorn, a thistle, a rose, and a shamrock.

Ginny waggled the tin—evoking a diffuse shushing sound and dropped it into a wide pocket on the front of her apron. "For later." She turned to the crate and pawed through. Her nails scraped against the bottom. "Here it is. Here it is." She tugged, but her fingers came out empty. She stepped back and made a childish pout.

Reaching in with both hands, Peter wrestled out a sleek, fiddle-shaped machine mounted on a three-inch-thick wooden base.

The machine dangled in his right arm, in jeopardy of falling.

Ginny hollered.

Peter froze. Ginny, the vigilant problem-solver, lifted the lower end of the appliance and leveled it.

She slid her fingers over the machine. Tears trickled down her face.

Peter steadied his boots on a flat rise of earth approaching the cabin.

"I want to see it, too." Kathleen edged her shoulder against Ginny's back.

"Let's get this inside. I'll bring in the rest of the things later. Say, maybe you would consider making me a new shirt." He picked his way up the cabin's steps.

Ginny shadowed him and hovered each step forward. "Yes, oh yes, Peter. I will make you a smart shirt. The collar will be keen, the sleeves will be tailored, and cuffs with slots for cuff links. Oh, you do like cuff links? Do you have cuff links? The shirt bottom's shape is very important too, and so many choices. Would you like it tucked in or left to hang out?"

Peter laughed. So, this is what Ginny sounded like when she was excited; running at the mouth, jumping from one, big, New York word to the next. Her work would produce a good quality shirt, painstakingly made. He would stake his grandfather's onyx cufflinks on it.

Had he and Ginny been alone, he might have planted a kiss on her forehead. But farmer and seamstress weren't alone, and he couldn't kiss her because he couldn't catch her.

She combed her fingers through her hair and tapped her lips. She clenched his elbow as she guided him.

Peter trod over the cabin threshold.

Ginny followed, her steps in synchrony. She darted from one corner of the front room to the next. "I want it right here. Right by this window, so I have good light."

"Okay, I will set it down, and then I will bring in the cabinet. After I put the machine in the cabinet, I'm leaving. Say, Ginny, I think there's been a mistake."

She arched her brows. "What?"

"This machine belongs to someone else. See, the name is right there—in big gold swirly letters painted across the top—Singer." The look of relief on her face made him feel guilty—at least momentarily.

"Why, Peter Nickles, you stinker!"

He held the machine tight against his chest and burst into guffaws.

Kathleen pinched his elbow. "Oh, please, Peter,

stay for dinner. Joseph made squirrel stew last night with fresh spring onions. We will have that with bread and blackberry jam." She rubbed his shoulder. "You need to indulge me since you didn't bring me a present."

He bit his lower lip and flinched.

"Yes, please join us, Peter. This is a time to celebrate." Ginny pleated her skirt in folds and twirled about the room. "And I saw you ogling those biscuits. We can have some for dessert. Once Joseph arrives, we can all eat together."

He set the machine on the floor and flicked his hands. "Okay, dinner. But, Kathleen, how about you set the table while Ginny has a few moments to see her new machine?"

Kathleen made a moue with her lips, but she went to the kitchen.

Peter lingered.

"Oh, merciful heaven. It is my dream." Ginny knelt and trailed her fingers over the gizmo on the right side of the machine and traced the fanciful curlicues painted on the machine's corners.

The shallow intake and the soft exhale of her breath resonated in Peter's ears and his heart. His awareness of her shut out the clatter of plates settling on the kitchen table, the smell of squirrel bubbling in dill sauce, and the feel of a soft May breeze against the earned sweat on his chest.

"Oh, Peter, thank you so much for bringing this to me." She stepped on the tip of her toes and clasped her arms around his neck.

"You're welcome." His tone parroted in his head as pillow talk.

She blushed and rolled her shoulders.

The advent of spring, or something like it, coursed through his veins and thrummed across his chest.

"Kathleen," she called. "Mrs. Sheridan sent it already threaded. It's ready to sew."

"That's Star in front of our house. Where's that rascal Peter Nickles?" Joseph's voice traveled from the porch.

"Come see, Brother. That rascal brought me a precious gift," Ginny yelled.

"What?" Joseph stuck his head in the doorway.

"Well, come and eat everyone. Everything is ready. Joseph, Ginny can tell you all about it once we sit." Kathleen wiped her hands on an apron and flapped a hand toward the table.

Ginny took a step toward the table and paused. She reached her arm straight back. Her fingers stretched to maintain contact with the sleek black dream.

Peter took her elbow and guided her forward.

The four sat and bowed their heads.

"Heavenly Father," Ginny began. "Thank you for friendship, dear Irene, and her generous gift. Father, thank you for the ships and horses it took to get this package to me, and thank you, Father, for our friend Peter who delivered it. Amen."

Peter added a private message. *Thank you, Father, for this gift coming from a woman friend. Amen. But who the hell is Wallace?*

****

In the days that followed, the women of the Dahlke house developed a tentative bond in their shared zeal for keeping the new Singer singing.

Ginny earmarked the gift of muslin as curtains for

the front room.

The evening she hung them, Ginny played peek-a-boo with Kathleen in the curtains, and they giggled like schoolgirls.

Kathleen held a store of fashion designs in her head, as well as scribbles on the flyleaf of *The Adventures of Tom Sawyer*.

Ginny bore the skills to execute them. Each day Ginny consulted Kathleen on projects, fabrics, embellishment, and a daunting pile of clothing in need of mending.

At the end of the day, Joseph would enter the cabin, weary and spent, hear the needle's rhythmic clacking, witness his sister and wife laughing and cavorting, and smile.

In her giddiness, Ginny took to singing, and Joseph chimed in. One of their favorite ditties was a seafaring chant.

As I was walking down Paradise Street

A young damsel I chanced to meet.

She was round in the counter and bluff in the bow,

So, I took in all sail and cried, "Way enough now."

At this, Joseph linked his arm through Ginny's.

Ginny swung him across the floor and sang,

So, I give you fair warning before we delay,

Don't ever take heed of what pretty girls say.

Ginny turned her hand, as if shielding her eyes to gaze on the sunny waves.

Blow the man down, bullies, blow the man down.

Blow the man down, bullies, blow the man down.

Brother and sister planted their feet on the make-believe ship deck and swayed with the music, and for the time being, peace shrouded each of the four mudded corners, the pine trusses, and the puncheon floor of their pioneer home.

Ginny sighed. *Please Lord, make this a lasting harmony.*

****

"Lucky girl," Annie Erhardt greeted Ginny at church the following Sunday. Annie carried a toddler on each hip, a baby burgeoning in the middle, and one hanging on the back of her skirt as she teetered past, heading down the aisle.

"Now I know who can make the wedding dress and the headdress." Ruta pinched Ginny's cheek as she walked past.

Packages arriving in crates seemed to make folks an instant celebrity. Ginny shook her head. *Had the news of her gift from Dansville, New York, traveled the continuous perimeter of Paris Township—Helena Road on the north, Finkle Road on the East, Huron Line Road on the south and Verona Road on the west?*

Father Graca opened his Bible. "From Mark, 4:14-20. 'The sower sows the word...In a similar way. These are the ones on whom seed was sown on the rocky places, who, when they hear the word, immediately receive it with joy.' "

How the heck had Irene's gift influenced the sermon of Father Graca, parish priest of St. Mary's in Parisville, Michigan, three hundred and forty-two miles from its original sewing room? Ginny pursed her lips. Once outside, blinking in the warm sunshine, Ginny felt a tap on her shoulder. She turned.

"Miss Dahlke?" Casimir Urdzela stood nearby, turning his hat in his perpetually gritty hands.

"Mr. Urdzela?"

"Yah." The big man's lips curved, revealing dimples and cheeks that puffed into crabapple shapes. "Miss Ginny, my missus, Sophie—she could use your help in making clothing for our family. Please, Miss Dahlke, call me Casimir."

"I would be pleased to help Sophie, Casimir." *Judging from the patched knees, too-short britches, undone collars, and tight-sleeved clothing on the spirited Urdzela clan, plenty of sewing needs doing.* "Casimir, you can call me Ginny."

"I will pay you—cured hams and sugar beets. Would that be okay, Ginny?"

Pinching his nose, Casimir shuffled what must be his Sunday-best shoes. "I will be happy to supply those foods to my brother's household. I understand you make your cured hams the old country way—a real delicacy. Ginny smacked her lips.

The big man blushed. "Well, I'll be off then. My missus will be glad. Spring makes the children grow, too." He held out a hand waist-high and moved the other hand above the other.

Ginny laughed.

"The boys, they are too tall for the *spodnie* they wear. Whoops, I mean pants. When can you come?"

"If it meets with my brother's approval, I will come after the planting is done and stay for a week. I can complete several garments in that amount of time."

Casimir stuffed his hat on his head and jogged back to his family.

Sophie stood on the wagon and waved.

Sidling into the Dahlke wagon, Ginny situated herself on the tarp Joseph put over the hay-strewn bottom. The cover made a crinkling noise.

"Ginny?" Father Graca stood below the wagon.

"Father?"

"Would you consider sewing a set of new altar cloths? If I may suggest, traditional Polish embroidery would be a nice touch."

"Yah, Father, what about the Polish crest with an eagle?"

Father inhaled deeply, swelling his generous beak.

"Oh, that would be magnificent. The Lord will be pleased to see you using your talents to honor Him."

"I will start on it right away, Father."

The corners of the priest's eyes wrinkled. "Thank you, Ginny."

Call it coincidence or divine intercession—Father was successful in sowing an idea in her head. On the ride home, notions percolated in her mind. If Casimir Urdzela would pay her in hams and beets, and Ruta Pawlowski was willing to compensate her, earning a living with her sewing talents was possible. The idea was thrilling and freeing, making the sky bluer as the sun shone on the steady backs of Buster and Blue.

Chapter 8

Chessie's barking cued Ginny's emergence on the front porch. A haze of dust billowed behind an approaching team of horses, wagon, and solo driver. Ginny raised her right hand to shield her eyes from the late afternoon sun and paused to inhale deeply, welcoming the scent of the blue moon phlox growing in the shade of the north side of the cabin entrance. It was another day of May radiance—the season of warmth, new, and still appreciated before flies swarmed in legions, when windows were bare and untended and no one complained of doors left open—not even, or perhaps especially, the door with the half-moon cutout on the south side of the barn.

Wide-strapped suspenders wrapped over oxen-straight shoulders gave away the identity of the incomer. Ginny waved and rose on her toes. "Henryk, hello."

A trio of lambs frolicked through the straw behind Henryk's seat. Their slender white faces, triangle ears, and fluffy bodies were pocked with hayseeds and grass bits. "Baa, baa, baa."

"I brought you some pets," Henryk yelled over the lamb's cries. "Ruta thought to pay you in advance for your sewing."

"They're mine?" Ginny squealed and clambered down the porch steps.

"Yah, these little lambs are all yours."

"Oh, I see mittens and socks."

"Whoa," Henryk hollered, and his matched team of workhorses stopped.

Her new pets slid like a line of dominoes—sidewise on top of each other.

Henryk hopped down and unlatched a gate on the back of the wagon.

The babies toddled to the edge. They balked. "Baa…baa."

Henryk swiped a beaten leather hat off his head and waved it over the lambs' behinds.

"Baa, baa."

"Stop." Ginny hiked her skirt and leaped on the buckboard. "Poor babies," she cooed. She cradled each one and set them, one domino at a time, in the yard.

"What's all this hullaballoo?" Joseph appeared in the barn doorway, wielding wire clippers and sporting a villainous smirck.

Henryk held up his palms. "Delivering Ginny's payment."

"We don't have any Cotswolds, only Shropshires in our flock. Thanks, Henryk." Joseph sauntered over to admire the all-white lambs.

"They are all just weaned, so they will need lots of feeding, and you'll need to keep a look on their tails."

Ginny gazed closely at the bloody stumps. Her stomach pitched. *Ugh.* She covered her mouth, ran to the barn, returned with a metal pail, ran to the well, and filled it. Sunlight gleamed off the bucket, and water splashed on her shoes as she carried the container to the barn's entrance.

The handle clacked against the side. Three curious

lambs ambushed her. Their hooves were sharp and clogged with mud, and all matter that dropped freely onto a barn floor, and all three smelled like what they stepped in. Their greasy fleece captured a layer of dirt from their ride down Parisville and Leppek roads, and Ginny's apron and skirt hem bore the proof.

But from the first "baa," Ginny fell in love. She plucked red clover growing by the barn and held it on her outstretched palms.

The lambs wagged their docked tails and knocked each other over as they staggered to reach the offerings from Ginny's hands.

She turned.

In jumbled crying chaos, the babies tripped on each other again.

Across the yard, Henryk tucked his hands under his black suspenders and snapped them.

Ping.

Ginny grinned. Henryk's sturdy shape didn't require any gimmicks like elastic bands to hold his pants.

"We have several more newborns in the barn. I've counted four calves, eight piglets, six Shropshire lambs, more kittens than I can tally, a bunch of rackety chicks, and two beautiful foals. Right, Mama?" Henryk scrubbed one of the mare's necks. "Yah, it's spring." He chuckled, punctuating his enthusiasm with another suspender snapping.

"Well, we have to remember, not only are new babies in the barns, but new offspring are in the forest, too, some of which would like to eat our barnyard babies." Joseph scratched his head and leaned against Henryk's wagon.

"Yah, more bear sightings along the Cass River." Henryk spat in the grass. "And we have to keep those foxes away from the eggs."

"They are tricky fellows. Which reminds me, I need to shore up our coop." Joseph turned and stared at the clucking hens scratching the barnyard.

"Ginny, Ruta wanted to know if you'd like to start sewing this week. We are looking forward to your visit." Henryk lifted one foot on the wagon and hoisted himself on the buckboard.

Ginny directed her gaze away from the antics of her new pets. "Joseph?"

"You can go the day after tomorrow. Tomorrow, we shear our sheep. Peter will help me, and I'll need you to scour."

"I'll be back, Ginny." Henryk led his team and exited the Dahlke homestead the same way he entered—agitating dust into a mushrooming cloud.

"Ginny, time to get supper. I'll put your new flock in the barn."

She skipped to the cabin. *After each cup and plate are back in their place tonight, and Joseph and Kathleen retreat to their bedroom, I will heat a kettle of water, go to the barn, strip and wash—top to bottom. Then I'll sit on the front porch, gaze at the stars, and let the night breeze dry my hair. Peter Nickles will be here tomorrow.*

Chapter 9

Ginny scurried, rattling bread baking pans, flipping eggs easy side up, grating baked potatoes, grinding coffee beans, and sprinkling Joseph's Sunday shirt. She rolled the garment neatly into a lozenge shape in preparation for ironing. She sighed and brushed tacky hair off her forehead with the back of her hand. So much to get done in one day—the high-pressure pace she paid for her pending escape. But the oppressive humidity and Kathleen kept getting in her way.

Kathleen sprawled on the settee and pulled the most recent edition of the *Huron Times* newspaper close to her face. "Oh, hell's bells," she booed. "Here's some news from Forestville: George Ruby and his paramour waived examination at Lexington last Saturday, so this sordid case goes over to the circuit court." She flogged the paper in the air. "If you ask me, he and she should be locked up until he provides for the suffering family those two left behind. Ginny, don't leave before you polish the floor, and for heaven's sake, don't leave any of your sewing stuff about. I don't want to step on any pins or see any loose threads blowing about the house."

Ginny shook her head. The novelty of the sewing machine waned, and, along with it, Kathleen's short-lived pleasantness.

****

Peter whistled. *Damn.* The place looked so much better—curtains hanging in the windows, rag rug at the door, some kind of purple flowers in pots on the porch, and a neat little trail to the necessary. He nudged Star's belly and rode close to the open barn.

Joseph faced the door. He knelt in the hay.

Damn. Joseph looked better, too—his face was fuller, and his clothes were spiffier. Peter wound around in the saddle and grasped a long sheath tethered across Star's back. "Hey. Are we ready for this, old man?" He withdrew a set of shears from the leather casing and held them above his head.

Joseph straightened and slid the clippers into the tool belt around his waist. He exhaled with a whoosh and rubbed the back of his neck. "I'm sure glad you're here, old man yourself. Could you have picked a less muggy day? The wool will be ten times stickier and heavier."

"Let's start with the biggest guy while we're still fresh, right?" Peter suggested. "How about that ram bucking against the wall? I bet you he weighs well over three hundred pounds."

"Yah." Joseph tensed his facial muscles. "We'll be wrestling these dumb creatures, and we better emerge the winners. Go put Star in the paddock."

Peter backed Star and nosed her toward the corral.

Star walked lazily forward.

Cold water pelted Peter's left side, from his face to his waist, and narrowly missed his hat. "Gah."

"Oh, so sorry," Ginny called from the porch. Her hands clutched a bucket. "I was in such a hurry. I didn't look."

Soapsuds and oatmeal remnants stuck to his

mustache, lips, beard, and shirt. *Damn*. He spit the concoction, rousing a whiff and a taste of maple syrup. Next time he would shout before he passed Joseph's doorway. He secured Star in the paddock and walked back to the barn. He brushed away the swill Ginny flung. He followed Joseph into the sheep pen and swatted the pre-selected ram's butt, compelling him to move into the smaller cell rigged for shearing.

Joseph flopped the ram onto its back and pinned it with his knees.

Peter paced forward with shears.

Full-blown baaing commenced—each flock member raising their voice in a discordant chorus.

"Shouldn't they be happy about this?" Joseph joked. "After all, we're making them more comfortable by removing these dense coats."

But the anxious beasts baaed and thrashed, jumped over one another, kicked one another, and scampered in a circle, dredging more debris in their lint-trapping wool.

"You can't reason with them." Peter huffed. He wrenched a shaggy fleece from a nude ram.

As the pile of fleeces grew, the men fell into a stoic determination to best each fresh sheep. Dumb as they were, the animals were strong and single-minded in their counter efforts to retain their wool.

Peter waited for the next sheep. He stood and stretched and let the devil have its due. "Roar," he yelled. He formed a mirrored L out of his index fingers and thumbs, rested his hands on his forehead, lowered his head, and stomped like a bull.

"Goll dang it, Peter Nickles!"

The next victim kicked Joseph's butt.

Peter wrapped his arms across his belly and hooted.

Joseph blew out a string of words unfit for congenial conversation and threw his hat in the straw.

Stumbling like a Saturday night drunkard, Peter doubled over in laughter.

A tiny, tinkling sound trickled through the moos, the baas, and the ba hahas.

Ginny maneuvered across the hay-strewn floor, fronted by a metal tray, topped with sweating glasses. "Joseph, I brought you both some cold tea." Dusky liquid contents sloshed against the insides of the glasses.

Peter drew a deep breath and slid his hands down the front of his pants. Ginny wore her hair tied in a loose braid, which hung over her breast. A shaft of sunlight highlighted the seductive curve of her eyes and the thick lashes framing them. *Damn.* She looked better too.

"Thanks, Ginny. Good time for a break, I guess." Joseph took the tray and set it on a haystack. He held the glasses and extended one to Peter. "This so-called friend of mine is trying to get me killed."

Ginny giggled.

Peter chuckled, and with his glass-held hand, swiped a trail of perspiration off the side of his face. "Shropshires, you like this breed, Joseph?" He brought his glass to his lips and sucked the cooling brew.

"Yah, good grade fleece and substantial meat. See the fat rump on that one, and the long shanks, good for roast, and leg of mutton, yah?" Joseph turned to his sister. "Ginny, you can do the picking and scouring after dinner. After the shearing is done, Peter and I will help you." He leaned his elbows into his knees. "How much time before we eat?" He set his glass back on the tray.

"About fifteen minutes."

"Peter, could you gather all the fleeces in a pile and stow the shears? I'll start the fire. I don't know about you, but I've worked up one hell of an appetite." Joseph rubbed his stomach and walked toward the yard.

Peter sat atop the hay bale. Joseph's shadow grew deeper and then faded away. For the first time, he and Ginny were alone—if he didn't count a barn full of bawling sheep, milk cows dunking their heads in feed pails, Buster and Blue lazily flicking their tails, and slinky cats prowling the hay. His breathing came ragged. His chest puffed. He bent at the knees, shoved his hands under the bulk of shorn fleece, slowly aligned his spine, turned toward Ginny, and lost sensation in his arms. He dropped the pile, scattering barn dust and errant wool strands.

She stood idle. The sunshine pouring through the slats on the barn's east side outlined her silhouette. The soft hollow in her neck swelled and emptied. A clothesline, bare for the warped wooden pins straddling it, swayed between its oak tree moorings behind her. She lifted the tray, set Joseph's glass on it, and held her hand for his drink.

"I'll wash your shirt. Sorry I spoiled it." She leveled her gaze to his.

He turned the glass in his hand. A single mint leaf stuck to the bottom. He fished it out with a finger and rolled the bumpy foliage in his palm, releasing its scent. He rubbed the leaf on his wrist and opened his mouth. He bit into the sprig, savored the fresh prickly taste, and swished it around his gums and teeth. He swallowed.

"Peter?"

He ignored her.

"Peter?" She barely whispered.

"Go ahead. I'll be a minute." He turned and averted his face.

The crunching noise of footfalls on hay and the pounding sensation of treads on packed earth resonated.

Peter shut his eyes and pressed his forehead against the scratchy pine wall. *Gawd.*

****

Following a cold dinner of rye bread and *chlodnik*, Ginny entered the lean-to and pulled a denim apron from a peg. Peter and Joseph had already left for the barn to haul the fleeces shorn this morning. She pulled the top knot in her hair tighter, shrugged into the denim cover and stepped outside. A breeze blew from the north, and smoke billowed about the cauldron hanging from an iron crossbar spanning the fire. The tedious work of picking and scouring shouldn't be put off. Raw fleeces left dirty would allow the inherent lanolin to congeal.

Joseph and Peter carried fleeces to a table outside.

Ginny plucked twigs, grasses, hay, and dung from the wool. Approaching the fire, she extracted a pocketknife and a cake of soap from her apron. Standing close to the washing pot, she whittled slivers of ash soap into the water. She dropped one fleece at a time into the pot, stirred it gently, and hauled the sopping, massive mess to the drying racks Joseph set near the porch.

Farmyard debris picked from the fleeces dotted Ginny's hair. Her apron and her dress were wet through, and grime spotted her apron. *I'm a mess.*

Please, Peter, don't stare at me now. Yet he did. Ginny sensed his gaze from the moment the men latched the barn door and approached her with the remaining raw wool.

"Peter, Ginny and I can finish up here. Thanks for all your hard work. Go on now."

"Ah, I'd like to see this job done. So, I'll see it through with you. Boy, we sure did come out the winners, didn't we?" Peter slapped Joseph's shoulder.

Joseph smacked him back. "Yah, we did. We showed them a what for."

Peter lifted a fleece from the cauldron. "Ugh. This is one of the trickiest farming jobs." He tossed the soggy mass on the rack and locked his gaze with Ginny's. "It helps to have a partner in this."

Ginny felt her heart swell. *Partner.*

Chapter 10

Nudging the front door with her bare toes, Ginny stepped outside, dropped back her head on her shoulders, and welcomed the rain showering her face and the fecund smell of the greening fields. Clouds scudded the horizon. Dismal darkness, songbird silence, and the advent of mud besieging the bottom porch step—none of these somber incidents could fade the glow of Ginny's mood. This morning, the first day of the prettiest months of the year, June, she was out of here. She would be earning money, and happy company was a guarantee. Peter planned to spend a few days helping Henryk shear his flock. Water pooled on the step and trickled over her feet. She grasped a post at the top of the step, executed two high kicks, and sang.

"Please pay attention and listen to me, Give us some time to blow the man down."

Pellets of rain, hard as chicken feed, drummed the porch floor.

Halleluiah. Na Zdrowie! Thank you, sweet Jesus.

Henryk would want to return immediately, rather than taking time for chit-chat with Joseph or dawdle over a neighborly cup of coffee.

She stepped inside, closed the door, reached for her boots, leaned against the wall, and leveraged herself to pull Joseph's castoffs on her wet feet. A tremor on the porch jolted her, and she grabbed hold of the door frame. With one boot on, she threw open the door and missed by a whisker's breadth a punch in the face.

Henryk burst into a pinging laugh. He stepped back and retracted his raised fist. Water sluiced from his leather hat and McIntosh rain gear. He reached behind her and thrust a pile of musty canvases into the house. "Ruta couldn't wait for the weather to improve. So here I am. You get things covered up, and I'll trot things to the wagon."

Ginny shoved her bare foot into the other boot. "Yes, sir," she replied in a voice that sounded like her ten-year-old self, accepting her first pony ride. Despite the dense humidity, the wooden crates weighted with a steel sewing machine, and a plethora of forged metal seamstress tools, Ginny skipped over the door. She ran to the wagon, parting the puddles with her jumping feet, leaped on the buckboard, and ducked under the umbrella Henryk offered. *Na Zdrowie! Thank you, sweet Jesus. Will Peter be there today?*

****

Ruta was a teakettle on steam—bustling, chirping, and smothering. Cinnamon essence permeated the kitchen and enveloped Ginny as she tiptoed over the threshold. Saliva pooled in her mouth. Her empty stomach rumbled.

"Ginny, come in, come in." Ruta licked her fingers and wiped them on her apron. "You must be soaked. Where shall we start? Oh, I have so many ideas. Or maybe you'd like to get settled first. Oh dear, I forgot to ask you if you've eaten yet. Can I get you anything? Oh my, you'll think I'm a terrible hostess."

"Mama," Nadia called from the parlor. "Mama, take a breath. Ginny likely needs to escape to the necessary. Then we can have the cinnamon rolls you made."

"Oh, of course." Ruta lifted a metal spatula, turned to the stove, and leveraged the fragrant pastries onto a crystal, cut-glass plate. She licked the spatula. "Nadia, take Ginny's satchel to Dawid's room. While she's here, he'll sleep in the lean-to."

"I don't want Dawid to give up his room." Ginny pressed her hands to her cheeks and shook her head.

"Nonsense. Already settled." Ruta turned to direct her husband. "Henryk, put Ginny's sewing machine in the parlor, by the front window."

"Okay, I think this is good." Henryk huffed as he nestled the Singer on a table. "What scenery! Ginny can watch me toiling away in the fields. Looks like an all-day cloudy day, Ginny. Ruta, you should light a lamp for Ginny. See you girls later."

Ginny followed Henryk out the door to make the trip Nadia suggested. On the way back to the house, she remembered Henryk's account of the new baby animals. She peeked into the barn. "Hello, again."

Henryk held the edge of long shears against a grindstone and pumped the turning mechanism with his foot. "One of these days, Peter will assist me with haircuts. Gotta be ready."

She giggled.

"Take a look in the first stall and you'll see a cute, little filly. We're trying to name her. What do you think?"

Ginny ambled down the barn corridor. From overhead, the muffled sound of rain spread over the roof.

A mare whinnied.

The sound registered reedy and high-pitched in Ginny's ears. "It's okay, girl," she whispered. "Fine baby you have." The foal teetered on bulbous, jointed legs. Her hide was greasy, and her dark eyes were crossed. "Well, maybe not exactly fine-looking, Mama." Ginny crossed her eyes and smiled. "Henryk, I'll think on it," she yelled behind her and dodged another rain burst on her way back to the house. She entered the parlor, patted her sleeves, and ran a hand over her wet hair.

The cut-glass plate packed high with frosted cinnamon buns set on the edge of her work table. A straight-backed chair stood behind her sewing machine, and two kitchen chairs flanked either side.

Ruta and Nadia perched on them.

"Help yourself to a bun, Ginny." Ruta selected a pastry from the plate, bit off a section, and wetted her lips.

"What's that song you're humming, Ginny?" Nadia balanced a teacup on her knee.

"I was humming?" Ginny pursed her lips.

"You have a dreamy face like you won a hundred dollars." Nadia swayed her head in unison with Ruta.

Ginny sighed and steepled her index fingers.

"These are the dress styles I like." Nadia leaned forward and displayed a paper with pencil drawings. "What do you ladies think?"

Ruta placed a fingertip on one of the sketches. "I am partial to this one. I like the shape of the bodice and the gentle slope of the bustle."

Ginny held the paper by one end. "My, what an assortment of fashion sketches. Where did you get the inspiration?"

"I copied these from Bette's collection." Nadia smoothed the page, avoiding the corner Ginny gripped.

"Bette's collection?" Ginny mumbled.

Nadia smiled. "That girl has a whole box devoted to wedding designs. She's been tearing up *Peterson's* and *Harper's Bazaar* magazines and *Lady's Godey* books her entire life. You know, I bet her dad would pay you well if you were to sew Bette's wedding outfit."

Nadia's words stung like a pearl necklace wrapped too tight. Ginny slid her steepled fingers to the juncture of fingers and hands. She pressed her palms together and folded one thumb over the other.

"How about we start with the veil?" Ruta stood and clasped her hands. "I want to leave the wedding dress until Annie Erhardt finishes the lace. And I already have the tulle." She patted a brown paper-wrapped package that extended from her waist to the floor.

"Yes, that is an easy place to start. I will begin by gathering the width of the tulle. Once that is done, I can position it on Nadia and determine the length. My fingers are tingling to get started." Ginny bit her bottom lip.

"Excellent! Nadia and I are going to the cellar to organize canning jars. See you in a little while." Ruta pulled a cloth from her apron and tied it around her head.

Henryk was right. The placement of the sewing machine allowed Ginny observation of the Pawlowski fields as she earned her three Cotswold lambs. In the landscape scene, soil soaked by drizzly rain darkened. The sky's texture and color shifted aimlessly from diaphanous silver to razor-sharp opaque. Ginny measured the springy fabric and fed the yardage through the machine. She put a pin between her lips and draped the fabric across her lap.

A knock sounded on the front door. Three more knocks dinged—louder each time.

Ginny plucked the pin from her lips, stowed it in her pincushion, and struggled to lift the yards of netting that spilled over the back of her sewing machine and onto the divan. She walked to the door and opened it. "Oh, it's you." Heat flooded her face. She clutched the door's edge for balance.

"Oh, it's you." Peter removed his hat, unveiling the uncrushable cowlick signposting his head.

"I'm here for a few days of sewing." Ginny stared at the aberration on his head and the childlike smirk below his mustache.

He peered through the parlor windows. "I see your sewing machine."

"It's my workhorse." She set her jaw on the door frame.

The favored felt hat hovered over his left thigh.

Rain dripped from his hair and wetted his face.

"Well, Peter, come in, come in." Ruta clambered to the front vestibule, wiping cobwebs from the scarf tied over her russet hair. "I forgot you were coming today. How about coffee? You like a lump of sugar, yah?"

"Well, sugar in my coffee is the most important thing to remember about me. And I think I detected cinnamon?" He walked past Ginny to the kitchen, scanning counters and licking his lips. "You didn't forget about me coming over. I didn't decide until this morning. Since it looked like rain, I thought it would be a good day to be inside the barn. Henryk promised me a morning of fishing in return for shearing help."

"You better be here for supper tonight since Ginny brought a prune cake." Ruta handed him a nut-studded, iced roll. "This can tide you over for a while."

"I would like that." He winked at Ginny, lifted his hand, and popped the entire syrup-dripping roll into his mouth. His Adam's apple bobbed, and he gulped. He rubbed his hands along the sides of his jeans. "Well, ladies," he mumbled, with bloated cheeks, "I will leave you to your day." He moved the first two fingers on his right hand in a snip-snip motion. "You know what I will be doing."

Ginny put her hands over her mouth. Warmth creeped up her neck and suffused her cheeks. *You'll welcome a glass of cold tea, Peter. And I'll welcome the chance to be alone with you in the barn.*

Ruta shook her head. "See you at dinner. We promise not to serve mutton."

Ginny blushed. *Will he sit by me again?*

****

Truth be told, Peter preferred the brand of farming that included animal care over the long, solitary days of plowing, sowing, and harvesting. Shearing was a welcome diversion for a gregarious bachelor. Peter did not own sheep, but he grew up in their presence on his father's Maryland farm. He worked in a woolen mill before he moved to Michigan and took up lumbering. Sheep unto themselves were not so much effort. Farm wives insisted on raising them for their wool. So even though he owned none, Peter assisted his farmer friends who did.

His payment was finished woolen socks or sweaters, and to Peter, receiving the finished woolen product offered a perfect arrangement. This year he expected a thick, cable-knit sweater from Ruta. Joseph hinted Ginny would be weaving some blankets. The reward seemed difficult to imagine on a warm day like today. Yet, Peter knew from experience the trade would be welcome once the Michigan winter set in.

As Joseph had, Henryk prepared a channel for the sheep to enter the shearing pen.

Peter selected a robust ram and shooed him through the passage toward Henryk.

The sheep lowered his head, ran full bore into Henryk, and knocked him flat.

Peter cupped his hands to relay his voice over the barnyard tempest. "Hey, old man, maybe I should send you a baby lamb instead?"

Henryk spit into the straw and pounced—mimicking a sparring prizefighter. He spit again and called over his shoulder. "Yah, bring him on."

For the remainder of the morning, the men exerted their muscles, psyche, and comedic moves.

"Looks like all the boys are done. Time for dinner. What do you say?" Henryk pulled straw pieces from his beard and smoothed the sleeves of his shirt.

"I could eat a bear." Peter flexed his shoulders and rubbed his stomach.

The men were flushed and sweaty and wore the grease and smell of lanolin.

"Go on to the well and clean up," Henryk called on his way to the house. "I'll fetch a couple of clean shirts and let Ruta know we're ready."

Standing on the pump platform, Peter tugged the sheep-slobbered, manure-smelling shirt over his head and threw it on the ground. The cold air hit his bare chest and stimulated hair and nipples to surge. Naked from the waist up, he stood vulnerable to biting flies, beating sun, and the unfamiliar gaze.

****

The front door banged open.

"Ruta? Could you bring two shirts to the porch for Peter and me?"

"Ginny, I have my hands full. Please do me a favor, and put these shirts on the porch?" Ruta called from the kitchen.

"Yah." Ginny rose from her chair behind the sewing machine. She walked to the kitchen, rolled her shoulders and stretched her neck from side to side. She arranged the folded shirts in the crook of her arm and opened the front door. The freshly laundered garments smelled of lavender, and Ginny paused to breathe in the scent.

The rain stopped, and a trace of sunshine provided a hint of Mother Nature's expanded color palette.

A corkscrewed track of purple-hued dragonflies flitted around the newel posts.

Reddish-brown feathered wrens preened on the fieldstones topping the well.

A shirtless Peter stood on the wooden platform within inches of the tiny birds.

On his torso, chest hair spread in a pattern resembling a burnished cross that appeared to continue below his dungarees' frayed waistband.

He bent, picked up a bucket, shut his eyes and poured water over his head. He turned slowly and blocked out the sun. Corded scars crisscrossed his back.

Ginny swallowed a scream. Newly washed, freshly starched shirts plummeted to the porch floor. She backed into the recess of the porch awning and stumbled. Covering her mouth with her hands, she zigzagged to the outhouse and avoided the route that trailed by the well. *What in God's holy name happened to him? Was he imprisoned and meted punishment? If so, what horrible crime did he commit? Was he injured by wild animals? If so, where and how? What else don't I know about this man?*

Chapter 11

Ginny slunk into the dining room like a ghost testing the creakiness of a floorboard.

Ruta pressed the tabletop and rose from her chair. "Are you all right, dear? We waited a while but went ahead and said grace."

Henryk stopped a loaded fork from entering his mouth. He raised his eyebrows and froze his expression.

Dawid wiped a milk mustache from his upper lip.

Peter buttoned the top button on his shirt.

Draping an arm over the back of an empty chair, Nadia pulled it from the table.

"Of course, I'm fine," Ginny lied. The smell of scalloped ham, welcome before she dropped the shirts on the front porch, invoked nausea. She picked her way to the empty chair next to Nadia and lowered slowly into the seat.

Ruta made a face and tucked her chin.

"Well, maybe a little headache," Ginny fibbed. *Good God, what happened, Peter?* She lifted a shaky hand, clutched a water glass and took a tiny sip. *Please stomach, don't betray me.*

From beneath her frizzy topknot, Ruta's frown deepened.

"Ah, that explains it…too much time sewing those rows of gathering stitches." Ruta sighed. "I insist you

107

rest and put your feet up for a spell after dinner, *kochanie*. I will make you peppermint tea."

"Ginny, I hope this doesn't bother your headache, but what is your idea for naming the foal?" Henryk righted his fork and stood it on end over his still-folded napkin.

What did Henryk say? Bless my soul? Pass the bowl? Heat with coal? Ginny twisted her neck. "I'm sorry, Henryk. What did you say?"

"He asked you, dear, what name you had in mind for the new foal." Ruta swiped the air. "Darn flies. I suggested Opal, and Nadia suggested Chestnut."

"Oh, yes, well…what about Penny? She is such a rich, coppery color, and she is brand new." Ginny folded her hands and tucked them in her lap.

"What about Penny Ann?"

Was that Peter's voice? Ginny gripped the wicker seat below her.

"Penny Ann?" Henryk arched his eyebrows and stabbed a pickled beet with his fork.

"Yah, then give her my last name, and she'll be worth six cents." Peter clapped.

"Oh, you, always making a joke." Ruta shook her head.

"Penny Ann it is." Henryk made a fist and thumped the table.

From Ginny's left side, Peter passed a platter.

She turned to receive it.

"I hope you like those, Ginny," Henryk remarked. "It's one of my favorite foods. Maybe you want the recipe from Ruta?"

"The trick is to cool the beets right after you boil them," Ruta chimed in. "So yesterday, after I made beets for dinner, I kept some from the table, added dill and salt, and put them in the springhouse. Today I cut them in small pieces and added them to the salad. They are nice and firm, yah?" Ruta emphasized her point by raising her fork. Speared beet chunks affixed the points of the tines.

Ginny smiled. Ruta twirled the utensil, like a drum major strutting a baton, before plunging it into her mouth and chomping.

"Chilling them draws the most beautiful color out of those drab old beets that hide in the cellar all winter." Ruta gazed at Henryk.

Henryk shook his head. "Such an imagination." He whistled low.

Ginny didn't miss Henryk's wink and Ruta's resulting blush. She knew little of the private things shared between husband and wife and wondered if she ever would. *What of Peter's back? Nokee would know.* She would return to Nokee's as soon as she could.

Nadia heaped dirty dishes.

Peter dipped back on his chair and sipped coffee from a cracked cup.

"How about a campfire tonight?" Henryk stood and stretched.

"Oh, yes, Papa. It feels so good to enjoy summer nights again." Nadia pierced ham slices with a meat fork and slid them into a crock.

"I could come back tonight after my chores are done. It all depends on Gertrude." Peter scratched his beard.

"Gertrude?" Nadia pursed her lips.

"My cow. Sometimes she is sweet-natured. Other times she is cranky."

"Oh, you." Ruta brushed crumbs from the tabletop, turned, and scowled.

Ginny curved her hand over the braid hanging over her breast. *Dear Lord, would it be a sin if I asked for Gertrude to be a contented cow tonight?*

****

A cupboard door creaked. Water splashed. Dishes rattled. Silverware tinkled. Ruta's and Nadia's voices, one animated and loud, the other chiding, trailed from the kitchen.

"All done here. A few more tasks and I'm done for the day," Ruta called. "Ginny, you too. Enough sewing today."

Ginny stood from her sewing chair, stretched her shoulders, wiggled her fingers, rolled her head, and covered her sewing machine with the yards of cotton sateen she spent the afternoon hemming. She gathered her shawl from the sewing chair, draped it over her shoulders, walked to the porch, and kicked off her shoes.

Dull in color, rude in raucous language, scavenger seagulls rummaged the turned fields, fronting a rosy-pink sunset.

Soft-cooing doves nesting in the porch overhang settled in for the evening like a pair of grandparents, seemingly content to rock and replay their day for each other.

Ginny mulled little nuances she shared with Peter and found a mass of assembled flirtations and specific preferences. Peter was a confirmed bachelor with a waiting list of women if he ever changed his mind. *Would he be back tonight*? She released a pent-up sigh. Lights came on inside the house.

Through the parlor windows, Ruta watered her African violets.

Dawid sprawled in a rosewood chair and opened a copy of the *Huron Times*.

The print was too small to be seen from the porch, but Ginny had little doubt Dawid sought the auction notices, zeroing in on horses—big, small, dappled, quartered, Belgian, ad infinitum.

The screen door opened and snapped shut.

Henryk walked past Ginny. "Going to start a campfire. I told everyone to come out in a little while, and that goes for you, too."

"I will be there."

The sky deepened.

Bullfrogs coughed their bass notes.

A wisp of smoke tinged with the odor distinct to Peter's hand-rolled cigarettes—a mixture of applewood and aged leather preceded him. He approached cat-like, in no hurry. His boot breached the bottom step, and he sucked in a smoke.

The cigarette's tip flared a devilish red. Ginny rocked on the balls of her bare feet.

Peter took a measured drag on his cigarette, dropped it to the ground, and crushed the flame with the heel of his boot. He tilted his head and stared at the sky. Hugging his arms to his chest, he rubbed each upper arm, inhaled deeply, and turned. His lips flattened into a straight line as he began his ascent. "Nice night." He stopped inches away.

She reached to pull the sag out of her shawl. "Yah, it is."

With both hands, he reached to cinch the garment in the soft hollows of her neck.

She moistened her lips and swallowed.

He moved his hands to her shoulders and squeezed.

She stood on tiptoe and closed her eyes. Applewood essence filled her nose and flirted with her taste buds.

Peter's fingers caught in the lace edge of her shawl. "Damn, I'm a fly trapped in a spider's web."

"Did you call me a spider?" Ginny giggled as she worked to untangle Peter.

"Hey, you two," Henryk called. "Get the others and come on out. I've got a roaring fire going." He turned back to the shadows.

That evening the pattern was set for the nights Ginny stayed at the Pawlowski farm.

Following an early supper, Peter left to care for his stock and then returned for the welcome camaraderie of the family and their itinerant seamstress.

"Not much moon tonight," Henryk remarked on the third evening of Ginny's stay. "How about we stay inside and play some games? He pulled a box of dominoes from a drawer underneath the Lady of Czestochowa shrine. "Who wants to play?"

Dominoes became an evening ritual.

"I think Ginny has an unfair advantage in this game." Dawid tossed a handful of tiles from one hand to another. "She has very nimble fingers. Does anyone here watch her plow through the pile of fabric across that chair over there?" He shook his head and grinned.

"I think you're right, Dawid. That explains why Ginny usually wins." Ruta smiled.

Using the very tip of her fingers, Ginny stood eight tiles on end. "Dawid, you guessed my strategy. I am happy to share my needles with anyone who wants to improve their game." She arched her eyebrows and shifted her gaze.

Peter held up his hands. "Not me. I'll take my chances."

Henryk chuckled.

Catering to sweet tooths also became custom. Every night the womenfolk brought out a fruity pie, an egg custard, fried donuts, or a crumbly cake.

On the fourth night of Ginny's visit, Ruta reached across the table and tapped Peter's hand as he played a domino. "How about dessert? Nadia and I invited Ginny into the kitchen today to give her shoulders a rest, and she made something very special."

"Yah." Peter rubbed his hands together, bent his knees, and stuffed his hands into his back pockets.

Ginny brought out a pie, set it on the table, and cut a large slice. She slid the piece onto a plate. "Here you go, Peter, quince pie."

"Quince? My mother used to make it. Boy, this looks good." He dug in with his fork and shoved the pastry in his mouth.

By degrees, Peter's expression changed—from happy, to confused, to shock, to disgust, and finally to repulsion. "Oh, dear, let me taste it." Ginny spooned a minute portion from the pie pan to her mouth. She pursed her lips and frowned. "Oh, something is missing."

"Allspice, maybe?" Nadia suppressed a snort.

"Salt, perhaps?" Ruta casually flipped a domino tile and set an elbow on the table and her chin in the palm of her hand.

"Sugar," Peter bellowed. He spit a wad of quince pie from his mouth.

Ruta giggled.

Ginny put her hands over her mouth.

Beside her, Nadia snorted—this time, with no restraint.

"Were you boys in on this?" Peter yelled and broadcast a threatening eyebrow-raising at Henryk and Dawid.

Dawid opened his eyes wide, shook his head, and burst into laughter.

"Let this be a lesson to you, friend," Henryk smirked. "Never let a woman know your weakness."

"Okay, you got me, and you got me good. But…" Peter jeered. "One trick is good for another. Everyone here"—he pointed a finger at Henryk, then Dawid, Nadia, Ruta, and lastly, Ginny—"should be on their guard."

Chapter 12

Ginny settled herself in the straight-backed chair behind her sewing machine, selected a spool of white silk thread, and glanced at the painting of the Black Madonna. The sainted patron's posture spiked a stiffening in Ginny's spine. But the holy impression couldn't sway her thoughts. Her contemplations this morning were as sweltering as the heat that evicted Nadia and Ruta from the kitchen, and her journal entry of yesterday, June 11,1881, confirmed her feelings.

Peter is expected to help Henryk with shearing the Pawlowski flock tomorrow. I know I'm acting like a silly school girl but just knowing the man will be in my presence makes me tingle. I find it hard to believe the first day I met him I found him uncouth. My, my, how my opinion has changed.

She ran a finger along the satiny-smooth wound thread. The section of hair that grew on Peter's face and lapped his ears was just as silky. He might be in the barn with Henryk and Dawid now. Her breath caught. She sighed. The men would welcome a cool drink. She rose. But the beadwork would take many hours of work, and she couldn't afford to dilly-dally. She sighed and returned to sitting. She unwound an eighteen-inch length and cut. Choosing a fine needle from her pincushion, she guided the thread through the eye, slid the opposite end over her tongue, and licked it. She wrapped the wet end over her left thumb and rolled the thread between her thumb and adjacent index finger. Tugging on the tangled end, she fashioned a knot.

Tiny paper boxes retaining clear glass beads of varying sizes lined her work area. She chose several beads, strung them on the thread, and pushed them to the knotted end. Following the penciled guide she had outlined on the tulle, Ginny embroidered a daisy flower shape on Nadia's bridal veil.

The screen door thumped against its frame.

Ginny flinched and knocked the paper boxes.

A thousand crystalline beads spurted onto the carpet. A thousand more flooded the wooden floor and rolled into a blurred pattern resembling melted snow.

"Ginny? We need a needle, as big as you have," Peter shouted.

Whack. Stomp. Stomp. Stomp. The vibrations on the porch triggered a silent alarm exploding in her head.

Yards of bridal veiling trapped her. She kicked her chair, lifted the tulle mass, and flung the translucent netting to the floor.

Whack. The porch shook.

Peter bolted through the doorway, skidded on the beaded floor, and scattered the glass ornaments into floor crevices. Blood spatters peppered his face, laced his beard, and wetted his denim shirt.

"Are you hurt?" Her heart hammered.

"It's one of the ewes, and she's with lamb. Henryk cut too quick." Peter panted. "Needs to be stitched. Bring what you have." He ran out the door and let it slam.

Ginny culled her pincushion and selected three of the stoutest needles in the lot. She grabbed the thickest thread from her sewing box, threaded the needles, knotted the ends, poked them through her bodice, and raced to the barn. Sheep bleats, anxious and pitying, permeated the barn in ear-splitting volume. Ginny lifted her skirt and strode to the men.

Henryk wrestled the bawling sheep.

Blood spurted from the ewe and stained straw, gloves, shears, and beards red.

Henryk jumped. "Dad gummit, Missus."

"Try this." Ginny pulled a threaded needle from the front of her dress.

"Ginny, we need you to help." Peter brought his head level with hers. He gazed directly into her eyes. His arms and back and thighs strained against the thrashing, bleating, bleeding sheep.

She knelt next to Peter, closed her eyes, inhaled sharply, and stretched her fingers against the coarse weave of her apron. She opened her eyes, stared into Peter's beseeching eyes, and nodded. Today she would stitch more than rows of tulle. The cut, long as the length of her hand, bared faint-blue fat bubbles and pulsing, blue-veined muscle. Hot urine and its acrid odor splashed over her skirt.

"Whoa, girl," Peter whispered. "It's gonna be fine, just fine."

Henryk grunted as he struggled to match the cut pieces of flesh.

She's with lamb, Ginny reminded herself, gripping a needle and stabbing through one side of the slice. She sucked a deep breath and gritted her teeth. *Pretend you're sewing a cured sheepskin together. Don't think of it as a live thing*. She pulled and drew slack out of the thread.

"I'll hold her," Henryk muttered through clamped teeth. "You two, stitch."

Peter blotted the cut with loose wool.

Ginny plied the needle through the opposite side, tugging until the thread laced the fissure together. She held her bloodied hand and clenched needle aloft and petitioned Peter with her eyes.

He wiped her hand and needle with the tail of his shirt.

Ginny lost count of the stitches, but she used all three lengths of thread. She tied off the last thread, tugged, and tested the knot.

The patient kicked, flinging straw into Ginny's mouth.

"Ick." She spat.

Peter wiped her mouth with his elbow. "Well done."

Henryk expelled a whooshing pant and wiped his face with his handkerchief. He kept one hand wrapped around the sheep's neck. "I'll take her to a separate pen and feed her a little mash to settle her. Hopefully, she'll take a good long rest. I know I could use one."

Blood sullied her dress and her shoes. Her braid grazed the floor.

Peter rocked on his haunches and harvested straw from her hair. "You're good with a needle, Ginny. Go freshen up. I'll bring a pail of water to the porch."

"Thanks, Peter. I'll go directly to the house." Ginny sensed a tug on her heart as viscerally as the tugging on the hide of a sheep's belly.

****

Ruta and Nadia, flushed from their sweltering morning in the garden, returned and prepared a dinner of pulled pork sandwiches and stewed fruit.

Ginny's valiant sheep stitching story capped the conversation during the noon reprieve.

"Not everyone could've handled what Ginny did today," Henryk said. "I don't mind confessing. That stuff makes me a bit queasy." He stared at his plate and shook his head.

"A bit?" Peter leaned forward on the table. "You just about passed out on the barn floor."

Ruta nodded her head. "Yah, when Nadia was a baby, I turned my head for just a moment. She rolled off our bed, banged her head, screamed, and Henryk did pass out."

Henryk hung his head. "Let's not mention that again, please, Wife?"

"Ginny, did you use any fancy stitches?" The adolescent fuzz on Dawid's lips wavered.

"Perhaps French knots, feather stitches, herringbone stitches, or turkey stitches?" Nadia arched her eyebrows and reached for the saltshaker.

"Ginny, you did a fine job on the ewe's belly today, even though the stitches looked like a kindergarten primer." Peter shook his head and chuckled.

Ginny tucked her chin. *Peter Nickles, you make me laugh, and that's not all.*

"Well, while you were all busy in the barn, Nadia and I took charge of garden invaders." Ruta held a knife upright. "We drowned about thirty-five green-horned tomato worms."

"The tomatoes are safe for now." Dawid spooned another helping of fruit onto his plate.

"Eww." Ginny scrunched her nose and shuddered.

"Good riddance, I say." Henryk beamed and snapped his suspenders.

"Well, we've all had a harrowing day. How about taking a little break this afternoon?" Ruta fanned herself with a napkin.

"Papa, can I ride Mystic over to the Nowakowski place? Michael said he'd help me train him." Dawid squeezed the bulb of his nose and wiped his hand on his pants.

"How about taking Sandy instead? I think Mystic should stay here. Perhaps Michael could come here one day and work with Mystic. By the way, son, thank you for cleaning the stalls. Did you tell your mama you scoured all the boards?"

"That's a good idea, Papa. Mama, guess what I did today?" Dawid didn't wait for Ruta's response. He pushed back from the table, grabbed a dinner roll, popped it in his mouth, and started for the door.

"Say hi to my sister for me, Dawid," Peter called.

"Thank you, son," Ruta added. "Now for you, Mr. Pawlowski, how about you spend a few hours by my side? I can read the paper to you."

"I would like that very much, Ruta." Henryk moved behind her, squeezed her shoulders, and pulled her chair from the table.

She giggled, rose, and lifted her eyebrows.

Henryk kissed her hand, took the dirty dishes out of her other hand, and walked them to the sink.

"Mama, Ginny and I can make the supper." Nadia kissed her mother's cheek on her way to the kitchen.

"Shoo and stay out of my kitchen." Ruta squawked. "You young people go for a walk. Now off with you and no more dawdling."

"Don't think twice." Nadia grabbed Ginny's hand. "Come along, won't you, Peter?"

"Sure, lead the way." He stretched from the table, allowed the girls to walk past, and shoved their chairs back under the table.

Outside, a southerly breeze drifted through the stagnant heat.

"Tad and I have worn a path here," Nadia called behind her.

Ginny traipsed behind, rustling the tall, sweet grasses in her path.

Peter brought up the rear.

Bottle-nosed dragonflies with iridescent gossamer wings flitted. Bluebirds soared in spur-of-the-moment updrafts. Black-eyed Susans, their circular faces fringed in black and sun-gold petals, nodded.

Nadia slowed at a place where a creek babbled, and sunlight filtered through a stand of oaks, leading them to a meadow lush with waxy white trillium, bright-orange butterfly weed, and the pretty pink but poisonous sweet pea.

An osprey shrieked its high-note, teakettle-whistling call, dropped to the creek's surface, and splayed its clawed feet as it targeted a fish.

An eagle pair flaunted their wingspans in dramatic escalation and soared above the water.

"Ah, such a perfect spot, Nadia." Ginny twisted her head and twirled her arms. Tension flowed out her fingers.

"Ahh...what a day." Peter sighed.

Standing behind him, Ginny cataloged Peter's exhalation as the sound of ash wood as it dropped into a lazy campfire. She bent and removed her boots.

Beneath her released toes, the cool earth beckoned a sense of abandonment and freedom.

Nadia leaned from her waist and flattened a grassy area. "Come and sit." She lifted her skirt, crossed her ankles, and lowered herself.

Ginny edged close to Nadia and followed suit.

Peter chose an area a body length away from the ladies and sank to the ground. He reached for a blade of grass and thrust it in his mouth.

"Come, Ginny. Turn around. Let me braid your hair." Nadia gripped the ends of Ginny's single braid and scooted on her butt until she was sitting behind Ginny. She pushed the bonnet off Ginny's head, unbound the plaited hair, and finger-combed it.

Ginny shivered and rolled her shoulders. The thick tresses fell below her waist.

"I've got some ideas how I'd like the horses decorated on my wedding day. Papa promised they will be scrubbed clean from their ears to the end of their tails. Once they are shiny clean, Mama will weave flowers and bells into their manes."

Nadia's voice procured the inflection of an enchantress. Ginny closed her eyes. The sensations of gentle pulling along her scalp and soft brushes along her face sent a provocative tingling along her skin. Nadia's ministrations mimicked the comforting touches bestowed long ago by her mother's able hands. Ginny's head slumped to her chest.

"Mama is tending a special flower garden, just for the wedding. We planted all my favorites—roses, of course, cosmos, carnations, hollyhocks, foxglove." Nadia yanked on the creation she fashioned in Ginny's hair. "Peter, what do you think of this style of braid for the horses?"

"H-h-horses?" Ginny shook her head and twisted the hank of hair from Nadia's grasp.

"Neigh," Peter bellowed.

"Horses?" Ginny repeated. She uncrossed her ankles and stood. "You were using me to practice bridal horse fashions?"

"Oh, hold your horses, Ginny." Nadia laughed.

Peter rolled on the ground, clenching his stomach. "Better watch out, Miss Seamstress. The next thing you know, the Pawlowski women will have you sewing gowns for the fillies and suits for the colts for this big wedding."

"Not this seamstress." Ginny pulled her bonnet back on her head and stuffed her loose hair inside.

Peter rose, rolled his shoulders, squatted, and uncoiled. He leaned his head to the right and the left and back to the middle.

Crack.

"Oh, that felt good." He repeated the neck roll.

Crack.

"Time for me to get back to work. I've got a garden to check for invaders, too." Peter brushed the seat of his pants.

Nadia glanced toward the house. "I can guarantee you Mama will keep Papa corralled until supper. It's a rare occasion, and Mama will take full advantage."

Ginny turned and glanced toward the homestead.

Skinny sheep grazed in the pasture.

Horses in the paddock lazily swished their tails.

"So, sit back, Peter Nickles. I'd like to get a man's point of view." Nadia waved a finger.

Ginny brushed the seat of her skirt. She didn't take

her gaze off Peter. *I need to hear this.*

"Uh, oh," he responded, and ran a hand down his face, from his ear to the end of his beard, right over the sweet, silky spot.

"C'mon, c'mon, we're all adults. I'd like to ask you a few questions, you being a man and all." Nadia rose to her knees.

Peter adjusted his weight from one foot to another. He put his hands in his back pockets and twisted his shoulders.

"Ginny would be interested, too." Nadia arched her eyebrows.

Ginny blinked and shook her head.

"Let me guess, something about politics, right, Nadia?" Peter's shadow stretched over the compressed grasses they rested on.

"Yes, you and I have had this kind of conversation before." Nadia grinned.

"Indeed, we have." Peter smirked.

"Well, Ginny and I have discussed a woman's right to vote. What do you think, Peter?"

Ginny sucked a deep breath and turned to the other woman moderating the question. Nadia's expression mimicked an empty ballot.

Peter sat and tucked his legs in an *X* formation. He pulled a hank of clover and chewed it. His jaws moved against the grain of his beard. "I think…I think…that a woman has the right to vote on what is served for dinner and what bonnet to wear on Sunday morning."

Nadia furrowed her brow and scrunched her face.

Ginny bit her lip and clenched her fists.

Silence hung between them.

Peter burst out laughing. "That's for the pie thing."

Nadia snickered.

"So, we're clear, a woman has equal rights in my mind, and I would cast my poll on that. A woman," he continued, "works as hard, suffers as much, and usually shows more smarts than any man."

"Well, thank you for your vote, Mr. Nickles." Nadia clapped. "As long as you're contributing your opinion, tell us what you think are the necessary qualities of a marriageable woman." She tucked a springy tendril behind her ear. "No more teasing. We are fair and square now."

"Well, maybe a truce for now." He chuckled, leaned back on his hands, faced the sky and squinted his eyes. "A wife should be strong."

"Like an ox?" blurted Nadia.

"Shhh…" interjected Ginny. Hot hair clung to the back of her neck. Hot air dried her tongue.

"Thank you, Ginny." Peter lifted his face and connected with her gaze. "A wife," he began again, "should be strong—in her loyalty, in her ability to shoulder difficult chores, and in her ability to stitch together what needs mending."

Ginny's heart tapped in her throat.

"Of course, the deal would be sealed if she possessed sufficient strength to be yoked and plow the fields too, Nadia. Every once in a while, Star needs a break."

Ginny jumped her gaze to Peter. *Peter Nickles, you are a stinker.*

Nadia swatted his shoulder. "Peter Nickles, no wonder you are single."

He offered the expected grin, turned his back, and shut his eyes. *What will be in my dreams tonight as I shut my eyes again?*

****

The day's heat gripped on into the night. Peter's ride from the Pawlowskis' was punctuated by ripening smells of beans, tobacco, oats, wheat, and rye. The odors invoked memories of his first married days with Franny. Their wedding anniversary was imminent and the one day of the year that could bring him to his knees.

He thought again of Nadia's question on marriageability. What he didn't utter was the yearning that pulsated through him—the strength he desired in his bed, with a woman who burned for the same. The only woman to share his bed was now in heaven, and the bed half she had warmed remained unendurably empty. He had taken no actions to fill it. He avoided the obvious resolution, wary of the effort it would take to remedy that ache. Instead, he filled his days with what he justified as actions to survive.

Unwittingly, today's events returned in waves, and the currents filled with visions of Ginny. She didn't flinch as the bucking sheep threatened to break loose from Henryk's grasp. Peter guessed at her mental sturdiness, as lines of determination sank in her brow each time she pulled the thread to tighten the stitches lining the bleating ewe's belly. Her steely strength transferred to him as she braced her thigh against his as they worked together, restraining the terrified sheep.

He rode Star to the barn, dismounted, and led her into the paddock. He envisioned Ginny as she appeared across the campfires on the Pawlowski farm. Her hair shifted almost invisibly, and yet he strained his eyes to keep track of every hair on her head. The rush of jealousy he endured this afternoon surged again, as his memory played the scene in the meadow of Nadia taking free reign of Ginny's scalp, raising the tresses, threading her fingers through its glossy fineness, and playfully manipulating it away from and around her head. Peter felt the same ache now. Shuddering, he gated the paddock and shuffled to his quiet home. The sweet intoxicating fragrance of the sentry rose bush filled his senses and pierced his heart.

Chapter 13

Peter sat astride Star and urged her down Parisville Road.

Last Saturday night, during their final round of whist, Henryk and Dawid shared Michael Nowakowski was coming to help Dawid train one of the Pawlowski colts.

Michael, my oldest nephew, my little buddy, now grown into a fine young man.

Silver clouds scudded the sky, and sunshine livened the hues of every leaf and berry on the route.

Star's mane rose and fell as she nosed into a southerly breeze.

St. Mary's Church came into view. The lot was empty—pretty typical for a Monday.

Father Graca walked through the parish cemetery's dappled shade.

Peter waved.

Franny and their baby rested under the overhang of a sugar maple.

The fall following their deaths, Ruta had planted orange daylilies, that bloomed more profusely each year over their grave.

Father arrived a year ago to assume responsibility for their parish and immediately made it his mission to nurture the cemetery. Elm and oak saplings swayed, and forsythia and lilac bushes bloomed.

Peter's throat constricted. *Happy Anniversary, my love*. He clucked to Star, and man and horse hustled past the church property.

Greenish-gold rye shoots shook and susurrated in the soft wind traveling over the Pawlowski fields. Peter turned into the lane.

Peter walked Star into the yard, stopped at a shady spot next to the barn, slid out of his saddle, gathered the reins, and wrapped them around a fence.

Henryk stepped across the drive that circled in front of the house.

Ginny followed.

"At least one of the girls is interested," Henryk yelled to Peter. He pulled his hat low on his head, stomped the twenty yards to the corral, folded his arms, and leaned them on the top rail of the enclosure.

Peter clambered atop the fence and sat cowboy-style—boot heels tucked behind the lower rail, anchoring him in place.

Dawid and Michael emerged from the shadow of the barn with a pinto pony between them.

Michael, Peter's first-born nephew, had grown. His gangly posture converted to a ranch hand's muscular stance, and his baby-soft face transformed to a heartbreaker's honed mug. Peter leaned forward and shook his head.

Michael held the colt's reins.

The three walked the inside perimeter of the corral, passing the spectators twice.

"Henryk, this is the closest I've been to a Medicine Hat horse," Peter called. "He's a real looker." Each time the trio passed, Peter registered a different view. Head-on, the medicine hat markings were apparent: a white face with an approximate four-inch, dark-brown band stretched between white ears; nostrils as pink as a pig's behind; eyes blue as flax flowers. From the side views, white legs and white body showed, sprinkled with dark-brown spots, as round and as big as a milking pail's circumference.

Henryk whistled. "You know, the natives consider a horse with Medicine Hat markings to have magical protective powers for their riders. I think that's why Dawid named the horse Mystic."

Peter beckoned Ginny to sit next to him.

She scrambled the skinny rails, settled her backside on the top rung, and anchored her feet in cowgirl fashion.

He leaned his shoulder against her. "Watch him. I've never seen anyone who can handle a horse like Michael can."

Michael led the colt across the paddock, ambling and leaving a generous slack in the reins.

Dawid shadowed Michael's moves.

Michael dropped the reins and walked away from the horse.

Snorting, pawing, and walking in jerky spurts, Mystic approached.

But Michael firmly shooed him away.

"What's he doing?" Ginny whispered as she inclined her body toward Peter.

"Shhh…"

The colt zigzagged around Michael and tried to cut in.

Powdered dust billowed and settled on the colt, the trainers, and the spectators.

Peter stared straight ahead. "The colt is confused

because he's used to getting affection and treats from Michael."

Mystic neighed and dipped his head under Michael's arms.

Michael continued to ignore the horse's attempt for recognition.

"Oh, poor baby...I think Michael's mean. Tsk. Tsk." Ginny expelled a sigh.

Peter turned toward Ginny. A slow, steady smile spread across his lips which threatened the security of the straw bobbling out of his mouth. He lifted his jaw and used the shaft of wheat as a pointer.

Michael retrieved the dragging reins and tightened the slack.

The colt stilled his Medicine Hat-marked head and snorted.

Michael stared into the animal's eyes and walked away.

The horse blew a puff of air from his nostrils, kept his lips close to the ground, and followed.

Michael turned and walked in the other direction.

Peter shifted his weight on the rail and whistled softly.

The horse changed direction and trailed Michael.

Ginny gasped.

Michael continued his fancy footwork, moving backward, forward, circling left and right.

"Keep your eye on the colt." Peter brushed his elbow against her rib and pointed. "He's licking and chewing, though he has nothing in his mouth. See Mystic tuck his head." He scrunched his shoulders and kept his gaze toward the corral. "See him following Michael like he was a little lamb?"

Ginny nodded.

"In horse language that's saying, 'Yah, you are my friend, and I trust you.' "

Michael stepped back.

Dawid pulled an apple from his back pocket. He opened his hand and offered the fruit to the colt.

Mystic opened his mouth, and his muscled tongue pulled the apple behind his forward embedded incisors. A wad of saliva dropped on the earth.

Dawid lavished praise and stroked the colt's bristly-haired muzzle. He reached over to Michael.

Michael took his hand and made a joke of shaking off the transferred horse slobber.

Dawid laughed.

From his standing spot behind the corral fence, Henryk thumped his hat on the rails. "Good show, boys."

Ginny elbowed Peter. "How did Michael know to do that?"

"I told you, that one, Michael, is a born horse trainer. Horses are naturally scared. They need to be sure you won't hurt them before giving you their trust and seeking you as a protector. Michael talks in a language the colt could understand. Now Dawid is learning the language."

What is the language you understand? Peter turned his contemplations to the woman who sat beside him.

As if reading his thoughts, Ginny licked her lips and lowered her chin. He swallowed a chuckle.

"What?" Ginny scrunched her lips.

Peter gripped the rail and bounced it.

She snorted.

What started as a snort grew into a hoot and then

erupted into a full-blown belly buster. The top rail wobbled.

Wobbling advanced to shaking.

Peter was the first to be unseated. He landed on the inside of the sandy paddock and turned in time to grasp a tumbling Ginny.

Laughter melted to silence as their bodies touched from shoulders to toes.

She's skinnier than I imagined. A tendon in her neck puffed out, pulsing and vibrating. He fought the impulse to bury his face and nuzzle her like a trusting colt.

"Show's over. Back to work, you two," Henryk hollered.

Peter jumped. *Which show did Henryk mean? The boys and the horse, or the boy and the girl?* "Yah, of course." He winked at Ginny. Then he did something he'd thought of doing since the afternoon he visited with Nadia and Ginny in the meadow. He grasped the tail of her braid and rolled it between his fingers.

Ginny covered her mouth and ran to the house.

Peter clapped his hat on his head and kicked corral dust on his way to the barn. *I'm not imagining this. She's feeling something, too.*

****

Henryk and Dawid came in from the fields for supper without Peter, explaining he fell behind on his chores and left.

Ginny sighed. She had come to look forward to the end of their day, filled with the agreeable company of the Pawlowski family and Peter.

Following a cold meal of sliced ham, pickled green beans, and potato salad, Nadia and Ginny restored the kitchen to order.

Ruta poured dried navy beans into a large pot to soak overnight. "Thank you, girls. I'm heading to my bedroom. I'll give my hair a good brushing and then I'll read for a while." She hung her apron on the peg by the pantry.

"G'night, Mama." Nadia hung a dish towel over the sink. "My journal is calling me, and my dear Tad deserves a letter."

Ginny sighed. "I'm going for a little fresh air." She walked out into the June evening and drifted aimlessly until she reached the corral. Once inside, she trudged through the sandy arena, smoothed horseshoe prints with her boots, and strolled to the spot Peter straddled earlier in the day. She climbed to the area she occupied before and tucked her feet behind the lower rung.

A low whinny echoed in the barn.

A soft snickering answered.

Moonlight illuminated the delicate gestures of a black cat licking her milk-soaked paws.

With persistent and beseeching meowing, a slatternly tomcat successfully romanced the ebony feline and lured her into the shadows.

Ginny thought back to the recent lazy afternoon she shared with Nadia and Peter. *I would've told you what I want in a husband, Peter Nickles. I would've told you a man with your hearty laugh, your ability to make distressing work fun, and a man who is loyal to his friends like you are. If we'd been alone, I would've asked you how the scars on your back came to be, and I would've kissed them in every direction.*

She rocked on the top rail of the corral and, with a trembling hand, shifted the braid hanging against her back to the swell of her breast. Rolling the tail in her hand, she eased off the fence and walked a solitary path back to the house, painfully aware of the coupled world about her.

Chapter 14

Rapid-succession slamming noises reverberated from the Pawlowski kitchen below Ginny's assigned bedroom.

"Mama, whatever are you looking for?" Nadia's voice streamed upward.

"My favorite cake pan. The one I use to make a birthday cake." Ruta's tone rose higher with each cupboard closure. "I've gotta get it done before your father comes in for the noon meal. I hate to heat the house, but it's for a once-in-a-lifetime occasion."

"Well, don't get all in a tizzy. I can help."

Ginny scrambled out of bed, hastily dressed, and hurried down the steps.

"Good morning, Ginny." Ruta knelt on the kitchen floor. The soles of her bare feet peeked out from the pouf of her compressed calico skirt.

A recipe book lay open on the sideboard, and a bottle of Dr. Price's Flavoring Extract stood next to an enormous mixing bowl.

"Shall I help you in the kitchen today or keep sewing?" Ginny pulled an apron from a peg.

"Henryk's birthday is tomorrow, June twenty-first. Good grief, fifty years old." Ruta clutched her knees. "I'm making a birthday supper and inviting some neighbors, but let's keep him in suspense. So, girls, it's a secret, yah?" She put an index finger over her mouth and arched her eyebrows. Ruta rose on her knees and reached for a countertop.

Ginny extended a hand.

Ruta levered her weight against it. "Thank you, *kochanie*." She moved to the stovetop and poured Ginny a cup of coffee. "I'll send Dawid today to ask your brother and sister-in-law and Peter to come. Do you think you could take some time from your sewing and help with a celebration, Ginny?"

"Sure." Ginny frowned. She pulled the apron ties tight around her waist.

"Oh, don't worry. I won't keep you all day from your sewing."

The party preparations weren't vexing Ginny. In Kathleen's menacing presence, Ginny was on niggling tenterhooks.

"Nadia, get the feather duster and attack the front room," Ruta barked. "Check the plants and trim the dry edges. Take the cushions and rugs outside. Whack them with the rug beater. After that, sprinkle baking soda on the carpets and brush them. Then apply cold tea to the varnished baseboards in the hallway. We need to make this whole house clean—so much dust. Get going now."

"Yes, Mama." Nadia rolled her eyes at Ginny.

"Dawid." Ruta stepped to the hallway leading into the front room. "Get your eyes off the horse sale column in that newspaper and fill a bucket with water and add a cup of vinegar. I want you to wash all the east windows—inside and out. But before that, take this cream to the springhouse and bring me some buttermilk. I'm baking your Papa a gingerbread cake. After the windows are sparkling clean, I need you to ride to the Dahlke farm and the Nickles farm to invite them to supper tomorrow night for your Papa's birthday."

"Now, Mama? Papa needs me in the barn." Dawid took a step toward the door.

"Well, now, who comes first in this house?" Ruta thrust a bottle of cream toward her son.

Dawid grimaced and took the glass from his mother.

"Not a word of this party to your father. It's a secret," Ruta shouted after him. "Come, Ginny, kitchen work for you and me. We'll make Henryk's favorites: pea soup, potato dumplings stuffed with ham, and of course, sauerkraut with sausage. June isn't the best month for a celebration. No fresh tomatoes, apples, pears, or corn are available. However, all those things will be in full harvest and ready for Nadia and Tad's wedding day."

"Mama," Nadia admonished. She brandished a feather duster above her head.

"I know, I know. It's always on my mind." Ruta threw her hands in the air. "You know, Ginny, I'm not one to pry, but I wonder how it goes between your brother and sister-in-law." She arched her eyebrows and bit her lower lip. "Now that poor girl doesn't seem to know the difference between a potato peeler and a spatula. I imagine things have changed for the better now you are there."

Ginny sighed and opened the utensil drawer. "Well, Kathleen is not fond of everyday chores. That is the truth. I think she fancies herself a fashion model or an artist, not a farmer's wife. She must have cooking talents, though I've yet to see her use them. When I first arrived, we had this marvelous brown bread with a pumpkin seed crust. I found the sweetest butter when I first went to the springhouse."

Ruta spun, upsetting a bowl of potatoes. "Oh, my." She twisted to grab the rolling spuds. "I can solve that mystery. I brought Kathleen some bread and honey butter the minute I heard you were arriving."

"Oh." Ginny laughed. "By the way, the stew and applesauce were great, too."

"Ginny, we never asked you." Nadia grasped a tin of baking soda from Ruta's clutch and locked gazes with her mother. "Did you have a beau in New York?"

Ginny gulped and cleared her throat. "Well, there was this man…" She continued to root in the silverware drawer.

"Yes?" Nadia breathed.

Ruta and Nadia moved close to Ginny.

She stepped sideways and faltered. Ruta's indulgence in things romantic blocked the ticking, birthday-party clock. *Would it be impolite if I steered her back to the tasks at hand? Maybe I can keep this story short.* "I did some volunteer work with a group of ladies in Dansville." Ginny smoothed a hand on the sideboard. "We would get together and roll bandages for the veterans and those in the hospital. One of the ladies has a son named Wallace."

"Wallace…" Ruta repeated, in a breathy voice, oblivious to flour spilling outside a tin measuring cup.

"How did the two of you meet?" Nadia sucked in a breath.

"One day, Wallace came to escort his mother home, and she introduced us."

"What's he like?" Ruta flapped loose flour off the table with her apron.

"Mama, let Ginny tell the story. Quit interrupting," Nadia scolded. "Is he handsome?"

Ginny's throat tightened. Nadia's unswerving scrutiny squeezed like a too-tight collar.

"Nadia…" Ruta reproached.

"Oops, sorry, Ginny." Nadia made a lip-buttoning motion with one hand and clasped a rug beater with the other.

Ginny widened her eyes. "Yah, yah, I would have to say, he is quite the good-looker Wallace is." She played to a reverent audience now. The center stage attention spurred her to exaggerate Wallace's attributes. She was taking a risk, but the chances of Nadia and Ruta ever meeting Wallace were as bona fide as a Polish cookbook without the word dill. Ginny continued. "Wallace has sleek, black hair. You know how some men have bushy eyebrows and hair growing in odd places like out of their ears and, well, you know, odd places? Not Wallace. Wallace's hair is absolute perfection, with no artifices." She blinked her eyes and exhaled.

A mixing bowl waited on the table. A rug beater stood abandoned just inside the parlor entrance. A birthday cake baking deadline loomed.

Nadia and Ruta sighed in tandem, melted into kitchen chairs, set their right elbows on the table, and pressed their chins into their upright palms.

"His eyes, oh, how could I describe the color of his eyes?" Ginny's voice turned husky. She scanned the kitchen.

Nadia and Ruta studied the kitchen.

Ginny sauntered to the windowsill and pointed. "That is the very color of Wallace's eyes." She lifted a bluebird figurine and caressed its glossy silhouette. "This icy blue is like staring Wallace in the eye."

"Ahh…" Nadia exhaled.

Ruta sighed.

"Wallace is so very bright and so noble. He's studying medicine at the University of Michigan. His father served as a surgeon on the battlefront for the Union soldiers. Wallace's entire family dedicates themselves to healing people. I very much admire their commitment." *Every word regarding Wallace's accomplishments and compassion was true.* Ginny bit her bottom lip.

"How very honorable, and you, too, Ginny, how laudable to volunteer like that." Nadia clapped.

The knife Ginny held in her hand clattered to the floor. *Oh, Nadia, I'm not worthy of your praise.* She stooped to retrieve the utensil. Tears clung to her lower eyelashes.

"Ginny." Ruta rose and stood next to Ginny. "You can finish the story another day, *kochanie.*" Ruta squeezed Ginny's upper arm.

"Mama, here's the buttermilk." Dawid tramped through the doorway.

Ruta reached for a pail and a bottle of vinegar. "I'll trade you, Son." She turned to Ginny and Nadia. "Perfect timing, girls, now to finish this cake."

Nadia walked to Ginny and hugged her. She reclaimed the rug beater. "It's back to work for me, too."

Ginny sighed. *Wallace is no more my beau than the sought-after Peter Nickles.*

****

The remainder of the afternoon and the next day,

Ruta, Nadia, Dawid, and Ginny conspired to keep the birthday dinner a surprise for Henryk. All three ladies took turns redirecting Henryk from the kitchen.

"It's such a beautiful day, dear. I've decided we'll have our noon meal on the porch. A little picnic, yah?" Ruta grabbed her husband by the elbow.

On the day of the party, Dawid furthered the ruse by urging his father to investigate a suspicious animal track in the field farthest from the house.

So, Henryk was well out of the way.

Ginny and Ruta bustled about with last-minute party preparations. The main dish of pork sausage and sauerkraut laced with caraway seed lay in a blue-and-yellow bowl, topped with halved, hard-boiled eggs, yolks side up, fried bacon, and bits of hard bread. The dumplings' crimped edges and translucent shells hinted at the spicy meat inside. The pea soup was vibrant with husks and pulped filling from Ruta's garden. The vinegary smell of sauerkraut and the flavorful aroma of bacon riddled the kitchen space.

Boot-shuffling clamor, backslapping, and loud guffaws reverberated from the front porch.

Ruta and Ginny poised with dishes in their hands.

"You old dog, you, happy birthday," Peter's voice boomed, followed by Henryk's suspender pinging.

"Yah, happy birthday, you old coot," Joseph called.

"Ah, Joseph and Kathleen must be here, too." Ruta nudged her elbow into Ginny's back. "Our company has all arrived." She set the dish on the table, wiped her hands on her apron, and inched through the doorway. "C'mon, Ginny, the party has started."

Kathleen entered the kitchen.

Ginny's jaw dropped. *Oh, Kathleen, no!* She

stiffened and fumbled the dish she held. Her top teeth bit into the skin below her lower lip, and she tasted blood.

"Lovely outfit, Kathleen," Ruta exclaimed.

"Well, it's Ginny's, but I think it looks better on me." Kathleen swirled in a prairie- brown-and-black-plaid skirt, revealing a series of small rips in the waistline. "I tried Ginny's blouses, but we don't have the same figure." She struck a pose, emphasizing her ample bust line.

Ruta pursed her mouth and cast a doleful glance.

The men crowded their way into the house.

"Let's all take a seat." Ruta brought a basket of freshly baked rolls from the kitchen and centered it on the table.

Kathleen chose a chair, smoothed the back of Ginny's best church skirt, and sat.

Ginny's stomach roiled. Her teeth hurt from clenching. She fought the inclination to bolt out the door.

At the side opposite of Kathleen, Peter pulled out a chair and beckoned Ginny to sit.

Ginny's heart swelled as he pushed her chair and claimed an adjacent seat. He smelled of cedar soap and something piney. His beard was mat-free, combed, and sprung loosely about his jaw. The cuffs of his denim shirt were rolled inches past his wrist bones, and his fingernails bore the evidence of a rough scrubbing. Ginny inhaled a breath that threatened to pop the glass buttons off her lawn shirt.

Kathleen's arched brow and pinched face gave Ginny a moment's triumph.

"Ginny is such a help. I asked her to come and sew

for Nadia's wedding. Not only is she a talented seamstress, but this girl can cook." Ruta added another dish to the table and took her place at the end of the table.

"Yah, this girl is a marvel. She performs veterinary medicine, too," Henryk chimed.

"I don't think it will be long before some lucky bachelor claims her."

Ruta's voice broadcast over the table like an auctioneer at a livestock sale. Ginny blushed, picked up her fork, and plied it into a pile of sauerkraut pocked with caraway seed. Her mouth watered.

"Well, marriage isn't all about sewing and cooking." Kathleen lifted her pointy chin.

"I suppose you're right. But a man must eat." Henryk rubbed his belly. "And a man does need his socks mended every so often, right, Ruta?"

"Yah, right. I finished darning a drawer full of tattered socks this morning. It is a birthday gift to my dear husband." Ruta smirked.

Joseph chuckled and rubbed his nose.

Dawid shook his head.

Water sprayed from Nadia's nose.

Ginny put her hands on either side of her face and grinned.

Kathleen sat straight as a pin.

"You can start on these next, Ruta." Peter held up one of his feet.

"Peter, find your own sock darner!" Henryk snapped his suspenders and slammed a fist on the table.

Cups, plates, and silverware at the opposite end of the table lifted and rattled.

Are those the same socks he wore Easter Sunday?

144

The hole was more prominent. Ginny sighed.

"Peter, if any dumplings are left, send them this way." Henryk smacked his lips.

"Here you go, birthday boy. These sure are sweet and kind of spicy." Peter leaned forward, passed the pottery bowl, and brushed his foot against Ginny's ankle.

Heat spread from Ginny's calf to her neck to her face. She tucked her toes behind the legs of her chair. *What was Peter thinking? And was he referring to the dumplings or her ankle?*

"Ginny, we're taking you home with us tonight. Kathleen needs your help." Joseph scraped his upper teeth over his bottom lip.

"Of course." Ginny clenched her fists beneath the table. "Ruta, if Joseph allows it, I will come back later and keep working on the wedding garments. Joseph?"

"Yes, Sister. You can make short visits." Joseph leveled his gaze on Kathleen.

"Yes, yes, we've got lots of time before the big day." Ruta stood and gathered plates. "So now, who can stay for cake?"

"My chores can wait a little longer tonight." Peter pulled a cigarette from his shirt pocket.

Joseph nodded.

Kathleen coughed.

"Good, you men can escape for a smoke while we settle the kitchen. After that, we will serve the birthday cake."

Nadia dropped dinner plates into a sink of soapy water.

Ruta poked five slender candles into the top of the pastry.

Ginny pulled small plates from the cupboard and forks from the silverware drawer, and she followed Ruta back to the table.

A sweet smell of tobacco mingled with the scent of ginger as the men reentered the kitchen.

Ruta motioned for everyone to sit.

"Happy birthday, dear Henryk." Ruta lit the candles and set the cake in front of the birthday boy.

Henryk puffed his dimpled cheeks and blew out the candles.

"Why don't we enjoy our cake on the porch? It's such a lovely night." Ruta pulled the candles and laid them on the sideboard. She moved the cake to the table and cut wedged slices.

Ginny held the plates as Ruta dropped a piece on each.

Everyone chose a plate and a fork and walked out the front door.

A bright splash of pink, swathed in deepening shades of red, polished the western sky. Barn swallows flit atop the roof. Bats zoomed into chestnut trees and disappeared among the ripening fruits.

"A good omen for tomorrow's work." Henryk stretched his shoulders, swiveled his arms, and gazed at the sky.

Ruta and Henryk chose the most worn chairs, placed side by side.

Joseph motioned for Kathleen to sit and then followed in a chair next to hers.

Nadia sat close to her mother and leaned her head against her mother's knee.

Dawid dropped on his haunches near the screen door.

Peter held the back of the remaining camp chair.

Ginny claimed it.

Peter squatted into a sitting position on the top porch step, opposite Ginny, and angled his knee to rest his boot on the step below. "Well, old friend, *Sto Lat*. Ruta, you chose well for a birthday cake. In New York, Ginny's friends"—he glanced at Ginny—"would call it gingerbread."

Ginny licked her spoon and nodded.

"We old Poles know it as *piernik*."

Henryk choked with laughter.

"Only you, Peter Nickles." Ruta snorted. She leaned forward and made eye contact with each person on the porch. "For those of you younger people, in Polish, *piernik* is a word with two meanings. It can mean a dough with cinnamon, ginger, cloves, and nutmeg, which is gingerbread cake, but it's also slang for old person."

Snapping his suspenders, Henryk bent his head over his chest and belly chuckled.

Peter threw his head against the railing and howled.

Dawid kicked his feet on the porch floor. "Hah, Papa—old man."

The glowing reds on the horizon melted into purple smidgins.

"Well, besides this wonderful party and socks made whole, I have one more birthday wish." Henryk reached under his suspender strap and into his breast pocket. He pulled out a cigarette.

Peter took a few steps toward Henryk, bent his knees, lit the birthday boy's cigarette, and reclaimed his seat.

"What is your request, oh, birthday boy?" Ruta

patted his thigh.

"I would like you to tell us a story. I love your storytelling, Wife."

Ruta's round cheeks flushed. She reached and squeezed Henryk's hand.

Fireflies flickered across the yard.

Silhouetted gladiola stalks framed the corners of the porch.

The heady perfume of lilacs wafted.

Ruta sighed. "I will tell you a story about my mama and papa. God rest their souls." She raised her right hand and made the sign of the cross from her forehead to her chest, across to her left shoulder, and to her right shoulder.

Henryk, Nadia, and Dawid repeated the movement.

"They lived in Sitki, in the region of Boronów. My father was a butcher. My mother, Izolda, would come to his shop to buy meat. They fell in love discussing kielbasa recipes."

Nadia snickered.

Dawid drummed the porch steps and guffawed. "Not very romantic, even I know that!"

Ruta cast her son a threatening scowl. "Well, back to the story. My father confided in his godfather—he had his heart set on marrying my mother." She sighed.

"Oh, I love this story, Mama." Nadia rocked back in her chair.

"*Kochanie*, your day is coming, you and your Tad." Ruta paused to blow a kiss to her daughter.

"On a Tuesday night, my father and his godfather went to my mother's house. They waited until dark, so no one in the village could see them and know their business, and they wanted to avoid the evil eye." Ruta stopped, made her eyes large, and flashed a wicked frown.

"Oh, Mama, there's no such thing." Dawid smacked a palm on his knee.

"Son, don't be so sure. I've learned to respect the evil eye." Henryk winked at Ruta.

"Yes, listen to your father's advice, Son. Now, where did I leave off?"

"They were about to get to grandmother's house." Nadia scratched her nose.

"Oh yes, my father and his godfather snuck over to my mother's home. All the lights were off, save one. They peered through the window. Grandfather sat alone at the parlor table, reading his Bible. My father's godfather rapped on the glass panes. Grandfather opened the door and let them inside."

Henryk made a fist and knocked on the floorboards.

Ruta rolled her eyes.

"As I was about to say, my father pulled a *gesiorka*—a bottle of vodka from behind his back. A floral bouquet sat atop the bottle, and a red ribbon was tied on the neck. My father offered the bottle to my grandfather, and then Godfather said, 'We hear you have a heifer you might be selling. We want to let you know we are very interested if you are willing to part with it.' My grandfather snorted and took the bottle. He told my father and his godfather to return on Thursday night for the answer. Now, this is the tricky part of the story." Ruta sucked in a deep breath and expelled it slowly.

"Yah, it sure is." Henryk blew a ring of smoke. "Go on, Mama."

149

Ginny sat forward on her seat.

Cigarette smoke lazed around Peter's head.

Ruta laughed. "My grandfather, he was okay with the match. But, my grandmother, not so much. She heard my father planned to immigrate to Canada, and she couldn't bear the thought of her beautiful daughter moving far away. So, my grandmother planned to break them up, but she did not want to go against my grandfather, so here is what she did." Ruta lifted her fork, carved out a bite-size piece of cake, and brought it to her mouth. She set the fork on the plate, closed her eyes, and chewed.

The soft gray, grandparent love doves peeked over the eaves and cooed.

Ruta rocked back and forth. She reached for the utensil again.

"Well, goll darn it, what did the woman do?" Peter hollered.

The fork clattered to the wooden porch floor.

Ginny giggled. *I'm not the only one sucked into Ruta's story.*

"All right, all right, I will finish my cake after the story." Ruta snorted. "On Thursday night…"

"Wait a minute," Peter interrupted. He leaned toward Ruta. "How do you know it was a Thursday night?"

"Shush, Peter, just listen." Kathleen wagged a finger.

"As I was saying," Ruta continued, "After Father and his godfather arrived for dinner on Thursday night, my grandfather brought out the *gesiorka*. 'Izolda,' he asked my mother, 'get us some glasses.' My mother was giddy with joy and brought the glasses right away.

My grandfather poured a drink for the men. The men told jokes and talked about the great harvest. Meanwhile, Grandmother carried out her plan."

Across the porch, Peter sucked his dwindling cigarette and snapped it away with his middle finger and thumb just as the stub threatened to burn his flesh.

Ginny flinched. *That was too close for comfort.*

Ruta stood and cupped her hands, fashioning a circle. "She placed bowls on the table." Ruta doled out pretend bowls. "Then she portioned out the soup." She mimicked the action with a pretend ladle.

Nadia giggled.

"Then she asked my father, his godfather, my grandfather, my mother, and my mother's sisters and brothers to please, please come and sit." Ruta motioned her ancestors to the imaginary table.

"My father and his godfather pulled their chairs from the table. My grandfather raised his head and sniffed the air. He gripped his bowl and stared inside it. His eyes shrunk in his head, and he yelled in an angry voice, '*Czaria*, is this duck blood soup?' "

Henryk fashioned his hands into a make-believe shotgun, fanned it across the night sky, and popped off a pretend shot.

" 'Yah,' my grandmother replied. My father's godfather grabbed my father by the arm and shoved him to the door. Grandfather shouted and cursed. My mother burst into tears."

"Why? What happened?" Peter demanded. He shifted his legs and leaned toward Ruta.

"Serving duck blood soup on the Thursday night a suitor called meant no wedding—we are not interested."

Henryk repeated his shotgun move.

Dawid chuckled and mimicked his father's hunting action. "Pow!"

"Oh, my." Ginny inhaled a deep breath. "I can only imagine how heartsick your mother must have felt."

Nadia shook her head.

Ruta sucked a deep breath. "Well, as you know, everything got straightened around since your grandpa and grandma did get married and had me. Now I have you children." She beamed at Nadia and Dawid. "But my grandfather had to make a big apology to my father and his godfather. And my parents moved to Canada, even though your great-grandmother tried her best to prevent that marriage and keep her daughter close."

"Thanks be to God they did move to Canada and then emigrated to Parisville." Henryk stroked Ruta's hand. "Well, now that my daughter is safely engaged, you could cook me duck soup, Wife."

"Well." Ruta whistled. "If you brought me a fat little duck, I would."

"I bet Chessie can retrieve a nice mallard once I set my duck blind, yah?" Joseph raised his arms and repeated Henryk's duck shooting mime.

Peter smacked his hat against his thighs and rose. "Well, it's time for me, I think, to say good night. Ginny, I wonder if I may have a word with you."

Silence held sway on the porch.

Ginny's cheeks simmered.

Peter faced her and moved his chin ever so slightly toward the paddock.

She stood and took three steps forward. The sound of her footfalls boomed in her ears. She hesitated and scanned the faces of each person on the porch.

Kathleen's eyes squeezed into mere slits and her lips rucked.

"Ginny…" Peter crooked a finger.

His husky voice mesmerized her and pulled her forward. She tucked her head, followed, and inhaled his scent—an exotic mixture of cinnamon, nutmeg, allspice and homegrown tobacco.

Peter reached the paddock.

Star pranced to the fence rail, neighed a welcome, and shook her lustrous mane.

Peter opened the gate, ushered Ginny inside and followed her. "Hey, Star."

Snorting, the horse pressed her face into Peter's outstretched palm.

Peter flattened his hand and smoothed it over the horse's muzzle. He repeated the petting again and again and again.

Something in Ginny spilled. Heat infused her face. Her stomach bubbled.

Crickets played their day-ending symphony.

A breeze pushed a wash of cleansing lilac scent.

Peter snatched his saddle from the corral rail, threw it over Star's rump, grabbed the saddle horn, and pulled himself onto the horse's back. He fitted his boots into the stirrups, took up the reins, and turned Star in a half-circle, kicking dust and scattering fireflies.

Ginny staggered. She backstepped. Her breath suspended.

"Ginny…" Peter gripped the saddle horn with one hand. He smiled a grin that spread across his lips and into the bristles of his sideburns.

"Yes," she responded in a mere whisper—as weightless as the trail of his cigarette smoke.

"Do you know how to make duck blood soup?" Peter leaned back in his saddle. He sat tall and pulled the reins taut over his worn jeans.

Ginny swallowed.

The waning traces of the setting sun slanted across the brim of his hat and illuminated the sawtooth pattern of the dangling shells. She balled her hands into fists and shoved them deep into her apron pockets. "No, I've never made duck blood soup."

"Well, that's a good thing." He dug his boots into Star's side. "Giddy up."

She watched him leave. Her heart flickered uncontrollably like the disappearing hairs on Star's tail.

Chapter 15

Sighing, Ginny wiped her hands and paused before the calendar hanging on the kitchen wall next to the blackened stovepipe in Joseph and Kathleen's kitchen. Oil spots resembling ants on parade festooned the June page. In three weeks, they would all be marching into July.

She moved to the sink, scrubbed the remnants of bean soup from the most giant pot in the house, and grimaced at the dishes, forks, spoons, pots, and pans bearing the traces of navy beans and noodles.

Kathleen and Joseph managed to turn the tidy house into a foul mess within a span of ten days. She carried the pot, trekked to the well, drew water, and filled the pot to the brim. On her return, Ginny passed the lavender plants. She set down the vessel, plucked a lavender shoot, and inhaled its sweet elixir, as if it was life-giving oxygen.

During the past week, leaf buds matured to green-veined shapes distinctive to their oak, elm, hickory, maple, or birch mother.

Grasses grew with recklessness.

Birds' nests dotted the landscape—sweet trilling bluebird families in apple tree cavities, lemon-breasted Kirtland's Warbler families in the jack pines, and the whistling, plump bodied, short-tailed Northern Bobwhites in the grasses and brushy pastures.

The air warmed.

The earth warmed.

Insects hatched and filled the sky with movement and the atmosphere with buzzing.

Ginny kicked off her boots and stowed them in the lean-to. She traced her footsteps back to the kitchen, made a fire on the stove to heat dishwater, and dropped dishes into the pot.

"Come see what I'm working on." Kathleen waved a brown paper scored with pencil drawings of the front, side, and back views of women's bonnets. "Could you make me one to look like this?"

Would the woman never take control of her own house? Ginny was less than one day back in the presence of Joseph and Kathleen, and already she longed for an excuse to get away. The time had come for another visit with Nokee. She assured Nokee she would return to learn more about medicines and herbs, and Nokee might have an explanation for the scarring on Peter's back. Ginny's stomach quaked as she recalled the angry red mutations on his virile body. First thing tomorrow, she'd ask Joseph's permission for another Nokee visit.

****

Rain fell overnight and well into the morning.

Stopping in the lean-to, Ginny slid her feet into her boots and draped a coat over her head. She opened the cabin door and closed it carefully.

Sunlight broke through the salt and pepper clouds hanging on the horizon.

Ginny zigzagged around puddles and stomped to the barn. *Please say 'Yes,' Brother*. She bit her lip and pulled the door aside.

Joseph held a lamb and a pair of nail clippers. "Great timing, Sister. I could use your help."

Ginny scooped her hand under the lamb's soft belly and lifted the struggling lamb onto her lap.

The baby kicked her sharp hooves and scraped Ginny's arm.

"Ouch! I'll hold. You trim."

Joseph slipped his fingers into the rings of the clippers and reached for a front leg of the lamb.

"Baaa…"

Ginny tucked the baby's head under her chin. "Joseph, I'd like to revisit Nokee. Gathering medicinal herbs must be well-timed, and I don't want to miss the chance to get the plants we need. Unfortunately, we'd have to wait a whole year to collect them, so I should go soon." Her words were rushed and delivered in a tone that wailed like a primary student begging for a horehound drop.

Joseph set the clippers on his knee. He sighed. "Ginny, you can see why long visits away are not good. Kathleen depends on you." He frowned and wiped his forehead on his sleeve.

The Cotswold lamb in Ginny's lap bleated and thrashed. Its baby heart mimicked the thud of Ginny's contrite affections. She stroked the baby's head and its quivering body until the creature's legs relaxed, wishing all the while she had the same power to quiet Joseph's worries. *Why, oh why, does he coddle Kathleen so fervently?*

"If you set things right in the cabin and have meals arranged, you can go tomorrow. But you'll have to walk this time, Sister. The creek has shrunk now that summer is here. Just follow the banks and take Chessie.

You'll have more than that dog for company. Be prepared for winged, blood-thirsty mosquitoes."

****

Yesterday, each ram, ewe, and lamb in the Dahlke barn thrashed and baaed their way through hoof trimming.

Ginny hummed, stretched her arms, and jumped out of bed. *Finished that job yesterday.*

A breeze flapped the curtains hanging over the kitchen window.

The floorboards were cool on her bare feet.

The day was perfect for burning through chores and walking to Nokee's. She dressed, ate a light breakfast of rye bread and strawberry jam, and headed to the barn. She clamped a hand over the neck of a rebellious chicken, grabbed the ax, and took both to the chopping block under a wide-leaved oak tree. She whacked the head and feet from the chicken and cooked the carcass in a pot of boiling water. She churned butter and made a large pot of *zurek,* fermented rye soup. While waiting for the soup to cook and the chicken to fall from the bones, she extracted clean wool from a canvas bag and carded the tangled fibers in preparation for spinning. She left no minute of the morning unworked. Joseph just had to witness her diligence and approve her Nokee visit.

After Joseph returned from early barn chores, he reviewed the prepared chicken and soup, the streak-free windowpanes, the shiny empty sink, and the tightly sealed lips on Ginny's face. Then, finally, he nodded and motioned her to leave.

Ginny leaped, kissed him on the cheek, and bolted out the door. "Chessie!" *I'll gain more knowledge of herbal medicines, but what I really what to discover is what happened to Peter's back. Ginny reflected on the first day she met Peter and observed the way he stroked the brim of the shell-decorated hat—as if the soft felt was the silky skin of his lover. Nokee handled the matching shells in her sewing box in the same loving manner. An intimate connection must exist between them, and Nokee must know the cause of Peter's scars.*

****

Nokee's ginger-colored cat preened herself on the stoop. "Hey, kitty, kitty, kitty," Ginny called.

Chessie bounded toward the Wilkowski cabin and barked.

"Meow." The cat's snarls and unbridled hissing stalled Chessie from advancing.

Nokee opened the door and laughed. "Ah, Ginny. Come in. As soon as I tidy the kitchen, I'll show you how to build a smudge fire, and then we will hunt in the woods. While you're waiting, you can walk around and gather a pile of dried pine needles. We'll need those to start the fire." Nokee rolled her sleeves to her elbows, reached behind the door, pulled out a canvas bag, and thrust it at Ginny. "You can use this. "Meet you by the fire pit next to the wood stack."

Ginny looped the bag's straps over her wrist and walked to a stand of red pine trees. A carpet of fire-ready dried needles lay at her feet. She opened the bag, threw fistfuls of needles inside, and sauntered to the stacked woodpile. She furrowed her brow and chewed on her lower lip. The raised welts on Peter's back flashed through her mind. *How do I ask Nokee such personal questions? Will she ignore me? Will she scold me for being nosy?*

159

"You look scared. I promise not to lose you in the woods." Nokee tapped Ginny's shoulder.

Ginny jumped. "Gah! I was lost in my thoughts."

Nokee smiled. "Let me distract you." She moved to the wood pile, selected a bundle of thin twigs, and bent to the stone fire ring on the ground. Placing the twigs in a teepee formation, she turned. "The fire takes a bit of patience, and I hate to stand close to a fire on a hot day like today. You'll be glad since we are moving into battle—a battle into the deep woods where our enemy, the mosquito, lives. Come over here and place the pine needles in the circle under the twigs, as if you were laying a rug on the floor."

Stepping forward, Ginny bent and dropped the pine droppings into the center of Nokee's fire structure.

Nokee pulled matches from her pocket and struck a match against a rock lining the fire pit. As she added layers of green pine needles, grasses, and cedar boughs, tiny orange glows flickered, ornamented the dry, and dismissed the green with a dump of ugly gray.

Acrid smoke billowed.

Ginny's eyes watered. Her lungs fought for air and beat against her ribs. Following Nokee's lead, she leaned from her waist and extended the entire length of her hair, allowing the mosquito-repelling smoke to infiltrate it. She moved her arms in large circles, fanning the smoke to penetrate her clothing. Like Nokee, she broke cedar bough tips and crushed them on body parts Nokee described as "your leanest and warmest." She rubbed the cedar around her neck's circumference, behind her ears, and over her wrists.

"Don't forget underneath, Ginny. Our enemies swarm from the ground." Nokee lifted her skirts, opening the fabric to the smoke.

"Oh, witches of the woods," Peter called. "What wizardry are you conjuring?"

Ginny jumped as if she stepped on the hot coals fueling the smudge fire. "Peter Nickles, what are you doing here?"

He reared back in his saddle and laughed. "I'm here to see if Lerk can help patch fences today. You still didn't tell me what you're doing, though. Nokee, are you turning Ginny into a sorceress?"

Nokee spun, twirled a finger, and pointed it at Peter's nose. "Peter, if you don't leave us alone, I will turn you into a tick on a donkey's behind."

He chuckled. "Lerk's fishing pole is not at your front door, Nokee, so I know where to find him." He kneed Star. "Hah."

As she doused the fire, Nokee coughed.

How long had she been staring after Peter? She turned to Nokee and intercepted her gaze.

Nokee slung a basket over her arm, offered Ginny a hand, and led her toward the woods. "This is an old lumbering road. Watch where you walk."

Ginny stepped onto a trail pocked with deep ruts and thick undergrowth.

Chickadees and gray-crested tit mouses soared from a bower of thick shrubs.

Crouching, Nokee fingered a plant with heart-shaped leaves. "Ginny, come and see, but be careful. This one has sharp prickles."

Lustrous red berries adorned erect woody stems. Shiny dark foliage complemented the bush. "Oh, my, this is a handsome plant." Ginny knelt beside Nokee.

"Yes, but what we are interested in is below the

ground." Nokee pulled a trowel from her basket and dug down about twelve inches around the plant's circumference. Then, grasping the top of the plant, she yanked. Grunting with the effort, Nokee extracted a tuberous root, the length of a man's hand.

A sweet smell, like root beer, filled the air.

Tilting back on her haunches, Nokee held aloft the plant. "Meet sarsaparilla."

"You mean the sarsaparilla the men put in beer to make it foam?"

"The same."

"What are we to do with it? Are you having me make beer, Nokee?"

"No, no, no. We will grind the root and store it. When you need to make a poultice for healing a wound, add some of this." Nokee scratched her fingernail into the root and lapped her finger. "Here, try it."

Ginny peeled away the bark and licked it. She closed her eyes. "Now, this I like." She swirled the saccharine taste in her mouth. The spice freshened her tongue.

For the next hour, the women dug and wrestled sarsaparilla plants.

"How about a little rest?" Nokee wandered to a moss-covered log with a stripe of sunlight warming its bark. She folded her legs and lowered herself.

Ginny sat alongside her. Nokee's expression grew serene, like the surrounding forest. In a spot like this, secluded from curious ears and the sun's clarity, secrecy protected confessions and revelations. "Nokee." Ginny tucked her hands into the folds of her skirt. "Can you tell me what happened to Peter's wife?"

"Ah…Franny." Nokee rolled a sarsaparilla root

between her palms. "Franny died two days after she gave birth to a stillborn baby girl."

Ginny gasped. Her stomach quaked.

A chipmunk sprinted across the forest floor, chittered his woodland song and furled and unfurled his multi-striped tail.

A woodpecker's knocking insulted the silence.

"Josephine Pyonk attended her. Have you met her, Ginny?" Nokee's voice lowered.

"Peter brings her to church, and she and I were both guests at the Pawlowskis' for Easter dinner."

"Josephine was the first midwife of your people here. She lives on the next farm from Peter, so she didn't take long to reach Franny. She stayed with Franny for two days before the child was delivered." Nokee took a deep breath. "Ginny, the only way I know this part of the story is from Josephine. The cord wrapped three times around the baby's neck, and when she was born, the poor baby looked like a stone—cold and gray. Josephine swaddled the baby and let Franny hold her. The placenta would not come. Josephine kneaded Franny's belly—gently at first and then rougher. 'Find Nokee Wilkowski,' she yelled at Peter, and he came for me. I grabbed my birthing tools and jumped behind him on Star's back. That horse galloped as if a panther had his claws in her rump and his teeth in her hind leg. By the time we arrived, Franny had delivered a piece of the placenta." Nokee dropped the sarsaparilla. She clasped her hands over her knees and rocked.

Ginny gripped the log seat. Bark bit into her palms.

"Franny writhed on the bed. Her skin turned the color of a ripe, red plum, and her arms and legs puffed up." Nokee stared through the forest canopy.

Ginny's throat swelled.

"Josephine and I tried everything. But the blood wouldn't stop. Then, finally, Franny died in Peter's arms." Nokee inhaled through her teeth and released a mournful whistle.

Chick-a-dee-dee-dee. Chick-a-dee-dee-dee." The quick-flitting, little birds trilled, darting over their mossy carpet.

Struggling to breathe, Ginny dropped her head on her chest.

"After Josephine and I prepared Franny and their baby for burial, Peter went for the priest, and then he went to the barn and made a coffin out of pine he milled himself. Father came and blessed the bodies. Josephine and I placed Franny in first, and then the babe wrapped in one of Franny's shawls and laid her face on her mother's breast. You know, I've never seen a prettier dead body, Ginny. That baby had the silkiest hair. I combed it myself."

Comprehending the extent of Peter's grief, Ginny shuddered.

"Peter brought the coffin cover. Then he left. I never saw him cry or flail or shout at the heavens. But deep from the woods, I heard a wild keening. It rent the air like a dagger ripping a tight canvas sail. Peter stayed away all that night. Then, in the morning, he returned. Josephine and I laid out fresh clothes for him and cooked breakfast, which he wouldn't eat. Henryk Pawlowski and James McGrarry came and nailed the cover and put the coffin in Henryk's wagon. We met with Father and many St. Mary's members. Henryk and James lowered the coffin in the earth in the church cemetery." Nokee sighed.

Ginny swallowed a sob. She couldn't stop her hand from shaking as she laid it on top of Nokee's.

"Afterward, I insisted Peter come home with me, and he didn't resist, but once we got back to my home, he would not come in. He preferred the outdoors and the starry nights. I watched Peter try to shrink himself and sink in the same earth that swallowed Franny and their tiny babe." Nokee drew her shoulders tighter and clutched both hands to her chest.

"Each night, you looked over him and protected him." Ginny reached and rubbed Nokee's shoulder.

Nokee huffed a sigh. "I thank God for the blessing Peter lived."

As if to rejoice in that truth, a tufted titmouse whistled above them "Peter-peter-peter."

"And I thank you, Nokee, for sharing the story of Peter's heartaches."

The older woman closed her eyes and nodded.

"I hear mosquitoes buzzing, but they aren't biting."

Nokee chuckled. "Yah, we are real sorceresses. Come, Ginny, I want to show you more medicines, like what you can find in those black gum trees."

She pointed to a cluster of twenty-foot-high trees with bark that resembled the illustration of an alligator's back Ginny once saw in a children's book.

Nokee put her right hand through the handle of her basket, adjusted the trowel, and led Ginny to the black gums. "Watch your feet. This tree prefers swampy areas. Now we will test the smoky mosquito net we wear."

Ginny tiptoed after Nokee. Her footprints created mushy impressions. Water leaked through her shoes as she reached the trees with dense branches leafing into shiny, elliptically-shaped foliage.

Nokee set the basket on a stump. She took the trowel and scraped the bark, letting the shavings fall into a newspaper page at the bottom of her basket.

"There's s-s-something else…" Ginny stammered. She licked her lips. "What do you know about the scars on Peter's back?"

Nokee's face crumpled. "Do you know anything of Peter's past?" She leveled her gaze at Ginny.

"Not much more than what you've told me today. But at the Pawlowskis', I saw him washing at the pump, and I got sick to my stomach."

"I need to move a bit first." Nokee stood, stretched her arms over her head, and swept them to her feet.

Ginny tilted her head right and left toward each shoulder and walked in a circle.

Picking a stick off the ground, Nokee plunged it into the earth, signaled Ginny to sit, and sank on an adjoining stump. "Peter married Franny out east and came to Michigan to do lumbering. My man Chet and my brother George worked in the same camp as Peter. One night, a few months after Franny died, some men ambushed George. They stabbed him with his fishing knife. Peter found him, tore his own shirt into bands to make a tourniquet, but my brother died."

"Nokee, I am so sorry." Ginny clutched her chest.

"Chet left the camp, bringing George's body. While Chet was gone, the men went after Peter. They tied him to a tree and whipped him. 'That's what we do to Injun lovers,' they yelled."

Ginny gulped, covered her mouth with her hands, ground her elbows to her knees, and rocked.

Nokee's arm brushed against hers as she flung the stick into the canopy above them.

Branches crackled.

A crow complained.

Ginny opened her eyes.

Nokee's stick wobbled in a leaf web above them and dropped to the forest floor.

"The next morning, other men in the camp found Peter. They untied him, cleaned his wounds, and made a shelter. When Chet returned to the camp after my brother's burial, he found Peter writhing in pain and delirious. At night, Chet returned to me. I went to the forest and harvested herbs. I picked sarsaparilla, Ginny, like this." Nokee pointed to the roots in her basket. "For the rest of that night, Chet and I made poultices for Peter. We had to convince him to live because after Franny died, Peter had no will to go on. It was a terrible time." Nokee squeezed her eyes and shook her head.

Inhaling a succession of quick, shallow breaths, Ginny dug her fingernails into the stump's bark. "Nokee," she whispered. "I see why Peter is dear to you. You saved his life, not once, but twice."

"As he has saved mine." Nokee rubbed her hands over her mouth. "Six months after George died, Chet died. My boys found baskets filled with deer, squirrel, and rabbit meat dressed and ready for cooking. Peter left the game."

Taking Nokee's hands, Ginny logged the gnarled knuckles, the slender fingers, and the rough tips. They were the hands that massaged healing compresses into the raw slices of Peter's back. They were the hands that this very day reached out to offer friendship.

"You should be on your way before dark." Nokee

stood and patted Ginny's back. You are becoming more and more useful. A man like Peter will notice."

Ginny exhaled softly. "But Nokee, whatever medicines we've reaped from the earth will not cure the hauntings carved on his back or in his heart."

"No, but I think your heart can, Ginny."

"Peter-peter-peter," warbled a stout-billed, gray-and-white bird in accord with the words of the older woman.

Peter, oh Peter, what you have endured. Will you ever love again?

Chapter 16

With the early demanding weeks of June past and the planting done, Joseph agreed to resume Sunday churchgoing.

Ginny woke before dawn to help him feed and water the stock. "Good morning, Mama Pig," she sing-songed and upended a bucket of swill into a metal trough inside the pigsty.

Sunshine glinted off the bottom of the pail—momentarily blinding her.

The sow grunted hello and returned her attention to the pinching, wriggling, and squealing of her eight curly-cue-tailed piglets.

Buster and Blue tipped their velvet-soft noses, whickered, and flicked their tails as she filled a pail with oats and corn.

A breeze swirled tail and pin feathers about the barn floor.

Joseph treaded through them. "Hawk." He stepped outside the barn and checked the sky.

"I'll get breakfast." Ginny scurried past him. The worry lines on Joseph's brow signaled trouble. "Joseph, thanks for putting the tarp roof over the pigs. That sun is getting so hot, and those babies need to be protected."

Joseph waved. "See you in a few minutes."

Following a meal of bacon and biscuits, the Dahlke ladies stepped onto the front porch in summer-weight frocks and brand-new bonnets. The headpieces that began with Kathleen's penciled doodles came to fruition in the paper roses and feathered birds Ginny affixed on the crowns.

Hitched to the wagon and persuaded by Joseph's rein snapping, Buster and Blue plodded across the drive and stopped in front of the bonneted ladies.

A paper rosette fluttered in the mane of each horse and rendered mellifluous shushing sounds. Ginny snickered.

"Joseph." Kathleen giggled.

He shook his head and saluted Kathleen.

Buster and Blue deserved special recognition today, too. Walking in front of a four-wheeled wagon must've felt like a vacation after a plow's resistance. Both horses gummed their lips, whinnied, and shook their floral decorated manes as the ladies alit.

Ginny nestled in the straw lining the wagon and opened the satchel she packed that morning. *Will Father Graca approve?*

The hitching posts aligning the north side of the church filled as the Dahlke family pulled close.

Father Graca will be in good humor to see so many parishioners.

Joseph maneuvered the team to an open spot between a set of dappled geldings and a set of matched bays. He lowered to the ground and looped the reins around a fence rail. He walked behind the wagon and raised his arms.

Kathleen put her hands on his shoulders.

Joseph braced his hands around Kathleen's waist, lifted her, and swung her to the ground.

Ginny leaped from her seat in the back and

followed Joseph and Kathleen into St. Mary's Church.

Joseph walked past the seated Urdzela family, stopped at the end of the next pew, and motioned Kathleen and Ginny to take a seat.

Ginny nodded to Casimir and smiled at Sophie's ministrations. The boys retained fresh-combed and slicked hair. The girls' braids were tight and muss-free. Up and down her pew, Ginny witnessed smiles and nods. She swiveled sideways and stilled.

On the opposite side of the church, Peter sat with Josephine and the Oberski family—Martin, Marta, and Bette.

Ginny's heart flip-flopped. Peter's wheat-colored hair was groomed razor short on the sides, with a longer hank of hair combed to the right and slathered with some shiny substance. *Pomade? That would explain the presence of the obnoxious fly Peter swatted.* Sitting hatless revealed the shape of his ears. They bowed slightly from his head. The man reviewed suddenly turned his head and caught her gaze. Heat slammed her face. She turned her attention to the tissue-thin hymnal laying across her lap, opened to *The Old Rugged Cross*.

Father droned the opening prayers in traditional Latin.

His speech induced sleep as effectively as a Brahms lullaby. Ginny fanned herself with a glove. The gentle movement caused the hair on her neck to billow.

An Urdzela boy climbed over his brothers and sisters.

"Ouch," one of the boys hollered.

The outburst resulted in his mother's swift rap on the side of his head.

The recipient of his mother's cuff glowered and

mouthed, "Well, he stepped on me."

Casimir patted the struggling boy's shoulder as he stumbled past him to reach the aisle.

As the Urdzela son walked to the front of the church and turned to face the congregation, Ginny crossed her fingers. *Please, Lord, let this boy shine.*

The boy's soprano voice floated through the church, singing Polish words lauding the heavens and earth and tiny sparrows.

Throughout the hymn, Ginny perused her fellow parishioners. Tears leaked from Casimir's eyes, and he unashamedly brushed them from his cheeks.

As the boy took his seat, a collective sigh mounted, heads swiveled, and smiles widened in praise of the gift this child exhibited.

Everyone, that is, except for the child's mother swatting another Urdzela boy caught wiggling a finger in his nose.

Father Graca faced his congregation and blessed them with the sign of the cross.

The altar boys, wearing matching black cassocks and white cotton surplices, held tall crosses and flanked the priest.

Proceeding down the center aisle, Father took his place at the front door to greet his parishioners as they exited the church.

Ginny lagged and waited to give Father the altar cloths she embroidered painstakingly with the Polish crest—an eagle with splayed talons and a head adorned in a yellow crown. She watched the congregation as they emptied the church.

On the opposite side of the church, Peter stood and offered his arm to Josephine.

The elderly woman pulled her cane from beneath her seat and rose clumsily.

With shuffling steps, the pair inched slowly toward the aisle.

The Oberskis followed.

Bette sidled up to Peter. Her face glowed, and her spun ringlets bounced. She mouthed something to Peter, and her lush breast grazed against his elbow.

He stumbled and threw Josephine into a tilted stance.

Ginny's lungs seized.

Marta reached to balance Josephine.

Martin lunged to stabilize Peter.

Father Graca pounced to help, upending the three-peaked hat, which fell from his head and bounced on the floor. The priest stooped to retrieve his hat, placed it back on his head, and frowned at the jumbled queue. "Josephine, Martin and Marta, and Peter and Bette, God bless you and go in peace."

His loud voice carried to Ginny. *Peter and Bette, the handsome couple, he of pomaded hair, she of sugar ringlets, blessed and directed to go in peace.* Ginny bit her lip. She shooed a fly with a vengeance reserved for a poisonous spider. She bolted for the wagon, hopped into the back, and folded and refolded the embroidery piece in her hands.

Kathleen walked to the wagon, straightened her bonnet, and stood stiffly as she waited for Joseph.

Joseph assisted her onto the wagon, jogged around the horses, took his seat, and clucked to Buster and Blue.

"Stop. Please stop." A red-faced Casimir ran after the wagon.

"Whoa," Joseph yelled and stilled the team.

Ginny fell forward, her chin just missing the bottom of the buckboard.

"Miss Ginny," Casimir began, "Crops are in. Will you come to our house this week?"

"Joseph?" Ginny crossed her fingers under the folds of her striped faille dress.

"If she gets all the laundry done tomorrow, Ginny may go Tuesday."

"I'll come by with my team, Ginny. My Sophie will be so happy." Casimir dropped a dusty hat on his head, turned toward his family's wagon and waved broadly.

Sophie beamed and clapped her hands. She turned to the children wriggling and romping in the hay behind her.

She moved her lips as if she were announcing they were all taking a day off and feasting on ice cream for dinner.

Enthusiastic whoops blast the air.

A little Urdzela girl blew Ginny a kiss.

Ginny's heart softened.

"Did Father like the new altar cloths?" Joseph adjusted the reins in his hands.

"Oh, I think they would be better if I added some petite roses in the corners," Ginny lied.

"But you were so intent on presenting them today." Joseph turned from his waist.

"The next time will be fine. Father didn't expect them today." Ginny wandered her gaze to Peter. Bette placed her slim-ankled, silk-shoed foot in the lee of Peter's interlaced fingers. She tossed her silver-haloed head and squealed as Peter clasped her wispy waist and sprung her effortlessly on the seat beside her parents.

"Yah, maybe next time." Kathleen waved as they passed the Oberski wagon, turned, and smiled behind her.

Why is Kathleen so thrilled Peter dotes on Bette?

Chapter 17

Ginny dropped her head into her pillow. The exuberant faces of the Urdzela family and the enthusiasm for her visit they displayed today kept her from sleeping. She kicked her feet.

A mosquito buzzed the perimeter of her bed.

She extended an arm into the darkness and swatted the stifling air.

The mosquito hum grew louder.

She yanked the bed sheet and pulled it taut—flattening her feet—jamming her toes. *Which of the two evils should she choose—suffocation or all-night itch?* She decided the former and jerked the sheet over her head. Or maybe she could run outside, build a smudge fire, and play witch of the woods as Nokee taught her. She giggled.

Behind the curtain partitioning her sleeping area from the remainder of the cabin, soft murmurs sounded from Joseph and Kathleen's room. The murmurs developed into mutters. The mutters grew into distinguishable sounds.

Ginny thrust the sheet from her head and sat.

"Every time she leaves, she neglects her chores," Kathleen whined. "She does owe us for putting a roof over her head."

"This is a turn of events," Joseph countered. "First, you fought with me because you didn't want her to live

176

with us. Second, by sewing for others, she is earning her keep. Let it be. Anyway, the visit will be short. She'll be returning after the Fourth of July picnic."

Huffing, pillow punching, and body-turning noises ensued, followed by silence.

****

Shuffling footfalls sounded on the puncheon floor.

Ginny cringed. She turned from the window and her view of an idyllic morning.

A backdrop of greening exploded across the sphere of her outside world.

Against the verdant landscape, russet-colored chickens bobbed their feathered heads as they scrabbled across dewy grass, and a gray bunny posed as he chomped a clover stalk. His pink nose wobbled and his stiff whiskers pointed as he consumed the sweet plant.

Kathleen slouched into the kitchen, walked to the sideboard, and lifted the coffee pot. She pushed her unbound hair from her neck and poured herself a cup of coffee. "Ew, coffee's burnt." She spat. She banged her cup on the table, grabbed the coffee pot, and threw it into the sink, which caused a clattering noise that startled the morning doves roosting in the cabin eaves.

Last night's disparity leached into the new day.

"Why is the floor sticky?" Kathleen stomped across the kitchen. "Someone didn't wash it last night. Ginny, your hair is full of burrs. For God's sake, use your comb."

The barbs, wounding as rapier-sharp leaves projecting from a rye plant, pierced their target. Ginny retrieved the coffee pot and opened the cupboard that held the coffee grinder. She stilled. *I'm not making more coffee. It's too damn hot for coffee. Kathleen can*

177

go without or make her own damn coffee.

Kathleen strode outside and slammed the front door.

Chessie barked.

Stepping to the kitchen window, Ginny gripped the counter and looked out.

Joseph stood outside the barn with a pitchfork in his hand. One of his suspender straps drooped across his chest. He took his hat from his head and waved to Casimir.

From the buckboard of his wagon, Casimir nodded. Dust plumed around the men and the massive workhorses pulling the Urdzela's family-sized cart.

Ginny vaulted to the lean-to, jumped into her boots, and shoved her satchels and sewing machine out the door.

Chessie continued to bark, sprung the porch steps, and sniffed Ginny's belongings.

As she rocked on the porch, Kathleen stared at the horizon.

Crick-crick-crick.

Casimir stood at the bottom of the front steps. "Good morning," he called.

"*Dzien dobry*," Ginny replied. *I haven't heard that old country accent since I left New York. Oh, mamma, this charming man reminds me of you and my aunties.* She smiled inwardly. "See you Monday, Kathleen." She gritted her teeth. "Casimir, my sewing machine is in that crate. Could you please carry it?"

"Yah, of course."

The big man lifted the Singer as effortlessly as he lifted a toddler to his shoulder. Ginny gripped both her satchels, one with sewing tools and one with her personal effects, as she hovered on the top porch step. She faced a vista of greening rye fields, broad-leaved maple and oak trees, and furrows of dark earth plowed by Joseph, Buster, and Blue.

On the south side of the barn, a fledgling garden welcomed the warmth of the sun. She sighed. *Please, God, remind Joseph to water the garden. Please, God, don't let him forget these precious plants below.* She gazed tenderly at the flowers, delineating the approach to the house. Ginny nurtured them through unexpected late frosts and Chessie's digging. Sweet William effused a sweet ginger scent. The pair of finicky rose bushes were what held Ginny's concern. Each day she examined the leaves for evidence of curling and twisting and blackspot. When she cleaned the fish Joseph caught, she applied fish guts to the soil surrounding their roots, as Nokee advised her.

Casimir cleared his throat.

Crick-crick-crick.

Alternately lifting and pounding her feet, Kathleen pumped her rocker in a staccato beat.

Ginny examined her progenies once more. The budding roses' beauty vied Kathleen's pure complexion. The prickly thorns jutting from the rose bush stems caricatured Kathleen's expression. Ginny vaulted from the porch. She lifted her bags into the back of the Urdzela wagon and climbed onto the buckboard.

Casimir hauled the crated sewing machine to his wagon. He settled himself next to Ginny and clucked to his team. "Nice day, hey?"

"*Przjemny dzien,*" Ginny replied.

Sighing, Casimir gripped the reins. "The missus,

she wants me to speak English in front of the children since that is the language used in school. I do better in the field. I'm not much good with book learning."

"I think being loyal to your family and providing for their needs is more important, Casimir. You can speak Polish to me anytime. I miss hearing it."

"Thank you, Miss Ginny. You are a good girl. Maybe you will find a husband here. But I think your brother and sister-in-law like you staying with them." Casimir stared down his bulbous nose.

He might claim not to be smart, but Casimir sure knows how to size a situation. But does he have a crystal ball?

****

A rope swing dangled from a shady maple tree.

A baby goat cavorted and stalled in its catch-me-if-you-can game with a small girl. The child's giggles caught in Ginny's heart.

Bending among the cucumber vines on the south side garden of the Urdzela clapboard home, a middle-sized girl adjusted her bonnet.

On the lowest board of the paddock gate, a small boy swung it closed by muscling his weight against it.

An older girl opened the front door with a book in her hand. "Papa," she called.

Beside Ginny, Casimir held up his hand and waved.

Children swarmed the wagon and ran next to it.

"Ho, Papa, I'll take care of Peggy and Abby. They both need a good curry job." The tallest boy took the reins from his father.

"Thank you, Stanislaw." Casimir climbed from his seat.

"I'll help Ginny." A gangly boy hopped on the wagon.

Standing in the entryway, Sophie held a broom in one hand and shielded her eyes with the other. "Thank you, Oskar. Good boy."

Oskar jumped from the wagon and offered his hand.

Ginny gazed at the front of the Urdzela home. A mix of benevolent mother love and exciting girlfriend visit tweaked Sophie's face.

"Welcome, welcome, Ginny. We're so glad you're here." Sophie grinned and hiccupped.

Smiling, Ginny put her hand in Oskar's and followed him to the porch.

A skinny boy elbowed his way through the bunch and pulled on his mother's hand.

"Oh, this is our musician, Jakob." Sophie's hands clasped the boy's shoulders.

Ginny nodded.

Jakob grinned, revealing missing front teeth.

"I remember your song in church, Jakob. I enjoyed it very much."

The little boy's cheeks pinked.

"*Dziekuje,* I mean, thank you." His blush deepened.

"I speak both English and Polish." Ginny bent close. "Jakob, I think you are lucky to know two languages." *I just hope I can remember more than two Urdzela names.*

Entering the house with Ginny's bags and within earshot of the conversation, Casimir winked at Ginny. As he passed her, he whispered, "*Dziekuje.*"

"Ginny, this is our oldest daughter, Anna. Halina, here is the middle girl. Julia and Teresa are our youngest." Sophie beamed.

Each girl curtsied.

Julia giggled.

Teresa frowned.

"This boy is Ludwig." Sophie pinched the boy's ears as he wrestled her. "Stanislaw is in the barn, but I 'spect he'll be in soon. Casimir, put Ginny's things in the girls' room. Thank you, dear. Ginny, I think it best you sew in the bedroom, since that way, you will not get stepped on or tripped over."

"Good idea. I need to be careful not to leave pins and needles about."

"Ah, here's my Oskar, who you have already met." Sophie motioned the gangly boy to approach. "Miss Ginny, do you know who this young man shares a name with?"

Casimir, on his way back from the girl's room, blurted, "The great, the one and only, son of a patriot, Union soldier, and winner of the National League pennant, one of our sons, a Polander—Oskar Bielaski."

Oskar, the Urdzela, shuffled his barefoot toes across the wooden floor. "Oh, Papa…"

"Go on, son. Tell Miss Ginny about Oskar Bielaski."

The boy stared. His protruding, adolescent Adam's apple bobbed in his skinny neck. "Oskar Bielaski is a remarkable baseball player, Miss Ginny. I want to be just like him." Oskar continued to swivel his feet against the floor and swallow in gulps.

"This boy's got a great arm, Ginny." Casimir held aloft his son's right arm. "Why this arm, right here, I've seen it whip a ball so fast the leather melted off. Why this Oskar here, his tossing is so hot, it sizzles." Casimir dropped Oskar's arm as if it burned him.

"Oh, Papa." Oskar laughed as his father grappled him into a hug. "Miss Ginny, my papa, he served as a Union soldier, like Oskar Bielaski. My papa, he is my hero."

Oh, Oskar, do you know how lucky you are to have a papa you are proud of? Ginny took a deep breath.

"Pshaw." Casimir twisted his booted foot on the floor.

"Mama, Mama, please kiss my finger. It got caught in Ludwig's teeth."

"Come here, my *kochanie*. Mama will make it better."

Toddler Teresa, the family's baby, grasped her mother's skirt and extended a chubby finger for her mother's healing.

"Tell Miss Ginny how old you are, Teresa."

The tiny girl with flossy white hair, matted in the back of her head, held up three fingers.

"Boys, boys, please don't shout," Sophie called behind her. "Don't forget your chores. Papa says to check the tack for oiling. The chickens need feed, and please kill any worms in the cabbage plants. I've got to get Ginny started on her sewing. Oh, I'll be waiting for one pail of milk. The rest goes into the milk house."

"Yes, Mama." Sounds of feet shuffling and door slamming followed.

A rag doll missing a button eye laid face up, legs askew on the floor, next to a rocking chair. A dusty fern struggled for existence in a cracked pot behind the front door. A hand-braided rug laid in front of the hearth could benefit from a curved needle and thread stitching loose sections back together. A mound of mud-covered shoes and boots crammed a walkway between kitchen and parlor. The stack of footwear smelled like an extension of the barn. Ginny pursed her lips and held her breath.

Sophie, with Teresa on her hip, stepped over them and turned to Ginny. "Where shall we start?"

"Let me begin by making a list of each child and their measurements." Ginny put her hands on her hips.

Sophie headed toward the kitchen. "Teresa and I will get paper and pencil." She tickled the sole of Teresa's foot.

The little girl giggled and pressed her head into her mother's breast.

By the end of the day, Ginny recorded each Urdzela child's name, and one by one with Sophie's direction, she took measurements of each child's shoulder-length, chest, waist, hip, arm length, back waist length, neck circumference, inseam, and length from waist to floor. From sixteen-year-old Anna to three-year-old Teresa, Ginny noted hair, eye color, and any physical attributes that would impact clothing choices for the children.

Ginny took inventory of the supplies on hand.

Sophie supplied twelve yards of denim canvas, six yards of pink, rose-printed dimity, six yards of blue-and-white gingham, and six yards of yellow-striped lawn.

The children's grandmother sent a jar of buttons, three spools of thread, several hanks of dainty lace trim, and four discarded dresses.

"My benefactor, Mrs. Sheridan, was kind enough to send me a variety of sewing patterns, which, good for us, includes guides for both boys' and girls' clothing," Ginny added.

"Oh, how wonderful." Sophie's shoulders lifted, accompanied by a peal of tinkling-hiccupping laughter.

By the third day of her stay, Ginny differentiated each child by more than their measurements.

Anna was obedient and serious-minded and a second mother to her younger siblings.

Stanislaw was loud and robust and the first to repeat disciplinary methods meted to younger brothers and sisters. He had the start of a mustache, and Ginny noted a manly odor as she wrapped the measuring tape around his chest.

Oskar was the first to chuckle, offset a sour mood, and cajole the younger ones into eating their dinner.

Ludwig was inventive, confident, and exasperating to his usually patient parents. Ludwig's name was the most mentioned, and the name was oft-repeated as "Ludwig, Ludwig, why would you do that?"

Halina, at nine, was an Anna in the making. She adored babying the younger ones and was the appointed family storyteller.

Jakob was the entertainer. He could suspend time with his melodious voice.

Julia, without question, spoke straightaway to her papa's heart. As soon as she heard him return from the fields, Julia was the first to jump in his arms and press her soft cheek to his sweaty bearded one. The little girl walked with a limp.

Ginny recorded the child's handicap to make clothing adjustments to accommodate the child's uneven gait.

Sophie confided Julia's deformity occurred during

a strenuous birthing.

Despite her handicap, Julia didn't consider herself exempt from difficult chores, and she volunteered to clean her daddy's boots and stir the sticky mass of morning oatmeal.

The entire family doted on Teresa, and her toddler tantrums were short-lived due to the multitude of people willing to quell them.

All the children, in one form or another, were interested in Ginny's sewing.

She learned to keep the machine covered when she wasn't near since Ludwig experimented with how the flywheel worked.

Halina tried changing the thread color and wasted yards.

Casimir discovered a loose thread weaving across his chair one day and followed it through two rooms to the sewing machine spool spindle.

Of all the children, little Teresa was the most enthralled. She begged to sit on Ginny's lap as the machine churned through the fabrics fashioned into clothing for her family. Day after day, the toddler approached Ginny. "I want to pull the pins, Ginny."

Ginny hoisted her atop her lap and secured Teresa between her body and the sewing machine cabinet. Teresa's tassel-silk hair caught under Ginny's chin, and the pressure from her little body warmed Ginny inside and out.

Determining the greatest need, she worked on pants for the boys. With Sophie's approval, Ginny selected the denim canvas for those garments. Denim weighed more than the dimity or muslin she used for the girl's dresses and blouses, and after a few hours working with the heavier cloth, the muscles in Ginny's shoulders ached. She stood, stretched, and rolled her arms.

The smell of freshly brewed coffee wafted into the girls' bedroom. She strolled into the Urdzela kitchen and poured herself a cup of coffee.

Sophie and Anna stood in front of a counter with a mountain of potatoes between them.

"Did you see this, Ginny?" Sophie pulled a dishtowel from the cupboard and handed it to Ginny.

Anna held a peeler and shook it toward her mother. "Mama," she protested. "I made it when I was eight, and it's not very good."

"Oh, pshaw, I love it," Sophie placed her hands on her hips.

"Anna, you did a lovely job. Your cross-stitching is even and tight. The feet on the ducks and the geese are so lifelike." Ginny guided her fingers along the tiny *X*s.

"Thank you, Ginny. I so admire your sewing skills." Anna tipped her head and smiled.

"Yes, thank you, Ginny, now maybe my Anna will believe my compliment. You are such a good girl." Sophie pinched her eldest daughter's cheek.

By the fourth day, two things were apparent. Oskar, the namesake of the baseball legend, had a crush on her. Secondly, every member of the Urdzela family harbored a strong opinion of Peter Nickles.

Yesterday, twelve-year-old Oskar left a bowl of strawberries next to her dinner plate. Each berry appeared blemish-free and conjured the smell of sunshine. Today, Oskar placed a feather on her sewing machine. He lined it symmetrically within the gold-leafed flourishes. The gift was the plumage of a blue jay, marked with royal blue, white, and black striping without a speck of dirt or insect dung.

"I imagined you could use it on one of your hats," Oskar said. "It is the same blue as your eyes."

Ginny held it aloft. "Well, thank you, Oskar. So it is. I will look forward to wearing it. Do you think the blue jay misses it?"

The admirer scratched the back of his neck. "I found it on my way to the field. I didn't steal it off his back."

"As long as he doesn't swoop to my head and try to reclaim it." Ginny arched her eyebrows.

Oskar laughed.

The laugh was caught between a child's giggle and the belly chuckle of a man. Ginny's heart stirred. *Dear, dear boy.*

As the family lingered over supper one night, the subject of Peter Nickles entered the conversation.

"That Mr. Nickles, he is a good judge of horses." Stanislaw broached one of his recurring topics of interest. "The last time Mr. Nickles visited, he showed me on Peggy how to tell the difference between good and bad bones. Do you know what the canon bone is, Papa?"

"I sure do not, Son." Casimir reached between Halina and Jakob to break up a pinching fight.

"The canon bone…"—Stanislaw scowled at Jakob and Halina and continued—"is the leg bone that carries most of the horse's weight. So, you can imagine, Papa, how important it is to know what a good canon bone looks like."

Casimir nodded and licked one side of his knife, flipped it over, and licked the other side.

"So, what you want to look for is a flat bone. That, Papa, is where you see the tendons stand away from the canon bone. It's not good if the tendons are tied too close to the bone. As soon as I've plenty of money saved, I'll ask Mr. Nickles to go to auction with me and help me pick the best horseflesh."

"Mr. Pawlowski said he would pay you as part of a threshing crew. He said he could trust you with the horses. You're a strong young man, now, Stanislaw."

Sophie's smile radiated from the opposite end of the table.

"Mr. Nickles always throws me in the air. He makes me giggle so much I could pee my pants." Julia hopped around the table, grabbing the back of each chair.

"Ludwig," Sophie scolded. "Don't spit your food."

"But Julia made me laugh so hard applesauce just spilled out, Mama."

Sophie tossed Ludwig a napkin.

Ludwig wiped his face, crumpled the napkin, and dropped it on the floor.

"I have to say, Casimir, that I am happy to be sewing for my reward of your cured ham. This is just delicious." Ginny reached for her knife and fork, cut another piece from the slab of pork on her plate, placed it in her mouth and chewed. The blended flavors of maple syrup, salt pork, and woodsmoke lingered in her taste buds.

"You are welcome." Casimir wiped his lips with the back of his hand.

"Yah, Mr. Nickles, he always plays tricks on us." Jakob's grin displayed burgeoning adult-sized teeth crowding the baby teeth remaining in his bottom jaw.

"Yah, he does." Halina crooked her index finger and tapped it on the side of her mouth.

"One time, he scared Mama coming out of the necessary. He jumped from behind the sumacs, and Mama screamed so loud we thought she fell down the privy." Anna laughed.

Ginny giggled. *He does have a wicked sense of humor.*

"Oh, ho, that boy. I always have to watch out for that one." Sophie hiccupped.

Casimir winked at his wife and leaned back in his chair. "Out of all the farmers around here, Peter is the one always to jump in and help. I know he stops by Mrs. Pyonk's farm and checks on her every day."

"He always brings her to church. I know she looks forward to that." Sophie gripped the handle of her teacup.

Peter really is a sweet, thoughtful man. Ginny bit her lip.

"He's a big meanie." Teresa pouted. She stood in her chair and wrapped her arms tight across her chest. "I don't like him because he scared my mama."

Everyone at the table giggled.

"Another fine dinner, Mama." Casimir pushed from the table. "Come, boys, let's check the stock and then call it a night."

"Go put up your feet, Mama." Anna stood and stacked a pile of dirty plates. "I'll finish things in the kitchen."

"Thank you, dear, and please light a candle from the stove and bring it to me. Halina, please help Julia and Teresa get their faces washed and change into their nighties. Come, Ginny, sit by me."

The sun faded in the western sky.

Anna lit a candle set on a side table next to Sophie's rocking chair.

Its glow reflected off Sophie's knitting needles.

She cast on fine woolen yarn the color of a buttercup. Yarn splayed over her fingers, and Sophie hummed.

Ginny joined in. "I remember that lullaby, but I only know it in Polish."

Tears spilled over Sophie's cheeks and plopped onto the yarn.

Ginny jumped her gaze to Sophie. A knot formed in her stomach. *Why is Sophie crying?*

The front door swung open and banged against the east wall.

The younger children rushed inside.

"Straight upstairs, boys. Pajamas on. Girls, straight to your bedroom and pajamas on. Then you can all say good night to Mama," Stanislaw barked as he herded his siblings.

Sophie's rocker creaked.

Ginny studied her list of children's measurements. She took her pencil and doodled collar concepts to use on a dress for Anna.

The children padded barefooted into the parlor and swarmed Sophie's chair.

She set aside her knitting. "Line up, one by one." Sophie checked each child for dirt behind their ears and under their fingernails and dispensed a kiss to each clean face. "Say your prayers. Sweet dreams, my darlings."

"Night, Mama. Night, Ginny." A chorus of voices caroled as each child passed taciturn Stanislaw waiting in the hallway.

Nine-year-old Halina hung back. "Mama? Can I trim the candle wick?"

"My little firebug." Sophie turned to Ginny. "Halina is fascinated with helping her papa and me keep the fire blazing, and she is quite skilled. I can count on her to notice the embers burning low."

Halina crimped the hem of her nightgown and twirled. "Then Mama or Papa let me blow the bellows. It makes a big whoosh." She demonstrated by puffing her cheeks, widening her eyes, and making a gusty noise.

Sophie chuckled. "Find me the douter, sweetheart. I think Papa left it on the mantel, next to his shoehorn, by the pinecone carving."

Halina skipped to the hearth, stretched an arm above her head, and reached for the tool.

"You're close, dear, but right now, you are touching the candle snuffer."

The little girl stepped to the right, stood on tiptoe, and swept her hand over the mantel.

Sophie turned to Ginny. "A wedding present from my aunt Mary Wright. Whenever I hear Father Graca ring the bells at St. Mary's, I think of her. She gifted us with that candle snuffer. A talented artist carved a bell on the cone."

"I found the douter, Mama." Proving her cautiousness and respect for the implement, Halina clasped the stunted scissors and moseyed to meet her mother at the table. The little girl arched her eyebrows, widened her eyes, and held her breath.

"Yah, go ahead, *kochanie*," Sophie whispered.

Halina touched the douter to the burning wick and

clipped the frayed portion. The lifeless snippet sizzled briefly and fell into the small bowl atop the scissors, held by Halina. The candle, however, continued to burn.

Sophie clapped.

Ginny clapped.

Halina beamed.

"Perfect. No soot, no spilled wax, and no runaway sparks threatening to raze the house. Child, you make me proud. Please put the douter in the silverware drawer, Halina. I want to keep it next to the shears."

"Yes, Mama." Halina's hazel eyes twinkled.

On the way back from the kitchen, Halina hugged her mother and flashed Ginny a smile. She plucked the sides of her nightgown, spun in a circle, and skipped to the bedroom she shared with her sisters.

Ginny gazed at the retiring Halina. *Firebug? Hmmmmm...*

****

Soft snoring and intermittent body-flopping sounds filtered through the floorboards. *All asleep, I think.* Ginny sighed.

The three adults indulged in a quiet visit on the porch.

Manure odor assaulted the air. Ginny waved a hand in front of her nose. Sophie owned no sweet-smelling flowers edging the front of the house.

"Ladies, please excuse me." Casimir stepped inside and returned with a tray and two glasses filled with amber-colored liquid. "Here you go, ladies, my brew of dandelion tea. As for me, *gesiorka*, vodka, yah." Casimir retrieved a bottle from under the porch. He sat heavily into the chair next to Sophie, uncorked the bottle, lipped it, and drank a long swallow.

Ginny hunched her shoulders and brought her drink to her nose. She caught a whiff of sunshine, sweet clover, and licorice. She inhaled again and savored the relief it brought to her nose. She swished the liquid over her tongue. *Hmmmm, tastes good. But if I drink it all, my nose will suffer and the manure blitz will continue.* Ginny pressed the glass above her breasts.

"Wheat's coming up, and lots of good shoots on the beans." Casimir gripped the vodka bottle and rested it on his thigh.

"I am so proud of you, dear. No one works harder than my husband." Sophie patted Casimir's hand.

They exchanged looks that warmed Ginny in the crossfire.

Muffled burping sounds discharged from the pigsty.

Casimir chuckled. "I added the last of the apples stored in the root cellar to their feed. That is the sound of happy pigs."

Sophie coughed. "I…"

Casimir set the bottle on the floor and leaned forward. "Sophie?"

Tears leaked from the corners of Sophie's eyes. She clasped her hands over her mouth.

Casimir leaped from his chair. "Sophie?"

"Please sit, dear. I'm fit as rain. Really, really I am."

Holding her breath, Ginny squeezed her fingers over her kneecaps.

"Mr. Humphries, the postman, brought this today." Sophie rose and pulled a letter from her apron pocket. She edged back to her chair and lowered herself.

Ginny took a breath.

Casimir downed a swig.

Pulling a pair of folded spectacles from her pocket, Sophie opened them, adjusted them over her nose, and fitted the sidebars around her ears. She upended the envelope and shook out a grayed piece of paper.

A crinkling noise broke baited silence. Then, clasping the document with both hands with the same reverence she displayed washing raspberry jam off the chin of baby Teresa, she read aloud:

"My dear family,

I hope this letter finds you well. Cecilia and I miss all of you and hope the summer season has thus far provided long, comfortable days to do the planting. Cecilia continues to make our cozy apartment home with her sewing and decorating."

Sophie turned. "Oh, my daughter-in-law Cecilia is so like you, Ginny, so good with a needle and thread. She is also an artist. You should see her floral paintings. They should be in a museum." Sophie wiped her cheek and continued reading.

"My work at the bank is quite agreeable. My supervisor tells me I have the makings to be a senior accountant. Mr. Dunning, the owner, has personally complemented my ledgers. He says I've got a real head for numbers."

"Yah." Casimir pounded his fist on the arm of his chair. "Zygmunt is so good with figuring, right, Sophie? He could track how many pounds of seed we would need for how many acres of rye and corn and beans from the time he was a little boy. Counting skills came naturally."

"We found a significant settlement of Polanders,

and we've made many friends here in Chicago. I'm sure you would like our church, Holy Name Cathedral. At the second service each Sunday, the priest says Mass in Polish."

"I bet you'd like that, right, Sophie." Casimir reached for her hand.

Sophie opened her mouth. She pressed her hands over her lips and let her head fall toward her lap. Her shoulders shook, and a torrent of tears seeped through her fingers. Her breath expelled in fitful huffing.

Knocking aside his chair, Casimir knelt beside her and stroked her hair.

Ginny ground her fingernails into the arms of her chair. *Please, please God, keep this family from harm.*

Sophie kept her face covered and lifted the letter with her hand.

Casimir took it and brought it close to his face. He scrunched his eyes, shook his head, and gazed at Ginny.

She took the paper, held it with both hands, and read aloud.

"This, Mama and Papa, is the church of the next Urdzela baby's baptism."

Casimir buried his head in Sophie's lap.

She caressed his hair and his big ears and lifted his head.

Tears flooded his face. "You and me, *kochanie*, we are grandparents!" He rose on his knees.

Spreading her fingers on either side of Casimir's face, Sophie kissed him full-mouthed.

Ginny waved the letter in the air. "Sophie, Casimir, I am so happy for you. If Zygmunt and Cecilia are parents like the two of you, that is one lucky baby."

"Thank you, dear." Sophie turned to Ginny. "Oh, a

new little one to love. I am so happy, so happy." Sophie wheezed, pulled her handkerchief from her bodice, and wiped Casimir's face and then her own. Once again, she took his face in her hands. "Casimir, promise me…we will go see our grandbaby before it is six months old."

Casimir lifted Sophie's hand from his cheek and kissed it. "I promise you, dear."

"We'll make some fine baby clothes." Ginny squeezed Sophie's upper arm.

"Oh, Ginny, I hoped you would say that."

A sliver of a moon glimmered.

Pigs burped.

Unfiltered fecund odors wafted over empty glasses.

"*Kochanie,* I am going to bed." Casimir tilted his head and drained the last of the bottle.

"Me too, dear." Sophie stood and stretched.

"I think I'll stay put and enjoy this fine summer night a bit longer." Ginny waved them both a good night. "*Dobranoc*, Grandma and Grandpa."

"Good night to you too, dear." Sophie stopped to caress Ginny's shoulders on her way to the cabin.

Fireflies dotted the inky-blue night. Star formations with their ancient lore twinkled crystal clear. Gentle hoots from the woods, deep twangs from the pond, and an occasional long-distance howl punctuated the silence. Sophie and Casimir, soon-to-be grandparents, were already parents of nine beautiful, healthy children. Sophie confided her first child, Zygmunt, was born when she was a fifteen-year-old bride, and that three-year-old Teresa arrived nine days after her thirty-fourth birthday.

Ginny couldn't match Zygmunt's counting

aptitude. Yet, she could figure her own life was quickly passing, and she had no children and no imaginable way to get them. Ginny strolled into the quiet Urdzela home, kicked off her shoes, added them to the dusty pile behind the door, and tiptoed into the girls' bedroom. She shed her fashionably tight-sleeved shirt, glazed cambric skirt and whalebone corset, donned her airy nightdress, and eased into the double bed she shared with Anna and Halina.

First thing in the morning, as she usually did, she would check the tomatoes in Sophie's garden. Globes of green hid under saw-toothed leaflets. *Was Joseph vigilant with their budding kitchen crops?* Tomorrow, following the Fourth of July celebration, she would return to Joseph's with a basket of sewing. She expected mounds of sullied dishes and dust-infused laundry, but maybe, more opportunities to see Peter. The Urdzelas spoke so highly of him. Ginny chuckled, remembering the one dissenting vote. *To three-year-old Teresa, Peter Nickles was a meanie. What would make him sweet on me?*

Chapter 18

Though inaugural- and second-generation Polish emigrants inhabited the community of Parisville, the Fourth of July, honoring the United States of America independence, was a highly anticipated day for celebration.

Out of all the holidays, Peter enjoyed this summer festivity over those requiring gifts and church-going. The Fourth of July parties provided a perfect opportunity to play games and drink beer. If anyone could combine barley, water, and hops to make a damn good brew, that man was George Worchok—Parisville's best cooper. Peter's mouth watered.

The first time he rode to the Worchok household to buy barrels, he pulled Star's reins short, sat back in his saddle, and scratched his head. Streamers of hop cones looped from the eaves overhanging the Worchok front porch to an oak tree twenty feet from the door. George was more than a keg maker. He was a hops master.

"Listen here, Nickles." George had pulled a pinecone looking object from his pocket. "Here's how you can tell if your hops are ready to harvest." George held the pod to Peter's ear. He shook it.

Peter inclined his head. "Holy crickets!" he hollered.

George chuckled. "Yup, if you hear *pinging* inside the cones, it's beer-brewing time."

Plans for the annual festivities had been in the making for weeks. Father Graca led the parish in prayer the Sunday before, asking God's grace for good weather for the get-together feted by the whole town and beyond. God granted the prayers and wishes of St. Mary's Catholic Church parishioners.

July 4, 1881, in Parisville, Michigan, proved a glorious sunlit day.

Peter volunteered to set tables and chairs for the crowd and enlisted Henryk and Dawid to help.

Ruta was in their midst—directing and pontificating. "Did you hear the horrible news? About President Garfield? Two days ago, two days before we celebrate this country's birth, our president is shot. May God protect him and give guidance to his doctors. That poor man, less than four months as our president, and a crazy idiot shoots him. Ach. It makes my heart sick." She wrung her hands. "It brings back nightmares of those frightful days of President Lincoln's death. Such a terrible, terrible time."

Peter nodded. Terrible days were stitched in his memory, as strong as the catgut lacings that tied the flesh of his ripped back.

Once the men arranged the furniture, Peter helped Ruta bring food to tables set under the church's east side grove of maples.

As each farmer's wife alit from her wagon, she hauled a covered basket and stumbled to the picnic area.

Family gatherings made him melancholy, but the sight of women staggering was funny, even in his apprehensive mood. *Ah, the womenfolk are all trying to outdo one another, and I will take full advantage of their efforts.* He knew to expect the sauerkraut preserved last fall and saved for this day, the jars of pickled beets, the egg sandwiches, and *pierogis* filled with spiced lamb and sausage bursting from their fork-etched seams. *Lord, I know there will be sweets—* mazurek *cake, flavored with almond and lemon; bite-sized, poppy-laced* kolacky; *sandwich cookies with strawberry jam filling; and Bette Oberski's sugar cookies.*

Men followed their wives with their substantial loads—cider kegs, bottles of home-brewed beer, and store-bought vodka.

Each time he noticed a new team pulling through the church lot, Peter raised his head. Several weeks had passed since he had seen Ginny. Last Monday, he'd stopped by Joseph's house with the ruse of needing to borrow a ladder, but Ginny wasn't there.

Kathleen had been tight-lipped after she revealed Ginny wasn't available, and she had not divulged more information.

Fronted by a matched team of dappled gray geldings and backed by a wagon full of boisterous children, George and Harriett Worchok came into view.

Peter waved.

"Crickets!" George shouted and pointed to two kegs setting amid his children.

Peter fashioned a megaphone with his hands. "Crickets!" he yelled.

On his final trip to the church shed, Peter stopped outside the entrance and extracted a cigarette from his shirt pocket. He fumbled in his pants pockets for some matches.

Buster and Blue approached.

Peter's heart lifted, and he tucked the unlit cigarette back in his shirt.

Joseph and Kathleen sat side by side on the board seat.

Ginny was nowhere to be seen.

Peter sighed. *Did she stay home? Is she ill? A chill ran up his spine.*

The Urdzela family approached. Homemade red, white, and blue flags waved from little hands, big hands, and from the four corners of their wagon. The children wrestled and chucked straw on each other.

Who was the tall girl? Her face turned to the sun. A cluster of orangey-red bittersweet dangled from the thick, plaited braid that circled her hatless head and highlighted the golden strands. Peter stood in the oak canopy with his arms crossed over his chest. *Ah, there she is.* He smiled and ran his hands down his thighs.

Ginny jumped from the wagon.

He gazed at the way her dress fit her figure. On the breast, stripes sewn into a V pattern broadened her bust. Pine boughs, lavender, and bittersweet branches filled her arms. She looked like an ad on one of those fancy-smelling soaps Tom Taraski sold in his Forestville General Store.

"Oh, Ginny, how thoughtful. You brought table decorations." Ruta's voice carried to the canopy.

The two hugged and set to work, dividing the décor among the tables.

In the shade of a cluster of elms and maples, fiddlers tuned their instruments. Smoke circling the end of their cigarettes swirled in tandem with the pluck of strings as each tuned his violin.

A lanky, silver-haired man sat next to the fiddlers

and polished a penny whistle. Despite the heat, he wore a tailored, tweed jacket.

Father Graca made his way to a clearing fronting the picnic area, and the crowd fell silent.

People bowed their heads.

"Most heavenly Father, we give you thanks for this great country. Thank you, God, for the bounty on these tables today and for the friendships you foster. Lord, we ask you to heal our president, James Garfield. Lord, a special thank you to the hearty men and women here and their families who sustain this parish in praise of the Blessed Virgin. Amen."

Father's last word sounded the same in English and Polish. In this great country, the expression of thanks rang the same as Peter's ancestors and those the St. Mary's parishioners used in their mother tongue. "Amen."

"I have an announcement," the priest shouted over the crowd. "Henryk Pawlowski thinks it would be a welcome break from this heat if we spend a day on Lake Huron."

Cheers and squeals erupted from the congregation.

Father beamed. "Yah, I thought so. See Henryk if you plan to go. He said he'd be willing to organize the horses and wagons to get everyone there who wants to go. If it is not raining this Saturday, plan on seeing your neighbors at White Rock, on the lake end of Ruth Road. Ruta Pawlowski is organizing the picnic, so see her if you are going."

Ginny stood behind a table, arranging the bowls and trays of food.

Peter sauntered to the picnic spread. "Hmm... smoked cheese, *biala kielbasa*, *kopytka*, *chlodnik*, *pierogis*, and plum cake." Saliva pooled in his mouth. *God, Polish women can cook*.

Ginny looked up.

A new spate of freckles dotted her cheeks.

She grinned. "Yah, lots of good Polish food, with lots of potatoes, cream, and meat. Everyone will need a nap after this feast."

He wanted to tell her she looked beautiful and that the sun agreed with her. But he disguised his thoughts by commenting on someone else he knew. "It looks like your brother gained weight. Does that have anything to do with your cooking?"

Ginny blushed.

"So, what did you bring to this table, Miss Virginia Dahlke?" He should just fill his plate and move along like the rest of the hungry people because his dallying would risk gossip. But today, he didn't care.

"Well, that would be the *chlodnik*. She turned and pointed to a pottery bowl setting on a lace doily. "I used strawberries from the Urdzela's vines. Cold soup is always refreshing on a hot day, no?"

"Yes, it is." He drew a bandana from his back pocket and wiped his forehead. Then, he dipped a finger into the soup.

"Why, Peter Nickles." Her eyebrows arched, but her lips puckered.

He raised his finger, licked it, stole a second lick, and jumped his gaze to lock with hers. The sugary taste of berries lingered in his mouth.

Blood ran to her face. She gripped her fingers on the edge of the table.

Round-bellied Ludwig darted to the table and angled his hand over iced cookies set on a cut-glass plate.

Peter clutched the boy's shoulder. "Does your mama know what you are about?"

"Oh, my mama, she said, 'You go feed yourself, Ludwig.' "

Peter laughed. "Well, I can't argue with that. Where is your mama?"

Ludwig pointed. "Under the linden tree, with my papa."

Ensconced in creamy white- and saffron-colored flowers so thick they buried the branches, the tree heralded its July beauty. The heady fragrance, a sweet perfume concoction conjured with honey and lemon essences, seemed to hypnotize the bees swarming it.

At the base of the tree, Ludwig's mama and papa reclined.

Casimir tucked a sprig of blossoms in his wife's hair and kissed her. The pair took no notice of their eight children's antics, the musician's fiddling, and the buzzing of the intoxicated bees.

Peter tipped his head sideways and met Ginny's gaze. "Kind of nice, yah? After all those years of hard work and sacrifice, a man and a woman can still feel like that."

"It is, Peter," she whispered.

"Wanna hear how loud I can burp?" The little boy pressed his hands against his abdomen.

Then, without waiting for an answer, Ludwig belched with the vigor of a chick pecking out of its shell. Peter laughed.

Ludwig grabbed a sandwich cookie, licked the strawberry filling, and ran to the other children.

"Peter, I think Josephine is beckoning you." Ginny

pointed to a table close to the church's front doors.

"Okay. See you later, Ginny." He strode toward Josephine, stopped, and turned. "Nice soup." Ginny's cheeks flushed as red-hot as the strawberries in the cold *chlodnik*.

From the bench where she sat, Josephine moved the corner of her shawl.

Peter backed up, folded his knees, and plopped next to the retired midwife.

An accordion player joined the fiddlers. The robust man threaded his arms through the straps and hauled the instrument over his chest. He grinned and stretched his fingers over the black and white keys. "A one and a..." He fisted the handles and drew out the serpentine shape. "Ladies and gentlemen, 'The Maple Leaf Polka' for your dancing pleasure!"

Josephine waved her hand-carved cane. "I love a good squeeze-box," she chortled.

Emptied beer bottles, played by patriotic papas, clanked on the tables in raucous harmony.

The music beckoned dancers, and people in pairs moved toward the music makers.

George and Harriett Worchok, ungainly to the moment they joined hands, became a graceful union with their fluid dance moves.

"Oh, there you are, Peter. You know I love to polka. This music is calling us." Bette, her white-blonde hair in spiral perfection, her breasts straining against a gauzy pink dress, glided across the yard and extended her hand.

He clasped her petite hand, squeezed it, and ran to keep up as she scampered toward the musicians. Her touch sparked currents that traveled below his waist.

His toes arched; his feet grew light. He pulled Bette close, savoring the scent of her familiar rosewater cologne, the impression of her familiar shape, and the acknowledgment of her unthrottled acquiescence. He forgot why he had been avoiding her.

****

Even their backs were beautiful—Peter and Bette. Had they been horses, they were a perfect match in their height, energy, and goldenness. Ginny could not compete with a ripe woman's figure, a family inheritance, or the history of intimacy Peter and Bette shared.

The golden couple's spins and shuffles played out on the lawn.

She tried to look away, but she couldn't turn from Peter's face as Bette drew sinuous swirls across his shoulders.

He closed his eyes and licked his lips.

Bette pressed her bosoms to his chest.

Ginny coughed and covered her mouth. Gorge rose in her throat. Still, she couldn't take her gaze off them.

Arching his shoulders, Peter brought his mouth close to Bette's ears.

Bette clutched his hand and snuggled her nose against his shirt.

Perspiration soaked Peter's hair. Heat and exertion colored his face and neck radish-red. He extracted a bandana from his back pocket.

Grabbing the red square from his hand, Bette waved it over his face, and blindfolded him.

He feigned fighting it away, but the whole pirate farce seemed to stimulate him. He gripped Bette tighter, bent his knees to level his face close and dipped her in a

207

dance move.

Ginny swung and shooed flies off the table. "That goes for you too, Ludwig Urdzela," she yelled as the boy approached the table.

Ludwig scuttled off.

A piece of Ginny's heart broke as she absorbed the startled look on his face.

"Oh, it's good to see that hard-working man enjoy himself." Kathleen picked a lemon tart from the table and sauntered close.

Ginny closed her eyes and clenched her teeth.

"They sure make a handsome couple, and all the money Bette will inherit. No wonder Peter has eyes for her." Kathleen grabbed a morsel off a plate and bit into it. "This *kielbasa* has a smokey taste. Could you get the recipe from Harriett and make it this way next time?" She wore a purple silk bonnet studded with velvet pansies.

The artificial flowers were a gift from Ginny's inventory of precious accessories sent from Mrs. Sheridan. They were so authentic that a honeybee lighted on and rotated its bulbous abdomen about the shiny yellow stamens. *What if the bee realized the duplicity, felt the sting of injustice, and became so enraged it dropped down the bodice of Kathleen's dress and stung the bejesus out of her?* Ginny giggled.

Kathleen frowned. "Don't forget to pack our basket, and it's only polite if we clean after Buster and Blue." With that, she collected her plate and sauntered toward Joseph.

Ginny sighed. *Where are the Pawlowskis?*

They were seated together, sharing a table with the Worchok family.

Ruta moved closer to Nadia and beckoned Ginny.

"This is your cucumber salad, isn't it, Ruta?" Ginny set a plate on the table and sat next to Ruta. "I recognize the bowl. You always make your salads so pretty. I love how you use the whole dill florets, and the flavor is so refreshing."

"I see you have some of Harriett's *kielbasa* and some of Marta's coleslaw, too." Ruta smiled.

The tempo of the music changed.

"We've had a special request," one of the fiddlers announced.

"I offer you James McGrarry singing 'The Kerry Dance.' "

Hand clapping echoed across the lawn.

The silver-haired, penny whistle polisher rose. He handed his instrument to one of the fiddlers. "Accompanying myself on the penny whistle is none other than Mr. Lonnie McFarlane. Now, Lonnie and I want to thank all of you for invitin' us to your Independence Day party. We might be the only old Irish guys here, but, hey, we are all Americans today, right?"

The crowd cheered.

"To top it off, I'd like to introduce you to Miss Marianna Gugsak. She has learned a bit of Irish dance." James spread his right arm wide, indicating a young girl.

Ginny smiled. *She's about ten years old, and more Polish than Irish judging from the rounded cheeks, thick auburn hair, and lack of copper freckles.*

James closed his eyes, and after a few trilling bars of introduction, sang:

"Was there ever a sweeter Colleen

In the dance than Eily More
Or a prouder lad than Thaddy
As he boldly took the floor
Lads and lasses to your places
Up the middle and down again
As the merry-hearted laughter
Ringing through the happy glen
Oh, to think of it
Oh, to dream of it
Fills my heart with tears."

The music was simple with a predictable, slow-paced upbeat, and Marianna executed her youthful, zesty steps. Her coarse braid bounced off her back as she stepped high on the toes of one foot while placing the other foot on the opposite knee.

The crowd clapped, nodded, and smiled.

Marianna beamed bigger and changed her steps with an impressive sideways shuffling pattern, all the while holding her spine erect. Her arms hung straight and still.

On the last line of James's song, "Fills my heart with tears," Marianna bunched her skirt and performed a straightforward, forty-five-degree angle kick, punctuating her flexibility and grass-stained bare feet. Then, Marianna curtsied and fell into James's embrace.

James wagged his hat in the air. "Thank you," he yelled. He grasped Marianna's hand and led her to the food tables.

People swiveled their heads and whispered.

Ginny jumped from her seat. *I don't believe it!*

A dapper-dressed gentleman picked his way through the crowd. He paused to shake hands and bent to speak to seated ladies.

"Oh, my goodness. It's Senator Conger," Ruta stood and rocked on the tip of her toes. "How nice of him to join our Fourth of July celebration."

He had already spotted Ginny. She knew by the startled look on his face, the stock-still stance he took—midway through a handshake with Father Graca.

"Miss Dahlke?" the Senator extended his hand.

"Senator Conger. How wonderful to see you again."

The older man shook his head, extracted a cloth from his breast pocket, and wiped his nose and mustache.

The scent of imported sandalwood appropriated the air, and Ginny breathed deeply.

The statesman's blue eyes twinkled. "What a pleasant surprise. What are you doing here?"

"My brother Joseph lives here." Ginny spread her hands wide. "After our father died, I came to live with him and his wife."

"Well, that is a loss for New York and the Dansville Relief Society's noble efforts."

"How is Miss Barton? And how are you progressing on establishing an American Red Cross?"

"As you know, Miss Barton is a formidable woman, and I am proud to support her work. It is one of the causes near to my heart. I know your contributions were appreciated, Miss Dahlke."

"Please give Miss Barton my best regards once you see her again. Her work is so important." *Oh my goodness, how wonderful to be recognized by the Senator for my efforts. Where is Peter? Did he notice?* Ginny stood, righted her shoulders and jumped her gaze around the perimeter of the crowd.

"With pleasure, Miss Dahlke. I'm glad I have an old friend new to my district."

Ginny dipped her chin and winked. "I don't think I am threatening any national secrets if I tell you my brother Joseph voted for you. Congratulations on your election to the United States Senate."

The Senator bowed and wiped the back of his neck with the scented handkerchief. "I can thank my fellows in the Michigan Legislature for that one."

Ruta pinched Ginny's leg.

Ouch! Ginny glared at Ruta and bit her bottom lip. "Oh, Senator Conger," she called as the man started to walk away. "Please allow me to introduce the Pawlowski and Worchok families."

After meeting two more families in his jurisdiction, the Senator moved on.

"Ginny? How do you know Senator Conger?" Ruta drummed her fingers on the table.

"Remember the day you asked me if I left a beau in New York?"

Nadia stared.

Ruta raised her eyebrows almost to her hairline.

Bending at the waist, Ginny giggled and held her abdomen.

"Well?" Ruta shouted. "Were you romantically involved?"

"No, no." Ginny shook her head. "Senator Conger was not a beau. He is a married man with a wonderful wife named Stella."

Ruta flapped her hands and wiped her brow. "Thank God for that."

Ginny smiled. "You do recall I told you I volunteered in the Dansville Relief Agency. The woman who founded the Relief Agency was a nurse named Miss Clara Barton. She petitioned Senator Conger to establish the American Red Cross, a humanitarian effort modeled after the Swedish Red Cross. I accompanied Miss Barton to some of her engagements, and through those meetings I came to know Senator Conger."

"But, my goodness, what a coincidence." Nadia rose from her seat and stood on tiptoe as she gazed at the senator's back.

"You think that is a coincidence. I've got an even better one." Ginny grinned.

Henryk set his glass on the table and rubbed his hands together. "I love a good story," he said, and winked at Ruta.

George plucked his pipe from his mouth.

Ginny wagged her head. "Here is a tale of genuine happenstance. Miss Barton served as a field nurse in the Civil War. She later met Senator Conger, and in pleasant conversation, they discovered Miss Barton nursed his brother at Fredericksburg."

"Imagine that," Ruta leaned her elbows on the table.

Ginny nodded. "Indeed. Since that awareness, Senator Conger has become even more dedicated to Miss Barton's efforts."

"Which reminds me, you've never finished the story about what was his name...the man with the bluebird-blue eyes?" Nadia twisted her shoulders and steepled her fingers.

Ginny sighed. "How about the next time I visit? Did you get the lace we need, Ruta?"

"Yah, Annie Erhardt crochets the most beautiful

hairpin pattern. Wait 'til you see the pieces she made."

"Well, I guess I better get back to your house and work on the wedding dress." Ginny rubbed her palms together and grinned.

"Don't forget the rest of your story, *kochanie*." Ruta pinched Ginny's cheek. "Who knows, maybe Mr. Handsome Blue Eyes could make a surprise trip to Parisville. Now, I better check on the food—before those Urdzela children awaken and go for their second dinner." Ruta laughed.

Ginny arched her brows. "Yah, I know how those children eat. If you see Ludwig, check his pockets. He could make off with a whole plate of *herbatnikis*."

Curses rent the air.

Conversations curdled.

"Who is that, Ruta?" Ginny leaned over the table.

"Oh, dear, oh dear, it's Louis Gugsak. He must've been drinking again. He's lit like a teakettle. That's his son, Louis Jr." Ruta pointed to a slight boy running with his head down. "His daughter, Marianna, is the darling little dancer."

The senior Gugsak staggered after his son. "Hey, you, am talkin' to you, you whittle b-bas-turd," he bellowed, slurring his words.

Ginny knew that face. The beady eyes hooded by gnarled eyebrows, the skeletal cast of his cheekbones, and the bluish lips illustrating the ogre in The Grimm Brothers' story, "The Devil with the Three Golden Hairs" had haunted her since childhood.

The boy stopped. His head hung on his chest.

The ogre fell on him, grabbed him about the knees, and knocked him off his feet. Then, kneeling over his son, Louis Sr. slugged the boy's head.

Somebody screamed.

Peter scrambled from the blanket he shared with Bette.

Leaping over Harriett's outstretched leg, George fell headlong into Ruta's picnic hamper.

James thrust his penny whistle on a picnic table, ran to the skirmish, and clenched a hank of Louis Sr.'s hair.

Grabbing Louis Sr. from Louis Jr., Peter threw the older man to the ground and stamped his boot onto the man's chest. "No, never," he shouted. Peter waved his hand in a come-here gesture to the men hovering in the perimeter of the scene. "This man needs cooling down." He looped an arm around Louis Sr.'s neck and pulled him upright.

Joseph, Henryk, and George Worchok formed a blockade, and together, the men dragged Louis Sr. to the watering trough.

Ginny held her breath and clenched her fists. *Jesus, Mary, Joseph.* She traced the sign of the cross over her forehead and chest. *Please, God, keep everyone safe.*

Tethered horses neighed and reared as the men dumped Louis in the shallow tank fronting them.

Louis emerged—spitting, coughing, swearing, and punching.

Peter dunked Louis's head, held it in the water, and repeated the motion again and again. He walked away and joined the other men.

Louis rolled out of the trough and lay prostrate in the mud.

Families packed their wagons.

Fiddlers snapped their cases closed.

Ladies tore the red, white, and blue buntings from

the tables and stowed them away for the next patriotic celebration.

From her seat in the rear of the wagon, Ginny turned and looked back. The last ones to leave the picnic were Irish tenor James McGrarry, driving home the now-sobering and thoroughly soaked Louis Gugsak Sr. and the Gugsak children, Louis Jr., and Marianna.

What started as a joyful day ended on a sour note. But Ginny was enlightened. She witnessed further evidence of Peter's compassion and the mutual sexual attraction between him and Bette. *How could I ever compete? I should've asked Senator Conger if he had current knowledge of Mrs. Dunbar and her son Wallace. Will I ever see you again, Wallace? If Senator Conger can appear here in the thumb of Michigan, why not you? And Please, Lord, take care of the Gugsak children.*

Chapter 19

Maybe wearing one less petticoat wouldn't matter. After all, they were spending the day at the beach. Ginny lifted her dress, peeled a damask underskirt from her waist, and let it drop to the floor. She sighed. Her bottom half's temperature dropped sinfully low on the border of propriety and hell's southern hemisphere. She threw her hair into a topknot and hurried to the kitchen.

Joseph left a note next to the coffee pot, signaling he would be ready to go after he tended the stock and found his fishing net.

Ginny opened a drawer and grabbed brown wrapping paper. Yesterday she baked sugar cookies, knowing one man with a sweet tooth would welcome them.

Kathleen sauntered in, grabbed a cookie from the wrapping paper, and bit into it. "You've never had a sugar cookie until you've tasted the ones Bette makes. Martin Oberski buys imported vanilla flavoring for Bette's baking when he visits the food markets in Detroit. So I would bet on my last dollar that she'll bring sugar cookies to the picnic today."

Cookie crumbs dropped from Kathleen's mouth and sprinkled the linen napkins Ginny laundered, pressed, and folded the Monday before. Ginny clamped her teeth.

"Hey, girls, your carriage awaits," Joseph called.

Ginny stepped onto the porch, inhaled a sweet breath of sunshine, and scanned the yard.

In the back of the wagon, Chessie jumped over Joseph's gear and stirred the hay.

"Joseph? Why is Chessie in the wagon?" Kathleen's shrill voice pierced the air.

"Chessie is a water dog, and we are going to the lake. I need to work with him before duck hunting season." Joseph shrugged.

Ginny followed Kathleen, jumped on the wagon back, and scrambled over a pile of rough-cut pines and an excited dog to find a place to sit.

Chessie pressed his head against Ginny's thigh. "Ew, Joseph. I'm glad this dog is getting a bath today. But, Chessie, you stink." Ginny held her nose and scratched the dog's head.

Joseph assisted Kathleen onto her front-row seat.

"Sorry for the crowded space, Ginny. We're stopping by the sawmill in White Rock while we're over that way. I'm planning to have these pines planed into boards. I can drop them off while we're enjoying the lake and get them on our way back." Joseph guided Buster and Blue onto Parisville Road. "We're building onto the cabin." He turned his gaze toward Kathleen.

Kathleen sighed and leaned her shoulder against him.

Joseph tipped his head. "We'll meet the Pawlowskis and Peter at the corner of Klug and Forestville roads and travel together. The men want to visit the sawmill. Nadia suggested the ladies visit Taraski's General Store while the men attend business."

Kathleen squealed.

Ginny brought her hands to her mouth and rolled

her shoulders. Months and miles had passed since she strolled the aisles of a store larger than William Engle's shop in Parisville, where Joseph got their supplies of vinegar, gunshot, and sugar. She rose to her knees and squeezed Kathleen's shoulders.

Shaking his head, Joseph continued chewing on a hank of grass.

Ginny sighed. *Whose cookies will Peter choose? Bette's or mine?*

****

The Taraski General Store couldn't compare with Bloomingdale's or Macy's, but Taraksi's lack of elegance more than made up for luxury deficiencies with the sheer number of pioneer curiosities. There were knives—knives for gutting, skinning, chopping, paring, buttering, shaving, slicing, and sawing, with serrated, scalloped, wavy, or beveled blades. Lining rough-sawn shelves top to bottom, all varieties of tools and powders, tonics and remedies claimed a cure for everything from pink eye to cancer, mange to mania. Ginny smiled. The old-fashioned selection of women's niceties—plain black stockings, plain white bloomers, and plain white petticoats offered a level of modesty prudent enough for the Felician nuns.

A collection of glass canisters rested on the end of a row of dishes and soaps. Striped candy sticks in an array of colors and flavors filled them. Ginny strolled closer, squeezed her eyes, and inhaled the aromatic scents of wintergreen, anise, peppermint, lemon, molasses, mint, licorice, and sassafras.

"What's your favorite?" Peter asked.

"Gah," Ginny shrieked. "You scared me."

"Well?"

His voice was thick as molasses and stirred her senses.

Peter reached a hand over her shoulder and hovered his fingers over the knobs on the candy jar tops.

"Sassafras." She stifled a giggle and clasped her hands over her mouth.

Grazing the top of her head, he removed the glass-dome lid labeled Sassafras and extracted a striped candy stick.

She stared at the floor.

"Ginny?"

"No, I can't accept a gift from you." She looked beyond him. *If Ruta or Nadia witness this, they will hound me for the rest of the day.*

"Here, I thought you were a modern girl." He returned the top to the glass jar.

The glass clinked loud enough to foist their innocent flirting into a surefire Ruta and Nadia observation. Ginny stepped back, knocking tubes of flypaper onto the floor.

Peter knelt, reached under shelves, and retrieved the errant rolls. Then, he stood and bent his head. "A gift of a candy stick is pretty harmless, don't you think?"

"Hey, Nickles, Peter Nickles, we need some help over here," Henryk called.

"Be right there, fellas." Peter thrust the candy in Ginny's hand, placed her fingers around it, and curled his fingers over hers. "I insist."

"Thank you, Peter. It's such a fine treat," Ginny whispered. Her hand shook. Her heart thumped.

"Yah, you, crazy Pole. Give us a hand here,"

Henryk shouted. "Let's get loaded and get to the beach. It's hot." He ran a hand over his head.

"Oh, I can't wait to put my feet into the big, cool lake." Nadia fanned her face.

"Got more tooth powder for Henryk since he favors garlic so much." Ruta held aloft a brown paper parcel.

"You folks, enjoy yourselves," Tom Taraski said. "Never seen a summer this hot and dry. We should all be glad for that big lake. We might all have to turn to it to get our drinking water."

Despite the heat, a chill ran down Ginny's spine. *What did Tom mean? Could things get that bad? Joseph's home was miles from the lake. How would they survive without water?*

****

Peter guided Star and followed Joseph's wagon to a verdant stand of maples. The temperature lowered at least ten degrees in the shade, and a steady breeze wafted through the foliage. He breathed in a sigh of satisfaction and the intoxication of sun and sand and fish and grass. *Father Graca was right. This respite from strapping hard work is a good idea.*

Lake Huron stretched to the horizon, topped with a sapphire sky and fleecy clouds. Wavy currents splintered sun reflection into shimmering mirrors of light.

Casimir pulled his wagon behind Peter's.

Urdzela children bounced over the sides as their papa maneuvered his team into the shade.

Chessie jumped from Joseph's wagon, barked the entire span of sand to the water, and leaped into the lake.

Ginny scrambled after Chessie and tossed her boots behind her. "Halina, Oskar, Julia, wait for me." She ran pell-mell with her bonnet hanging on the back of her neck, and her skirts pulled to her knees.

All four splashed into the lake.

The children's shrieking rent the air.

Peter tethered Star, pulled oats from his saddlebag, and held them in his outstretched hand.

Star gummed his palm and shook her mane.

"See you later, girl. Enjoy your rest." He scrubbed her nose, removed his boots, rolled the bottom of his jeans, and sprinted to the water. Peter slunk next to Ginny, who stood in knee-deep water. "I followed the scent of sassafras."

Silver minnows darted about her ankles, and their gills flashed in the sun.

She jumped. "Oh, Jiminy, that tickles."

Peter laughed. "Be careful. They can pick pieces of flesh."

"Oh, no," she screamed. She turned toward shore and clambered over the slippery rocks.

Peter held his middle. Laughter swelled his ribcage.

Ginny turned and scowled. "Oh, you."

"Well, miss, did you think they've got teeth?" Peter tipped his head and grinned.

"Fair enough, Peter, but remember, I lived in a city until I moved to this wilderness. The only fish I'd experienced was either on the back of a cart or headless on a platter." She walked back to the shallow water and squinted. Then, she leaned over the water, plucked a stone from the lake bottom, and handed it to Peter.

"Ah, this is a fossil." He rolled it in his hand and

brought it close to Ginny's face. "See the imprint of little leaves and tiny lake creatures?" He traced the marks with the tip of his finger. "They were trapped in the rock when time began."

"I'll take that." Ginny scooped it from his hand and stowed it in the pocket of her dress.

"Hey, look." Peter pointed toward a line of canoes gliding over the lake in a southerly direction.

Ginny lifted her hand and shielded her eyes.

"It's the Odawa, Nokee Wilkowski's people, probably checking their traps, or maybe just enjoying the day." Peter moved his arm in a sweeping motion. "See that huge rock, straight out?"

"Yah."

"That rock is a marker of the Indians' territory to the United States Government in the Treaty of 1807. It designates the northeast corner of the ceded area. But long before that, the rock became sacred to the natives. They gather there, in their canoes, and honor their creator. They leave baskets of food and tobacco as offerings."

"Do many of them live here?" Ginny brought her hands to her mouth and gazed at the horizon.

Is she afraid of them? Is she expressing a disparaging opinion of the Odawa? Peter stiffened his back and sucked in a deep breath. *I can't abide being with a person who views the natives as less than themselves.* He cleared his throat. "Before the first explorers came, before we Poles came, and before the lumber companies came, these people were the only inhabitants. A tribe lives north of here. I see them tapping maple trees in the winter. The women make baskets and sell them at Taraski's store."

"They are very thoughtful and talented people. I so admire their respect of nature and the loving relationships among their families." Ginny rubbed her upper arms. "My eyes have been opened since I came here to Michigan." She looked down at her feet. She bit her lip and gazed again at the scene around the large white rock. "I wish the rest of the world realized they deserve equally the things we all want—good health, freedom of religion, a safe place to live, and food to eat."

The Odawa plied the lake. They executed graceful, coordinated movements, plunging their paddles into the depths and raising their elbows parallel to the surface while holding the paddles motionless. They worked in unison as a flowing caravan, skimming the metallic water.

Peter hung his head. He breathed a deep sigh and squeezed Ginny's shoulder. "Yah."

"Do you like to fish, Peter?" Ginny stepped forward, slipped, and her skirt dropped into the water.

Peter grabbed one of her elbows. "Let's get you back on land."

She met his gaze.

The tip of her nose was burnt. In the illumination of the sun, strands of red sparkled throughout her braided hair. She was as natural looking as a field of sunflowers. He extended his arm.

Ginny clasped his hand and leaned on him as she teetered back to shore.

"Yah, I like fishing." He picked a stone from the beach and brushed sand from its edges with the side of his hand. He dropped to his knees, sat, and nudged his rump. He settled himself in his hollowed-out seat. "Ah, just right." He winked and beckoned her to sit.

She flattened her skirt, sat in the sand, and tucked her feet under her skirt. She busied her hands, tunneling through the sand, lifting it, and filtering it through her fingers.

"I grew up along the Chesapeake Bay." Peter turned his head. "I have a brother who lives there. We spent a lot of time hunting in the marshes—kind of like those young fellows Mark Twain writes about."

Ginny's hands stilled.

"Ever eat turtle soup, Ginny? It's delicious. I like oysters too. But crabs, crabs are my favorite."

"Yes, but eating crab is such hard work...all that shell breaking...give me fish any day." Ginny scrunched her freckled nose.

"Imagine the plight of the poor crab." Peter chuckled. "As he grows, he has to shed his shell and grow another. It's an all-day affair. He starts by finding a safe place to disappear, maybe for privacy?"

Ginny giggled.

"Well, then he has to kick." Peter demonstrated by jumping and booting sand. "He has to box." He clenched his fists and drove them into an imaginary punching bag. "He's gotta bust his way out."

Ginny clapped her hands over her mouth.

"Crabs don't have bones, so they can do this a little easier than me, but you get the idea."

"What's next?" Ginny tilted her head and smiled.

Peter sighed and looked at the beach. "Well, now the poor crab is naked...helpless, easy prey for any hungry otter, osprey, or turtle that shares the marsh. So, for the next three hours or so, he hides out."

"Oh, tsk, poor crab...I never realized." Ginny flung

her arms over her chest and laughed.

Peter feigned a terrified, defenseless crab and stared from behind closed fingers.

Ginny squealed with laughter and kicked her feet in the sand.

"Within five hours, he has a brand-new shell, and now he's ready to face the swamp again." Peter dropped to his sand seat, panting from his antics and the grip of Ginny's laughter on his heart. She was so childlike in her enjoyment of the sun raining on her skin. Her eyes shone like the minnows that looped around her ankles. Her vulnerability triggered a long-lost memory. He had been just a boy, but the story, now recalled, was vibrant.

One day, trolling among the marshes, creeks, and crays with his brother and grandfather, Grandfather pushed his bucket hat to the back of his head and stared at both boys. "Hear that?" He cupped one of his ears and motioned lip buttoning.

The boys quieted. He hadn't been aware until his grandfather called attention to it, but he heard the sound—a tinny cacophony that grated on the watery peace.

Grandfather whistled through his nose, ran his hand over his beard, and crouched in the tall grasses.

Peter and John sprawled in front of him.

"Girl crabs are making that noise."

He and John covered their ears and frowned.

Grandfather chuckled. "Oh, those sooks, those girl crabs are pretty darn desperate. Their bellies are full of eggs, and they need a jimmy, a boy crab, to squirt his, ah, fertilizer on the eggs. That way, the eggs can hatch into baby crabs. Do you follow me, boys?" His grandfather stroked his beard. "Boys, those jimmies sure like to help out those sooks." Again, the older man chuckled.

Peter's face burned. He shifted his butt in the sand.

Did Ginny know the saga of crab mating? What if he told her this story? How would she react to his telling her that once the sook attracts a jimmy, she becomes a swooning, passive companion and begins her molt?

Grandfather had been quite poetic in the final chapter of his story. "Jimmy demonstrates his gentlemanliness. He cradles her tenderly as she gyrates and twirls and shucks her shell with all the gusto she can muster. Then she lays herself, spineless and bare, to her male protector—her spawn's chosen father. As the hours pass, sunlight to dark, they stay locked together in the coupling, male to female. Once those hours whirl away, Jimmy remains a few more days, as his love grows a coatdress of armor to safeguard her life and the lives she carries. Once Jimmy senses his protection is no longer needed, he swims away."

Peter crossed one leg over the other.

"Yah, boys, that is the way it is." Grandfather chortled. "Life. Ah, it's good, but remember the jimmy's job, and that be you two." He made a clucking sound in the back of his throat and ran his pipe-holding hand over his bristly face. "Your job is to protect and love the sook...girl. Now you see."

Ginny threw some sand. "Peter, I think you are getting too much sun. Your cheeks are as red as a cardinal."

Oh, Gawd, if only you knew, Ginny girl. More than my cheeks are affected by the thought of you as my sook. "Gotta cool down." He shucked his shirt and tossed it on the sand. He ran to the water, waded to his waist, and dove headfirst in the lake.

"Hey, look out, here I come," Joseph ran across the beach, cast off his shirt, and hobbled over the stones.

Chessie followed Joseph and paddled behind him.

"Yah." Joseph spit and lunged toward Peter.

Lake water rose in a crescendo and spattered their heads, shoulders, torsos, and arms.

Peter flexed his biceps and hollered. He jumped on Joseph's back and pushed his head underwater.

Joseph hooked an arm around Peter's neck.

Taking a running leap and wincing as his feet grazed over the rocky lake bottom, Oskar plowed through the water. "Water fight. Water fight."

Jacob screamed and ran behind his brother. "Papa, come help us. We want you on our team."

"Graa." Casimir plunged into the water.

Joseph struggled to stay upright. "What the hell?"

"Yay, Papa. Get his foot!" Oskar hollered.

Joseph rose to the surface. "Let go of my foot, you old Polish farmer, you." He laughed and spat water. Then, he jumped on Casimir's shoulders and straddled his waist.

Casimir shouted something in Polish.

Twisting toward shore, Peter caught the women's reactions.

They clamped their hands over the nearest child's ears and shook their fists in the men's direction.

Peter stumbled toward shore, forced his feet over the slippery rocks, and breached the line of Urdzela children darting the shoreline.

Ludwig chased his siblings with a crablike creature

held aloft in his hand. "He'll pinch you. He will rip your nose."

Snapping his pincer, the button-eyed creature waved his menacing antenna.

Sibling shrieks and screams bounced across the shoreline.

"Ludwig Urdzela, if you don't put that poor beast in the lake this minute, you will spend the rest of the day tied to the wagon next to Abby and Peggy!"

The boy hung his head, faced his mama, and tossed the creature over his shoulder toward the lake.

More shrieks and squeals ensued.

"Mama, Mama...Ludwig hit me with a crab." Halina ran toward Sophie.

"Ludwig Urdzela, now!" Casimir strode across the sand. "Halina, he's not a crab. He's a crayfish."

Halina stuck out her tongue at Ludwig as he skulked to the Urdzela wagon.

Julia shook a finger at the crayfish tosser.

A stab of commiseration struck Peter's heart. *Poor Ludwig*.

"Papa, can I take Abby and Peggy into the lake? They would like to get a cool down, too," Stanislaw said.

Casimir finger-combed his wet hair, withdrew a drenched hanky from his pocket, wrung Lake Huron from it, and blew his nose. "Yah, why not, son? You take Abby's halter, and I'll take Peggy's."

Stanislaw unyoked the team and put a lead on Abby. He walked her north on the beach, gained distance from the crowd, jumped on her back, and dug his knees into her flanks.

Traipsing over the slimy rocks, Abby stayed

upright until water met her belly. Then, she tucked her legs and swam.

Stanislaw hugged the horse's neck and floated over her back.

They stayed that way, bobbing in the great lake— boy and horse, wave and sky. Peter sighed. He placed his hands on his hips and arched his back. *What a perfect day. Nothing more peaceful than a boy treating his horse to a well-deserved float in the lake.*

Casimir waited with Peggy, who paced along the shoreline, switching directions each time Abby and Stanislaw turned from north to south and back again.

Even from where he stood, Peter could see the deepening hole Peggy dug on the gravelly shoreline with her anxious pawing and the threat it crafted to Casimir's balance.

Placing his hands on either side of Abby's neck, Stanislaw pointed her to the shore.

The sleek-muscled animal rose from the lake, tread over the Lake Huron rock beds composed of Puddingstones, Petoskey stones, and other aggregates, shook her mane and tail, and flung water droplets that rained on anyone within a ten-foot radius. *Her muzzle is lowered, and her ears lay flat. That is one beautiful, relaxed horse.* Peter whistled.

Stanislaw vaulted from Abby's back.

Sophie gathered Stanislaw in a hug.

The onlookers offered the eldest Urdzela son handshakes and hat swings.

Nodding briefly, Stanislaw busied himself, bending to check Abby's hooves. He rose and switched the horse's reins with his father.

Sophie stood on the shoreline and shielded her eyes

as she gazed at Stanislaw and Peggy swimming. She rolled her sleeves past her elbows, placed her hands on her hips, and rotated her shoulders.

Sneaking from behind, Casimir scooped her in his arms, and strode straight to the lake.

"Casimir, Casimir Urdzela," Sophie shrieked. "Put me down, right now," she squealed as the bustle of her skirt dipped in the water.

Her band of children waded in Casimir's watery steps.

Peter jumped in behind them. *I gotta see this.*

"Papa, put her down, right now," screamed toddler Teresa.

"Right now, you say?" Casimir smirked. "Okay." He answered his question and dropped his writhing wife in waist-deep water.

The entire Urdzela family vaulted and splashed into the water.

Oskar swept Teresa to his shoulders.

Anna held Julia's hand.

Casimir bellowed with laughter.

The older children hopped on their father and pulled him to his knees.

"We got him, Mama. Your turn." Anna lifted Julia in the air.

A soaking Sophie, her normally prim top-knotted hair, now hanging in dripping strings, swayed through the water and palmed her husband's head. "Oh, you." Sophie draped her arms across her husband's lake-level shoulders, planted a big kiss on the top of his sunburned head, and lowered herself to his lap, her skirt and petticoat billowing around them.

Casimir, you old crab. Peter shook his head.

Ginny, you sweet sook. He blushed.

****

Ginny straightened her fingers and made a cover for her eyes. She put her other hand on a hip and leaned back, digging her toes into the sand.

The sky was piercingly blue—a hauntingly cloud-scudded eyelid cupping the earth. *I suppose I should sit like a dutiful woman.* She sighed and turned.

The men lingered uphill by the teams. The only movements they expended were lipping cigarettes and blowing smoke.

Ruta, Nadia, Kathleen, and Bette nestled downhill on a blanket under waxy-leaved beech trees. Grosgrain ribbons knotted under their chins anchored poufy sunbonnets on the women's heads. The recesses of gingham shade obscured their faces.

Shuffling her feet and moving at the speed of a crab shucking her shell, Ginny approached the women.

"My goodness, Ginny, you've got freckles popping out everywhere, your nose, your ears, and oh, my, look at your hands." Bette pursed her lips and frowned.

"Did you roll in the sand, Ginny? It's caked all over the hem of your dress." Kathleen lifted her skirt and brushed the surface.

What's in your hand, Ginny?" Nadia stretched her neck.

"Peter called it a fossil." Ginny moved the stone close to Nadia's face. "Notice all the impressions and the mixture of embedded materials?"

"Oh, that Peter, he loves teaching kids about nature. He always leaves the beach with a pocketful of rocks for his nieces and nephews." Bette stretched her long-tapered fingers, wove them together, and ran them over her lap. "Peter has a younger sister. He's so fond of her. It's so cute he feels that way about you." She exhaled with a soft *pffft* sound.

Bette's coquettish smile flattened into a hard line. Ginny clenched her fists. Clinging sand grated her fingers. Triumph glared in Bette's shrouded blue eyes. An impermeable lump, like an age-old silt and sand aggregate, polished by the currents of a Great Lake and entombing a tiny water creature, lodged in her throat.

Chessie, awash in the odor of dead fish, leaped on Kathleen and shook sand on every seated lady. "Joseph! Come and get this smelly dog." Kathleen screamed, slid her bonnet over her forehead, and pinched the brim under her chin.

"Git!" Ruta jolted off the blanket, covered her face with her hands, and knocked into Ginny.

"Chessie," Joseph ran to the women and grabbed Chessie's neck. Man and dog skidded to the lake. Joseph splashed Chessie, roughed his fur, stowed him under his arm, walked him to the wagon, fashioned a leash, and tethered him to the undercarriage.

After shaking himself and walking three times in a circle, Chessie dropped on his belly with a harrumph.

Maybe I should have tried Chessie's approach. At least it would have gained me an escape from harpy scrutiny.

"Hey, everyone, time to eat," Henryk yelled.

Families carried picnic baskets to a grassy bluff thirty feet from the lakeshore.

Poplars and birches and a few sturdy oak trees provided shade for the sun and water-soaked revelers.

"I'll be stopping by my sister's, so I'm leaving, right after I eat this." Peter bit into a cookie from the basket Bette offered. "Mmmmm…my favorites." Sugar crumbles trailed on his lips.

"I made them with you in mind." Bette wiped his lips with her sand-free hand.

Peter gazed at her and grinned. "I want to see how Linda's family is doing in this heat." He scratched his neck under his beard. "My brother-in-law Leon grows tobacco. Yah, he's a good friend to have." He winked and held a pretend cigarette to his lips. "My sister, Linda, is with child. Her…" He stopped to count on his hand. "Whoops, two hands now. Let's see. I think this makes six."

"Oh, Peter, you've got presents for the children, right?" Bette smiled in the shade of her lace-trimmed, gingham bonnet.

"Yah, right here." He patted his shirt pocket. "Beach glass, a fish skeleton, and fossils."

"Sure, you go on, Uncle Peter." Joseph laughed. We'll see you in church tomorrow."

On the ride home, Ginny laid in the wagon back and gazed at cloud formations. Seagulls trailed them to their inland destination. Their squawks punctuated the air and broke through Ginny's reflections. She imagined a lively family of six children, all clamoring over their uncle Peter.

How easy it was to link from uncle to daddy in her ruminating. She could picture them, the children she and Peter would have, robust and bright, strong and resilient, with a side of dimples. But more likely, Peter's children would be recognized by their raucous, sugar-spun hair and their delight in the vanilla-flavored cookies served by their freckle-free mother.

Ginny reached in her pocket and clenched Peter's

fossil as if it were a combustible lightweight confection she could easily crush. But the ancient stone history of tiny animals and the short-lived history of a day begun in romantic promise denied deconstruction.

She rose on her knees from her hay-strewn seat and flung the stone into the dusty wake of Buster and Blue's homeward-bound trip.

Chapter 20

Peter dismounted Star, pulled loaded saddlebags from her back, and dragged them into the Dahlke barn.

The horse shifted her weight and pawed the ground.

"Happy to be rid of that, right, girl?" He returned to the horse and moved a hand over her muzzle. "Yah, you just carried a new roof. Fancy that, girl—a might heavier than last week's delivery of beach fossils." He led Star to the paddock.

The morning sky appeared bland as mashed turnips. In relief, stands of trees materialized black and lifeless.

Ebony crows screeched and circled.

Humidity gripped his temples. He lifted his felt hat from his head and ran a hand through his drenched hair.

Buster and Blue whinnied hellos and clamored to the fence.

Pulling carrots from his saddlebag, Peter opened the gate and let Star inside. "You horsies play nice."

Star guzzled a carrot, broke into a trot, and circled the inside perimeter.

Blue, the lightest steed, gobbled two carrots, snorted, and steered quick stops and turns. A game of chase ensued.

In the grassy field beyond the paddock, Joseph's flock grazed. Tufts of fleece dotted their hides.

Behind the kitchen window, Ginny's head bent over the sink. She looked up.

From twenty feet out, Peter could see the smile lines fringing her eyes.

She waved.

His heart went light.

The screen door squeaked.

Joseph stepped on the porch and stretched. "Mornin'." Holding a coffee cup with one hand, he reached behind his head and scratched the nape of his neck.

"Wheat's about three feet. Sheep are filling out again. Your new shingles are in the barn," Peter called.

"Great, how about coffee?" Joseph held his mug aloft.

"Naw, I'm all set. Let's get this building underway." Peter shifted the tool belt circling his waist.

Joseph had established a workstation close to the lean-to. He handed Peter a shovel. "I've already got the post lines marked. I think about eight inches down, yah?"

Peter nodded, plunged the shovel, withdrew soil, and waited.

Joseph snugged the first pole, paused, and held a level along the edge of the stake.

A pile of dirt grew. A line of poles emerged.

"Hey, old man, we are ready for the sheeting." Joseph set the level on the ground and pumped his fist in the air.

"Hey, *starzec*," Peter returned in the Polish vernacular. "Don't make me wait too long." Joseph curled his fingers like a princess holding the reins on a high-stepping stallion and pranced like he was in a parade.

The walls went up quickly.

Hammering thuds eclipsed the air.

Nailheads protruded from Peter's lips. The iron bits leached an unpleasant taste, but it wouldn't be manly to stow the spikes anywhere but between his teeth.

Joseph tapped him on the shoulder. "*Starzec*, Ginny's beckoning. Looks like dinner's ready."

Peter spat the nails and followed Joseph to the house. "Smells good in here." He rubbed his hands down his thighs. Ginny wore a new dress. He recognized the fabric. The last time he saw it, it lay on a table at Taraski's General Store. Her hair shone as if she had just scrubbed it, and her cheeks were steamy pink.

Pulling a chair from the kitchen table, Joseph sank onto the seat.

Kathleen placed bowls in the table's center.

Looks like chlodnik, strawberries, yum. What would Ginny do if I stuck my finger in the bowl?

Kathleen sat next to Joseph.

Peter pulled a chair, waited for Ginny to sit, and claimed the seat next to her. "You are a lucky man, *starzec*." He spooned thick chunks of onion and noodle pieces into his bowl.

"Peter, how are your sister and her family?" Kathleen tucked a napkin on her lap.

"Like the Urdzelas, they are blessed with a large family. Their oldest son, my nephew Michael, is a horseman I've never seen the likes of." Peter rested his elbows on the table, steepled his fingers and rested his chin atop his joined hands. "He's training his horse, Bertie, as a trotter, and the connection with boy and horse is like something right out of a storybook. Michael insisted on giving Star a full inspection—teeth, legs, back, ears, hooves. I'm pretty sure Star fell in love and would be happy living with Michael." Peter chuckled. "I made another stop on my way home."

Joseph, Kathleen, and Ginny looked up.

"George Worchok has been having fox trouble, too. He lost pretty near every chicken he owned. That's why they missed the trip to the beach."

Joseph shook his head.

"George told me a troubling story about Louis Gugsak." Peter blew out a long breath and ran a hand over his beard.

"What?" Kathleen dropped her spoon.

"He shot Worchok's dog. His aim was straight."

"What did Worchok do?" Joseph moved from a hunched position to a straight stance.

"Nothing yet, but he's mad as hell." Peter scooped strawberries from the *chlodnik* and dropped them onto his plate.

Ginny twirled her fork. "Louis has two children, doesn't he?"

Peter gazed at the strawberries still on his plate. "Yes, a son, about twelve, Louis Jr., and a younger daughter, Marianna. She danced at the Fourth of July picnic. Louis's wife died two years ago of influenza."

Ginny leaned her elbows on the table. "I worry about those children."

Peter sat forward in his chair. He ladled strawberries into his mouth and reached for the coffee pot. He drew in a deep breath. *Ah.* The brew was fresh, not what you'd expect from a lazy cook. But then, Ginny hadn't exhibited shortcut maneuvers to any task.

Stretching across the table, Ginny tossed a lump of sugar in Peter's cup.

Peter lifted his spoon and stirred the beverage.

Kathleen's scowl loomed over the table.

What the hell is wrong with her? "Going to the race next weekend?" Peter took a sip of coffee. "Stanislaw Urdzela and Michael are running their horses on Atwater Road. I'm betting on a big crowd. Both boys are natural horsemen."

"You bet. Wouldn't miss it." Joseph slapped his palms on the table.

Ginny nodded.

Kathleen pouted.

Joseph peered out the kitchen window, pushing back from the table. "Sky's a shade darker. How about getting back to work?"

Peter stood and touched Ginny's hand as she cleared plates.

She slowed.

He caught her gaze for a moment, and then with renewed effort, strode to the door.

"Hey, old man," Joseph called. "Before I forget, I want to pay you for the shingles. Five dollars, right?"

"Yes, thank you." Peter pulled a drawstring bag from his back pocket.

Joseph took the bag and went into his bedroom. "Meet you outside."

Ten feet in the air, both men straddled the roof joists.

The temperature plummeted, and wind gusts swirled sawdust into Peter's eyes. The sky curdled into a churning, yellow tempest. Within seconds, rain beat in gritty pellets biting his head, arms, back, and legs.

"Peter, there's a tarp inside the barn. You're closer to the ladder. Can you get it? I'll keep tacking the sheeting," Joseph hollered.

"On my way." Peter backed to the ladder. *That sky is wicked. I hope this ladder holds.*

****

Standing in front of the kitchen sink, Ginny thrust aside the curtains, stood on tiptoe, and gazed at the yard. She gasped, ran to the front door, and threw it open. Wind whipped her hair and scattered sawdust in every direction.

Kathleen darted to the porch.

"Kathleen, Ginny, we need help," Joseph yelled from atop the addition. "The hammer fell. Get it for me. It's somewhere in that pile of rope. Bring it now."

"Joseph, please," Kathleen whined. "I'm afraid of heights."

"For God's sake, go back in the house."

Fighting the wind gusts, Ginny stumbled to the bottom of the ladder, and found the hammer stuck in a clump of red clover. Clasping the hammer in one hand, she grabbed the ladder's third rung and attempted to climb. The weight of her rain-soaked clothing and the savage wind thwarted her efforts. With each attempted ascent, layers of skirt and petticoat alternately ballooned and clung. Joseph's position was perilous, and the costly lumber was in jeopardy of ruin. Ginny stepped away from the ladder. She shucked her skirt and petticoats, scrambled up the ladder, and lugged the hammer. Grasping the tool by the last fingerbreadth of the handle, she extended it to Joseph.

The gap between their reaches was too great.

"You can do this, Sister."

241

Rain blew in icy fragments and pummeled her face. She bent one knee and eased on top of the raw construction. Then, belly to the unfinished roof, she inched herself across the span and passed the hammer to Joseph.

"Got the tarp," Peter shouted from the ground.

Jesus, Mary, Joseph. Ginny turned toward the top rungs of the ladder that listed on the joists. They jiggled with every advancing step. Onions and noodles roiled in Ginny's stomach. She shivered and gripped the wood frame anew.

"Here, grab this corner." Peter wrapped a calloused hand around Ginny's foot.

Shock waves coursed through her exposed sole and ignited every nerve cell from the bottom to the top of her leg.

"What the hell?" Peter yelled.

Ginny closed her eyes, reached back, and snatched the tarp.

Joseph grabbed a corner from Ginny.

The tarp unfurled and caught in the wind like a spinnaker on a New York harbor schooner.

"All secure," Joseph hollered. He rose on his knees and held aloft the claw hammer.

Peter backed down the ladder. "I'm holding the bottom."

Just leave. I'll take my chances. Her last step was a hurried hop. Once her feet were on the ground, she dashed past the discarded skirt and petticoat and leaped to the top porch step without touching the bottom two. *Oh, my goodness. I left nothing to his imagination. Gah!*

****

Swiss chard and lettuce leaves lay bent in the kitchen garden. Other than that, Peter's property looked none the worse for the beating rain.

A rainbow lit the western sky.

Chickens squawked at their reflections in the deep puddles outside the barn.

I can't wait to get out of these wet britches. Bouncing in the saddle and wearing the same saturated pants and shirt he wore stepping from Joseph's ladder was a sensation he looked forward to ending. He dismounted Star, pulled aside the barn door, and led her to her stall. Then, he removed her reins and hung them on the tack wall. He wagged his head and laughed low. He couldn't shake the view of Ginny's almost naked body. Through the lightweight underthings, her skin was as pink and wriggly as the bottom of her bony, mud-stained foot. *How the heck did I keep my balance climbing down that shaky ladder after what I saw?*

He ran a hand through his hair. *Besides a whole lot of pink, I saw something else today. Ginny chose to save the lumber over preserving her modesty.* The choice bypassed his male organs and spoke to his heart.

He shrugged the saddle from Star's back and moved it to its wooden frame. A rectangular-shaped tin—topped with the English Queen Victoria's coat of arms and side decorated with rear-standing lions, a chained unicorn, a thistle, a rose, and a shamrock—fell into the hay. He lifted it and pried it open. The spicy smell of molasses escaped. His nose wrinkled as he held the tin away. Lumpy, brown cookie pieces filled the container to the brim. He sighed.

Pigs'll like 'em.

He curried and watered Star, milked Gertrude, and

243

took the tin. Then, he walked to the house, stopped in front of the pigsty, and flung the stinking molasses treats to the squealing piglets and their mother. A paper stuck to the bottom of the tin. With the edge of his fingernail, Peter scraped it free.

Happy birthday, Peter. Many happy returns. Ginny. He grimaced, threw back his head, and laughed. *Ruta must have spilled the beans.* Then, withdrawing Joseph's coin payment, he tossed it into the prior residence of *Superior Reading* biscuits. Satisfied with the weight of the coins, he secured the lid. Then, he walked back to the barn, brushed hay from the trap door, lifted the flap, and stowed the tin inside. It was money in the bank and a small measure of security. He sighed. His chosen way of life, farming, was fraught with surprises and held no guarantee of a reliable future. *All the more reason to stay single.*

Chapter 21

Joseph rode Blue and headed north on Parisville Road. "Hey, Sister," he called behind him. "It sure is a perfect day for a horse race. I bet there's a lot of excitement in the Nowakowski and Urdzela families today. I bet most of the parish will be there."

"It's going to be a great show between Michael and Stanislaw." Ginny sat atop Buster. A pleasant breeze, originating from the Canadian coast and blowing west, penetrated the cambric blouse Ginny wore and riffed Buster's nose hairs. "And you sure deserve a break. You've been working day and night on the new addition. I can't believe how much you've gotten done in the ten days since you and Peter roughed it in."

Joseph turned on Premier Road.

Ginny pulled Buster's rein, kneed his left side, and followed in Blue's hoof prints.

The fields brandished willowy rye, dainty, blue-flowered flax, and stalks of tight, green mufflers concealing ears of corn.

Leaf-trimmed orchards sheltered maturing apples, pears, walnuts, peaches, and chestnuts.

Shropshire and Cotswold sheep, their new coats sheer and gauzy, grazed on waning-days-of-summer-height sweet grasses.

Cows, calves in tow, lowed and flicked flies with their tasseled tails.

The warmth and suppleness of the leather saddle caressed Ginny's thigh, and the rhythm of Buster's gait jarred her spine in a way that invigorated her spirit.

Joseph came alongside her. "Wanna race?"

"You bet," Ginny yelled. Boat rowing wasn't the only thing she had learned at Auntie Valentine's. She dug her heels into Buster's belly and braced herself upright.

The horse lurched, whirling from a walk to a canter.

"Yah." Joseph kneed Blue into a canter and accelerated into a gallop.

The Dahlke horses sped past Eppen and Stafford roads.

People assembled along the seam of Premier and Klug roads and parked their carriages and wagons on Atwater Road.

Ginny waved to the Erhardt family.

"There's Father Graca." Joseph tipped his hat.

"There's the Pawlowskis," Ginny sing-songed.

Joseph held out his hand to Henryk Pawlowski, who slapped it in an energetic hello.

"Hey, Joseph. Over here," Peter hollered. "Tie Buster and Blue with us and hop on. Hurry! It looks like things are starting." He pointed to a pregnant woman standing near him. "This is my sister, Linda. I'll introduce everyone later."

Joseph whipped the reins of Buster and Blue around the wagon tongue.

Grabbing Ginny's outstretched hand, Peter pulled her onto the wagon.

Joseph jumped onboard behind her.

Bang!

Heads turned north.

Smoke cleared a revolver.

Two figures, their faces masked, burst a homemade bunting stretched across Atwater Road.

Bertie, ridden by one, and Peggy, ridden by the other, lifted their legs and pounded the dirt. Glossy coats skimmed powerful equine muscles—Bertie's a rich mahogany color, and Peggy's a dove gray.

The riders molded their bellies to the backs of their mounts and tucked their heads.

Ginny's heart thumped with each hammering hoof beat.

Peter grabbed her elbow.

Nose to nose, the two horses steamed toward them. Their nostrils flared with each exhale.

Deep blowing sounds rent the air.

"Go, Michael."

"Go, Stanislaw."

"Go, go, go."

The crowd jumped, clenched their fists, and smote the air.

Anna Urdzela stood below her family's wagon and clasped her hands together in prayer.

Marianna Gugsak and Annie Erhardt's oldest daughter, Lorna, grabbed each other and screamed.

Peter tugged on Ginny's wrist.

The horses returned.

They ran swifter than the north breeze that whipped their tails and held the long fibers parallel to Atwater Road. As the riders and horses passed, all equine legs floated in the air. Ginny held her breath.

Peter tightened his squeeze. He dropped Ginny's arm. "Michael's got Bertie under wraps. He's purposely losing." Peter clamped his lips.

Linda swatted her brother. "Why?"

"I don't know, but Peggy, not Bertie, won," Peter shouted.

A roar let loose.

A shot fired.

Exhilaration flowed like vodka at a betrothal.

Peter grabbed Ginny, pressed her to his chest, and kissed her.

He's trembling as if he galloped the entire route with his own legs. Ginny closed her eyes.

Time, and motion, and breathing stopped as Peter's lips lingered against hers.

The winning jockey took a victory lap around the inside perimeter of the juncture of Premier and Klug Roads. He completed the square, threw his hat in the air, and tore off his mask.

People rose on tiptoe and jumped atop wagons to see.

The cheering subsided, and a gasp rippled through the crowd.

Peter whistled long and low. "Well, goll darn."

"What?" Linda sidled to Peter and stretched onto her toes.

"That's Louis Gugsak Jr. and not Stanislaw Urdzela on Peggy. Now I see the reason for the masks." Peter shook his head.

"Peter, can you explain this?" Linda braced her hands on her back in the traditional pregnant pose.

Peter sighed and scratched his head. "I suspect Michael and Stanislaw did this to give Louis Jr. a day of glory." He combed his fingers through his beard. "When I visited your family, Michael told me he felt bad for Louis Jr. The kids in school tease him about his father's drunkenness. Michael and Stanislaw are making up for that. You should be proud of that boy, Linda. Michael intentionally lost that race. Most people wouldn't notice it, but he purposefully held back Bertie. Michael's a good boy." He rubbed a hand under his nose.

Linda jumped on Peter. "I couldn't be more pleased. He's just like his uncle."

For the second time that day, Peter was kissed by a woman.

"So, Peter, now that you've kissed this girl on my wagon, don't you think you should introduce her?" Linda turned to Ginny with a teasing smirk that mirrored her brother's.

"Linda, this is Ginny Dahlke."

If ever she felt like being inspected under the lens of a microscope, it was now. Linda's gaze bored into her as if she were puzzling her background, motivation, and soul.

"Hello, Ginny Dahlke. Nice to meet you."

Ginny bent her head. "Hello," she mumbled.

"Hey, Ginny, let's ride," Joseph stood below, holding the trailing reins of both Buster and Blue.

She waved goodbye to Peter and Linda and hopped to the ground.

Teen girls congregated around the horsemen.

Teen boys punched each other.

Anna Urdzela and Michael Nowakowski stood toe to toe. Their faces were animated and their gestures exaggerated. Their youthful abandon tugged at Ginny's heart. *What a darling couple they were, with a world of possibilities lying in every direction.*

The walk home was lazy and unhurried. Buster and Blue clomped companionably along, their easy affection for each other apparent to their riders.

Ginny's hips rolled in tandem with the movement of Buster's shoulders. Her feet lolled in the stirrups. She held the reins lightly. The hardest working muscle in her body was her brain. Ginny's accumulated kiss experience left her questioning and wanting. She leaned forward and pressed her lips into Buster's mane. *Was Peter's kiss just an emotional climax to a thrilling horse race? Or was he kissing her like he'd kiss a little sister?*

****

Peter strode into the barn.

Damn. I kissed her today. I kissed her in front of my sister and God knew who else.

What if I'm in love?

Damn.

In the waning daylight, he tripped over a stump and skinned his leg on the sawn-off remnant of one of the many stumps dotting his property.

Damn.

Like most thumb pioneer farms, the remains of white pines gleaned for ship masts and furniture lumber littered his acreage. He stumbled on the path he knew intimately. *What is my problem? A man alone needs to stay sharp. His survival depends on having a clear mind.* He knew what the problem was. It was a she, and that she was a pert, freckle-faced, animal-loving seamstress named Ginny Dahlke. He retrieved the milking stool from behind the barn door and strolled to Gertrude.

"Moo." She turned her head and stared with

piebald eyes.

"Good evening to you, too, girl." He crouched, lowered himself to the stool, and commenced their twice-daily shared ritual.

"Whaa," Gertrude complained as a swarm of biting flies landed on her rump. She snorted, kicked, and lashed her tail in retaliation.

Peter fell backward against the coarse barn wall.

Rip...

He twisted his neck and assessed the damage. From one hip pocket to the other, a clean slice marred the canvas. "Now, look what you made me do. I know, I should have changed out of my best pants as soon as I got home. But damn, my best pair of overalls and a split clear across my backseat. Damn."

Peter knew who had the right machinery and skill to fix them. A man needed his overalls. No one would question his desire to have them in good working order. Her brother Joseph would relate to that. Joseph Dahlke was a lucky man. He had a pretty, if not practical, wife, but he also had a fine sister to fatten him, sew his overalls, wash his laundry, haul in the firewood, and Ginny knew how to tell a joke and make people laugh. Her kiss today left him hungry for more. Peter groaned.

Tomorrow, his priorities would be getting his ripped pants sewn and seeing Ginny.

In the light of day, Peter mustered a bit of self-control. He worked slowly, methodically dragging out the most mundane tasks. He tidied his kitchen, fed the stock, checked the well level, washed at the pump, went inside, and put on a new shirt and his second-best set of overalls. He stowed the ripped pants in his saddlebag and a two-bit coin to give Ginny in exchange for mending. Peter blinked and tipped the brim of his hat low.

Along the countryside, sun brilliance bounced—bedazzling oat kernels golden, chokeberry shrubs ruby, bean vines emerald, and bluebirds sapphire.

The temperature had shot up since dawn, and the second-best overalls he wore were warmer than the ripped ones in his saddlebag. Sitting atop a thick, leather saddle heated by Star's exertion was damn uncomfortable. *Damn.* He slid from her back and bounded the three steps to the Dahlke porch. He ran a hand over his sweaty beard and knocked on the door.

Kathleen opened it.

She wore a dress he recognized, but it was tight on her and lapped the floor. On Ginny, the garment fit perfectly.

"Well, Peter, how grand to see you. What brings you here?" Kathleen stepped on the porch and closed the door.

She sure shut the door in a hurry. "Where's Ginny? I've got a favor to ask her. You can see I need her help." Peter pinched the waistband of the injured pants and held them as if they hung on a clothesline.

"Yah, something needs to be done with those pants." Kathleen laughed. "They are much too revealing in that condition. But Ginny isn't here. She is at the Pawlowskis' for a bit of sewing."

"Okay. I'll just take these to her." Peter started down the steps.

"Oh, don't be silly. Leave the pants here. It was so good to see you dance with Bette at the Independence Day celebration. It's pretty clear that girl worships you, Peter."

Peter stilled. He stared.

"She has her cap set on you. Everybody thinks you two make the perfect Parisville pair, and my, what a farm to go with it."

Blood coursed to his temples and beat against the backside of his forehead and inner ears. He balled his ripped pants and thrust them at Kathleen. "Tell Ginny I hope she can fix these. And here is a little something for the trouble." He gritted his teeth and placed a coin on top of the pants. He turned and stomped off the porch. *Was the whole village assuming he would wed Bette for the advantage of her inheritance?*

He didn't even take the time to water Star at the Dahlke trough. In his haste to skedaddle, he almost overshot his leap onto Star's back.

She neighed and backstepped.

Gripping the saddle horn, he took the reins and squeezed his thighs into her belly. *I promise you a thorough curry job and a cold drink once we reach home again, Star.* He did what he always did to get his mind clear. He dove into work. Taking a pine billet from the stack drying behind the livestock, Peter walked to the barn and gathered a saw and two sawhorses.

Setting everything underneath a broad oak tree, he wiped his forehead. He rolled his sleeves and laid the billet atop the sawhorses. Channeling all his weight onto the saw, he bore down and pushed the saw teeth into the wood. Out of each thick, wood slab, he could harvest three eighteen-inch bolts. Then, using the wedge-shaped blade of a frow, he split the bolts into one-half-inch-thick, eight-inch-wide shingles. He clamped each shingle to a bench and tapped one end at a time with a shingle shave. For each thousand shingles Peter made, he could earn five dollars. Once he had enough money, he would face his log cabin with clapboard lumber.

He eased his hands into the everyday work, and he took to whistling a tune—the same ditty James McGrarry had sung—the same one that had set Marianna Gugsak's feet dancing. Peter had other plans for the shingle earnings. First, he would cultivate more rye and alfalfa, and lately, he had considered raising sheep and even adding a crop of flax. The last two additions would please Ginny since both yielded fibers to develop into textiles.

What would five dollars allow me to buy Ginny? Fancy ribbons for her hair? A brush and comb set? A silver thimble? His breath calmed. His chest went light. Exhaling heavily, he lifted the floorboard in the barn, extracted the heavy tin, and popped the lid. He culled his fingers through the coins and listened in satisfaction to the *clank, clank, clank, clank* thuds. If he married again, it wouldn't be out of greed. If he married again, he would marry for love.

Chapter 22

Flies buzzed about the humid kitchen.

Ruta swatted one as it landed on the rim of a bowl filled with oil, vinegar, sugar, and sliced cucumbers. "Ginny, it's good to have you back. I am just no good at the delicate sewing you do and all the figuring it takes for garments to fit right. You are truly gifted, Ginny, and I am so excited to see the gown on Nadia."

A weight lifted in her chest. Ginny held her shoulders more erect. "Thank you, Ruta. Your words mean the world to me. What about right now?" Ginny put her coffee cup in the sink. "The men are busy in the field and out of the way, right?"

"I'd like that." Ruta pressed her hands on her apron. "But, first, girls, we must gather flowers for the Black Madonna." She made the sign of the cross over her forehead. "Today is August twenty-sixth—Our Lady of Czestochowa's feast day."

"Of course." Ginny walked to her sewing machine and grabbed her scissors. In the kitchen garden, no dewy blooms or buds nodded. Instead, the earth below them and the stems that supported them were dry as paper. As she cut a stalk of roses, the leaves crumbled and dropped to the parched earth.

Ruta frowned. "I'm sure the Madonna would be happy with my wheat weavings, yah?"

"Good idea." Ginny squeezed Ruta's shoulder.

"Let's get out of this heat. I'll put these roses in a bit of water, and you bring a weaving. If you gather the wedding dress and take it to Nadia's room, I'll bring my pincushion."

"Nadia, come here. Ginny wants to do a fitting," Ruta called.

"Just finishing dusting the Madonna, Mama."

"Perfect. The Lady is all ready for her big day. Thank you, daughter."

The women gathered in Nadia's stuffy upstairs bedroom.

Blue-and-white-striped wallpaper punctuated with pink peonies as big as Ginny's fist decorated the angled walls.

Ruta sat on the edge of a nine-patch quilt.

Three square pillows rested at the top of the bed. Ginny fingered a straw-colored linen top, petite needled and symmetrically spaced, stitching spelling out Nadia Izolda Pawlowski, September 1, 1859, Parisville, Michigan, in an elaborate font popular in New York advertising. Her mentor, Mrs. Sheridan, had used the same style in the announcements she posted in the Dansville newspapers. Ginny ran her fingertips over the stitches, admiring the artist's skill aligning the wool threads with no evidence of crimp. Any seamstress worth her thimble provided a back closure to extract a pillow form for cleaning. Amateurs stuffed the decorative pillow and sewed the opening shut. Ginny turned the pillow. A French envelope finish, complete with corded buttonholes and wooden buttons, highlighted the reverse side. A three inch in diameter fluted-edge medallion decorated the right side of the closure. Gilded letters across the medallion's center spelled out *First Place Needlework Division Michigan State Fair 1879.* Ginny dropped the pillow. She closed her eyes and pressed her lips together.

Outside Nadia's bedroom window, squirrels chittered. Their squabbling blared through the silent room.

Ginny raised her head and gazed first at Nadia and then Ruta.

"Mama made it for me. She entered it in the State Fair two years ago." Nadia pressed her lips together and looked at the floor.

Tears leaked from the corner of Ginny's eyes. She covered her face.

Ruta chuckled, leaned over, and squeezed Ginny's hands. "*Kochanie*, it's just a little fib. Look how things turned out. You are doing such beautiful work, and you are saving my fingers from pinholes."

Nadia coughed and looked away. She reached for the hem of the dress draped across Ginny's lap. "Oh, Ginny, it's so fine. I know wearing it will make me cry." The bride-to-be smoothed the feather-light satin fabric.

"Oh, that's a good thing, of course." Ruta clapped. "We want a long and happy life for you and Tad. Any good Pole knows a bride who doesn't cry at her wedding will cry later."

"Well, maybe I could leave some pins in the seams, and then you might let out some high-pitched screams and cries, and no one will worry about your wedded bliss." Ginny laughed.

"No, no, I'll let the screaming go on later." Nadia winked.

"Oh, ho, so let's salute that." Ruta bounced her

backside on the bed, sat upright, and rolled her shoulders. "Oh, girls, I do remember my wedding day."

"Ginny, make yourself comfortable. Mama's got another story." Nadia flapped a hand toward the rocking chair fronting the window.

"Pa, come and see what Mystic can do." Dawid's voice carried from the paddock.

Ruta leaned out the windowsill and waved. She sank back on the bed. "The harvest was in, and everyone welcomed rest after so much hard work. Our godmothers baked the wedding cake. Oh, it was the loveliest cake I had ever seen. But then again, my godmother was a true artist. She could draw anything. Our godmothers made the cake from fine wheat flour. Then my godmother fashioned forms of a man and a woman like a little gingerbread couple to look like Papa and me, and she put them on top of the cake. My godmother even made your papa's nose look like his own. She put an extra lump at the end. Hah."

Ginny covered her mouth with her hands.

Nadia giggled.

Ruta leaned against Nadia and pinched her cheek. "Your papa's godmother pressed poppy seeds into the cake—making a sign of the cross. Then they decorated it with little apples—a symbol of love—and walnuts—a symbol of fertility. See how that worked? Your papa and I've had much love and wonderful children."

Lord, I love this family. Thank you, Lord, for putting me in Michigan and giving me such dear friends. Ginny squeezed Nadia's hand.

"Mama, you and Papa have walnut and apple trees. You can use their fruits in my wedding cake, too. Tad and I want a big family, so put on a peck of walnuts."

Nadia smiled.

Ruta chuckled. "Of course, we will, *kochanie*. Now, let's see how this dress fits."

Nadia disrobed and reached for the dress.

"Here, let me help you with that." Ginny guided Nadia's hands through the belled bishop sleeves.

"Oh, I do like that natural waistline." Ruta rubbed her hands together.

"Mama, tell us more about your wedding day."

Ginny turned to Nadia and tweaked the shoulder seams.

Ruta settled on the edge of Nadia's bed. "The night before our wedding day, my bridesmaids came to my papa and mama's house. Oh, I wish I could see those girls again. I wish they could be here to see this wedding." Her eyes grew misty. "Well, my mother laid her best white tablecloth on the kitchen table, and as the girls arrived, each brought rosemary, myrtle, and lavender plants. But oh, to smell all those herbs would take me right back to that night and to the next day when I wore them circled on my head. My friends sang sweet songs and teased me about becoming a married lady."

"Let's figure this neckline." Ginny manipulated the fabric on Nadia's chest. "With a V shape, it's important to make sure the shoulder seaming is form-fitting, so your dress stays up. You've got good shoulder shape, Nadia, but the left shoulder dips a bit."

Nadia stiffened like a wooden soldier. "Will that make my dress look bad?" she moaned.

"No, no, I will compensate for the dip with a small tuck, and your shoulders will look straight across."

"Like an ox yoke, yah?" Ruta clucked.

"Mama, you know Tad and I are not having that kind of marriage. Just because my grandfather asked to buy a cow from your grandfather doesn't make me one." Nadia gusted a breath.

Ruta swiped her hand in the air and laughed. "Pshaw. You are right, *kochanie*. No, you are a smart, modern, beautiful girl, and Papa and I love you with all our hearts." The older woman clasped her daughter's chin in both her hands and squeezed each cheek before kissing them.

Wrapping her arms across her mother's shoulders, Nadia nestled her head on her mother's breast. "I love you, Mama."

"I want to check the length." Ginny crouched on her knees. She scrutinized the distance from the floor to the bottom of Nadia's gown. Her eyes clouded. *Mama, I miss you.* "I have what I need now, Nadia." Ginny leaned back on her feet and swallowed a lump of melancholy. "You are free to step out of this pinned trap." She spread the bottom of the dress and widened the gap for Nadia to pull her head through. The satiny fabric splayed over her fingertips. "Be careful."

"How about a cup of cold tea, girls? I need to get dinner on anyway, so let me see to that, and I will bring us a little snack." Ruta stood and stepped gingerly around the bride-to-be.

Ginny carried the dress to the parlor and draped it on the chair behind her sewing machine.

Nadia joined her.

Ruta brought in the tea set. "Ah, this is nice." She sat and lifted her feet.

"Mama is more relaxed while you are here, Ginny. She never takes a moment for herself. She works so hard. You are a good influence in many ways."

"And dear as a daughter to me." Ruta glanced over the rim of the glass. She fanned herself with her hand. "This awful unending heat is forcing me to move slowly."

"Now, Ginny, you promised. What about this man named Wallace?" Nadia set her tea on the end table adjacent to her chair.

Ginny sighed and wrung her hands. "I am embarrassed to tell you this, ladies, but I led you to believe that Wallace Dunbar was a beau. He never was a boyfriend." She bent her head and closed her eyes.

Ruta cleared her throat.

"I will say that at one time, I was quite fanciful in my imaginings." Ginny jumped her gaze from Nadia to Ruta. She rushed her words. "But Wallace is no more to me than the son of one of my mother's friends." Ginny's words trailed off. She raised her shoulders and looked in her lap.

"*Kochanie*, that's part of growing up and becoming a woman." Ruta reached and pressed Ginny's cheek. "You know, Tad is not the first man Nadia had eyes for."

Nadia slammed her teacup on the side table.

The cup and saucer rattled as her hand retracted.

"Mama," Nadia groaned.

"Well, there was the dashing Andrew Rogger. I was quite smitten with that curly-haired, blue-eyed, beguiling, good-smelling man. Andrew owns a haberdashery in Cass City, and he's a real sharp dresser. He always wore a fine set of cufflinks when he came courting."

"And there are not enough adjectives in the world

to describe him." Nadia shook her head and rolled her eyes.

"Oh, oh." Ruta moved the back of a hand over her brow. "Lonnie Mitchell. He always brought me wild roses or violets or a tin of cookies, and once, he brought me a book of nonsense poetry by Edward Lear. Lonnie had the voice for reading poems —so mellifluous. I'll always remember the way he said 'runcible spoon.' " Ruta giggled. "Romance just dripped from his mouth. Ahhh…"

"Mama! That is quite enough!" Nadia harumphed and plumped the pillows surrounding her.

"So, Ginny, I have a resounding arsenal of bachelors if you want help getting over your youthful fascination with Wallace. If those two don't meet with your satisfaction, perhaps I could suggest a certain…"

The smell of acrid sugar wafted into the parlor.

"Not the berries, Mama," Nadia moaned.

"Oh, girls." Ruta jumped and ran to the kitchen. "Looks like we need to put away the sewing and get this mess cleaned. Your father and brother will be here sniffing for their dinner, and they won't be happy if it's burnt. Hurry!"

Ginny brushed tears from her cheeks and followed Ruta. *A certain who or what?*

Chapter 23

Kathleen slid her bare feet across the floor, loosened her hair, and twirled in a transparent gown. The movement directed a tiny current along her body that was naked underneath. She could set aside modesty. Ginny was sewing at the Pawlowskis'. Life had become so much more bearable with someone else to do the household work. Heaps of foul laundry, a bare larder, curtain-less windows, a scant garden, and soiled bed linens once existed. Now snow-white, Priscilla-style curtains draped the roughhewn window frames, hand-polished floorboards were underfoot, and the marinated green tomatoes Ginny canned a few days ago lined shelves.

A deboned chicken was ready for a stew pot, and crocks of dried berries and hand-churned butter waited for oven-warmed rolls. A vase of ferns, daisies, and forget-me-nots sat tidily on a tablecloth of Irish linen. Lavender-scented sheets stretched across their beds, and a year's supply of soaps and candles made by Ginny's hands nestled in a cupboard. The money to afford the house addition came from earnings from Ginny's sewing. If Ginny married and left them, all those niceties would disappear.

Peter stopped by twice this week, first with a lame excuse of needing his pants sewn and then pretending interest in the crops. Both times he arrived clean-shaven, hair pomaded, and wearing clean clothing from the neck down. He didn't need to waste shaving powder on a fellow farmer to discuss seed and rain. Kathleen saw right through the ruse.

This romance must be snared and whacked dead like a fly buzzing against the screen door. *And I am in the mood to do some whacking.*

The following morning, before the dew evaporated, she donned garden gloves, took a basket from the porch, and stepped to the flower garden. A familiar neigh sounded.

Peter rode Star into the yard.

His muscular body sported a tidy pair of coveralls, and he approached like a single-minded suitor come calling. *Peter Nickles, you cannot fool me.* Kathleen clamped her lips together.

"I wondered if Joseph wanted to go fishing tomorrow." Peter turned his head and scanned the grounds.

"You can find him in the alfalfa field. I'm surprised you didn't see him on your way to the house."

He leaned back in his saddle. "Is Ginny in the house?"

Kathleen removed her gloves and put them on top of the cosmos and nasturtiums in her basket. "She hasn't returned from Pawlowskis' yet. Why Peter Nickles, you've sure found plenty of reasons to visit lately." She straightened the flower stems. "Are you smitten with Ginny?" Peter's jaw worked as if he were juggling a rock with his tongue. "She isn't a girl for you to get giddy over." She pounced with rehearsed words. "She's way too plain for a fine-looking man like you. Some women have it all, while others have nothing at all." She lowered her lashes and sashayed into an exaggerated curtsy.

****

Peter shifted in the saddle. "I make my own decisions. Surely, you know that, Kathleen." He leveled his gaze and clamped his teeth so tight the taste of blood filled his mouth.

"You do know Ginny's promised, don't you?"

Kathleen's voice shattered the air like a stray bullet splintering an empty beer bottle. Peter pulled hard on the reins and turned his upper body.

Star whinnied.

The roof's overhang cast a shadow over Kathleen's face. She stood straight as a ramrod. "To a man in Dansville, New York. He helped Ginny when her father became ill, and they became close. Ginny keeps a book he gave her right by her bed. She must treasure it."

Peter clenched the saddle horn.

A bevy of flies toyed with Star's ears.

She shied.

"His name is Wallace, Wallace Dunbar."

"I never heard that. So why did Ginny come here? Where is this Wallace Dunbar?" Peter barked.

Star pranced and shook her head. Her whirling forelock scattered the insects.

"Well, he's in the military, and Joseph said she could stay here until he came to get her. You did know she didn't plan on staying here forever, didn't you? Besides, Peter, you know how it is with the old Poles. The marriage contracts made between Ginny's father and this man would have to be honored. To break the contract would be a huge disgrace to Ginny's father. She would never dishonor his memory."

He turned Star from the biting flies and the Dahlke homestead. "Good day, Kathleen." The mid-morning sun beat his hatless head, tightly overall-strapped shoulders, and cuffed sleeve-covered arms. The brutal heat spawned rivulets of sweat down his head, neck, and back.

Star fought against the bit, lolling her tongue.

Had he not been so taken aback by Kathleen's revelation, he would've tracked Joseph to discuss the water level in his well. Now he rode dejectedly, worried about the weather, the heat, and his weary heart. Had he misread Ginny? Looking through the lens of Kathleen's account, he could view Ginny's demure reluctance to accept a candy stick as the reaction of a committed fiancée. Her off-putting manner, whenever he got physically close, now appeared a clear message. *Good God.* He had kissed an engaged woman. Ginny avoided his touch and emotional entanglement, and damn it—he should, too.

Chapter 24

Henryk stood in his withering wheat field. A frown dented his dimpled face.

Ginny sighed. Her view from the Pawlowski porch prompted shared concern. Wheat—the plant yielding flour for apple dumplings, semolina for cereal, sap for vodka, and straw Ruta wove into intricate wheat weavings—refused to grow in a climate over ninety-five degrees. For days on end, stagnant air enveloped them, smelling of sunbaked manure and ripening pears. The wheat dithered, immobilized in its inherent quest to reach its full height of four feet. The stalks and heads turned yellow. The seed heads drooped to the ground.

Tomorrow was Ginny's last day at the Pawlowskis'. Nadia's wedding veil was laden with beads. The dress was a masterpiece. Ginny had only one more thing on her to-do list, and that was to confront Peter. Something festered, and she was heartsick, trying to discern what it was. Then, three days ago, she opened the door in response to Peter's knock, and his censoring gaze both wounded and mystified her.

"I didn't expect to see you. Give this to Henryk."

He dropped a sledgehammer at the bottom of the front steps, turned on his heel, and strode away. Tomorrow would be the last chance for a long time to come since Peter, like every farmer, would be tied to harvesting until they baled and stored the final stalks or took them to the docks for sale. Ginny bit her lip.

The following morning, she awoke early to the sounds of the screen door slamming and footsteps pounding up and down the porch steps. *What's going on?* She threw a wrapper over her nightdress and hurried to the front of the house.

Ruta hunched over a chair and dragged it through the front door.

Outside, the sky blackened at the horizon line, and a band of starlings flitted about the morning glories hugging the porch lattice. Ginny moved to the side of the chair. "Ruta?"

"Ah, *kochanie*, good morning. It's your last day here, and I will miss you." Ruta reached and pinched Ginny's cheek.

"Where do you want this?" Ginny crouched and grabbed the chair's legs.

"Next to the wall by the others."

Someone had moved the dining room table to the front porch. *When did that happen?* Chairs lined the walls.

"Mama," Nadia called from the yard. "Papa wants to know if you're ready for the quilting frame. He said he needs to sharpen an extra scythe in case Peter stops by today."

Ginny's heart seized. *Please, please stop today, Peter.*

"Tell your father now is good." Ruta stood and stretched. Her face flushed, and her auburn hair crimped in the humidity. But her eyes sparkled as she caught Ginny's gaze. "I thought for your last day here we'd have a party. And what would be more fitting than a quilting party?"

Ginny put her hands over her mouth. *Merciful heaven, how sweet this family is to me.*

"Besides, I needed some help to finish a particular project." Ruta reached for a parcel on the sofa. She unfolded it and held it up. "For a particular bride-to-be."

Henryk and Nadia walked over the threshold, carrying two twelve-foot-long wooden planks and two four-foot planks.

"Mama." Nadia halted.

Henryk stumbled.

"It's the log cabin pattern. It's beautiful, Ruta." Ginny clapped.

Henryk shored the planks and beamed at his wife. "Such a marvel, Wife. Good job." Perspiration beads trickled below his collar. He pulled a hanky from his pocket and mopped his head.

"I love it, Mama. How did you keep this a secret?" Nadia gripped the ends of the boards.

"It might not seem like a secret once you look closely." Ruta laughed. "I had the help of a little spy." She winked at Ginny.

"Well, this spy needs to get dressed now that you know my alias. I'll be right back to help."

"Why don't you wear your new dress?" Ruta called.

Ginny stopped and turned. "You think of everything, don't you?" She scurried to Dawid's bedroom, with her heart in her throat, and changed into the castoff dress Ruta gave her just two days before. Ruta had insisted Ginny take a break from wedding sewing and repurpose the day dress to fit Ginny.

The project had been fun, with both of them able to discuss complex sewing techniques openly, now that Ruta's skill level was no longer clandestine. On the way to the parlor, Ginny viewed her reflection in the mirror by the umbrella stand. The pleated collar framed her face as if she were a model in a portrait. She pulled her hair high at the temples and secured it with hairpins, and despite the heat, let the remainder cascade down her back.

She bounced her gaze back, and she recognized the giddiness and the anxiety there. *Please, Peter, be here today. I have to speak to you.*

Sawhorses supported the ends of the quilting frame. Chairs flanked the long sides.

Nadia and Ruta basted the quilt edges to the muslin drops on either side.

"Do you know the story of the log cabin pattern, Nadia?" Ginny tipped her chin.

"No, but I'd love to hear it."

Ginny came alongside and pointed to a one-inch red square, dead center in an arrangement of concentric strips. "This represents the hearth of the home. The burning fire provides your home with warmth—a place to gather and enjoy each other's company at the end of a long day."

"Oh, I see." Nadia traced her finger atop the red square.

"Now look, all the way going around the hearth are logs." Ginny guided her fingers over the thin, one-inch-width lengths sewn adjacent to each other. "See that on the other side of the hearth, the logs are dark prints, representing shadows cast from the fire, and on the opposite side, the logs are light prints, like the light from the hearth." She rubbed a finger along an outside edge of a block. "Here's a scrap of fabric from your wedding dress lining on the light side."

"Oh, how thoughtful, Ginny." Nadia sighed. "I'll treasure it always." She leaned into Ginny and kissed her cheek.

By ten o'clock, horses and buggies started to arrive, and each one delivered cheerful women and excited children.

Ruta reigned over the ado, directing the placement of incoming food baskets, crated infants, and older children to a swing in the backyard.

Ladies pulled aside the chairs, sat, pulled thimbles from pockets, and reached for the lengths of ready-cut thread and needles culled in felt squares laying on top of the basted quilt.

"I know my stitches are not tiny as they once were, but I'm happy to be quilting with you girls." Josephine Pyonk shook her head and held aloft a needle.

"Don't let her kid you." Ruta stood looking over the elderly midwife. "I count fourteen, maybe fifteen straight and tiny stitches per inch here." The party's hostess kissed Josephine's wrinkled cheek, stepped back, and wrinkled her nose.

Ginny had caught a whiff of the older woman as Harriett Worchok accompanied her inside the parlor. In a chair at the opposite end of the table, within close range of a vase of roses and phlox, Ginny inhaled their sweet scents and stuffed a pang of guilt. The older woman's stitching might still be tight, but her hygiene habits sagged. The conversation rolled and looped and shuffled around the rectangular shape of clamped boards stretching a pieced quilt top.

"Marta, what an ornate thimble."

"*Tak*, my man, he always finds such treasures for me."

"What Mama means is Papa always brings home useless knick-knacks." Bette snickered.

"Ruta, can you give me your recipe for *borscht*? Casimir is crazy over it."

"Sure, don't go home before I write it down."

"How about some ideas for cold meals? Way too hot to cook."

On each side of the table, heads nodded.

"Sophie, do you need boy's shoes, size eight?"

"Does anyone know Father's plans for First Communion this year?"

"I think I recognize this stripe, Ruta. Don't you have a bonnet made from this fabric?"

A babe cried.

A woman excused herself.

Before being snatched by the suspenders and disconnected from a tangle of legs and skirts, a child darted under their sewing tent.

"No playing hide and seek under the quilt," Marta hollered.

Giggles erupted.

Needles were rethreaded.

Caught in the gaiety meant to honor her, Ginny was distracted by her worry that Peter wouldn't show. The opportunity slipped away as Bette quilted across the frame. Ginny squinted. She cataloged Bette's attributes—heart-shaped, blemish-free face, expressive, doe-like eyes, delicate hands that executed minute running stitches through the light and dark prints. Bette was a beloved woman at St. Mary's Parish. She offered a kind word to each guest and received reciprocal hand squeezes and cheek pinches.

Thus far, Ginny's reputation relied on owning a modern Singer sewing machine, but that didn't warrant the community love and affection bestowed on Bette.

"Was that Peter Nickles's horse I saw by the barn?" Marta looked up.

Ginny jerked her head and stabbed a finger with her needle. *Ouch.*

"Star pattern on the muzzle? Three white stockings?"

"Yah."

"Surely, that is Peter's Star."

"Tsk…" Josephine whistled. "Poor Peter, that poor man, all alone, so handsome, too. I don't know what I would do without him. In the last few days, he fixed a hole in my roof and got rid of a hornet's nest under the porch. And yesterday, whilst I collected eggs, I found a silver coin under a hen. Now, who do you suppose put it there?" The old lady's eyes teared.

A mouth-watering aroma floated from the kitchen.

Harriett sniffed the air. "Annie Erhardt's bean casserole."

Annie looked up from her stitching and grinned.

No doubt every lady in the group knew the recipe by heart. Ginny smiled. Navy beans grew sturdy in the thumb of Michigan's soil, and beans were a relished staple in all her neighbors' larders. Annie's version of bean casserole included ham hock, maple syrup, and sweet potato.

Ginny turned her gaze from the quilt top to the front hallway each time the door swung open, hoping to see Peter's face. She had learned to read his expressions. Now she knew the feigned sober look before he delivered the finish to a joke. She knew the difference in his reaction to a funny story he told of someone else, and a travesty sprung on him. His laughter was more boisterous for the latter. What she could not figure was the stare of disdain he had recently leveled, nor the frigid impression he left in his retreat. The uncertainty frayed her nerves and snarled her thoughts. Ginny sighed.

"Gotta get up again, ladies." Annie Erhardt braced her hands on the seat of her chair.

"I remember those trips to the necessary." Harriett chuckled.

"Getting pretty close, right, dear?" Josephine cleared her throat. The old midwife watched Annie waddle toward the door.

"Yah." Annie panted.

The quilters bent back to their work.

The hinges on the front door creaked.

"Oh, thank you, Peter." Annie fluttered a hand over her flushed face and shuffled to her chair.

He looked taller and thinner and, oh, so much more handsome. Ginny fought to breathe.

A fresh round of cackling sounded around the quilt frame.

"We were just talking about you." The bride-to-be grinned.

"Yah, trying to marry you off." Harriett winked.

Ginny blushed. All gazes were on Bette. The clucks and the elbowing fixed on the pretty woman across from her. Ginny's hands grew cold. Her mouth felt dry as the cotton batting sandwiched between the log cabin top and the backing fabrics. She fought the urge to run. *But where?*

****

Whew. Peter shut the door behind him. He groaned. One at a time, he could buffer their infernal matchmaking. But a whole covey of them, consorting together, intimidated the hell out of him. Henryk would have to ask them himself or send another messenger to ask when they intended to stop for dinner.

Hell, not even all those sugary treats baked and brought to the quilting party could entice him to stay. His head hurt like a bachelor party afterglow, and his shoulders ached from a nocturnal wrestling match with his bedsheets. Franny had stormed his dreams.

This time, no provocative prelude softened the message. This time Franny communicated her displeasure with stoic silence. He tried to humor her, conjuring a mimic of Gertrude chewing her cud. But she ignored him. The dream ended as she turned to him, sighed, and shaped her mouth into a melancholy moue. The haunting stuck in his throat like a fishbone.

He felt the same throat constricting now. He'd held the door for Annie, walked inside, and there sat Ginny, looking so fine his heart jumped to his throat, closing off the air. Her gaze met his, and he read confusion and hurt in it. If he had to guess, he would've said she was on the verge of tears. *Was it guilt? Embarrassment? Regret? Probably all three. Shame on her and shame on me.*

Chapter 25

A trifling breeze rippled the front room curtains.

Joseph had advised Kathleen to leave the window coverings pulled shut to block as much heat as possible, but the panels lazed parted, exposing the room to strong shafts of sunlight.

Ginny reached to close them.

"I can't abide being so cooped up. I feel like one of our egg layers." Kathleen opened the curtains again and defied Joseph. She flopped on the settee and gathered a letter she received from her mother. She folded the stationery in several crosswise folds, pleated the paper's edges, and fanned herself. "Oh, Lord, it's so hot I hate to put on anything. If it was only Joseph and me..." Kathleen stopped short of finishing the thought aloud.

Sweat streaked Ginny's bodice. She wished she could peel fabric from wherever it encased her body. Instead, relief came from tying up the curls framing her moist face and neck. "I'll check the stock." Before she reached the barn, she veered to the now-familiar path leading to the cross-carved stone.

Clusters of wildflowers lay wilted on its surface. Ginny withdrew a vial of water she smuggled from the pail in the kitchen. She wetted the thirsty plants and plucked weeds threatening them.

The pigs lay in the shadiest area of their pen.

Joseph had turned the dirt, allowing the earth's

coolness to provide comfort for the hairless animals.

Chickens wheezed in their sleepy roosting.

Chessie snored in a shady spot near a haystack, and his pink tongue lolled between his open jaws.

A sea of dust clung to Ginny's skirt hem and filtered into her boots. The old-timers said it was the hottest summer they could recall. She had discarded the August calendar page three days ago. Shouldn't that alone guarantee cooler temperatures?

Perhaps Joseph could take them for a trip to the lake. She imagined the horses would enjoy a lingering rest in the sandy-bottomed lake. Maybe Joseph would take pity on the pigs, sheep, cows, and chickens, too. She pictured their whole bundle of livestock taking a holiday on Lake Huron banks—the hens feasting on sand fleas, the pigs rolling in the cool sand, the sheep lapping water with their rose-pink tongues, and the cows shrieking as their udders breached the cold waters. But Ginny knew little time remained for leisure.

Joseph hustled from sunrise to sunset—worrying over the lack of rain that threatened the soon-to-be harvested crops. He neared the well, attached the bucket to the rope's end, and turned the style to lower it.

Ginny gauged the time it took for him to begin the bucket's return. Even from across the yard, she could read the concern stamped on his sunburned face. Joseph shared what he knew of the consequences of extended, oppressive heat. Crops shriveled, making them more vulnerable to ravenous insects. Well levels sank, forcing water rationing for stock and humans. The arid grounds and vegetation presented another level of worry. They were agents of fire.

Joseph raised his head. He held aloft the bucket.

A cold drink would do them all good. Ginny nodded and followed Joseph into the house.

He pulled his hat from his head and hung it on the peg next to the front door. "I stopped to greet the new farmers the next two plots over. They've recently emigrated from Goderich, Canada, and are anxious to sow a fall crop. So, as terrible as this heat is, they were both burning to clear their land."

"Oh, no. Couldn't you talk them out of that?" Ginny cried. "Don't they know how dangerous it is to be burning now? With everything so dry? Good, Lord."

Joseph shook his head. "I also stopped by Eddie and Annie Erhardt's place. I don't know how they can suffer that extra heat, but Eddie is determined to burn a huge section east of his barn to prepare for a crop of winter rye."

Ginny wrapped her arms across her chest and scowled.

"I know, I know. I did tell Eddie that even though the winds were calm now, they can be fickle. I've seen Lake Huron when a north wind blows in. After that, all hell can break loose." Joseph rubbed his forehead.

"How is Annie?" Ginny chewed on her lower lip.

"She complained of trouble breathing." Joseph frowned. "Her pregnancy is well advanced. She looked ready to burst, and she had two other little ones dragging on her skirts."

From the rocking chair, Kathleen sighed. She ran a hand over her belly.

Joseph moved behind her. His hand clenched the back of Kathleen's chair. "Ginny? I've got something to tell you. Kathleen and I are having a baby."

"Jesus, Mary, Joseph." Ginny jumped to embrace

Kathleen and then her brother. Joseph's embrace was wooden, almost off-putting. *Why aren't they smiling?* A chill ran over Ginny's spine.

Kathleen stood and went to their bedroom.

Joseph watched her, turned, and left the house.

Jesus, Mary, Joseph.

****

Nightfall brought no relief from the stale, unremitting heat. Ginny slept fitfully. She raised her head, plumped her pillow, and flailed an arm.

"*Bark, bark, bark.*"

Chessie's alarm pierced the log walls and Ginny's tormented whims.

Clunk-clunk-clunk.

Ginny shot open her eyelids. She made the sign of the cross and rolled out of bed.

In his nightshirt, Joseph streaked past her bed, snapped his gun from its mooring spot, and flung open the door.

"*Bark, bark, bark.*"

"Out, out, be gone," Joseph hollered and ran into the night.

Ginny threw a wrapper over her nightdress and dashed out the door. The landscape held no moon, and Joseph's nightshirt showed as a ghostly specter. "Brother, what is it?"

Chessie darted past, snarled, and vanished into the abyss, where a formidable forest lived in the light of day.

"Wolves! Get back."

Still, Ginny followed, screamed, and wagged her hands high above her head.

Joseph disappeared into the chicken coop.

279

High-pitched squawking ensued, followed by soft cackles.

Joseph's gun blasted, and a silver filament illumed the blue-black atmosphere.

A scrawny wolf leaped through the doorway, sprawled ten feet from Ginny's bare feet, and died.

Ginny pulled her wrapper from her shoulders, stretched it, and swooped to gather three dazed hens flopping outside the coop.

With his gun brandished, Joseph cut a path around the house and the coop.

Kathleen emerged with a bedsheet. "Here, Ginny, grab an end."

The women walked through the yard, using the sheet to gather loose chickens. "Nine accounted for," Ginny called. Her shoulders ached from the struggle, and her bare feet stung from running pell-mell over gravel and jagged sticks.

Chessie returned from his foray and circled the women, herding them back to the house.

"Good boy." Joseph bent to scratch the dog's ears.

"Wait here. Let me go in the coop first." Joseph emerged, shook his head, and wiped the sweat from his brow. "No sense crying."

"Oh, no," Kathleen moaned.

"We'll put the remaining chickens in the house for tonight. I'll fashion them a crate. You ladies go on into the house. I've some work here." His shoulders drooped, and he stared straight. He put his index finger to his closed lips and nodded toward Kathleen. "Ginny, with small mammals perishing for lack of water, the bigger predators suffer, too. Wolves this hungry and this willing to reveal themselves are not a good sign."

Ginny tucked her chin, sighed, and stumbled to the house. *God help us all.*

****

As the sun ascended the next day, the red-hot orb reinforced another wave of suffocating temperature.

"Ginny, don't use the stove. I'm going outside and build a small campfire to boil water for coffee. As much as we can, let's prevent heat from entering the house." Joseph spoke softly behind the curtain delineating Ginny's sleeping area.

She rose and followed Joseph to the door. *Good God. Joseph aged ten years since he stepped from the house last night.*

"I'll check traps. I'll probably be bringing you a rabbit. Get the Dutch oven ready, and I'll cook dinner in the yard."

Kathleen staggered toward them. Her hair stuck to her neck, and her face bore the indentations of dehydration. "Joseph, please, I can't spend one more day here, trapped in these walls. Please take us to church. It's the first Sunday in September. Surely soon, the heat will break."

Joseph bounced his gaze from his sister to his wife. "I don't want to tire the horses. We should stay home and preserve water." He turned his back, shoved his hands in his overall pockets, and gazed at the barn.

"Joseph..." Kathleen whined.

"Okay, we'll go to church today, but, on one condition." Joseph ran a hand through his hair and planted his feet. "I'm making a decision as head of this household."

Ginny furrowed her brows and grabbed the back of a rough-hewn chair.

Kathleen put her hands on her hips.

"You ladies have to learn to use a gun."

"It's not proper, Joseph, and I don't have the strength to pull a trigger," Kathleen wailed. What if the powder erupts in my face?"

Joseph drummed his fingertips on the door frame. "Well, as long as one of you knows how and promises me that she will use it if needed." His gaze leveled with Ginny's.

By default, she would be the new gunslinger of the household. Ginny's stomach trembled. *Dear God.*

****

At church, Sophie, with toddler Teresa wedged on her hip, led her gaggle of children into a pew.

Casimir held his hat in both hands and brought up the rear.

Chubby Ludwig attempted to sit atop Jakob.

In a move of self-preservation, Jakob shoved his older brother's backside.

Ludwig's face puffed like a marshmallow over a campfire, but he held his tongue.

Oskar, ever the diplomat, allowed his younger siblings to scrabble across his lap before they were all settled.

Anna's gaze flicked right and centered forward.

Yet, Ginny caught all the furtive glances aimed at the handsome eighteen-year-old Michael Nowakowski.

Four-year-old Julia, ever her daddy's little girl, seized the opportunity of claiming him all to herself and snuggled against his right arm.

He kissed her upturned nose, and she giggled.

The Felician nuns attended church today and would be making visits to each parish member that week.

Women saved goose feathers for the nuns who stuffed them into comforters for orphans.

Ginny groaned inwardly. Sister Vincentine and Sister Nepomucene must be suffering stuck in those ovens of black-and-white habits. She made a mental note to set aside white cotton batiste yardage to give to the sisters, with the hope they would use it for their own relief, not just the comforters they made for orphans. Ginny remembered Ruta saying the nuns would be staying with them.

The high-ceilinged church offered more comfort than the squat cabin that was home. Or maybe the ease came from a parish full of fluttering fans. Women flapped little folded papers they tucked into the pages of their Bibles. Or perhaps it was from the continued soft huffing from singing hymns. The very young and the very old were falling asleep in the oppressive heat. The soothing sounds of humming mothers and geriatric snorting further mollified the congregation.

Blobs of sweat ran down the face and neck of the Roman-collared Father Graca as he faced his lethargic parish.

If he'd asked her, Ginny would've recommended the theme of a refreshing biblical psalm, such as the twenty-third, with its imagery of green pastures and still waters.

"I say unto you…sin is the misery and ruin of the soul. It will turn the soul into a fiery furnace of fire and brimstone. I quote Matthew, 3:12: 'His winnowing fork is his hand, and he will clear his threshing floor, gathering his wheat into the barn and burning up the chaff with unquenchable fire.'" The priest slammed the pulpit.

Josephine backhanded the dribble on her furry chin.

Sophie shot upright, squeezing a slumbering Teresa.

Stanislaw and Michael, clothed in floor-length altar boy cassocks and flanking Father, switched their facial expressions from comatose to stricken.

Dormant paper fans flapped to attention.

The organ wheezed and was reborn with the called-into-action pedal pumping of the organist, Harriett Worchok.

Ginny hazarded a furtive glance toward Peter. His face appeared as hard as the pews they sat on, and he maintained his steadfast focus on Father. Her stomach plummeted.

Peter bore dark circles under his eyes. He was alone in the worry of his farm. In times of fear, married couples fared better than loners. A concern shared was half the worry to bear. She wished she could clasp his head to her breast and soothe his troubled brow.

Following services, parishioners lingered. All that waited for them at home was unbroken heat.

Teams drowsed in the shade of oak trees.

The men lounged against the wagons.

The women gravitated to the shade of mature elm trees, where they kept a watchful eye on their men and their children.

Ginny sat away from the crowd and rested her head against the fissured bark of a wide-leafed oak.

"Ginny?"

Ruta approached.

"Ruta."

"I wondered if you would join me this afternoon.

I'm going to Josephine's. The poor dear needs help. Peter cares for her farm, but I'm speaking of the personal help only lady friends can provide. She sorely needs a bath, and I can only imagine her house needs a bit of your brand of spitfire and polish."

"Oh, Ruta, of course. I will come."

"Once I get the nuns settled, I'll be on my way to pick you up. I see Henryk signaling, so I'll be off." Ruta sighed and squeezed her shoulder.

Honk, honk, honk.

Overhead, a flock of low-flying Canadian geese narrowly missed the peaks of the oak trees surrounding the churchyard. Their bodies were massed together in frenzied escape, and to Ginny's ears they sounded threatened. Despite the unwavering heat, a chill ran from her heels to her shoulders.

****

Peter crossed over the church threshold and clapped his hat on his head.

Ginny sat on the ground, her back and head leaning against a shaded tree.

"Ginny, Ginny, look at what Mrs. Pawlowski gave me for my birthday."

The child's voice rang loud enough for him to hear.

Halina Urdzela skipped toward Ginny holding a colorful paper the size of a playing card.

"Oh, my, let me see, sweetheart." Ginny leaned forward and stretched her hand.

"It's my very own holy card. Mrs. Pawlowski said it's to remind me my guardian angel always looks after me. Isn't it the most beautiful thing you've ever seen in your whole life, Ginny?"

"Indeed." Ginny studied the holy card and returned

it to Halina.

Peter knew the picture well since he had witnessed Ruta pulling it many times from her satchel. The watercolor illustration depicted a winged adult angel observing a little girl and boy picking wildflowers in front of a cascading waterfall with a lone, white pine standing sentinel in the background.

"I know pink is your favorite color, birthday girl." Ginny loosened a ribbon band on her hat. "Let's see how this looks in your hair." She threaded it through Halina's curly braid. "Oh, I think it's perfect."

The little girl leaned over Ginny and hugged her. "Oh, Ginny, I love you." Halina kissed Ginny's cheek and fingered the ribbon. Then, the little girl turned and ran. "Mama, see what Ginny gave me..."

"Happy birthday, Halina," Ginny called after her.

She is a natural. Does Wallace Dunbar know what a prize you are? Peter strolled to the circle of men.

"Corn's in, potatoes next." George lifted his straw hat and scratched his head.

"Hot or not, I've got to burn more fields to discourage deer from getting too close to the rest of the garden." Martin fanned his ruddy face with a handkerchief.

A new Canadian neighbor shuffled his feet. "Yah, hot as it is, best to burn off rubbish."

"Fire is the only way to get rid of those stumps the kids are always tripping over." Casimir lipped a cigarette and blew a smoke ring.

"And there's the missus and her chores. Tomorrow is Monday, and that means washday." George shook his head.

"Yah, my missus, she wouldn't put off wash day if

all the fires of hell busted loose on us." Martin winked. "Cleanliness is next to godliness, she says."

Each man nodded his head.

Monday was washday for all the missuses.

Peter spoke to the ground. "I've got all my wheat threshed. So, I figure now is a good time to take a trip to Brockway Centre. I'll be leaving early tomorrow."

"That's quite a ride, Peter. What's so important in Brockway Centre?" George rubbed his face on his sleeve.

"A new woolen mill—a German family named Andreae built it, a father and two sons. They had a mill right on Lake Huron in Lexington, but now that the Port Huron and Northwestern runs through Brockway Centre, they're moving the operation. The rails come right up to their front door, and a stream runs behind it. I hear they will scour and card our fleeces for a trade of raw wool."

"How long will you be gone, Peter?" Martin spat a wad of tobacco.

"I figure a day to get there and a day to get back." Peter drew a cigarette from his shirt pocket. "The Andreaes might be looking to hire on. I've got some experience, and I might be looking for a little extra money now that folks prefer store-bought shingles." He accepted a light off the end of Casimir's smoke, brought the cigarette to his mouth, and took a huff.

"Let us know what you find. If we could get the washing and carding already done, it would make the spinning, weaving, and knitting go faster for the missus. And it's soon enough we'll be needing the winter socks and overcoats," Henryk said.

"Sophie would like to knit Zygmunt's wee one

some blankets and baby things." Casimir wrinkled his nose. The corners of his mouth lifted.

"You're going to be a grandpa, Casimir?"

"*Tak*." The new-to-be grandparent grinned broadly.

Peter clapped Casimir on the back. "Congratulations, my friend." After he took Josephine home, Peter let his thoughts drift. He gave vision to Ginny in the glow of soft firelight, a contented cat purring in her lap as she wrapped a loop of yarn around buffed wooden needles. Her hair hung loose. Unruly wisps, burnished in the hearth light, brushed her cheek. She rocked, humming a lullaby. The words came to him *Spij laleczko moja mala, czas na ciebie juz*…Sleep, my little baby doll, it is the time for you now…" He wished the picture was a scene in front of the fieldstone fireplace in his cabin, and God help him, he wished the baby she knitted for was his.

Chapter 26

Ruta chuckled. "Oh, my goodness, if there were an award for snoring, I'm sure Sister Nepomucene would claim the trophy." She clucked to the team, guided them into Josephine's yard, and stopped just short of the front porch railing. "I fed both nuns a roasted chicken dinner when we got home from church this morning and right after that they disappeared upstairs for naps."

"I've thought about them and wondered how they can endure this heat, wrapped in those black-and-white habits. Poor dears. No wonder they are exhausted." Ginny jumped from the buckboard and tethered the team to the Pyonk porch.

Reaching in the back of the wagon, Ruta pulled forth a satchel, tucked it under her arm, and joined Ginny.

Ginny paused at Josephine's front door and knocked. Mud pellets and tads of dried grasses peppered her bonnet, bounced off her shoulders, and dusted her feet. "Watch out, Ruta!"

"Too late." Ruta brushed bird nest debris from her shoulders.

Plunk–plunk–plunk. "Coming."

The thud of her cane pulsated stronger than the voice of the beloved midwife.

Josephine drew open the door.

A woolen shawl draped her slumped shoulders and smelled of urine.

Ginny fought the inclination to cover her nose.

Ruta wrinkled hers.

The look on Josephine's face quelled any revulsion Ginny bore.

A smile lit one end of her toothless gums to the other. "Come in. Come in," the midwife said in clipped English. She stepped back and echoed Ginny's greeting during her first visit to the Pawlowski home. "*Gosc w Dom. Bog w Dom*," Guest in the home is God in the home.

"Josephine, I brought you soft biscuits. Why don't you have a snack while Ginny and I tidy up a bit?" Ruta took Josephine's elbow and kissed her head.

The old lady's lips quivered. Her head shook. Tears leaked from the corners of her rheumy eyes.

"There now, dear." Ruta handed her a handkerchief and led her to a threadbare sofa.

Josephine laid her cane on the floor, backed to the settee, and toppled backward.

Ruta righted the elderly woman's shoulders, sat beside her, and caressed her cheek.

Josephine nodded, took Ruta's hand, and kissed it.

Ginny opened the oven, stacked wood in the bottom, and lit a fire. She filled a teapot and a large cooking pot with water and put them on to boil. She fastened an apron over her most lightweight muslin dress.

Flies droned and tiptoed along the surfaces of dishes strewn about the kitchen.

With two energetic women tackling the cobwebs and dust, the cabin was clean within an hour.

"I found the tub, Ginny," Ruta called from a bedroom.

Together, Ruta and Ginny dragged the tub to the front room.

Ginny dipped her elbow into the stove's simmering pot. "Water's ready."

With the tub full and fresh linens stacked next to it, Ruta helped Josephine disrobe.

Standing behind Josephine, Ginny threaded her strong arms under Josephine's flaccid arms, stood to her full height, and held the midwife's weight.

Ruta braced her left shoulder against Josephine and wrapped her left arm about the older woman's back. She used her feet to nudge Josephine's feet to the shallow end of the bathtub. "Here we go, now, slowly…" Ruta lifted her chin.

Nodding, Ginny continued to hold Josephine by her shoulders.

Ruta picked Josephine's feet off the floor.

Josephine's butt drifted into the water.

Placing the old lady's hands on the edges of the tub, Ginny lowered onto her knees.

"Ahhh…" Josephine murmured. She closed her translucent eyelids and leaned her head against the tin bath.

Ginny poured water over Josephine's scalp and massaged castile soap through the older woman's hair. Tears poured over Ginny's face. *Sweet, sweet woman. All the love and reassurance you have gifted women in their most vulnerable moments. Josephine, you are such a treasure, dear.*

From her position at the end of the tub, Ruta knelt and lifted one of Josephine's feet from the water. She rubbed between each crimped toe and around each leathery heel and repeated the motions on the other foot.

"My bonnie lies over the ocean…" Ginny sang.

Ruta joined the refrain and splashed the bathwater. "My bonnie lies over the sea…"

Over the opposite ends of the tub, Ruta and Ginny shared a smile as the old lady snored.

Goose bumps rose on Josephine's skin.

"Josephine…" Ginny whispered.

The midwife startled and stared with a vacant gaze. "Oh my, oh, I had the most vivid dream."

"Well, tell us about it as we get you dressed." Ruta reached for the towel and tucked it under her arm.

"My Aloysius was there." Josephine wheezed.

Ginny leaned forward and thrust her arms under Josephine's armpits. She raised slowly from her knees, hauling Josephine upright.

Ruta gripped Josephine's feet.

Once Josephine stood, Ruta moved to Ginny's end and assisted in lifting Josephine from the tub.

Ruta unfolded the towel and dried Josephine.

"Oh, he was the most handsome I ever remember. He wore a dark shirt, and it fit him tight across his strong shoulders." Josephine's eyes watered. He said, '*Kochanie,* I looked for you everywhere, and here you are, the prettiest girl from Pomeria, along the Baltic Sea.'"

Tears seeped from Ginny's eyes. *Yes, you are the prettiest girl.*

Ruta's chin quivered.

Slipping a nightgown over Josephine's head, Ginny threaded the elderly lady's arms through the sleeves, and fastened the gown's closure ribbons.

Ruta combed Josephine's thin hair and braided it.

After a light supper of biscuits, soup, and chamomile tea, Ginny kissed Josephine and helped her into bed.

Ruta tucked a flannel sheet around Josephine's shoulders.

"Aloysius, Aloysius," Josephine murmured. The fine whiskers on her upper lip trembled.

Sweet dreams, Josephine. Sweet dreams.

Chapter 27

Louis Gugsak Sr. tilted his camp chair, lipped a bottle of vodka, and leaned his head against the front of his wretched house.

It's so damn hot.

Peeling paint crackled against his neck. He swore and brushed the crumbling pieces onto the rickety porch. With his free hand, he directed a rolled cigarette into his mouth and sucked a long draw.

The vodka delivered the expected burning sting. The cigarette left too long in his shaking fingers caused him to swear again. The irony of self-punishment by heated objects was lost on him. He was so damn tired. Tired of his tiresome kids. Tired of his meddlesome neighbor. Tired of the thankless work. Tired of the damn heat.

Marianna started in first thing this morning. He hadn't even had his coffee yet.

"Papa, may I please go to church?"

He ignored her.

"Papa, I need to go to church to find out about school starting. I can run over to Mr. McGrarry's and ask him to take me." She wheedled and cried.

Finally, he silenced her by cracking her across the face. After that, she left him alone. The hell he would go to church. Bunch of teetotaling, interfering jackasses. Didn't Marianna remember they almost drowned him and stood in the way of disciplining his own damn son?

And the old man, always coming by, uninvited. He was so damn tired of hearing the old man's opinions. If he were as cautious as the old man insisted, nothing would ever get done. Louis was a product of taking risks. Experience showed him the way to proceed in life. He hadn't settled for his father's expectations to live his life in the bowels of a coal mine. At least he had that. Louis busted his ass, lived with courage, and accepted the consequences. He wouldn't live with fear. Now his nosy old neighbor spied on him, tracked his every move, and ran over every time he got a whiff of smoke.

What business was it of his if Louis fertilized his field with sheep manure rather than horse manure? What did he care if rain weathered his wagon? Who could prove he shot Worchok's dog? Tomorrow, if the old man came by, Louis would threaten him with his gun, and by God, he'd shoot him if he didn't hightail his sorry old ass right back home.

Tonight, by God, he would burn more stumps lying in the path to the rye field. Grunting in disgust, Louis plucked the cigarette from his mouth, tossed it in the grass, and lipped the bottle—intent on deadening every angry reflection in his brain.

Chapter 28

Monday, September 5, 1881, started the same way as any other day for Father Graca. He rose well before dawn in his sparse living quarters in St. Mary's Catholic Church's rectory. As was his custom and his holy obligation to fulfill, he began his day praying. By canon law, the character of the Morning Prayer was praise. Father recited a canticle taken from Zechariah:

"In the tender compassion of Our Lord
The dawn from on high shall break upon us,
To shine on those who dwell in darkness.
And the shadow of death,
And to guide our feet into the way of peace.
Glory be to the Father
And to the Son
And to the Holy Spirit,
As it was in the beginning,
Is now and ever will be forever.
Amen."

Father ate a breakfast of rye bread and tea—elderberry with two teaspoons of honey. Then, just before six, he walked the short distance to the church belfry. He pulled the rope hanging from the bell above him. With each tug, the bell swung on its fulcrum and struck the clapper on the backswing. Three times he executed quick and even drags on the rope, straightened his body, paused for a count of ten, and twice repeated the triple clangs, a pattern recognized in all the homesteads surrounding St. Mary's as an all-is-well message. Father stepped into the barn's shade after a walk through the church property, which included an exterior inspection of the church, barn, and cemetery.

A soft whinny welcomed him. "Hey, girl," he murmured. "How about a crunchy carrot, huh?" He pulled the vegetable from his pocket and allowed Maisy to lip it off the palm of his hand. Then, he stood for a few moments, enjoying the quiet commune with his horse.

Maisy angled her ears backward and patiently listened to his one-way conversation.

She was the one being privy to the outpourings of the priest, who was, despite the adoration of the members of St. Mary's Catholic Church, first and undeniably a mere man, incapable of changing fate.

****

Bette tied an apron over her muslin dress. Because of the large pockets on each side of the skirt, it was her favored washday apron.

Papa had saddled a team and was gone by six that morning. He liked to stay out of the way of womenfolk's laundry work, so for as long as Bette could remember, Monday was Papa's day to go to town to run errands and catch up on the news. Against the better wishes of her mother, who had asked him to stay home and rest during this heinous heat, he brushed aside Marta's concerns and traveled to Forestville to see if the horse-drawn rake he ordered from the *Montgomery Ward* catalog had arrived.

It would be another blazing hot day. Already the ground was rid of dew, and the air was thick as a winter muffler. Bette contemplated the futility of cleansing clothes while the ones they wore became soaked with sweat, as well as saturated with the permeating, laundry-fire smoke that encircled and attempted to suffocate her. Lacking a breeze, the smoke from the fire that kept the water boiling would settle back on her clothing and hair. It was a pointless task, yet Bette knew her mother would brook no argument. Cleanliness, or at least the pursuit, was long entrenched in her Polish mother's fervent devotion to St. Clare of Assisi, patron saint of laundresses. Besides, it will be worth it tonight after Peter arrives, Bette reminded herself and shook her hips.

Her father had been thoughtful enough to set the logs under the kettle before he left. Papa's kind-heartedness extended to leaving Bette a gift of sorts, a novelty not yet seen in Michigan's thumb. He purchased the item the week before during a trek to Taraski's General Store. Tom Taraski, the shopkeeper, flaunted a new product he sold, and Papa couldn't resist.

Bette imagined the scene and chuckled.

"Lookee here, Oberski, brand new…from a company in Ohio."

Tom Taraski, as Papa liked to describe him, was a Midwest P.T. Barnum. According to Papa, Taraski had a natural propensity for hawking gimcracks, trinkets, and knick-knacks.

Bette smirked. Her papa was an easy target for a salesman offering items of curiosity. Moreover, the junk Papa hauled home often exasperated her mother.

Mama would sigh and call him incurable.

As she recalled Papa telling the story of Taraski's

newest gadget, Bette grinned.

Supper leftovers had been stored in the icehouse.

The day turned into evening. The setting sun flared in the western horizon and illuminated the pointed-hat tops of jack pines, the rounded canopy of apple trees, and the rectangular fence posts marking the division between the paddock and the drive.

Papa settled into his easy chair. "Mama, Bette, please come here. I want to show you something special. It will take your breath away."

"Oh, pshaw, please, please, no more junk. I can't think who will take it off my hands or where we will put it." Mama entered the living room, sat next to Papa, and swooped her hands, emphasizing the organized clutter that filled every shelf, cupboard, drawer, and wall.

Bette followed Mama and sat on the sofa, opposite her parents' chairs.

"Now, Mama..." he leaned forward. "This item is quite small..."

"Oh, Martin." She whacked the folded newspaper on her knee. "You cannot get me with that one. You called that baby goat small, and he grew bigger and made a big mess of my flowers. He ate the big hollyhocks and the small petunias. So size doesn't sway me, Martin."

"Now, Bette, you surely want to see what I brought, don't you?" Papa's eyes shone and the wrinkles bookending his eyes cut deep.

Bette found it increasingly difficult to resist getting pulled into the net of his good humor. Her papa was so dear, even if he riled her neat-as-a-freshly-starched doily mother.

"One more clue, Mama. It's something you've always wanted for your left hand."

Marta sucked a deep breath and put her hand on her chest. "Martin," she whispered.

Papa reached and gathered Mama's left hand from her breast. He caressed the fingers that spent the day yanking potatoes rooted into a sunbaked garden, darting into a dozen egg-laying boxes, twisting and chopping the neck of what became their dinner and, early that morning, succumbed to Papa's whining about his itchy back.

"Enough of this silliness…those beets won't jump in the sink and scrub themselves. For God's sake, Martin, what is it?"

Papa withdrew a box from his overall pocket. His big hand eclipsed the small package hidden in the grip of his fingers.

Mama's gnarled fingers trembled. Her translucent cheeks blushed.

"Well, my dearest, here you go."

Mama shuttered her eyes.

Martin opened his hand. "A diamond!"

"What?" Mama leaned toward Papa. She gripped either side of her chair and compressed the arms' stuffing to half its depth.

Papa's belly jiggled with a burgeoning laugh. He slid open the box and extracted a single matchstick with a bulbous head. He held the stick on its blunt end and moved it within Mama's close visage. "This is a blue diamond match."

Bette stared at the small piece of wood Papa held.

Mama stared at Papa.

Papa split his gaze between Mama and her. "The

man who built this match company called it a diamond. See the shape of the top."

"Oh, Martin." Mama burst into laughter. "Oh, you had me that time. Shame on you, you big tease." Mama had swatted Papa's shoulder.

Well, the blue diamond wouldn't ornament her mother's finger, but it did serve a purpose. Bette pulled the Ohio-made matches from her pocket and struck one against the flint on the side of its container. She tossed it onto the wood under the cauldron. Striking the match let her relive a fun memory to help pass the time on wash day. As the fire took hold, she let her mind drift and collect happy thoughts.

Last Monday night, as she and Mama folded laundry, Peter had stopped by. The Oberskis shared the diamond match story. All four laughed so hard and talked so fast that spitting and hissing and back-thumping and tummy-holding ensued. Mama had started hiccupping, which led to more laughter.

She sighed. When Peter put back his head and laughed with no inhibitions, tingling sensations coursed through her body.

Reflecting on that night and all the times she and Peter were together, Bette was no less frustrated in her ability to intensify romantic overtures. She weighed the signs. Peter dropped by their house, but he didn't stop by specifically to see her. Instead, Peter would grin and nod, acknowledging the trim of her dress or the pouf of her hair. But he never gave voice to compliment her appearance. She had tiptoed into her parent's bedroom after her mother retired for bed.

Fronting a mirrored dressing table, Marta sat on a tufted cushion. The soft glow of a candle lit the satin folds of Marta's gown and emitted the scent of bayberry. A recent gift from Papa, a silver-plated comb, rested on the tabletop.

"What else can I do, Mama?" Bette pouted. "Perhaps if I go to his house and throw off all my clothes?"

Marta dropped the matching, silver-plated hairbrush she tugged through her waist-length braid. The heavy brush clattered on the glass-topped table, and Marta flailed her arms. She pinched her lips and sputtered. "Elizabeth Maria Oberski, don't even think that."

Bette laughed.

"Oh, you're a big tease, like your papa. I'll tell you what we'll do. We can expect Peter to stop by next Monday night like he sometimes does after Papa returns from his shopping expeditions. You and I will make a hearty Polish dinner. That's the way to a man's heart, right, sweetheart? I'll make sure you get all the praise for the cooking. Then, right after supper, your papa and I will excuse ourselves, maybe take a little walk to the orchard and stay a while, so you and Peter have privacy. You just need time to be alone."

Bette had taken advantage of the days in waiting to strategize. She was ready.

Mama was preparing the dough for the apple fritters—a dessert usually reserved for special occasions such as baptisms and holidays.

Bette chose the fruits from their supply in the root cellar before plucking two eggs underneath Henrietta, the early morning layer.

For the past six days, Mama fluttered around, intent on making the house shine to set the perfect courting backdrop. She expunged every speck of dust from the ceiling to the floor and every foul smell from the dank cellar to the musty attic. *I'm sure Papa was relieved to hitch the wagon today and leave.* Last night Mama had brandished a broom at her unsuspecting papa as he entered the house with dust flaking from his clothes after his walk from the arid fields.

A sudden gust scattered smoky debris beneath the kettle.

Hot ash seared a hole in her mother's chemise.

Bette swore.

The erratic wind dropped tiny fireballs on her father's wool socks. But, unlike her mother's cotton chemise, her father's wool socks shrugged off fire like a child fending off a dose of Dr. de Jongh's light-brown cod liver oil.

Bette drained the cauldron on the fire and hurried to the house. She donned her most becoming dress, constructed of a white lawn print speckled with blue cornflowers. Next, Bette heated curling tongs, wrapped the short wisps of hair framing her face, and fashioned spiral curls. Finally, she wetted her lips with berry juice. *I'll see you tonight, Mr. Peter Nickles, and I will fill your senses with my desirability. Tonight will be a night to remember.*

****

"Why was Peter hell-bent on going all the way to Brockway Centre today?" Joseph mumbled. He scratched his head and loomed in the door of the Dahlke homestead. "I've never seen him so tetchy. For all he's been through, Peter's a reasonable guy. But yesterday afternoon after church, Chessie and I stopped by, and I sure as hell can't figure what's gotten into him. Peter kicked chickens and whacked firewood like he was an executioner. He yelled at Chessie and might've kicked him, too, if I hadn't punched him first."

"Oh my God," Ginny whispered.

"His face got all mean lookin', and he asked me something strange. Geeze, maybe the heat has made the old boy snap."

"What did he say?" Ginny's breath caught.

Joseph bit his lip and cocked his head to one side. "He asked me if I condoned cheating."

"Cheating? What could he mean by that?" Flashbacks played through Ginny's memory, including Peter's grim expression and avoidance of her the day before.

"Cheating between a man and a woman, he said. He wouldn't explain anything else, just scowled. I thought to tell him to go to hell when he asked me to watch his stock for two days. But he is a good neighbor, and he's a damn fine carpenter, so I'll do it, but he could've waited 'til the weather cooled. I guess he was wise to leave so early in the day. He might be running into a bit of rain, though. The sky in the west is showing gray clouds. Lord, I can only hope we get a good dousing here, and I sure as hell hope Peter's in a better mood once he gets back." Joseph blew a breath and shrugged.

A wad of nausea stuck in Ginny's throat. She folded her arms across her chest and rubbed them. *What is making Peter so angry?*

"After I do the milking, I'll be off to Peter's." Joseph sighed. "I 'spect I'll be back in time for the noon meal, but don't wait. Buster and I will walk. He'll tire easily in this heat. I hope you don't mind building the wash fire, Ginny. I moved the wood and set the cauldron for you." He spoke in an undertone and looked frequently at his closed bedroom door.

"That's fine, Joseph." Ginny swept sticky hair from the back of her neck. Faint lines of worry stamped the corners of his eyes, etched like a dry creek bed. Ginny ached to reassure him, but how could she?

No one existed to soothe her, either. Instead, suffocating heat gripped and enclosed her like a full-body corset. Dust seeped through every crack in the floorboards and seeped through every pore of her skin. Dust had become an invader that had no antagonist, and dust won.

Ginny hunted for discarded hankies and socks under the settee. She rummaged through the lean-to for aprons, dishtowels, and socks and rifled through drawers and cupboards. All the while she hunted through the cabin, she combed through her knowledge of Peter, seeking answers to what caused his indifference and his uncharacteristic nastiness. But, unfortunately, she admitted, her mind remained as parched as their neighbors' fields.

She left a breakfast of a hard-boiled egg and rye bread on the table for Kathleen and ambled outside with the laundry basket. Handling the steaming wet clothing today was a loathsome chore, and she moved sluggishly. The job routinely took an hour. But this hellish morning, the effort commanded twice the time. Laying the clothing to dry usually evoked a feeling of satisfaction. Yet, with temperatures nearing one hundred degrees, completion of the task elicited little comfort. She gripped the cauldron and tipped the soapy water to smother the fire.

A braying bear cub sprinted past the barn.

Close behind, a second cub and its mother followed, undistinguishable against the sky, now as black as their eyes, snouts, and fur.

The cauldron fell from her hands and thudded to the dehydrated earth, sounding an eerie moan as it rolled into the ebbing fire.

"Kathleen," Ginny howled.

Her words were broken apart by the strength of the wind whipping her skirts and blowing the laundry off the maple limbs. "Kathleen," she screamed. She lifted her skirt and tripped across debris dumped by cyclonic winds. "Kathleen." Ginny's shriek vied with the wind's cacophony.

She fell inside the cabin door and found Kathleen, seated in Joseph's overstuffed chair with her bare feet tucked under her. She lifted her sister-in-law's hand that scribbled on the last week's *Minden Post* cover page.

"What?"

The pencil in Kathleen's hand fell to the floor and rolled into a crevice in the puncheon floor.

Chapter 29

Sister Vincentine and Sister Nepomucene sat in Ruta Pawlowski's front parlor, sipping imported, black English tea and waiting for Henryk to squire them throughout the parish. Already, they had collected several pounds of goose feathers from the good wives of Parisville. Each parishioner called on had been big-hearted in the nuns' mission to gather feathers to make down-filled comforters for orphans.

Earlier in the day, Henryk dropped a full wagon of dry hay in the front of the house and assured the sisters he would be back.

"I'll look outside and check if I can see him." Sister Vincentine stepped on the porch, looked to the west, and witnessed the sky darkening in a succession of deepening shades. She crossed herself. "Dear God, this might be premature, but thank you for the rain." Sister Vincentine opened her arms and lifted them to the sky, exposed her hands from her habit's long black sleeves and offered a silent prayer of thanksgiving.

Sister Nepomucene stuck her head through the doorway. "What is that noise? It's very faint, but it sounds like a sound of distress. Perhaps someone is in trouble behind that row of trees."

"It could be a wild animal. Mr. Pawlowski said he set some traps. Or it could be a stricken cow…"

"Dear God, I hope it's not a person." Sister

Nepomucene brought the figurine of the crucifixion of Jesus to her lips and kissed it.

****

Shortly before noon, Father Graca stood from the dining room table, walked to the kitchen, and placed his plate, fork, and teacup from his midday meal into the sink. He retraced his steps to the church belfry and repeated the nine-stroke, bell-ringing arrangement. Then, as farmers in the field, housewives in the pantry, and children playing outside, Father Graca knelt and recited the Angelus, a tradition practiced by Catholics for more than four hundred years. "Hail Mary, full of grace, the Lord is with thee. Blessed art thou amongst women and blessed is the fruit of your womb, Jesus. Holy Mary, Mother of God, pray for us sinners, now and at the hour of our death. Amen."

The priest rose and ambled back to the rectory, intent on washing his dishes and preparing a letter to the bishop to give a financial report of St. Mary's.

A herd of deer leaped from the concealing forest.

The stags trumpeted.

The does nipped their fawns' heels.

They are running from something. From what? Father Graca prided himself as a learned man devoid of superstitious thought—an ideology that pervaded the Polanders he ministered.

From the barn, Maisy bugled an unrecognizable sound.

The hair under his stiff Roman collar bristled.

Father's brain disavowed science and seized the simplest of mammalian reactions—gut-twisting fear. He ran to the barn, threw open the door, and wished he had acted upon church board member Henryk

Pawlowski's insistence to carry a gun. But, instead, the priest had resisted, claiming he was no hunter, nor was he a killer.

Maisy screamed, tossed her head, bucked her back legs, and kicked.

The threat was apparent. It had no claws, teeth, or venom. Instead, it encompassed all the menace of perdition. The most gruesome imaginations of the combinations of all evil eyes were manifested.

Hell was upon him. The end of the world was here, and God had unbridled every mount of Lucifer to spew the embers from the devil's habitat across the freshly reaped fields of the Parisville Poles. For the third time that day, Father ran to the belfry. He grabbed the rope hanging from the bell and, looking up, witnessed blackbirds and black bats enveloped in a swirling, black smoke cross over the bell.

Father jumped and hurled all his weight in the downswing that sounded the distress call. *Clang-clang-clang-clang-clang-clang-clang-clang-clang-clang…*

Do not stop in the fields to genuflect my people. Run, run, run, run, run, save yourselves. Clang-clang-clang-clang-clang-clang-clang-clang…

The church, I must save the church. A wall of flame towering over one-hundred-foot-tall trees bore down on his church. He yanked frantically on the rope.

The bell tower fell in around him—raining sizzling, jagged wood chunks.

Stumbling from the church, Father clutched his bloody scalp and staggered to the graveyard. He prostrated himself, made the sign of the cross, and surrendered himself to the will of the Lord.

****

Ruta peered from the kitchen doorway and wiped her hands on her Hardanger-stitched apron. "What is it, sisters?" A low murmur surrounding the house escalated into a dissonance of rasping bellows, piercing shrieks, and deafening booms. Ruta burst out the front door.

The nuns huddled together on the porch, transfixed as a whirling mass of burning twigs bounced forty feet in the air and zoomed toward them.

"Sisters," Ruta yelled. "Quick, in the house." She grabbed the door handle and fought against the wind constraining it closed.

Running past Ruta to the parlor, Sister Vincentine snatched the picture of the Sacred Heart of Jesus, and bore it back to the front porch. The oil painting's vivid browns and oranges punctuated with the thorn-studded heart played against the flames approaching the homestead and the easy prey of a wagon loaded with parched hay.

In turn, Sister Nepomucene mustered the painting of Our Lady of Czestochowa from the parlor wall. Then, handling the holy archetype like a shield, she struggled to the porch and faced the Madonna into the oncoming maelstrom.

Ruta crossed herself and followed the nuns.

"Holy Mother of Czestochowa," Sister Nepomucene prayed, contemplating the beloved icon's face. "Thou art full of grace, goodness, and mercy. I consecrate to thee my thoughts, words, and actions—my soul and my body. I beseech thy blessings and especially prayers for my salvation."

The wind rattled the painting. Sister gripped tighter. "And dear Mother, protect us from this rage of nature." She turned the painting and kissed the infant's face in his mother's painted arms.

"Sisters," Ruta screamed. She grabbed a handful of habits with each of her hands. "Dawid," she yelled toward the barn, cupping her hands to compete with the earsplitting wind. "Nadia!"

"My wedding dress." Nadia flew into the parlor with the garment in her hands.

"Mama." Dawid slammed the front door behind him.

Together, the five scrambled into the cellar amidst the recently canned jars of tomatoes, corn, and green beans.

"Ten days ago, we celebrated the feast of Our Lady of Czestochowa. Surely, she will keep us safe. She has protected her beloved Polish people for many centuries," Sister Nepomucene murmured.

"Surely, surely, she will." Ruta clasped her arms around her children.

The five people in the cellar clung to each other as the likeness of Our Lady of Czestochowa stood guard at the cellar door.

****

Nokee plied a needle into a pair of her brother Thomas's dungarees. Maybe taking in the waist would help keep them on. He had grown so thin. She sighed.

The Cass River gurgled and rippled over embedded stone and shocks of water grasses in front of her. Behind her, sounds of hammering and whistling echoed.

Chet Jr. and Lerk assisted Thomas in patching his roof.

Fire!" Lerk screamed.

Chet Jr. lifted their uncle on his shoulders.

Nokee grabbed Lerk about his waist, tucked her head, and propelled her son toward the murky waterway.

A muscular, curly-haired, web-footed dog with amber-colored eyes ran ahead. He reached the riverbank, raced back and forth in short bursts, barked, snapped, and whipped his head backward.

Lerk bent and grabbed the fur ruff around the dog's neck. "Come on, boy." Then, he thrashed into a brigade of towering, skin-and-fur-pricking plants flanking the riverbank.

Wild rye, little bluestem, sand reed, and goats-beard grasses, the latter with its distinctive fluff-ball fruits, obscured access to the life-saving water.

Nokee followed and beat back the foliage. She slowed, turned, and held aside the wayward plants.

Nodding to his mother, Chet Jr. plowed past and carried his uncle to safety.

As flames shot higher than the tallest jack pines in sight, Lerk skidded into the river.

Bringing up the rear, Nokee fell in the slimy embankment, crawled to the water's edge, and belly flopped into the Cass River. As she shook water from her eyes, she jumped her gaze to her younger son. Wavering in the current next to Lerk, a black bear sow shot a wary gaze on the boy and her doused cub. *We are all in this together.* Nokee clasped her hands.

"Gichi-manidoo," Thomas prayed as the animals of the creator's making slithered, dropped, swam, or thrashed into the dank water alongside them.

Fox, beaver, squirrel, deer, otter, muskrat, dog—all creatures presided by Gichi-manidoo, hid in the river, where the raging fire could not reach them.

****

"Fire! Springhouse, now, Kathleen—now," Ginny shrieked. From inside the cabin, she grabbed the door handle. The lever didn't budge.

Outside, the wind squealed and sucked the door, sealing it shut.

Ginny gripped the handle with both hands and yanked. "Kathleen!" She gritted her teeth and rooted her feet.

The door inched open and creaked like a ghostly forewarning.

Kathleen grabbed Ginny's braid.

"The sewing machine. I have to get my sewing machine." Ginny turned and reached her arms toward the Isaac Merritt Singer.

"No," Kathleen begged. She whimpered and dug her fingernails into Ginny's shoulders.

You're right, Sister. Damn the sewing machine.

"The Bible!" Kathleen shrieked.

Grabbing the family Bible from a cupboard, Ginny tucked it under her arm. Then, she clutched Kathleen's hand and alternately dragged and pulled her uphill toward the earth-shrouded springhouse. They approached the chicken coop.

Squawking noises punctured the air, and through the small grimy windows, feathers flew.

Ginny tightened her grip on Kathleen's wrist and lunged toward the coop. She flung open the door and dropped Kathleen's hand.

Kathleen spread her apron and captured a fleeing chicken.

Jamming the Bible into the waistband of her skirt,

Ginny grabbed a hen with each hand. Then she drew her apron around them, cinched the folds over the struggling chickens, and made a knot with the ends of her apron hem.

Kathleen reached for Ginny's free hand.

They continued hand in hand, with squawking chicken bundles between them, uphill to the springhouse.

The door listed open on its rusty hinges.

"Ginny, your hair." Kathleen untied her apron and thrust the chickens into the springhouse. Then, she unknotted Ginny's apron strings and shooed the chickens into the shelter. Finally, Kathleen pushed Ginny through the door, knocked her to the floor, and stomped on the end of her burning hair.

The acrid smell jammed Ginny's sinuses. She sneezed, crawled to the entrance, and pulled herself upright. She slammed her body against the door.

The latch grated and locked.

Kathleen gripped Ginny's shoulders and turned her.

"You're so brave. Joseph is so lucky." Ginny opened her arms and enveloped Kathleen.

"Sister." She cleaved to Ginny's breast.

The baby moved against her belly. Ginny gripped Kathleen's shoulders. "Oh, my niece or nephew is saying hello," she whispered. A tremor ricocheted through her heart. *Brother, I promise to protect them.*

"Yes." Kathleen skimmed her hands over the stirring mound. "Ginny, I never told you." Kathleen took a gasping breath and lowered to the floor. She gazed at Ginny. "Joseph and I had a baby before this one, and he...he died before he was one day old. We can't lose this one. We just can't. Every time I see that little stone with the cross I want to die, Ginny."

"Shush," Ginny collapsed to her knees. *My comfort stone…all these days, I've known about it, and now I realize it honors my sweet little nephew.* Ginny made the sign of the cross over her forehead and chest.

"Ginny, your beautiful hair," Kathleen wailed.

"We're safe. That's what's important. Now we wait."

"And pray," Kathleen whispered. "Heavenly Father, and Our Lady of Czestochowa, protect us. Guide Joseph back safely and keep him safe. Ginny, can you recite that poem, the one Mrs. Sheridan sent you?"

"The one by Elizabeth Barrett Browning that starts with 'Speak low to me'?"

"Yes, please." Kathleen lay on the floor.

In a faltering voice, Ginny recounted from memory: "Speak low to me, my Savior, low and sweet." She knelt next to Kathleen and whispered the remainder of the poem. Then, she lay on her back, the cold floor leeching to the very marrow of her bones. She nestled Kathleen to her breast amidst the wind's shriek, the crashing trees, the thrashing animals that seethed outside, and the soft clucking noises from the corners of a stoutly built springhouse.

Chapter 30

On Finkle Road, George Worchok stared into the rapidly darkening western sky. "Harriett, we can't wait any longer. Hold onto Isabel." He gathered his older children. "Edward, Maude, Gilbert, Herbert, join hands. Come with Mama and me."

"Papa, Papa, look! Fireballs!" Edward broke away.

Baseball-sized fire nuggets vaulted about them. One hit the earth inches from Edward, burst into a million fragments, and fizzled. More balls hit the ground, swallowed dry twigs and shafts of grass, and swelled into football-sized orbs. As they grew, the ravenous globes etched black strips across the yard.

"Mama, I can't hold hands. My tooth is wiggling, and I need my hand to hang on to it," Herbert wailed.

Grabbing her younger brother's neck, Maude sprang ahead and shoved Herbert forward.

George scooped four-year-old Edward under his arm and took one-year-old Isabel from his wife's arms. Then, he ran to the well. "Harriett, you first."

Harriett scrambled over the fieldstone abutment and scrabbled down the slippery rock.

"Maude, you're next. Don't worry, don't worry. You will be safe." George set Edward and Isabel at his feet and eased his eleven-year-old daughter over the side of the well. "Feet first now. Mama will catch you."

"Mommmmmaaaaa," Maude screamed.

"Big boys now…Gilbert, Herbert," George shouted.

Gilbert rushed to his father's side, lifted his arms, and scrunched his eyes as George lowered him.

Herbert clung to his father but silently obeyed as George carried him to the well and dropped him.

"Now, Edward…" George lifted his son and pinched the sturdy little boy's shoulder blade.

The four-year-old bawled and kicked his father. "I don't wanna. Papa, you always say 'Don't climb in the well.' "

"I know, Edward, but we all have to get in." George pressed him to his chest before dropping him into his waiting family's hands. "Now, Isabel." He scooped the baby from the ground and grasped her around her tummy.

The baby wriggled, clawed, and cried as her father released her into the hole.

"George, get in, please," Harriett yelled. Her voice pinged against the cavern.

But something stirred the father to pause and scan the field about him.

Through the blinding smoke, three figures charged.

The smallest figure fell.

The largest one lifted it, and they ran hand-in-hand to George Worchok's well. The glint of a polished penny-whistle gave away the identity of the largest runner.

"Jesus, Mary, Joseph." George grabbed two children and dropped them into the well. "James, you, too," George yelled over the sobbing wind. He grasped the older man's hand, grabbed him by the waistband of his dungarees, and shoved him to the well.

317

James climbed over the top and disappeared.

George placed three timbers over the well and slid an open space, barely large enough to squeeze his body through. "Look out below."

Water splashed.

Air gusts twisted above.

Harriett embraced her husband.

"You must be brave, *kochanie*," he whispered. His heart thumped against his ribs.

She squeezed his hand. "Louis Jr., Marianna, you're safe." She folded the Gugsak children in her arms.

"Papa, Papa," Marianna moaned. Her shoulders shook.

"We tried to move him, but we couldn't. Mr. McGrarry couldn't, either. So, we ran." Louis Jr. raked his fingers through his hair.

"Mama, I'm squished," Edward whined.

"Children, Mama and I will take turns holding you in our arms. Mama has baby Isabel. Edward will sit on my shoulders, and Herbert, come here. Papa will hold you for a while."

"George, thank you for throwing this table in here. It is a little island for us to rest." Harriett cradled Isabel to her exposed breast.

"Papa, I have to go wee," Edward whined.

"So, whoever has to go wee, turn your back on the rest of us and go wee on that side, under the highest rock jutting out." George made yet another decision for the group whose lives depended on him. George filled the bucket he had fashioned with his own hands as a cooper and began the first of many treacherous treks to the top of the well, balancing the sloshing vessel with one hand, grabbing for a handhold with the other. He heaved the water with the arm of most muscle—his left, long accustomed to exerting pressure on metal bands that fashioned a barrel out of wooden slats, wetting the lid of timbers to further safeguard those at the bottom of the twelve-foot deep well.

"Papa, you're throwing water on us," yelled Gilbert. "No, Papa, no, stop. I'm so cold," the child cried.

"Sorry, sorry," George responded as a rain of water and ashes filtered through the planks and blanketed all below.

"It stinks so bad in here." Maude sneezed. "Did Isabel dirty her diaper?"

"I'm scared, Mama...why is it so dark?" Edward whined.

"I'm hungry," Gilbert shouted.

"Ah, here it is. My tooth!" Herbert jumped and waded through the water. "Please, Mama, put this in your pocket and save it."

"I've got a big pocket right here, Herbert." James McGrarry lifted the little boy and held him.

"Mama, can we go home, now?" Edward whimpered.

With each syllable muttered, an echo vaulted in the murky tube.

Overhead, the wind screamed.

The most profound darkness descended.

But despite the veil of blindness, George was aware of the movements of his wife's lips as she brushed the tops of their children's heads in a trillion kisses.

****

Henryk Pawlowski, like every good Catholic, was reluctant to refuse a request from a nun. Sister Nepomucene would cast him a scalding scowl if, once he returned home, he reneged on his earlier pledge to haul both nuns to the northern portion of the community to glean more feathers. But the older the morning became—the more Henryk felt a growing anxiety. He wasn't the only one feeling it. He rode Mystic, the Medicine Hat colt, and the horse seemed overly skittish today. He should've chosen another mount.

Noon drew close, so Henryk wasn't alarmed when he heard the church bells peal. God, he reckoned, wouldn't mind if just this once he said the midday Angelus on horseback. He was almost to the church cemetery when he spied a lone sheep, bawling and running loops. It had to be his. The only other Cotswold sheep in this village belonged to the Dahlkes. *How did it get here, all the way to the church cemetery? Stinker.* He had to go after it.

He reared Mystic tight and goaded him left to circle the sheep. "Yah." Henryk stood in the stirrups, pulled a length of rope from the saddle horn, and spurred the colt into a zigzag pattern as he maneuvered to seize the bawling sheep.

The ewe darted and halted.

Mystic zigzagged and stalled.

The sky turned black as the ewe's nose. Smoke, as thick and curly as Cotswold wool, enveloped the ground.

The sheep slowed and laid in her tracks.

Henryk slid off Mystic's back, tied the rope around the ewe's middle, and lashed the other end of the rope to his saddle's rear-rigging metal rings. He guided Mystic in a one hundred and eighty-degree turn, retraced their steps, and headed home.

Crack-crack-crack...

Trees snapped.

The wind rushed.

The sky curdled so darkly it obscured the sun.

Clang-clang-clang-clang...

What the devil? That was not the Angelus Father was ringing.

Mystic reared, snorted, and bugled.

Henryk pulled the reins so tight he felt the bit slam into the Medicine Hat colt's jaw.

Acorn-sized fireballs bobbed on the ground. Lightning flashes illuminated the rows of hauntingly white headstones.

A figure shrouded in black fell on his knees and stilled.

Father Graca. Henryk pushed his boots in the stirrups and squeezed his thighs into Mystic's heaving belly.

They rode to the priest.

Henryk jumped to the ground, grabbed Father, threw him crosswise over the top of the saddle, and wedged himself back into his seat. He and the magical horse completed their second miracle rescue of the day.

Did miracles, like births and deaths, happen in a series of threes? A superstitious person of Polish heritage would expect that. *So what the hell would be the third?* Henryk choked on a wad of fear and dug his heels into Mystic's belly.

****

Leon woke, kissed Linda a good morning, and

patted her swollen belly. "If you need me, send one of the kids to the tobacco field."

Now, three hours later, he blew out a deep breath, wiped dripping sweat from his brow, and assessed his farm. Four acres of harvest-ready, cash-crop tobacco leaves quivered in a light, southern current. The hay was mowed and stored in the barn. Witch grass had been burned and cleared. Sinuous vines hung heavy with rich, concord grapes.

The harvest was all a man could want—income to provide for his family, a sweet rolled smoke, and a glass of wine at the end of a muscle-stretching day. *Fall is coming, and days are getting cooler. This heat will break.* Leon scanned the horizon. *Looks like rain.*

****

On her first trip of the day back from the outhouse, Linda rested, hands-on-hips, and scrutinized the landscape. A hatless Leon stood chest-high in his pot-of-gold—his favorite expression to describe the plot of densely packed, lush, green plants. Tobacco was a handsome plant with its stacked fronds bending toward its thick stem, leaf blades thick and enormous in dimension—twenty inches in length, ten inches in width, and edged in a whimsical sawtooth pattern.

The Nowakowski family spent their summer in this burgeoning tobacco forest. The children topped heads and flowering stalks, inspected under leaves for signs of rot, and killed trespassers—cutworms or grasshoppers. They had done well.

Leon projected they'd make enough money to spare for shoes for each child and the new plow he needed to till the loamy soil on the south side of the milk house. He had assured Linda they would utilize the recently cleared land to fulfill her plans for garden expansion. Soon, they would have another mouth to fill.

Linda flexed her shoulders and pressed her palms in the small of her back. The pot-of-gold land held other sweet, family memories. The little ones had played hide and seek, and their taunting cries of "can't find me" had waffled through the furrows. Their giggles had rolled off the leaves like cylindrical cigarettes tumbling from a farmer's coverall pocket.

The second time Linda traipsed to the privy, she dragged along her two-year-old to sit by her on the double seat, hoping only one child wore diapers by the time the new baby arrived. On her third trip from the outhouse, the sky turned so dark Linda relied on the worn path's familiarity to guide her.

Leon waved his hands and ran. A wind from the north blew with such force it sent him staggering. "Grab buckets. Grab mops. Bring blankets and quilts. Now." He grabbed Linda's hand, and together they ran to the house. "Children! Go to the well. Now!"

As each of the older children ran past the well, Leon doused them and the blanket they carried. Next, he filled buckets with water and motioned his family to run to the tobacco plants. "Lie down under the leaves and cover yourself with your blanket." Leon upended the buckets over their tobacco roof.

The sky soured brackish black. The wind swirled, changed direction, and swooshed through the giant fronds that shrouded the prostrate family. Fire crystals disguised as innocent fireflies pelted them.

"Mama," cried the children as scorching fire drops branded them.

Their mother or their father reached with a wet

mop and snuffed each winged blaze.

Beast cries beat against their ears. Cat screeches, cow brays, vulture shrieks, pig squeals, and horse bugling rent the apocalypse surrounding them.

"Bertie," Michael howled. The boy sat upright, beat away the tobacco plants, and scrambled to his feet.

"Michael," Leon yelled.

"Lie down," Linda screamed.

But Bertie's voice moved Michael more.

He jumped from the tobacco cover and ran to his horse.

****

Uninvited, the fire entered the house. Striking quickly, it overtook the most powerless ingredients—those made of pulp from the trees it had already decimated.

The family Bible, the record keeper of births, marriages, and deaths, flashed and crumbled into ashes.

A copy of *Peterson's* magazine took the sole lifeline to a world of current fashion and beauty to its collapse.

A handwritten copy of Ruta Pawlowski's recipe for borscht burned before the dish had a chance to bubble over the range.

A children's reading primer disintegrated before the youngest child in the house grew old enough to decode the symbols.

After it fed on paper appetizers, the intruder reached for the household's textile fibers. It licked the hand-braided rug shielding the plank floor. The fire withdrew and sought more appealing things. The arrogant fire traveled on, stretching its forked tongues to suck on ruffled curtains, the Belgian lace repurposed from a grandmother's trousseau, a pair of bloomers discarded under a bed, and a beet-stained apron listing on a peg extruding from the lean-to door.

Finding scarcely enough air to sustain its force, a tendril of fire skulked into a closed closet. Working slowly at first and conserving energy, the fire wisp touched a uniform, already miraculous in its two-decade survival, a symbol of a cruel war fought on a battlefield four hundred miles south of where it now hung. The tendril recoiled, not for a show of patriotism, but a criticism of the Union quartermaster's fiber choice. The smoky curl skipped across the government-issued jacket and pants and found a man's cotton shirt to its liking. It started with the cuff closest to the floor. It lapped the tiny stitches made by a loving wife, spitting the whalebone buttons and letting them fall one by one to the floor.

Ping-ping-ping-ping.

Gluttonous now, the fire slithered to the heart of the home, where the cheery crackles and pops of fire provided warmth and a place to draw the family together at the end of the day. It savored the soft pine mantel, supplely licking the bas relief pinecones hand-carved by the man of the home. It glided from one mantel keepsake to another: a figurine of a plump bluebird with a glass eye and a glossy beak, a birthday present—a card, not the type used to play solitaire or whist, but the kind to protect an innocent child, a triptych of Our Lady of Czestochowa, a gilded teacup, and a chipped saucer. It jumped lithely to the more mundane flotsam of a large family, placed high on the mantel to prevent the toddler of the house from putting them in her mouth: a mother's hairpin, a father's shoehorn, a spool of thread with a needle piercing the length, and a Montgomery Ward catalog with a handwritten list bookmarking a page.

Fire management tools, including a tin of matches and a pewter candle snuffer, hid behind but stood among the other mantel paraphernalia.

The fire ravaged all the items setting above the heart of the home.

Items of plant or fiber origin burned rapidly.

The candles surrendered quickly.

The breathier flames in the onslaught, finding no resistance to toy with since the mantel lacked a douter, blew the wax with dervish delight.

Liquid candlewax flung against the Lady of Czestochowa, fashioning a macabre mustache.

Those items of more complex derivation succumbed to the auxiliary peril of heat combustion. They blew apart, spewing a million atoms of powder and fragment, triggering an unmusicality of shrill staccato, bombastic timbre, and sibilant shriek.

The fire's dismantling of one item held unique irony. Caught in an unexpected raid and ambushed on all sides, the one soldier left in the house to exterminate the fire was deftly disarmed and molten, deformed and unable to perform its sole duty of extinguishing the flame—the wedding gift handcrafted in Switzerland stamped with a bell—the candle snuffer.

Chapter 31

Mounted on Star, Peter sidestepped potholes, manure droppings, and men cementing hitching posts up and down the village streets of Brockway Centre, Michigan. *Can't wait to get out of this saddle. It's been a long day's ride.*

The Port Huron and Northwestern had laid rail intersecting Main and First Streets, and wagons weighted with building materials—bricks, timber, shingles, and buckets of nails sprung and clacked as they forded the steel runways.

A poster advertising *Help Wanted* hung behind a street-view window of *The News*'s newspaper office.

From the open door of the C. Cooper blacksmith shop, sparks flew, and the clanging of axe on anvil rang.

A pair of women let the screen door flap as they exited the W.H. Palmer General Store.

A clapboard building on the creek side of First Street bore a sign over a set of large double doors. "*C. Andreae and Sons Woolen Mill.*"

Breathing deeply, Peter savored the smell of fresh-cut pine that infused the air around the mill.

A white-haired man sat in the shade of an elm tree between the building and the rail line, probing his teeth with a toothpick.

Peter jerked Star's reins and stopped. "Would you

be Mr. Andreae, sir?"

"Yah, Charles is my first name." The man rose and tossed the toothpick into the dried grass on the perimeter excluded from leaf cover.

For an older man, he appeared lean and straight. He dressed elegantly in a bowler hat trimmed with a satin band, a crisp white shirt, and spotless, center-creased, striped woolen trousers. His leather shoes shone, and the hair on his head and above his plumy lips displayed fastidious trimming. Other than his overly large ears, he was a handsome man. Peter dismounted and tethered Star to a hitching post.

Charles offered his hand.

Peter experienced the grip of a seasoned working man. "Peter Nickles. I own a farm in Parisville, forty-seven miles north. Are you ready for business?"

"Yes, we will scour and card your wool. Our fee is one pound of wool per every twenty pounds we process."

"And Mr. Andreae, would you be looking for help, sir?"

The older man took his time eyeing Peter. "You worked wool before?"

"Yes, sir. I worked in the scouring room in the Allen and Pearson Woolen Mill in Cecil County, Maryland. I even made straw boss." Peter shifted his weight and rolled his shoulders.

"I tried to figure your accent, son. You kind of drop your Rs like folks on the east coast."

Peter chuckled, stretched, and rubbed his back.

"That's a long way from here, son."

"Well, and that's a long story, sir, but judging from your accent, you're not from here, either."

The older man stuck a finger in his ear and dug in the ear canal. "What breed of sheep wool did you work with?"

"Mostly Cotswold and Shropshire, sir, my preference being Cotswold."

The old man spat. "Yah, and why do you say that?"

"Because they're not so baaaaaaaaaaad," Peter drawled.

Charles looked up and laughed. "Yah, you make a good joke, Peter Nickles. Let's get out of this heat. Let me show you around. The picker room." He led the way into a room with four men stacking fleeces on a table.

"More customers, Father?"

Thanks to the repeated ear shape, the man holding a handful of black wool bore an arresting resemblance to the senior Andreae. Peter grinned.

"Just showing this man a tour. Say hello to Peter Nickles. One of my sons—Rudolph."

Rudolph waved and turned back to the laborious task of plucking barnyard debris from the fleeces.

"Ah, scouring room," Peter remarked. He followed Charles into an area with four-foot-high kettles on slatted wooden flooring. "This room alone is a welcome sight to every Polish and German farmer alike. They would be thrilled to turn over this job to your pots, Mr. Andreae."

"We plan to expand our operations—even add a tailoring service. Every man needs woolen trousers and a winter overcoat, here, yah?" Charles pointed to the pants he wore and turned to display the sewn-in belt loops. "We've been talking to a man by the name of Otten. He comes highly recommended by the J.L. Hudson Company in Detroit."

"That is something." Peter shook his head. "Good for you, Mr. Andreae." He knew a highly recommended sewer, too. He breathed deeply. His heart swelled. "Would you be looking for other talented tailors?"

"Yah. C. Andreae and Sons plan to be in business here a long time." The old man whistled as he led Peter outside. "You best head back to Parisville, young man. Look at that sky and see how much it has darkened in the past few moments. With all this heat, it reminds me of how things were before the big fire of 1871."

Sawdust surrounding the new construction, and sand exposed from digging posts and foundations, blew in whirligigs around the C. Andreae and Sons Woolen Mill entrance.

Star chomped on her bit and staggered sideways, tugging on her tether. She whinnied.

"I will, sir, and thanks for showing me your operation." He threw a leg over the horse. "Good day to you."

"Peter?"

He turned in his saddle.

"I'd welcome you working here. Come anytime."

"Thank you, Mr. Andreae." He pulled the reins across his lap and held aloft a hand. By eleven o'clock, Peter left Brockway Centre and headed homeward, traveling first east on Burtchville Road. He reached the lakeside town of Lakeport in the early afternoon and followed the road straight to Lake Huron. He tethered Star to a poplar tree bordering the beach, found the *pierogis* he had packed in his saddlebag, and sat to eat.

Lake water ebbed the shoreline in calm, flat-gray ripples and lent an atmosphere of tranquility.

But other weather signs foretold turmoil.

Flies bit.

Hoary clouds scuttled on the northern horizon and abolished light.

Seagulls beat their wings, skimmed on the brink of the lake's surface, and screeched their alarm call. *Ha-ha-ha*.

Peter led Star into the lake.

She hobbled over the rocky bottom, lowered her head, and lapped Lake Huron.

Still gripping Star's reins, Peter sat, tugged off his boots, and waded into the cool water. He dropped to his haunches, splashed water on his face, submerged the canteen, and waited for it to fill. Then, he mounted Star and headed north along the lake-bordering road.

A temperature-plummeting north wind whooshed across the lake's surface. Its force sucked the color from the fresh-water sea and propelled the gray mass into rolling, churning waves.

Peter shivered. "Yah, Star." He drove his knees into either side of her belly.

The wind whipped around them and dictated the directions appropriated by hurled leaves, branches, and grasses.

Noise alternated. It was cavernous and thunderous, with the shrieking and shrilling of birds and mammals. It was soothing in intermittent silence.

Between Lakeport and Lexington, no towns existed. *Can we make it to Lexington to shelter?* As far as Peter could determine, the lakeside village existed five miles away. It would all depend on Star. *Will she last another hour?*

Star pranced. Her lips foamed. Her eyes rolled—the whites gleamed against the smoky haze surrounding them. She whinnied and bucked and went down on all fours.

Peter had only time enough to leap from his saddle. He reached for his canteen, pulled off the cap, wetted his bandana, and stretched the cloth over Star's muzzle.

She swung her head back and forth but finally settled.

Peter spent the night huddled next to Star and slept the sleep of the damned. He woke deep in the night, disoriented and stiff. Dreams of Ginny as a sorceress haunted his consciousness. She moved sinuously around a smudge fire and taunted the flames licking about her feet. A long braid tapped against her back.

Ginny, oh Ginny. Please, God, keep her safe. Please, God, keep her safe. He had wronged her, not the other way around. He should have questioned the words of that selfish sister-in-law of hers. Ginny was incapable of deceit and coquetry, and she had feelings for him. He would find a way for them to marry.

The black sky above lapped the earth.

Stars twinkled through traces of smog.

He raised his right hand, extended his index finger, and traced the luminous dots. "One, two, three, there it is—the ladle. One, two, three, four, and the bowl—the Big Dipper."

Grandfather taught him to focus on the two stars farthest from the handle to find Polaris, the North Star. "That will always point you north so you can find your way."

Repeating his grandfather's nightfall demonstration comforted him. *North, now I see my way, and in the first light of day, I travel north to Ginny.*

Chapter 32

By morning, the winds ceased.

Ginny pushed open the springhouse door. An eerie quiet engulfed the land.

The world smoldered—a skeletal silhouette of what was once a backyard of tall, forested stands.

The barn was whole.

The house still stood.

The outhouse survived intact.

Ginny collapsed to her knees and made the sign of the cross with her right hand.

"Joseph!" Kathleen staggered behind her.

Ginny cupped her hands together. "Joseph!"

"Oh, my good Lord, the smell." Kathleen covered her nose with the hem of her sleeve.

The released chickens squawked and ran through the women's legs. Their peeps subsided as they hopped through the open chicken coop door.

Ginny heaved a sigh. A mournful mooing sounded from the barn. "Back with you soon, Mrs. Mulligan." *Poor, poor thing. You must be set to burst.* "Perhaps Joseph is asleep in the house, Kathleen. You look there, and I will look in the barn."

Kathleen stumbled and ran to the cabin.

A scorched path of earth, as black as a moonless night, bordered the pigsty and snaked throughout the roots of the maple trees where Ginny had flung the last of Monday's wash. Not a stitch of clothing remained. Not a blade of greenery shone through the blackened swath. Ginny bit her bottom lip and tiptoed to the pigsty.

The dead pigs lay bloated.

The living pigs lay on their sides—eyes shuttered, snouts quivering. Every hoof had melted.

Ginny retched.

"He's not here, Ginny. He's not here." Kathleen lifted her skirt with one hand, pressed her hand against her belly with the other, and started down the front steps.

"Go back in the house," Ginny ordered. Her voice was steely. Her muscles were gelatin.

Kathleen faltered and stilled.

"Now, go now, I said," Ginny screamed. Her voice surged with the fervor of a snapping whip.

Tears streamed Kathleen's stark white face. Finally, she turned and scrambled up the porch footings.

Ginny reeled into the lean-to and pulled the gun from its mooring.

All the target shooting in the world could not prepare her for this. "Bless me, Father." She amassed the gun powder, the ramrod, and the wadding. "For I have sinned," she continued as she paced to the pigpen. "In the name of the Father." She held the gun upright and poured the black powder down the throat. "And the Son." She plunged the ramrod straight down the barrel. "And of the Holy Ghost," she whispered. She forced the wadding after the powder, leveled the gun, aimed, and jerked the trigger.

Eight blasts burst the artificial calm.

Ginny threw down the gun and fought every inclination to run and never look back. Kathleen and the baby were dependent on her. She owed it to Joseph. *Where was he? What of Peter? What of...What if she and Kathleen were the only survivors of all the people she knew?*

No sign of any living human existed as far as she could see. *What must come first?*

Kathleen needed food and rest. Ginny covered her nose with her apron and took a deep breath. *Jesus, Mary, Joseph.* She tucked her chin, fisted her fingers, and walked without stalling to the Dahlke cabin.

Kathleen paced in the bedroom she shared with Joseph. Her dark eyes were dull, and her movements were jerky.

"Please, dear, lie down, and I will prepare some breakfast." Ginny removed Kathleen's shoes and stockings and tucked her under a coverlet.

"Yes, Joseph will be so hungry once he returns."

"Of course, he will. We know Joseph has the appetite of a bear." She kissed Kathleen on the brow and slunk from the room.

Keep your hands busy, Ginny. Don't let your worry show. Joseph is safe.

****

"Please eat, Kathleen." Ginny brought the sugar bowl to the kitchen table and placed it in front of Kathleen.

"I'll wait for Joseph." Kathleen gazed at the door. She pressed her hands against the mound in her lap.

At noon, Ginny warmed tea, rewarmed the oatmeal that had grown cold, and brought the food to Kathleen. "You have to keep your strength, dear. I added lavender honey to your tea—your favorite."

"I'll try, Ginny." Kathleen sipped from the teacup.

Ginny's anxiety held additional burdens. For Joseph's sake, she must do all she could to protect his wife and unborn child. The stock needed feed and water. Dear God, she would have to check the crops. *Where was Peter? Was he on the road back, or had he been caught in the fire?* Nausea clotted her throat.

"Maybe I could eat some eggs." Kathleen sighed.

Ginny found the three remaining chickens, huddled together, clucking. No eggs waited under the first two hens she unseated. "Of course, poor dears, you've suffered a terrible time." The third nest dive produced a treasure. It was small but a breakfast miracle for a pregnant woman with a craving. "Oh, thank you, dear," Ginny whispered. Then, guarding the egg as if it were a ten-dollar coin, she started back to the house.

She rounded the chicken coop. "The strawberry plants. Oh, you survived." The mother plant and her trefoil-shaped babies glistened with lush green. "We'll have berries next year." Tears wetted her dusty cheeks. She knelt in the dirt and massaged the leathery leaves and the delicate sinewy links connecting them. Then, she laid the solo egg on the ground, pulled a pocketknife from her apron, and cut away the runners from the established strawberry roots. She had one more task before she returned to Kathleen.

Clenching her hand over the pocketknife, Ginny registered the metal coldness and its uncorrupted strength. She pulled the charred braid of her hair and extended it as far as she could. It barely reached her chin. Her hair had been a thing of beauty, her most treasured asset. She had felt so comforted as her mother stroked it. She remembered the girlish giggling she shared with Nadia as the bride-to-be used Ginny's tresses to imagine her wedding grandeur. Again, she felt the visceral thrill of Peter taking her braid in his calloused hand and twirling the end. Ginny dug the knife blade into the earth and hollowed a hole. She curled the lock of singed hair in her hand, caressed it, sawed it off with the blade, dropped it in the grave, and covered it with a handful of earth. *Useless tears.* She rubbed the drops from her cheeks.

****

Tom Taraski stood sentinel in Forestville. He knew full well the history of the first general store in town. In the fire of 1871, it burnt to the ground. All day yesterday, Tom worried and paced. The anguish of not knowing if the same fate waited harbored in his stomach. He had not slept. By morning, he knew the fire spared him and his store. With guarded optimism, he opened his shop doors. By midmorning, his store was a refuge.

Boats with anxious captains docked, and their crews entered, looking for answers.

Wagons carrying crazed pioneers and fronted by horses divested of hair and tails rolled into view.

"What do you need?" he asked.

"Shovels," replied a bent man with sullen eyes and blisters bubbling on his forehead.

Tom doled out the tools as a company of men left without thanks and attended to the thankless job of burying the dead.

Others required no questions. He pulled bloomers, shirts, pants, underwear, and blankets to clothe the naked.

"Marie, start cooking." Tom directed his shocked wife.

Marie grabbed groceries meant to sell—packages of eggs, iced fish, and loaves of bread she baked yesterday. She ran inside and returned with dresses, petticoats, and socks, then dispersed them to shivering people milling about their store.

"God bless you. God bless you."

Tom heard the thanks over and over.

"I could use some help in the kitchen," Marie called.

Several women stepped forward and followed her inside.

Marie returned to the store, bustled through the apothecary section, and pulled ointments, salves, and bandages from the shelves.

An old woman tugged at Tom's sleeve. Her jaw was set in resignation and her stance was that of a commanding soldier.

"Let me offer my assistance. I was a Civil War nurse. Esther is my name."

Tom nodded. He lifted a wooden chair, carried it over the heads of the crowds merging through the aisles to the back of the store, and motioned Esther to sit. As injured victims approached the store entrance, Tom ushered them to Esther's makeshift nursing station.

Esther brushed away sand fleas from the ooze and mucus of charred and exposed wounds. She unwound yard after yard of gauze and covered countless pairs of suffering eyes.

Eyes flashed with hell's heat and eyes clouded from the barrage of smoke and eyes that had witnessed that which could never be unseen. Tom bit his lip and covered his ears to the aftermath of Esther's ministrations—the subsequent shrieks and howls.

The northbound *Dove* was a day late. Now Tom's worry expanded beyond land and fixed on friends he knew who traveled the lake, no doubt in danger from the disorienting darkness created from the inferno on land. How would the *Dove* crew find the docks? *Could the fires of hell fall upon an innocent ship and swallow it in flames just as it had to the boats docked onshore? What could he do to guide them in or know their fate?*

But Tom had little time to worry about his sailor friends. The land drifters, the bedraggled, and their dead kept appearing at his door. Each brought with them a different story of horror and grief.

Marie handed a toddler one of the ragdolls she had made to sell.

The child clutched the toy to her smoky clothing, sat on the floor at Marie's feet, and rocked.

Her mother offered Marie a wan smile and returned her attention to an infant suckling her breast.

"Taraski," one of the survivors called after him. "Look outside at your new farm."

In addition to the stranded, homeless, battered humans making their way to his store, a pathetic collection of chickens, pigs, sheep, horses, and cows, with hair, fur, and feathers singed away, hobbled to Tom's property. Tom looked on in horror. Many of the animals walked on burned-away hooves or feet. Steeling himself once more that day, he returned to the back of his store for guns and a barrel of ammunition.

****

On the second day of Peter's attempt to return home, he would try something different. After he buckled the saddle on Star, he ripped his neckerchief in two and fashioned blinders. Then, he tied them on either side of her eyes, lay forward in his saddle, and scrubbed the horse's neck.

But the horse refused to move.

Peter spent the day letting Star graze and had little trouble picking off a wild turkey with his gun. Then he built a beach fire, gutted the bird, and roasted it on a spit.

Ginny filled his every thought. He recalled the day she doffed her skirt and petticoats and straddled her brother's threatened roof. He chuckled. *Who had been more surprised?* He had been so startled he almost fell from twelve feet to the muddy yard. He never told her how he admired her ability to drop the pretense of propriety in deference to getting work done, and he tried to imagine any of the Parisville women having that courage. None measured up to his Ginny.

Night fell.

Star bedded down.

Peter unrolled his blanket and lay close. The ground was soused, slippery, and cold. *Do I have a bed left in Parisville? Where is my Ginny tonight?*

****

The Worchok family, the Gugsak children, and widower James McGrarry spent what they later determined as two days in the well. Sunrises and sunsets, and the natural rhythms to mark the day's hours, were obliterated in the smoke-choked atmosphere.

The fear the parents had for their children was great. The longer they stayed in their safe place, the better their chance of survival.

Finally, George climbed out and surveyed his farm. He knelt ten feet away from the cavern that saved their lives. The relief his body felt for settling in a repose position after days of remaining upright was welcome. But no spiritual comfort refreshed George Worchok. Every sturdy log, planed board, and the sixteen glass panes on the home he built were gone. George returned to the well. "Harriett, praise God, we are all alive," he shouted in a broken voice.

His children would grow old to tell the stories of what they saw that day and how their parents steered them to choose gratitude over despair. The life lesson was one that few would ever know as dear as they did.

As they approached the barn, Louis Gugsak Jr. waved a hand and pointed. "Oh my gosh, look at that!"

A black bear and her cub lay side by side, sleeping the same fire-induced death as the cow in the barn and the pigs in the pigsty.

What other ironies and horrors awaited?

****

Peter trundled from his camp blanket, rubbed sand from his eyes, and bolted upright.

Star stood, shaking her mane and slashing her tail.

If she'd been stabled at home, she'd be knocking her nostrils against her feed pail. It was her way of saying, "Let's move. Time's a-wastin'." He stood and laid his face against hers, circled his arms around her neck, and scrubbed her ears. "All right, girl." As Peter came across intact fields, with graceful hickory saplings soaking up the sweet rain, hope inched into his heart. *Ginny, my Ginny, I can't wait to see you.* He rode across stretches of land lacking a twig or moss or feather, and his thoughts took on a desolate tone. *Ginny, my Ginny, are you still alive? What've you endured these last days? Why did I leave?*

Rain fell and slid off the perimeter of his hat, creating a stream of cold water that chilled his weary shoulders to the marrow.

The baked earth turned slippery as drizzle struck clay and sprinkles melted sandy hills.

Star's gait fluctuated.

The white star on her muzzle shone in stark contrast to the darkness of the dowsed hairs on her nose.

Light and darkness. Hope and despair. Life and death.

****

Two days north of their homeport of Port Huron, Michigan, Captain John Speck navigated his command, the *Dove*, through pelting rain. Runnels of water splashed across the deck from starboard to lee. They traveled light since they expected to load a large wheat inventory—the money crop of Michigan's thumb.

As they reached Fort Gratiot, then Lakeport, the landscape became astonishing. All along the shoreline, the effects of firestorms were evident. Trees, ninety feet in length, thirty feet in limb width, lay tossed on the beach. Odd items floated in the water alongside them: a peck of crabapples, a toeless sock, a cracked canoe paddle, a tree limb supporting a mudded bird's nest, a tiny, sleeveless nightgown, a leather satchel hand-tooled and stamped with the initials S.M., and a rowboat with cotton roping neatly coiled in its bow.

Sailing north along the coast of the fire-wracked thumb, Captain Speck wondered about his friends—the men he looked forward to sharing a beer and a smoke with once the *Dove* docked. Captain John Speck pondered the plights of the farmers, the shy wives, and energetic children. He weighed the risks and perils these people faced and how fickle nature could be. *How many miles inland had the horror gone?*

Smoke curtained the land and the lake and impeded the captain's vision of destruction. But his other senses detected the aberration and the hell.

Spine-chilling shrieks and earth-shattering splits rang in his ears.

Roasted flesh assaulted his nostrils.

Ghost-like phantoms purled and ruffled the hair on the back of his neck.

"St. Christopher, patron of travelers." A third-mate officer stepped below the mainsail, reached inside his jacket, and withdrew a medal hanging from a chain around his neck. He kissed it and stuffed it back inside his shirt.

The bow of the boat plowed through a bobbing mass of beaks and feathers. Hundreds of lifeless birds, their plumage spread like resplendent water lilies on the ash-choked surface, shifted with the current.

With each passing nautical mile, Captain Speck's prayers grew more fervent. His head throbbed from teeth clenching and squinting into the smoky specters. In forty-five nautical miles, the *Dove* would reach Forestville. *Finally, my questions will be answered, and Dear God, may my fears be for naught.*

****

A somber group of men marshaled in Forestville to search the woods for survivors and victims.

Overhead, the death trackers arrived. Each species was distinct in its feathered span, length of tail, and

343

wing. Yet, each species was alike in its purpose. They were there to dispose of the dead. The eagles, falcons, buzzards, vultures, harriers, and hawks flew in clusters. With its long black tail, a turkey vulture—wings aloft in the shape of a *V*, Lilliputian pink head with its sharp eyesight and bald dome—flew wobbly circles. Others of his ilk feasted in a frenzy below and fought over the bounty with their rapier beaks. The vulture swooped his graceful wingtips and landed on a bloated body. Gorged and sated, the birds paid little heed to the rescue party coming through—the desolate creatures making their way with shovels and crosses.

The human death trackers found the body of Martin Oberski, twenty feet from his wagon loaded with knick-knacks and gewgaws sound as the day they left the shelves of Tom Taraski's General Store.

"Oh, God," Tom cried, hearing the news. "He told me his wife sure as heck would give him hell for bringing all that stuff home. Well, sir, the way I see it, Martin Oberski got to heaven. He was a real good man, always lookin' out for his neighbor, you know what I mean? I never heard him cuss. I never heard him say anything foul. I'll sure miss that old guy." Tom hung his head. *How many more fatalities?*

Chapter 33

A kerosene lamp, its wick turned low, rested on a ledge overhanging an oak desk.

Opened to the thirty-day month of September, a wall calendar hung from a spindly nail.

A greased rag for daily maintenance on a newly minted Remington Number 2 Standard Typewriter lay neatly folded in half and then again next to the key succession QWERTY. Four glass panes—two feet high, four feet wide, and ten feet from the floor—broke the wooden monotony of solid mahogany paneled walls, one floor above the main offices of the *Dansville Steam Print* in Dansville, New York, where a staff of two struggled to write a news release.

"Colleen, I can't imagine the suffering of those people. It's just horrible." Monica scrunched her face and pushed back the springy hair escaping the chignon brushing the back of her collar.

"I know." Colleen organized a row of sharpened pencils on her desk and rubbed her fingers against the smoothly turned and aromatic cedarwood.

"Let's go over this writing again." Monica tapped the papers she held against a desk. "Miss Barton wants it posted to the newspapers post haste. You and I are responsible for the editing. How about reading it to me?

"*Michigan's Terrible Disaster. Dansville Society of the Red Cross Begs for Your Help.*" Colleen looked over her wired spectacles. "Those are the headlines we decided. Now here is the text. Monica, it has to sound imploring. See if we've captured that." Colleen locked gazes with Monica. "Here's the rest:

Our Michigan friends are in dire need of our help. Just days ago, an unimaginable natural disaster occurred. Fire fueled by a cyclonic wind swept across the thumb area of Michigan and burned through an area of over two thousand square miles. More than two hundred people died. Homes burned, leaving over one thousand people homeless. Crops meant to feed families and stock were destroyed. Senator Omar Conger has just returned from the burnt region."

Typewriter claps and thuds sounded in a next-door office. "Who is covering obituaries today?" a voice called from the hallway.

Colleen frowned and moved to close the door. "Monica, we've got to try to find words to describe the horror, don't you think? We need to move people to open their hearts and, more importantly, send their cash."

"How's this?" Monica pushed her spectacles farther up the bridge of her nose.

"The suffering is immense. The situation is dire. The future is bleak. Winter is coming on. The Society of the Red Cross of Dansville pleads with the good citizens of this city and surrounding communities to help. Money is desperately needed."

"Good. Did we hear back from Mrs. Sheppard if she will manage clothing and bedding donations?"

"Yes. People can take those items to Mrs. Sheppard's Sewing Machine Agency. Mr. Faulkner will handle cash donations through the First National Bank."

"Colleen." Monica lined the edges of her paperwork together and ran a finger to straighten them. "I think all we need now is to add the instructions on where to take the donations, and we can get this information to the editor."

"The sooner, the better, those poor, poor people." Colleen shook her head.

"Monica, I remember the young woman you mentioned—Ginny Dahlke. What a wonderful, hardworking young woman, so bereft following her mother's death that she immersed herself in making bandages and baby blankets. She took it upon herself to review every donated article of clothing and mend or refashion it if needed. She possessed such admirable seamstress skills. Ginny moved to the thumb area of Michigan to live with her brother. I wonder how she is faring."

"Maybe we should try to discover if she was affected by the fire."

"Oh, that's a wonderful idea. Perhaps Miss Barton could send an inquiry with her field staff. Let's finish this Cry for Help piece and have Harold put a rush on it."

****

Kathleen wobbled. The ballooned weights of her pregnant breasts and belly bent her normally ridgepole-sturdy posture.

Ginny's stance changed, too. She carried a new weight. Joseph's shotgun slung across and bit into her chest. Three days ago, she and Kathleen emerged from the spring house, and still, they knew nothing of Joseph's whereabouts or fate.

The women's world was incomprehensible—the

sky so unbroken it blinded their eyes, ground so charred it tested their balance, air so vile it choked their lungs, isolation so intense it birthed Judgment Day hysteria.

Fear aggrandized sounds, smells, visions, tastes, and touches.

A cooling breeze drifted the stink of death.

A hawk's cry catapulted Ginny into flinging the butt of her gun necklace.

The shadow of a solitary stag elicited an excited cry from Kathleen. "Joseph!" Kathleen pursued it. She stepped erratically, and her hands fluttered. She halted, put her hands on her knees, and bent her head. She rose slowly, opened the privy door, and stepped inside.

Ginny picked her way to the outhouse, waited outside, and took Kathleen's arm when she emerged. "How about we go check on the chickens?"

Kathleen nodded and leaned into Ginny.

Oak branches overhanging the driveway creaked.

The thrum of hoofbeats advanced and chafed every nerve along Ginny's spinal column.

She stepped in front of Kathleen, leveled the shotgun, and stared down the barrel.

Two strange men on horseback rode into the yard. "Is this the home of Joseph Dahlke?" one of the men called.

"Who's asking?" Ginny positioned her finger over the trigger. *Jesus, Mary, Joseph, keep my hand still.*

The men held up their palms.

"Ma'am, I am David Hunter, and this is Alexander Black. We are part of the Port Huron Relief Society, and we have news of Joseph Dahlke."

"I am Virginia Dahlke, Joseph's sister." Ginny pointed to Kathleen. "And this is Kathleen Dahlke, his wife."

Both men regarded Kathleen's round belly.

Kathleen sidled to Ginny and put her arm around her waist.

"Mrs. Dahlke, ma'am, your husband is alive, but he cannot come to you because of injuries he suffered in the fire."

Kathleen's arm fell away from Ginny, and she collapsed on the drive.

Bending to support her, Ginny turned to the men. "Where is he, and can you take us to him?" Nausea ruptured in the back of her throat. *How bad are his injuries?*

The men tipped their hats and waited.

Ginny strode to the barn and saddled Blue. She helped Kathleen into the saddle, jumped behind her, and stretched her arms across Kathleen's high waist.

As they rode, the men recounted what had happened to Joseph. An immigrant family, recently moved from Ontario, Canada, found him wandering along Minden Road and sheltered him in their root cellar. He hallucinated and insisted that he 'save Kathleen.' He hadn't been able to tell the family his name or where he lived. Joseph could not see. When the fire subsided, the family continued to care for him, hopeful that he would be able to reveal his identity. The day before, a search party from Port Huron made rounds and stopped at this home. The men from the search party agreed to take him to Forestville, where a medical team evaluated fire refugees. Once in a doctor's care and provided with nourishment and compresses for his eyes, Joseph remembered his name and his home location. He pleaded for someone to investigate his house and tell him if his wife and sister had survived and let them know of his condition.

"Has Joseph's vision been restored? Has he suffered burns? Is he in pain?" Ginny tightened her grip on Kathleen.

"Ladies, Joseph is in good hands. Some of the nation's best doctors are deploying to Lexington."

Ginny drew in a sigh.

"Oh, thank God," Kathleen murmured.

"Do you have any news of a man named Peter Nickles?" Ginny screwed her eyelids shut.

David Hunter pulled a sheaf of papers from his pocket and inspected them. "No, sorry, I can tell you your nearest neighbors, the Pawlowskis, escaped with little injury. Mr. Pawlowski will be glad to know you ladies are well. We explained we were traveling here to find the kin of Joseph Dahlke and that if we did, we were to take you to him."

Ginny pressed her face into Kathleen's back.

Kathleen squeezed Ginny's hands.

The belfry of St. Mary's no longer etched the sky. Instead, smoking rubble surrounded by collapsed rock and mortar stood in its place.

Clusters of men, shovels in hand, chucked dirt into a growing mound within the cemetery gates.

Ginny shuddered.

Blue walked with his head down and assumed the gait reserved for a funeral procession.

The twin maples marking the entrance to the Oberski orchards were gone.

The house stood, as well as the outer buildings.

Choking, Ginny made the sign of the cross over her forehead. She would know the fate of Peter Nickles soon. Icy fear knotted her stomach. She stared at the rumps of the steeds of David Hunter and Alexander Black. Both horses were muscled beauties. She knew men who would appreciate them—Stanislaw Urdzela, Michael Nowakowski, Dawid Pawlowski, and of course, Peter—Peter, the man she loved.

Blue broke into a canter.

He knows this place, and he expects a treat.

Kathleen arched her back.

Ginny gasped.

Gossamer tendrils of smoke marked the site of Peter's hand-hewn cabin.

Ginny motioned the men to stop. "This is Peter Nickles's home. Has the property been searched?" She trembled. Her heart stilled. She ran her fingertips over her forehead, chest, and shoulders.

"Yes, we searched this farm and found no sign of life or human remains. Unfortunately, we found stock remains."

Kathleen gripped Ginny's hands and then turned in the saddle to stroke Ginny's face.

They plodded on. A once-massive pile of stones marking the end of the intersection of Leppek and Forestville Roads had been blown apart and strewn as if they were grains of sand. Enormous stands of deracinated poplars lay horizontally on the baked earth like a party platter of spring vegetables for a gathering of giants.

A sibilant breeze blew, shuffling soot upon their hair and clothing. Attempts to brush it loose proved futile as the horses' movements resulted in an unending swirl of ashes under their hooves. The masks Ginny fashioned from Joseph's handkerchiefs were a barrier but provided little hindrance to the smells of the fire's aftermath.

"Do you have any news regarding a family named Nowakowski? They grow tobacco." Ginny squeezed her eyes shut and moved her hands to her thighs.

Alexander Black scanned his papers and gazed directly at Ginny. He cleared his throat. "The Nowakowski family suffered a loss. My list is not total, but it appears that the Relief Society sent a burial team."

Ginny slapped a hand to her mouth. *Oh, God.* She pulled a hanky from her pocket and retched.

The three horses whinnied.

A yearling colt and a skeletal nag, harnessed as a team thrashed and misstepped, causing the wagon they fronted to roll in jerks and fits.

Two men hunched on the board seat.

One held the reins loosely in his hands. Holes, rimmed in black, pocked the shoulders and sleeves of his coat.

"Oh God, p-p-please no." Ginny bit her bottom lip.

Casimir Urdzela raised his head.

Ginny quailed. His face was as old as a fossil. "Casimir," she called.

The wagon driver stared and shook his head.

"No, no, no," Ginny wailed as Blue came alongside. Nine blanketed forms lay on the floor, the largest almost six feet long—Stanislaw. Ginny knew the shapes intimately. She knew their height, their chest, waist, and hip circumferences. She knew their color preferences, and oh, God, the sound of their voices. Jakob, your sweet, trilling voice is silent. Anna, your balletic grace and your sweet laugh have vanished.

Halina, the pride you put in drawing little creatures, is depleted, and your imitation of their sounds is hushed. Dear Oskar, how you had a boyhood crush on me—how sweet your unfettered love. Baby Teresa, your sweet little soul with your sweet exuberant kisses, is no longer here to gladden your papa's heart.

A limb twisted off a linden tree lay across the shape of Sophie. Its twigs were bare of the summer blossoms in which she had adorned her hair and inhaled its nectar as her husband kissed her.

Casimir's gaze met hers. For the rest of her life, Ginny would remember the view into his soul. His eyes were vacant and devoid of tears. But then, Ginny remembered, dear Casimir cried when he was happy. *Peter, where are you?*

****

"Joseph!" Kathleen ran to her husband, fell to her knees, and cradled his bandaged head to her chest.

Husband and wife rocked together, suppressing words and sounds, and conceded to the intimacy of touch.

Joseph reached for the swell of his wife's belly, stroked it, and nestled his head there.

The onlookers turned and allowed them a bubble of privacy.

Kathleen stood and motioned Ginny to come.

"Dear Joseph," Ginny crooned.

"*Myszka*," Joseph murmured.

Brother and sister embraced and swayed.

"Thank you for keeping her, for keeping them safe." Joseph coughed.

"You'll be well, Joseph. You have so much joy in your future."

"I wish I could see you both. You are both so dear to me." Holding the hands of his wife and sister, Joseph choked on his words.

"As you are to us, Brother."

Kathleen sat. Tears streamed her face.

Ginny took a deep breath and clenched her hands. "Joseph, the day of the fire, did you take Chessie to Peter's when you went to check the stock?"

"Chessie," he wheezed. "I dropped him at Nokee's so Lerk could take him hunting."

Ginny shut her eyes. *Thank you. Thank you, sweet Lord.* "Joseph, I know Nokee's family is safe, though their home is lost. Chessie must be safe, too." She squeezed his hand.

The Relief Medical Team evaluated Joseph and deemed he required expert and extensive medical attention.

The next day, he and other seriously injured sailed from Forestville on the steamer *Saginaw* southward bound to Port Huron, Michigan.

Kathleen accompanied him.

Ginny embraced both on the dock, and once the *Saginaw* sailed from sight, she mounted Blue and rode to Parisville—a place she no longer recognized.

****

The closer Peter got to his homestead—the higher the dread rose in his throat.

Turning west on Atwater Road, he noted the fate of his fellow St. Mary parishioners. He came to the corner of Atwater and Eppen and scanned north and south. Acres and acres of land, whole months of toil, were scorched. Five days ago, he left ripe fields ready for harvest. On Sunday, he had stood with friends and discussed yield results of potatoes, onions, and rye. *How would they eat? How would they feed their stock?*

He passed orchards where fires had laid an absurd branding pattern. Fruit trees were crisped and blackened. Others bore eerie blooms as if it were May, not September. Twenty feet away, pears stood with baked fruit rotting at the stems, coated in swarming flies. Amongst them, a rail fence stood unaffected. A pair of mourning doves rested on it. Their long-scalloped tails created an ebony shadow on the gray earth. He turned north on Finkle Road and then west on Leppek Road. He watched for the landmark of St. Mary's steeple.

The entire structure was gone.

Peter turned north on Parisville Road. He stiffened, terror gripping him. He stroked Star's neck. "Ho, girl, ho."

Peter had been separated from his home and neighbors by wind, smoke, fire, and fog for five days and four nights. He leaned back his head and raised his shoulders. Every part of his body ached from the pressure he'd had to exert on a typically easily led Star. His thighs and butt were numb, and he was faint from hunger. Guilt weighed in his stomach like a fieldstone. So why had he chosen to go on a lark of a trip? He knew. He meant to put space between himself and Ginny. What price had he paid for his angst?

Ginny. He would go to her. He would ask her to forgive him for his brutish behavior of the past weeks. He would beg for understanding. He would throw himself at her feet. He would not leave until she agreed to be his wife. He would do it today.

****

"Praise the Lord," Peter murmured, seeing the Pyonk farm intact.

A row of cucumbers dangled on a vine.

Chickens pecked through the ones closer to the ground.

Dismounting Star, he ran to Josephine's cabin. "Josephine," he yelled, knowing she was hard of hearing. "Josephine," he repeated. Next, he entered the kitchen, the parlor, and lastly, the room she shared with Aloysius.

She lay as if prepared for her coffin, her skin clean, her gown unstained, her hair neatly combed and braided and draped across her still breast. Peter approached and smelled the nostalgic scent of castile soap lingering on her scalp. He fell at the side of the bed and wept. The fire had not besieged the Pyonk cabin. But its scent, the perfume of inferno, had poisoned the air.

****

Where his house had stood was nothing. All that remained of the buildings on Peter's property were globules of molten glass—contorted and gnarled—and iron nails that were gnawed and spewed.

The fire mauled Franny's tintype photo.

The only traces of the trunk that preserved her meager wardrobe were the metal locks, which now were bereft of a purpose. And so it was for so many remnants of Peter's life. No purpose remained in the softened stove pipe, the scattered, misshapen forks, or the bones of chickens, swine, and Gertrude.

He went to Star and removed a shovel from his saddlebag. After he dug a trench behind the vestiges of the barn, he steeled himself for the gruesome task of burying the stock. He owed them that. These creatures who depended on him, listened to his babbles of despair, and his exclamations of joy deserved a proper burial. *Oh, if only I'd stayed.* He would've protected them or at least spared them the lingering agony they must've borne.

After a day of internment, Peter paced the perimeter of the house he had built with the dreams of having a family occupying it. And then, he remembered the tin. *Is it still there? Did it matter?* He knelt and, with his bare hands, scraped the place he had stowed the reward of hours of monotonous work. The soil was softer here, and he dug quickly. The tin festooned with rear-standing lions, a chained unicorn, a thistle, a rose, and a shamrock appeared. Inside was a hefty deposit of one hundred silver dollars and the faint smell of ginger and nutmeg. He knelt on his haunches and clutched the container, ran his fingertips over the raised lettering, and wished he could turn back the world to the time the biscuit tin held an offering of molasses cookies.

****

At nightfall, Ginny returned home and secured Blue in his stall. After tending to a frantic Mrs. Mulligan, she stumbled to the cabin, exhausted in body and soul. More than any feeling that coursed through her was utter loneliness. The last six days had been so intimate with Kathleen and comrade fire survivors. The sheer act of survival and safeguarding Kathleen fortified her mind from progressing to dark recesses. The jubilant feeling of seeing Joseph still alive further occupied her mind.

But now she was alone, with nothing but moonlight to accompany her to the eerily quiet house. She brushed soot from her outer garments, reluctant to take any residues of hell into their home's sanctity. She opened the door and reached for the coat pegs by feel. She had no intention of lighting a lamp, even though the night was lit only by the tiniest sliver of a moon. Bed was the only place she wanted to go. She passed the hearth and gasped.

A man slumped in Joseph's chair.

His head sagged on his chest.

Charred-at-the-tips boots covered his feet. Pants pocked with holes encased his legs. *Was he dead, or was he alive? Who was he?* She had left the gun at the door. *Should she scurry back for it?* Ginny shrunk to her knees and crawled across the floor.

The man raised his chin.

Ginny peered into the phantom eyes of Peter. The wall of lies, the warped suspicions, the desperate hours of not knowing the fate of the other crumbled between them.

Peter rose and pulled her on his lap. "Ginny," he breathed. He rubbed his bearded face against her short-cropped hair.

"Peter." She gasped and stroked his shoulders. Then, the tears that had withered in her like the fried earth burst forth.

Peter sifted his fingers through her ashy, smoky hair. He curried it, combed it, and smoothed it. Finally, he snorted, pulled her hair savagely from her face, and thrust his tongue in her mouth.

She inhaled his skin, hair, and body's stench as if it were life-giving oxygen.

He dried her tear-studded cheeks with his parched lips.

Her blistered fingers stroked the slope of his nose,

his cheeks' prominences, and the hollows below them. She wet his chapped lips with the sweetness of her own and welcomed his masculine taste on hers.

"You've suffered…your hands, your hair…"

"Oh, please, don't look at my hair." She raised her hands to her head.

"To me, you are the most beautiful woman in the whole world. Ginny, I didn't know if you were dead or alive." He cupped her face and ran his hands over her short, springy hair. His hands moved to her waist, and he continued kissing her, drawing her closer, flattening her breasts against his palpitating chest.

Ginny panted, threaded her arms about his neck, and pressed against him.

Lifting Ginny from him, Peter moaned, pulled them both to a standing position, and shucked every scrap of soot-plastered clothing from her body.

Ginny held fast to his neck.

He kicked off his boots, dropped his pants, and tore off his shirt. He lifted Ginny's buttocks with one rough hand and pressed one of her ankles around his back. His tongue plunged into her mouth.

She locked the remaining ankle in a bracelet encircling his waist.

Tipping her head back with a rough finger pad, Peter gazed into her eyes. "Ginny." He choked.

"I want this, too, Peter," she said in a voice that rung strong and unbreakable.

He entered her swiftly and harshly. Peter held her, rocking and thrusting and expunging anguish, hopelessness, and despair into her body. "Ginny," he murmured in a ragged whisper. "Ah, Ginny." He laid her gently on the floor.

"Shhh…" She lay beside him. *He is mine, and I am his*. She sighed in raspy chuffs, stroked his hair, and smoothed the softest spot on his face, between his ear and the top of his jawbone. *Lord, what have I done? Please have mercy on us*.

****

Dawn broke across the village of Parisville, ushering in a welcome chill.

Peter shivered and drew a blanket tighter across Ginny's slumbering form, lying next to him on her bed. He took Ginny's hand, brought it to his lips, and kissed it. "Ginny, girl, I shouldn't have."

She silenced his apology by firmly placing her finger over his lips. Then she stamped his lips with a kiss.

He sighed and drew her close. "I've every intention of marrying you. The hope of you being my wife is what carried me through these terrible days." He leaned back, ready to read her expression.

Ginny put her hands over her mouth.

But he could see the "yes" in her eyes before he pulled away her hands and kissed her ear-to-ear smile. He drew her close again and closed his eyes. He had questions to ask and wondered how much heartache one could endure. "Joseph and Kathleen?"

Ginny related how she and Kathleen survived the fire and how they were reunited with Joseph. She told him Joseph and Kathleen were on their way to Port Huron seeking treatment for Joseph, and no one could tell them how long the recovery would take. He cupped her chin and kissed her on both cheeks.

"Thank God. Thank God."

"Pawlowskis?"

"All alive. Henryk, Ruta, Nadia, and Dawid were all quite shaken. The fire came almost to their front door, split in two, and then headed north. The Felician Sisters survived, as well."

"Oh, praise God." He tipped back his head, drew a long breath, and closed his eyes.

His chest rose and fell.

Breathe in and breathe out. Breathe in and breathe out.

Sunlight patterns defined by the silhouettes of barren oak trees filtered through the windows and gamboled across the walls.

"Father Graca?"

"Alive—found wandering in a daze in the cemetery and rescued by Henryk. The belfry collapsed around him. By the grace of God, Father escaped with only a slight head wound."

Peter made the sign of the cross, brought his clasped hands to his mouth, and kissed his thumbs. "Erhardt family?"

Ginny closed her eyes.

"Erhardt family? Ginny?" Peter grasped her hand.

"Annie and the baby she carried burned to death. The other children and Eddie were found suffocated in their well."

"Jesus, Mary, Joseph," Peter whispered. "My sister Linda's family...the Nowakowskis?"

"I don't know." She averted her eyes and bit her lip.

"Oberskis?"

"Marta and Bette are accounted for. Martin succumbed to the fire."

Above the cabin roof, the hoarse kee-eee-arr

screams of retreating red hawks sounded.

Peter brought his hands to his face. "Dear God…"

"After I've fed you some breakfast and lay out some of Joseph's clothes, why don't you take Blue and go see your sister? Leave Star with me, and I will spoil her with a lengthy curry and some juicy apples."

"Thank you, Ginny." He took her in his arms and kissed her. "I don't want to leave you. Are you sure you will be all right?"

"I am now that I know you are alive."

But how will we live?

Chapter 34

Harvest-ready tobacco leaves billowed.

Seagulls soared overhead. Their voices lent a feeling of normalcy as Peter approached the Nowakowski home. The house, the barn with its distinctive gamble and gray-tiled roof, the chicken coop, the pigsty, even the privy with the double seat his sister had insisted on, stood just as he remembered. He permitted himself an expansive sigh of relief. *Praise God.*

Bertie, Michael's beloved horse, neighed a welcome. *His tail swings loosely. His hooves land heel first. Praise God, Bertie is fine.*

A mournful howl wobbled through the sibilant tobacco plants.

The hair on the back of Peter's neck stood up.

"Awhoo…"

Keening rose to a crescendo and crashed like a spear shattering a winter's icy glaze.

In the richly fertilized soil, Linda knelt alone amid the tobacco plants. Their viscous fronds flapped over her shoulders. She tucked her head over the pregnant curve of her belly and shrieked again.

Peter jumped off Blue and leaped through the rippling fronds.

"He did it. He did it again…"

"What, love? What did who do again?" Peter

lowered to his haunches, leaned in, and stroked her back.

"Michael, your crazy nephew. He held Bertie. He held back Bertie. I screamed, Peter, I screamed as loud as my lungs allowed." Linda shuddered. "Bertie's legs are so strong. Remember how fierce he ran that race on Atwater Road, Peter?"

Peter nodded. Tremors caused his hands to shake.

"And you know Bertie's hooves are so sharp. Michael checked his hooves every day, every day, never missed a day." She swiped tears from her face and rubbed her hands over her thighs.

"Bertie was so scared. He fought Michael. He fought and he fought and he fought." Linda wrapped her arms around the crest of her extended belly and lowered her chin. "Michael's dead, Peter. He's dead…" Sobs escaped Linda's lungs and wracked the air.

Nausea gelled in his throat. He gripped her shoulders and positioned his face next to hers. His skin turned hot and then cold and then quivery.

Linda butted her head into his chest and repeated the motion, over and over and over again.

Peter held her and rocked. The uncle remembered the boy's love for his horse and the horse that would forever miss the boy's spirit. He spent the rest of the day with Linda's family. The silence of the usually boisterous nieces and nephews splintered his heart.

Following a relatively untouched supper of potatoes and noodles, the group separated and stumbled to sleeping spots.

Uncle Peter traipsed to the barn, climbed into the musty haymow, lay exhausted, and dreamed fitfully of Ginny and foaming horses.

****

Sunlight streamed through slats on the east barn walls.

A rooster crowed.

A spider hung from its nocturnal creation.

Peter swatted the insect. He rolled from the hay and jumped to the barn floor. Then, without saying goodbyes, he mounted Blue and ventured forth. *Ginny, Ginny, I'm on my way, but I've got a stop or two to make first.*

A black crepe wreath hung on the front of the Oberskis' clapboard house. He knocked. A haggard-looking Marta opened the door, and Peter's heart faltered at witnessing her condition.

"Ah, Peter, thank God you are alive...Bette, come, Peter is here."

"Peter." Bette pressed her cheek against his neck. She dressed all in black, and a dark-print scarf shrouded her hair.

"Bette, Marta, I heard about Martin. I am so sorry."

Tears ran fresh down drawn cheeks.

"We've buried him in the churchyard, but we haven't done a proper funeral yet."

"Martin was a thoughtful man and a trusted friend. I will never forget him." Peter embraced each woman in turn.

"Dear boy, I praise God for sparing you." Marta bowed her head and squeezed his hand. She touched his bearded chin with a fingertip and raised her head to gaze into his eyes. "How is your farm?"

He hung his head. "All gone."

"Oh, Peter, son. I am so sorry." Marta hugged him again.

"Oh, Peter, all your hard work and your dreams…" Bette joined in the embrace.

Peter broke away. "Would you like me to take a look in the barn and through the fields?"

"Thank you, Peter. I managed to milk the cows, but other than that…" Marta's voice trailed off. "Bette and I will prepare the noon meal. You come back, and we'll have a nice dinner together."

He spent the rest of the morning at the Oberskis' feeding and watering the stock, mucking the stalls, and familiarizing himself with the fields' and orchards' conditions.

After dinner, Marta cleared her throat and gripped the table in front of her. "Peter, you are welcome to stay. We've plenty of space. I will clear the back bedroom." Her gaze locked with Peter, and then she looked at her hands. "They're quite full." Her voice faltered and vanished into a full torrent of tears.

Tick-tock, tick-tock, tick-tock. A maple-leaf-motif, mahogany-carved pendulum of a wall-mounted cuckoo clock swung back and forth.

Marta cleared her throat. "They are full of stuff Martin brought home. I'll make up a bed. You need a place to stay, and we sorely need your help."

He tried, but shaping a smile, even a fake one, met with a resistance he could not control. He lifted the linen napkin to the right of his plate and wiped his mouth. His stomach rolled. A band of pressure clinched his temples. "Thank you, Marta. I will consider it. But first, I need to check on other folks, like the Pawlowskis."

Marta nodded.

Bette bit her lips.

He moved his chair from the table. The scraping noise resonated as loud as curses. He went to the barn, saddled Blue, cantered to the end of the Oberski property, and turned the opposite direction of Henryk's farm.

Pawlowskis could wait.

****

Quilts, blankets, curtains, and women's clothing clipped to a clothesline danced in the breeze. Ginny crouched on hands and knees, sleeves rolled to elbows, in front of a pail. Her backside blocked the doorway. His gaze fell to her feet. They were pink and bare, and the sight stirred his greedy desire. *Gawd.* "Ginny."

She jumped, spilled water, and ran to him.

He slid off Blue's back and into her open arms. "I love you, Ginny girl," Peter murmured into the cloth bandana covering her cropped hair.

"I love you, Peter," Ginny whispered. She rose on tiptoe and wrapped her arms about his neck. "Mrs. Mulligan's finally giving milk again. So come in for a cool glass. And I made shoofly pie this morning."

He took her hand, and she led him inside. Peter sat at the table while Ginny brought the pie and milk from the kitchen.

"Linda's family?" Ginny prompted.

Peter hung his head. Great gulping sobs erupted from his chest.

Ginny went to him.

He pushed back his chair from the table.

She lowered herself onto his lap and put her head on his shoulder. She stroked his back and tugged her fingers through his beard.

His breathing slowed, and he swallowed. He

rubbed his eyes and cleared his throat.

She pressed her cheek against his.

"Michael," he mumbled. He took a deep breath and shuddered. "Michael," he whispered in a strangled voice.

She smoothed the hair on his head and stroked his chin. She gazed into his eyes.

"Michael's dead."

Ginny clutched him and nestled her head to his chest. "I am so very sorry, Peter. I know you loved him. I can't imagine how horrible a loss this is for you and your family."

He wiped his face on her sleeve. "God knows how many people are grieving. I spent some time with the Oberski women."

"Dear Martin, my first Parisville friend." Ginny's voice cracked.

"I want to ride over to the Pawlowskis' and see for myself how they are." Peter's jaw moved against Ginny's elbow.

She sighed. "Henryk stopped by last night and said there's a meeting early this evening at his house. As a parish, we need to determine how to get through this together. Children are without parents. Parents are without children. Some people have no roofs over their heads, and some stock has no one to take care of them and winter's coming with no crops left." She shivered.

Peter squeezed her hand. "Yes, we have much to consider and much to do."

Ginny brushed her cheek against his shirt.

His muscled arms gripped her shoulders. He kissed the top of her head and turned her to face him. He paused. "This I know, right here." He took her hand and placed it over his heart. "Forever and ever and ever."

"Forever and ever and ever." She returned her face to the warmth of his shirt.

He ran his fingers over her cheeks, her brow, through her hair, and down her back, cataloging every curve and texture. "Ginny, love, until we are married, I cannot stay here another night."

She sighed and gazed at the floor. "I know."

"I will see you at Henryk's." Peter held her shoulders.

Ginny stood and took his hand.

He pushed himself from the chair. He walked into the sunlight, strode to the paddock, saddled Star, and guided her from the yard. He rode upright in the saddle with his heart in his throat.

****

"Peter!" The Pawlowski family fell upon him. One by one, Henryk, Ruta, Nadia, and Dawid kissed him. Then they all spoke at once. "We're so sorry about your farm. So sorry about Josephine. So sorry about Michael."

An abject group met that night. They filled the Pawlowski house with their presence but not with their characteristic Polander noise.

Henryk held a piece of paper and waved it over his head. "Ruta and I made a list of people needing a place to stay and a list of people who might take them in. Maybe you already have some solutions, but let's make sure tonight everyone has shelter."

"I'd take Louis Jr. and Marianna Gugsak, but I think they would be better off with a woman to care for them." James McGrarry stood and rotated his hat in his worn hands.

"Bette and I could take them." Marta Oberski sat forward on her seat.

Murmurs of approval traveled through the room.

"I've offered a room to Peter," Marta added.

Bette nodded and set her curls in motion.

The sight of the spun-silver tresses protected and uninjured by the fire that mauled their lives spawned a queasy feeling in Peter's stomach. The same disaster had struck the hair of his beloved, and he hadn't been there to snuff the sparks. Ginny's short-cropped hair framed the face he burned to hold in his palms. A wad of regret lodged in his throat.

"Peter needs a place to stay, and Bette and I sorely need a man's help about the place."

That arrangement struck a chord among the group.

Harriett Worchok, seated next to Marta and Bette, reached to hug them.

Peter hung his head. *Ginny.* From his position in the hallway, he tilted his head to see her.

A succession of emotions crossed Ginny's haunted face. Then, finally, she turned her focus to the braided wool rug on the Pawlowskis' parlor floor and flattened her chin against her chest.

Peter's heart plunged.

"Since Joseph and Kathleen will be gone for an extended time, Ginny will stay with us." Ruta bit her lip. "Father Graca could live in Joseph's home, for the time being, so he's got his privacy."

The rules of respectability regarding the unmarried are still met. Peter bit his tongue and scrunched his hands into fists. *What about the privacy Ginny and I deserve, now that we have professed our love for one another?* He felt small for the thoughts, but they came, nevertheless.

It was late, but now that the decisions were made, to follow through before the coming day made sense.

****

Peter rode with James McGrarry to gather the Gugsak children.

Marianna rode behind Peter.

Louis Jr. swung behind James.

The four of them entered the Oberski home, where the ladies waited.

A mouth-watering odor of baked sugar and vanilla permeated the air. Peter's stomach rumbled.

"Marianna, Louis Jr., I think you know Mrs. and Miss Oberski. They will take care of you now." James guided the children by their shoulders.

Louis Jr. held back and fixed his gaze on a wall shelved with an assortment of multi-sized tins that bore carnival-type fonts advertising biscuits and tooth powder and smelling salts.

But Marianna rushed to Marta.

"There now, child." Marta patted the little girl's back.

Bette extended a hand. "Louis, I never had the chance to tell you what a great horseman you are. I will never forget the race you won this summer."

Louis Jr. gazed at his feet. He clenched and unclenched his hands.

"Children, your father died a good Catholic. You can find solace in that. Peter told me how he was found with his rosary, surely saying prayers for all of you as his last thoughts. You can be proud of him, children. Surely, he is in heaven." Marta made the sign of the cross over her chest.

That declaration shredded the resistance of Louis Jr. Weeping, the boy turned and pressed his head against James McGrarry's shoulder.

Peter pulled a handkerchief from his back pocket, pried open Louis Jr.'s fist, and tucked the fabric into the boy's hand.

After a snack of Bette's sugar cookies and a glass of milk, the Gugsak children were both safe and sleeping in clean beds.

Peter excused himself to check the stock. A bed waited in an Oberski bedroom, but he was in no hurry to occupy it.

****

James McGrarry said a silent prayer. *Dear Lord, I long ago stopped questioning why. Tonight, dear Lord, I thank you for this turnabout in these children's lives. Amen.* He let his silver-haired head drop back on the rocker pitching on Marta Oberski's front porch.

She sat beside him.

Crick-crick-crick.

James pumped his feet on the floor.

Marta fingered the pages of a Bible in her lap and gazed at the moonlit silhouettes of apple, pear, and plum trees. "James, you don't have to say, but I suspect you've been a guardian angel for Louis Jr. and Marianna since the time their mama died."

"Hmm…" he replied, with cherry-wood-scented pipe smoke circling his ears.

"Marianna told me how she would find crocks filled with butter and cheese, loaves of rye bread covered in clean cloths, jars of jellies and tomatoes, and bags laden with potatoes and carrots. She also told me how you were kind to her papa when no one else was."

James responded by blowing a smoke ring over the porch rails.

"It would be the act of a real guardian angel to place a rosary on the neck of a dead father. That's what I'm thinking, James McGrarry."

James stood and knocked the ash from his pipe into the ground.

"What tune are you humming, James?"

" 'God save Ireland.' It was a favorite of your Martin's."

"Oh, James, thank you. You were a dear friend to him."

"Dear friends are treasures."

"What was Rose's favorite?"

"Sing it with me, Marta. Her brow is like the lily," he sang in his tenor voice.

"Her cheek is like the rose," she joined in her high soprano voice.

"And fair as the daffodilly, her yellow hair flows."

****

In the course of a week, Peter had yet to see Marta or Bette step into the barn, and neither one seemed to have an inkling regarding anything in the fields. Instead, their world dwelled in a small perimeter fanning their front door—the garden, the kitchen, and the fussy parlor.

Peter's uneasiness extended to a variety much more personal and much more complex than the physical aspects of the Oberski farm and field—the matter of Bette's intensity. The woman took painstaking efforts to appear with her hair dressed, her cheeks rouged, and her toilette sweet-smelling of lilies of the valley. He dreaded the smell of the diminutive, bell-shaped flowers, and now it left a cloying odor in his nose.

Bette trailed closely on his daily inspection of the grounds where he counted the heads of their flock of Romney sheep and black-and-white Holstein cattle. As the days wore on, Bette became disturbingly seductive.

One morning, she tracked Peter to the orchard.

"Peter."

He turned to answer.

She withdrew a ripe pear from a loaded branch. She stared, bit into the fruit, nibbled it, moaned, and laved on the stem. "All this could be yours." Juice slid down her heart-shaped chin. She brandished her hands to point to the domain of orchards she would inherit. On another occasion, Bette snuck upon him in the barn.

He had removed his shirt and was mucking stalls.

She came behind him and trailed her pampered fingertips over the raised cords on his back.

Her touches ignited a guttural defensive reaction. He swung and narrowly missed driving the pitchfork through her. "Your shoes are getting soiled," he sneered through clenched teeth.

Bette covered her face with her hands and fled. Her footsteps had raised dust and chicken squawks.

He cast aside the pitchfork and leaned against the barn wall.

Ginny, my Ginny, Lord God Almighty. I miss you, girl.

Chapter 35

Leon Nowakowski turned up the lamp wick, pulled a set of eyeglasses from his shirt pocket, and unfolded a copy of the *Minden Post*.

The crackling noise intruded the silence of Peter's conscience wrangling.

"Now, this here is good news. Three weeks since the fire occurred, and our countrymen haven't forgotten us." Leon peered over the top of his lenses.

Linda, heavily pregnant, eased into the chair across from her husband. "You okay, brother? It can't be easy living away from your homestead. You can stay with us anytime, you know." She moved a hand over the rise in her lap. "Ouch. That one was sharp. Not much room in there anymore." She sighed.

Peter stared at her abdomen. *Jesus, Mary, Joseph.*

Leon half rose from his chair.

"No, no, normal baby moving, nothing more. So, what were you saying, Leon?"

"Let me read you this." Leon sat and scratched his nose. *"The Red Cross promises to continue aid to the most grievously affected thumb of Michigan."*

"What's the Red Cross?" Linda furrowed her brow.

"It's a new, national relief agency, modeled after one in Europe." Leon adjusted his glasses. *"Hundreds of people barely lived through the most disastrous fire recorded in that area of the country and are left without the means of survival. A team headed by Miss Clara Barton's field chief, Wallace Dunbar, will be arriving within the month."*

Wallace Dunbar? Peter's body tensed from the muscle operating his eyebrows to the multitude of intersecting bones in his feet.

"Mr. Dunbar will assess the need for sustained medical attention as well as supplies of food, materials for rebuilding homes, and reestablishing farms."

"Oh, Leon, that is good news. Imagine people as far away as New York wanting to help us." Linda laced her fingers and stretched them.

Wallace Dunbar. God is giving me direction. I know what to do now. Wallace Dunbar. I know what to do. "Linda, don't get up, but tell me where I might find writing paper and a pen." Peter stood.

"You'll find them tucked in the top of my sewing basket right next to the chair you're sitting in."

Peter lifted the cover of the wicker basket and extracted the writing materials. He walked to the empty kitchen table, brushed away a crusty dollop of mashed potato, sat, and composed a letter.

Mr. Wallace Dunbar, care of The American Red Cross, Dansville, New York

Mr. Dunbar,

My name is Peter Nickles, and I reside in Parisville, Michigan. I read in a local newspaper you are coming here to aid fire survivors. Thank you for your noble work. I am an acquaintance of Miss Virginia Dahlke. I am happy to tell you she is well, but, Mr. Dunbar, Ginny's life would improve by leaving Parisville. I understand you are quite fond of her, and I hope that affection would be strong enough to return

Ginny to the safety and prosperity of New York when you return home.

Sincerely,

Peter Nickles

Folding the letter, he slipped it into an envelope. He carried it to the barn, where he stuffed it into his saddlebag. *Maybe Joseph and Kathleen will want her to stay. Maybe she'll fight leaving. And God knows I want her more than I've wanted anything in my life. But there is nothing here for her. She has friends in New York. She has the skills to make herself a life.* He slipped from the barn and walked to the perimeter of Leon and Linda's pot-of-gold tobacco acreage. Peter fell to the ground and covered his face with his fire-pocked bandana. Sobs wracked his ribs and propelled the contents of his stomach into the blanched earth. Tomorrow, he would ride to Tom Taraski's General Store and temporary post office in Forestville and send the message post-haste to Mr. Wallace Dunbar.

****

As the days progressed, the deaths continued. The very young and the very old died from the aftermath of smoke inhalation. Pregnancies aborted from aftershocks of stress, dehydration, and grief.

Father Graca performed more funerals than he had in his entire priesthood. But on his calendar, a date had long been reserved for the joyfully planned and much-anticipated marriage of Nadia Pawlowski and Tad Sterling.

"How can we expect anyone to overlook their sorrow and attend a wedding?" Henryk asked his wife. "It's too soon."

But Ruta pressed for the couple, and in the end,

Henryk came to agree that imparting a bit of happiness was beneficial for all of them.

For St. Mary's Catholic Church members to witness the marriage of Nadia Pawlowski and Tad Sterling was a respite from their suffocating, communal grief.

Nadia and Tad married twenty days following the Great Thumb Fire, in a month that ended in *R*, an affirmation of a deep-rooted Polish conviction. Good marriages began in a month ending in a consonant that spoken in their native language trilled off the tongue, like a flowing lace train.

This wedding might not be the one of my dreams, but Lord, I thank you for sparing my family. Ruta's eyes shone as her daughter entered their parlor on the arm of her father as they passed the painting of their guardian, Our Lady of Czestochowa.

The bride braided her hair in a style matching a coppery-colored filly's.

She wore a dress that draped expertly from her slightly mismatched shoulders and was trimmed in cascading rows of lace crocheted in a hairpin pattern by a sweet, silenced woman.

Ruta cried tears of gratitude and tinged in sadness for who was in their midst and who was not.

****

Henryk caught wind of Casimir's intention to leave Parisville unnoticed. So, he spread the news to the good people of St. Mary's Parish.

Casimir planned to travel by train. He would leave from the Port Huron and Northwestern Railway depot in Adam's Corner and stop in Chicago, Illinois, to see his son, daughter-in-law, and baby granddaughter.

Ruta and Nadia packed a hamper with rye bread, cheese, plum tarts, and molasses cookies.

Henryk tucked a bottle of vodka alongside the food.

Ginny enclosed the offerings with a linen towel embroidered in French knots and feather stitches depicting a pine tree, a lake trout, and a friendly-faced black bear.

Harriett Worchok culled through care packages sent by the Port Huron Relief Society, selected men's clothing in Casimir's size, and packed them in a scuffed, donated suitcase.

Well-wishers thronged him. They had little to say, yet their presence said it all.

Whooooo.

One prolonged blast signaled the train arriving.

Casimir faced his friends, coughed, and cleared his throat. "The missus, she made me promise." He shut his eyes, pinched his nostrils, and clenched the handle of the scarred suitcase. He gazed into the crowd. "She made me promise that we would see our new grandbaby before it turned six months old." His voice quaked.

Wind scuttered and blew the meager hairs on his hatless head straight.

Casimir made a fist and punched the sky. "By God, I'm keeping that promise."

The train whistle thundered.

Neighbors passed Casimir from bosom to bosom.

The promise keeper broke away and hopped on the bottom step of the Port Huron and Northwestern car.

Ginny gripped Ruta's hand. She froze her gaze on Casimir as he seized the stair rail with the resolve of a man pledging a lover's vow and disappeared into the cavern of the train.

Whooo.

One short blast.

Train leaving.

****

Joseph regained his sight in time to witness the birth of his daughter, Angel Valentine Dahlke.

The baby inherited her mother's shiny raven hair and her papa's jade-green eyes.

Her birth date of October 15, 1881, was recorded in the family Bible, which had for a short interval, hid in the springhouse her papa had built of sturdy planks on the high side of the farm she would one day inherit.

Peter was in Forestville when he heard the news, and he rode over to the Pawlowskis' farm to share it.

Tears streamed Ruta's face with the information that Kathleen delivered a healthy baby. "I've been praying for that girl for ever so long. It was in God's hands, but Kathleen suffered and withdrew from affection as if she sealed herself in a tomb. Praise God. Did you hear when Joseph and Kathleen and the baby will return?"

Peter shook his head.

"You can do me a big favor. Ginny will surely want to hear the update about the baby. She's over at Joseph's now. Why don't you ride over and tell her?"

He had avoided Ginny, hoping Wallace Dunbar would arrive and whisk her away from the smoldering wasteland of Parisville before his resolve weakened. But there had been no reports on the Red Cross arrival when he asked on the docks today, and no one had any leads on the story from the *Minden Post* that appeared a few weeks before.

"Why the glum face? I would think you would enjoy giving Ginny happy news."

He rocked on his feet and took a drag on his cigarette.

Ruta continued to scrutinize his face and his moves.

Best I move on. I've never been any good at secret-keeping and Ruta is an expert secret-extractor. The longer I linger, the more likely she is to figure something is amiss. He plucked the cigarette from his lips, threw it on the ground, stomped on it, took a running leap for the corral, and jumped on Star's back.

The landscape greened, building shelter for field mice, weaving soft mats for wolf footfalls, and painting a vision of hope and renewal for the tired eyes of Parisville neighbors.

Trees undamaged by the fire navigated by the correct season.

Leaves fell from the deciduous brands.

Cones dropped from their coniferous cousins.

The movement of Star's hooves scattered desiccated maple, oak, poplar, and aspen droppings.

Peter had seen Ginny at Nadia and Tad's wedding and Casimir's goodbye. Each time, he read the message *Please, Peter* in her gaze. Still, he stood steadfast in his decision to discourage any exchange of affection. Each time Peter denied his love, he forfeited a piece of his heart for her future.

Her sweet demeanor switched to a steely veneer, and he knew it to be a measure of the heartache he forced on her.

Joseph's farm came into view.

Peter's throat tightened.

Buster swished his tail and rested his muzzle against Blue. Three days following the fire, Buster had been found wandering a mile from the Dahlke homestead and returned to his paddock.

Horse dung and matted straw, spread on the tines of a warped pitchfork spewed from the open barn.

Ginny stepped out. She gripped pails on each side of her body.

Grime caked her cheeks.

Peter slowed Star and allowed himself moments to memorize every detail of the woman he loved. Her presentation of freckles, short-cropped hair, shapeless, soiled dress, and her brother's muck boots were far more fetching than the artifices Bette wore. His heart swelled. *God help me. I love her so.*

Chessie bounded from the other side of the barn and barked at Peter's presence.

"Hey, boy, good to see you," Peter called.

Ginny turned. She locked gazes. A smile lit her face as she squatted and rested the pails on the ground. She wiped her hands on her skirt and reached to smooth her hair. "Peter!" She lifted her skirts and ran.

Bette would've flown for cover to primp, but Ginny's greeting was as natural as sunshine raining on a field of tender shoots, as inviting as a wife pining the absence of her husband as he nurtured those shoots. He dismounted Star and let the reins trail loosely across his hand. Peter delivered his message in a monotone voice and devoid of emotion. He clenched his jaws. A thick rope of constraint throbbed in his neck muscles.

A dark cloud crossed Ginny's face, and she stopped abruptly ten feet from where he stood.

"I'm so thrilled to get the news. Thank you, Peter, for coming here to tell me. I'm sorry I can't visit. Father Graca will need a meal once he gets back from the Worchoks." She stooped, picked up the buckets, and stumbled.

He lunged and grabbed her wrist with one of his hands.

Tears spilled over her cheeks and her chapped lips.

Tin pails spilled sheep manure over his boots.

She stared at the hand clutching her wrist and breathed shallow, chuffing snuffles. She blinked, shook her head, and lifted short, damp hair tufts with the movement.

Peter maintained his grasp and fingered the elbow of her opposite arm. He squeezed his eyes shut, obliterating the pleasure of viewing her earnest eyes, the slope of her nose, and the airiness of her brow. He bowed his head and held his breath, disallowing the indulgence of smelling the sweat on the roots of her hair. He clenched his teeth, pressed his lips together, and withheld the kisses he had no right to endow. Finally, he dropped her arm and backed away.

A cow lowed in the barn.

"Mrs. Mulligan needs milking, and I need to get back to help Ruta. Please give my regards to Marta and Bette."

Her words were rushed and stilted. Her movements were jerky.

She turned her back to Peter and walked erect into the barn's shadows to soothe Joseph's cow and torment the agonized man who continued to spurn her.

Chapter 36

The United States Postal Service restored mail delivery to the village of Parisville.

Henryk returned from town one day at the end of October with a letter from Kathleen. He gathered Ginny and Ruta in the parlor.

With trembling hands, Ginny ripped the sealed flap free from the envelope.

Tears splattered her cheeks.

"Ruta, Henryk, I have wonderful news. Joseph, Kathleen, and Angel will be here within the week."

"Praise God, praise God." Ruta grasped Ginny to her breast and kissed her cheeks.

"I must return home and make things ready. Henryk, can you take me tomorrow?"

"Of course, dear." Henryk squeezed her shoulder. "I'll stay a while and check the stock, the barn, and the outbuildings. Ginny, you don't need to worry about housing Father Graca. The bishop granted him a leave of absence so yesterday, Father left to visit his family in Detroit. While he's gone, James, George, Dawid, Peter, and I will restore the rectory."

Following an early supper of borscht and meat-stuffed dumplings, Ginny sat beside Ruta on the Pawlowski sofa and faced the west parlor window.

Across the bare rye fields, the wind gusted, and leaves twirled against a darkening sky.

A frigid draft ebbed at her feet, and she pulled her shawl tighter across her shoulders.

"Do you think Marianna will like this dress? I cut it down from one of Nadia's." Ruta held a flax-flower-purple garment fastened with yellow buttons at the neckline.

Ginny's heart slammed in her throat. She saw the dress as Nadia wore it, the day she, Nadia, and Peter rested at Pawlowskis' pond. Ginny sighed and stroked the baby dress in her lap. She fingered the lace remnants from Nadia's wedding dress that she applied to the little gown's hem.

Ruta reached and squeezed her hand. "Ah, so much sadness, yah, *kochanie*, but this baby will brighten your days."

Wiping her tears on her sleeve, Ginny smiled. "Yah, I am so happy for Joseph and Kathleen." She reached for an afghan draped on the back of the sofa and folded the hand-knitted wrap over her knees.

"Cold?"

"Yah, a little bit." Ginny sighed.

"I will miss our time together, *kochanie*." Tears dashed Ruta's cheeks. "You must pledge to visit often."

Ginny leaned over and embraced her. "I promise," she whispered and kissed Ruta's cheek.

"Henryk might be losing another friend." Ruta shook her head. "Peter is considering moving to Yale to work in that woolen mill he toured the day of the fire."

Ginny's heart lodged in her throat and she gasped. She dropped the baby garment atop the afghan and cinched her hands over her lips.

"But Peter is worried about Marta and Bette. He says they need a man full time. Who can do it? No spare men are left." Ruta held a copy of *The American Woman's Home* by sisters Catharine Beecher and Harriett Beecher Stowe across her knees and drummed her fingers on the book's cover.

Outside, an impenetrable blackness sequestered the household from the rest of the world. The wind propelled a denuded limb to brush against the glass. The noise was barely audible, but it rent Ginny's heart.

Ruta's monologue continued, but Ginny comprehended only fragments: a homeless family of eight moved into Josephine's home, a shortage of vinegar, trouble sleeping.

"Ah, Ginny, big day tomorrow, yah?" Henryk entered the parlor.

Ginny forced a smile. *Dear Henryk*. The man had aged. At his fiftieth birthday party, which seemed a lifetime ago, he had no white hair. He did now.

"We will miss you." Henryk closed his eyes.

Ginny's lips quivered.

"Well, ladies, I'm turning in." Henryk snapped his suspenders.

"Me, too." Ginny stood and embraced Ruta and Henryk.

"Take that afghan with you, and you know where the extra blankets are."

Once alone in Nadia's old bedroom, Ginny lay in Nadia's vacated single bed. Her body felt foreign as if she shed it like a molting crab. She had no tears. Tears were exhausted, banished, like the hope that bled from her heart. Peter was leaving.

****

Early the next morning, Henryk drove Ginny to the Dahlke homestead.

Frost clung to the shriveled tomato vines and the withered rose petals bordering the path to the door. Dried aspen leaves skittered across the porch. Ginny pulled her shawl over her head and alit from the wagon.

Henryk tipped his hat and turned the team—no smile, no suspender pinging.

Choking on a lump in her throat, Ginny waved at Henryk's back. She stood in the yard, dropped back her head, closed her eyelids to the sun, and put her hands on her hips. She had work to do. She treaded the porch steps and threw open the door. She removed curtains from the window frames, the quilts from the beds, every single item of clothing tucked away in trunks and wardrobes, and took a whole load of linens to the yard. Next, she built a fire under the laundry tub and blanched every fiber moving back into a house where a family attempted to rebuild itself. Ginny reached for the pocketknife and the bar of soap in her apron pocket. Leaning over the kettle, she shaved slivers from a congealed lye and ash combination and watched stoically as the pieces drifted into the simmering water.

Minute bubbles formed and cleaved to the kettle's belly. Then, each bubble ripped into the chaos and churning of a cacophony of swelling suds. A myriad of water buds climaxed as they exploded through the tension of the erupting surface.

She wrestled with the question. *Did Peter use my body only for a physical release? Kathleen was right. I am no competition for Bette or her father's farm or her vanilla sugar cookies. Damn Peter Nickles. Damn him.*

A tiny quaking gripped Ginny's stomach.

Her lungs fought for air.

She masked her face with her foul-smelling apron

as her sobs swelled in cadence with the bubbling mass.

****

The Dahlke family resettled in their homestead.

Joseph's strength returned, as did his assumption of caring for the surviving stock.

Ginny moved the Singer sewing machine to a new location. It fronted an east window and allotted morning light to illuminate the favored task of fashioning feminine baby dresses.

Squirrels reappeared outside the window, chittering from spared oaks and harvesting their acorns for their winter nests.

Chessie brushed his paw over his nose from his post on a braided rug laid on the porch.

Of all the post-fire transformations on the Dahlke property, the changes in Kathleen were the most manifest. Kathleen's once shrill opinions were now subdued observations. The sharp angles of her brows and lips softened. Instead of searching for scandalous gossip in the *Huron Times* pages, Kathleen chose lighthearted stories to read aloud to Ginny and Angel. "Here's a good one. The title is 'Uncle Ephraim,' and it's about a widowed mother trying to find suitable matches for her three unmarried daughters."

Ginny rocked Angel and hummed "*Spij laleczko moja mala, czas na ciebie juz…*Sleep, my little baby doll, it is the time for you now." Ginny swept her hand over the child's silky scalp.

Kathleen fluttered the newspaper.

Crick-crick-crick.

The gliders' thud and the motion of the rocking chair lulled Angel into gentle slumber as Kathleen's voice droned.

Ginny's head dropped forward.

Crick-crick-crick.

Kathleen read with inflection and volume adjustments as if she were auditioning for a stage part. Ginny smiled.

" '*Oh, yes, he will,' cried Coral. 'That won't make a bit of difference. And his fortunes have fallen, too. He's the rich bachelor's head gardener now. Head gardener,' gasped Mrs. Sparkler. 'Head gardener,' exploded Miss Cassandra. 'Head gardener,' wailed Miss Theodora.*"

"Head gardener?" Ginny raised her head and laughed.

Angel spit bubbles from her tiny lips.

"Now, little one, Auntie Ginny is giving you back to your mama. I've got a secret task, and no, as curious as your mama is, I'm not telling her anything." Ginny winked at Kathleen. "But, little one, I will give you a clue," she whispered in the baby's ear. "It has something to do with your christening day." Ginny walked behind the curtain that separated the great room and her private space. She opened her sewing basket, removed a pair of scissors, and laid them on the floor. She knelt before her steamer trunk and strained to open the domed lid.

The top fell back on its hinges.

Ginny leaned over and pulled a gown from her trunk. She fingered the silk and the rows of ruching, brought it to her nose, and inhaled. The gown had rested on her mother's breast and had held Ginny's hopes and dreams of donning it someday in a month that ended in *R*.

She took a deep breath, raised the shears, and made

389

the first cut. *No better way exists to honor this long-preserved dress than to make you a christening gown, Angel.*

The garment fell away, releasing the love she felt for the man who would never wait for Ginny at an altar. She placed the scissors back on the floor and leaned deep into the trunk. She swept her hands over the bottom. She grazed her fingers over a bumpy surface, grasped the object, withdrew it, and rolled it in her calloused palm.

On a perfect summer day, when the world was lush and shining and promising and beckoning love, Peter had culled the pocked gray stone in his sturdy hands and dropped it into her waiting hand.

She had stowed it in the deep recess of her dress pocket.

Ginny knelt, leaned back, and raised the ancient stone that held the history of a world gone by and a perfect day of reveling in love.

This rock had survived the ebb and flow of ice, winds, sand, and time. And it had managed to find a resting place here—in the depths of her trunk, despite Ginny emptying her pocket that perfect day that turned imperfect. She had thrown the contents of her pocket into the dust clouds of Buster's and Blue's hooves.

Yet, this fossil had escaped the purge.

Rising, she dropped it to the bottom of the trunk, stepped back, and flinched as the weighty top slammed shut.

****

Marta, accompanied by Bette, came for a visit and brought pork-and-mushroom-stuffed *pierogis* and a dainty, pink sweater, cap, and pair of matching booties.

"Come, come." Ginny moved two chairs to flank the rocking chair where Kathleen sat facing the gladdening comfort of soft burning embers in the fieldstone fireplace. Pops and hisses ripped the serenity.

Faint hiccup noises sounded.

Kathleen lifted Angel from her crib and handed her to Marta.

The older woman choked. Tears leaked from her eyes. Marta pressed Angel's downy head to her cheek. "Oh, I remember it like yesterday. Your papa loved you so." She turned her face to Bette. "Ah, life goes on. The fields are God's testimony. The fire cleansed the earth, which is now fertile and prepared for a new life." She pointed a finger.

Angel wrapped her baby fingers across the older woman's twisted ones.

"Peter just finished a crop of winter wheat. It is God's promise for a new beginning." Marta sing-songed as she played finger games with Angel. "Peter said to give you all his regards. Oh, and Ginny, Peter thought you should know that Nokee Wilkowski, her family, and their people intend to leave tomorrow for a new home."

Ginny jerked her head.

Bette gripped the frame of her chair seat and frowned.

Kathleen leaned over Marta and tickled the baby's feet.

"She's had a bit of colic, but Ginny figured it was probably my penchant for cabbage that caused Angel's discomfort."

"Yes, Joseph and I both told Kathleen she could not eat any more cabbage until she weans Angel."

Ginny shook her finger as if she were scolding Chessie for chasing chickens.

A ripple of laughter split the air.

Cabbage and colic expunged the tension.

"Ginny has been such a help. She can calm Angel when I'm in a frazzle. I don't know how I would cope without her."

Kathleen's praise was sugary but curdled in Ginny's stomach. Even before the fire, Ginny had struggled with the guilt of leaving Kathleen and Joseph. But, now that both Kathleen and Angel depended on her, the feeling of responsibility was as sealed as the ground was burnt. Ginny bit her lip. The more she nurtured baby Angel, the more she yearned for a baby and a family of her own.

The dimples in Bette's cheeks deepened.

Her face was more angelic than baby Angel's. Ginny twisted her hands and laced her fingers together. The love she and Peter shared was destined to be yet another calamity of the fire aftermath. God's promise to Ginny was as empty as the four chipped teacups sitting on the table fronting the hearth of Joseph and Kathleen's log cabin home. She clamped her lips as yet another piece of her heart shattered.

****

More losses must be endured. Losses not as cruel as death but just as permanent.

Ginny went to see the Wilkowskis. She carried a burlap sack filled with squash and cucumber seeds as a parting gift.

Chessie bounded at her side.

"Nokee." Ginny greeted.

"Come with me, Ginny. I want to tell you a story."

She led Ginny to a flat boulder and sat.

Ginny clambered beside her and stared into the dark depths of the Cass River.

"In the days following the fire, my brother Thomas, Chet Jr., Lerk, and I made campfires at night. Thomas told us of the visions he had while we stood in this river during the storm." Nokee stretched her arm and fanned it across their line of sight. "Thomas saw a fair-faced woman wearing a gown and a bonnet as sheer as dragonfly's wings. She sang and twirled about a fire, the smoke drifting through her clothing. As she sang, she plucked boughs from a cedar tree. She broke off the tips and rubbed them on her neck and wrists. She bent low and rubbed the fragrant fronds on her ankles, which bore a circlet of silver minnows, strung like beads and joined by the jagged teeth to the tail in front of it. A horse's body appeared through the haze, and the woman could see the shape of a star, seared and branded above its bright blue eyes. She called to the steed. And as it neared, she saw a man astride it. The man's head had no face. Three loops of a rope caught about his chest and tethered him to the horse. The woman threaded her fingers through the stallion's mane, straddled her thighs behind the faceless man, clasped her hands around the man's middle, and righted herself atop his mount. With the riders on his back, the stallion leaped into the northern sky. The woman untangled the rope wound around the man and heaved it, lassoing the bottom handle star of the Big Dipper. She reeled it in. She pulled a flashing needle from her gauzy bonnet and sewed the star onto the man's face. She did this six more times, snagging the remaining stars in the Big Dipper's stem and the four of the ladle.

Each star glowed faintly on his face until the man had two eyes, a nose, and four stars curving in the shape of a smile. As the last star was stitched, all seven burst in a light that flowed into the man's heart and made him turn on the horse and face the woman. The man removed the woman's bonnet and saw with his star eyes that the woman had no hair. So, he took the rope that bound him and swiveled it around and around their heads, netting stars, moons, and silvery-tufted titmouse feathers. He spat on it, and the rope turned to strands of gold. Then the man crowned the woman's head and sprinkled the catches of the net over her golden hair." Nokee placed her hands on either side of Ginny's bonnet and slid it from her head.

Ginny shoved her hands to cover her hair.

Nokee took Ginny's hands and kissed them, and then she kissed Ginny's brow.

"Take care of each other," she whispered.

Her solemn eyes gazed into Ginny's, leaving a blood memory so searing it transcended the weighted chain built of sorrow links. From the elevated seat she shared with Nokee, Ginny watched Peter approach. Her heart strummed inside her chest.

****

If only I could paddle away with them. Peter swallowed, removed his shell-trimmed hat, beat it against his thigh and, with the tips of his calloused fingers, gripped the rim as if he was applying a vise.

Nokee stood, brushed the seat of her skirt, and walked through bowed grasses and a tangle of knotted undergrowth. Finally, she stopped within inches of Peter.

"How many days will it take you to reach Walpole

Island?" he asked.

A line of burdened canoes bobbed at the shoreline. Children scrabbled to the boats' centers. Adults climbed to the bow and stern positions.

"About seven days."

His heart plummeted as he viewed her impassive face studying the horizon. This parting was hard enough, but without her usual soft expression, this good-bye formed a weight on his heart so heavy he found it hard to breathe. Peter raised his arm holding the hat and moved it in a horizontal line. "It's good you will be with your people—all together." He waved to Lerk. "The fishing must be good there, yah?"

"They say the waters around the island are full of perch and whitefish." Lerk shuffled his feet.

"Nokee." Peter's voice started strong but trailed to a whisper.

She turned.

Her eyes were as black as obsidian and her face as constrained as the rock face she had risen from.

"You are a strong man, Peter." Nokee grasped each of his upper arms. She jumped her gaze to Ginny and spoke loud enough for her to hear. "There is a woman who loves you with the strength to get you both back to a place of happiness." She touched the tip of Peter's bearded chin and gazed into his eyes. "And there is a woman who will be calm once you acknowledge love again. So, let Franny rest in peace, Peter. She will stop haunting you once you realize you can love again." Nokee turned her gaze to Ginny.

"I will always remember you, Nokee. Go in peace, my friend." Peter plucked a shell that had passed through her hands a lifetime ago.

Chet Jr. knelt in the bow of a canoe.

Lerk waited in the stern with a paddle across his knees.

Nokee climbed into the canoe's middle.

Following the leave goers to the bank of the river, Ginny tapped her left leg.

Chessie heeled against it and sat when Ginny stopped short of the water's edge.

Kneeling in the marshy earth, Ginny stroked the curly hair covering the dog's ears and buried her nose in the soft fur covering his head. "Dear, dear, Chessie." She muffled a sob, stood, and swept her left hand toward the water. "Go," she commanded.

Chessie leaped from her side, dove into the river, raising a waterfall of river water with the swimming motions of his curly, multi-layered, created-for-retrieving body, and paddled to the stern.

"Chessie is going with me?" the boy cried.

"Joseph said he belongs with you. Chessie's a water dog, and you are a water boy."

"Thank Joseph for me." Lerk bent and pulled the dog on board.

Peter stepped over the rocky river bottom and pivoted the stern to point west. He gave the Wilkowski canoe a thrust.

The raven-haired sons dipped their paddles in the waterway that had been a sanctuary to the creatures of Gichi-manidoo.

Nokee never looked back.

Godspeed, my friend. Peter clamped his hat back on his head and took Star's reins.

****

By the end of the week, Peter came to see baby

Angel.

Ginny's maiden heart swelled.

He was so very handsome. He wore a sweet-smelling, blue cambric shirt that flaunted expertly pressed cuffs, front placket, and collar, and no telltale wrinkles appeared between the whalebone buttons running from the base of Peter's neck to the vanishing point under his waistband. His hair bore new streaks of silver.

Someone had recently cut it. Someone had stroked it, massaged it, and combed his hair.

That someone was not her. Stifled tears leaked from Ginny's eyes.

Kathleen stood from her rocking chair, gripped Angel under the baby's arms, and walked to Peter. She thrust the baby forward.

He balked, stepped back, and raised his palms.

Kathleen laughed, reclaimed her seat, and cradled Angel in her lap.

Peter shook his head, smiled, and retraced his steps. Finally, he drew a one-dollar coin from his pocket, stuffed it into the folds of the baby's gown, patted the infant's chest, and retreated.

Nodding to Kathleen, Joseph opened a cupboard door, and extracted a bottle of vodka and four glasses. "Will you make a toast with me for my new daughter?" He set the glasses on the table and poured the rye-based alcohol into each.

"Yah. To life. To Angel." Peter raised a glass.

Gripping the goblet, Joseph clinked it against Peter's glass, winked, and tilted his head back. "To all of us," he roared and downed a swig.

Kathleen smiled, opened her lips, tipped her glass

and blinked her eyes.

Ginny held her nose and swallowed the fiery liquid. *Gah!*

Angel hiccupped and flailed her baby fists and spindly legs.

Peter chuckled. His Adam's apple lifted.

Turning her head, Ginny locked gazes with Peter. His vacant stare shattered her heart. She glanced aside. *Don't even look at me. Stop toying with me. Go to Bette or go to Brockway Centre. Just go.*

Chapter 37

Peter chafed his hands and blew air into the hollow between his thumbs. He pulled the collar of his coarsely woven jacket up around his ears and finished wrapping Star's reins around the hitching post fronting the Taraski General Store. *It's been weeks, Lord, since I sent that letter. Maybe I'll find an answer today. It's killing me to shun Ginny.*

A trio of well-suited, dandily groomed men stood out from the bedraggled refugees congregating at the south end of the shaded porch.

Tom Taraski stood with the mustached men and gestured toward the stable behind his store.

The men nodded and shook Tom's hand.

"Does anyone know the whereabouts of a young woman and family from Parisville, their last name being Dahlke?" asked one of the men, stopping people and repeating the question.

Peter scrutinized the questioner. *Who was he? Would the Dahlke family benefit from the appearance of this man? Could this be Wallace Dunbar, responding to his letter?* The man was persistent, tapping shoulders and waiting for responses from folks examining apothecary bottles inside Taraski's store to fishermen on the lakefront, wearing snug wool caps and bulky knit sweaters. Peter followed him to the beach.

Lake Huron breached the shore, traversing shells

and pebbles, and left a soft shushing in its wake.

The man was frankly handsome. His black hair was thick with not a trace of gray at the temple, and he moved with the air of a respectable, educated elite. His fine wool suit bore neatly executed seams and accentuated the wearer's military-precise physique.

Peter stared, straightened his back, and brushed his arms over his sleeves. He drew a deep breath and stepped forward. "I know a family named Dahlke in Parisville."

The man turned abruptly. "How did they fare?"

He drilled Peter with the look of a man resigned to accept a jury's verdict. "They survived." Peter's gaze skimmed the man's length.

"Oh, thank God." The man grabbed Peter's hand and pumped it. "Miss Dahlke has many friends in New York who've been greatly concerned regarding her welfare. What did you say your name was?"

"Peter Nickles. I am a friend of the Dahlke family." He doffed his hat. "Who are you?"

"Oh, pardon me. Wallace Dunbar."

"Wallace Dunbar." Peter echoed the name and shifted his weight. *Here we are, face to face.*

"Yes."

"So, you received my letter. Have you come for Ginny?" Peter's lungs seized.

The man tilted his head. He met Peter's gaze, extended his lower lip, and frowned. "Pardon me, ah…Mr.?" Wallace ran his hand from the front of his scalp to the back of his head.

"Peter, Peter Nickles. Have you come to take Ginny?"

"Take her? Does she need to be escorted

somewhere? What letter?" Wallace squinted his eyes and smoothed his mustache. "Mr. Nickles, I am here with a group representing the American Red Cross. Miss Clara Barton asked me to lead a team to assess the survivors' needs in the wake of the horrific fire you experienced here. I wasn't aware of a need to transport Miss Dahlke, nor is that part of my mission here. But I would certainly not be a gentleman if I were to overlook the needs of one of my mother's friends."

Peter scratched his head. He peered into Wallace's eyes. *Is that how you refer to a woman you love?* "Your mother's friend? Ginny?"

A breeze rippled Wallace's hair.

A pair of sharp-eyed ospreys tucked their long, crooked wings and landed on the craggy rocks in front of them. They snarled and ripped the soft flesh off molting crayfish.

Peter cinched his eyes.

"Yes, Mr. Nickles, my mother's friend." He motioned for Peter to return to the dock and started walking in that direction.

Peter took a rushed breath. "You are not betrothed to Ginny?"

Wallace turned. He shook his foot and flung a layer of wet sand from his leather shoe. "Indeed, sir, I am not betrothed to Miss Dahlke. I'm betrothed to Miss Hattie Simpson of Ann Arbor, Michigan." Wallace brushed his hands down the lapel of his jacket.

"Well, thank you very much, Mr. Dunbar—for your work with the Red Cross. There is no need to worry about Miss Dahlke." *Damn, damn, damn. I am such a damn fool.* White hot rage suffused his chest. Peter took large strides through the grass, over the dock, and back to Star.

****

On his return to the Oberskis', Peter shifted his hips in the bowl-shaped saddle. He brushed his hand over his beard and scratched his head. *Ginny is incapable of duplicity. So how did I fall for Kathleen's ruse regarding Ginny's old-world betrothal?*

Kathleen had tricked him.

Damn it. I'm just as responsible for hoodwinking. I'm guilty of sometimes fueling, instead of snuffing Bette's romantic whims. I've gotta make this right.

****

"Oh, Peter, there you are. Come and sit." Marta set salt and pepper shakers on the dining room table. "James is visiting. He's in the barn with Marianna and Louis Jr. Supper is ready." She turned, bustled to the sideboard, and grabbed a long-handled spoon. "Bette made one of your favorites—sausage and fried potatoes."

Potato chunks dropped from the spoon and landed in a bowl rimmed in a pattern of Oriental pagodas.

"Oh, and Peter, Bette made apple dumplings." Marta turned her face and smiled over her shoulder.

Bette swiveled from the sink. "Hi, Peter. How was your day?"

She chirped, sounding to Peter like a loyal wife greeting her husband as he stomped dust from his boots, hung his hat on a peg, and reached for a kiss. Peter balled his hands into fists.

"Any news from Forestville, Peter?" Marta motioned for him to sit.

Peter eased his behind onto the hard wooden chair. His throat constricted. The weight of regrets lay on his

402

heart and made his shoulders sag.

Checking her reflection in the window over the sink, Bette unbuttoned the top button on her dress and sat next to Peter.

She put her elbows on the table, her chin in her hands, and a seductive moue on her lips. He feigned interest in the scene outside the window where Marianna laughed and threw a pile of leaves at her brother.

"Yes, any news, Peter?" Bette trailed a finger over the back of his hand.

He retracted his hand, bracing his feet on the floor and his back on the chair. The odor of baked apple, usually enticing, evoked a wave of melancholy. "Red Cross folks have arrived. It seems they are committed to furthering aid to fire survivors here."

"Oh, that's wonderful. So much help is needed." Marta rubbed her hands on her apron.

Marianna skipped into the kitchen and ushered in autumn evening chilliness. Tidy braids tamed Marianna's thick hair. Ribbons wrapped the tail ends.

James held the door for Louis Jr.

The young man's face had grown fuller, in tandem with the development of a wider smile that emerged with increasing regularity. "Hi, Mrs. Oberski. Hi, Bette." The tone of Louis Jr.'s voice synced with the expression on his face. Peter smiled.

Marta smoothed the back of her skirt and sat.

James pushed her chair and sat across from Peter.

Marianna scraped a chair across the floor, sat, gripped the seat with both hands, and bounced the chair close to the table.

Louis Jr. slid onto the remaining chair, spat into his

hand, and flattened his hair.

"I'd like to offer the prayer tonight." Peter steepled his fingers together and drew a shaky breath.

"Of course, dear." Marta bowed her head.

"Dear Lord, we don't always approve of your plans, but we trust you." Peter brought his joined hands to his face and lined them from his chin to his forehead.

"Amen," murmured James.

"Lord, we trust you for safekeeping Louis Sr. and Martin. They were good men."

Marianna slumped on Marta's shoulder.

"We see your goodness in the earth's renewal. And Lord, bless Marta and Bette who have opened their home to Louis Jr. and Marianna and provide for them so well." Peter grasped the top of Bette's hand. *And Lord, please, take care of this woman. She deserves a good life. We both know that I'm not the one to give it to her.* He patted her fingers and felt the softness of her skin for the last time.

"Amen to that, Lord," James said.

Marta brushed a tear from her cheek. "Well, let's eat." She lifted a fluted ceramic bowl and passed it to Marianna.

The dish, laden with buttered noodles, was passed hand to hand around the table.

Slurping, burping, and chatter sounds filled the room.

Bette leaned into him. "You look particularly handsome tonight." She brushed her leg against his.

Peter plunged his fork into a bite-size chunk of sausage. The odor of pork, onions, and garlic assaulted his nose. His stomach roiled.

The fork clattered to the table.

Tensing his backside muscles, Peter thrust back his chair. The jarring sound and Peter's tipsy attempt to right himself forced him into center stage.

"I'm not a mosquito." Bette laughed and reached to steady him.

"My goodness, are you okay?" Marta fussed.

"How about a game of dominoes tonight?" Louis Jr. asked.

"I'm in." James slapped a palm on the table.

"Me, too." Marianna wiped apple and crust crumbs from her face.

"Peter, you wanna play?" Louis Jr. arched his eyebrows.

The hopeful and tentative smile on the boy's face pierced Peter's heart. Louis Jr. had suffered more than most, and the boy deserved whatever happiness that could be mustered from these bleak days. Peter managed a limp smile for the boy's sake. *Lord, I don't want to put any more unpleasantness into these children's lives, not when they were finally getting their feet on the ground and signs of happiness dawn on their faces.* "Bette, I'd like to speak to you, please." He pushed himself from his chair, tramped to the entryway, moving as if he bore a bag of mortar on each boot toe, and turned.

"Of course. "Please excuse us," she said and jumped like an unleashed puppy through the doorway.

He dodged the blitz of her bosoms and the grasp of her arms by vaulting to the edge of the porch.

Bette closed the door.

Peter gripped the railing with both hands and turned toward her. His stomach lurched. He drew breath from the depths of his lungs. "Bette, you've been a good friend, and I hope you always will be. But I will never be more than that to you."

The wind rustled a loose shingle.

"Peter." Bette stretched her hand.

He blocked her touch and stepped away.

"Peter?" She gasped. "Friend?" she whispered in a ragged breath. "Friend?" She shrieked.

All the days of terror, frustration, anger, and regret boiled and erupted on the Oberski porch.

"Damn you, Peter Nickles, and damn that Ginny Dahlke. Damn you for falling in love with her, and damn her for coming here. Why couldn't she stay in New York?" Bette fell on him, slapped his chest, and scratched his face. "You were mine...mine...until she came here."

He raised his hand to caress her hair and changed his mind. *No, no more charade of affection. I want this thing done and holding her to soothe her would be cruel in the long run.* Still, a piece of his heart shattered as Bette's sobs resonated in the farmyard.

James and Marta appeared in the open doorway.

"Ah....whoo...."

Bette's sobs dissolved into pitiful moans.

Peter fumbled his hands in his pockets.

James held open the door. "Go to your daughter, Marta."

Marta stepped onto the porch and reached for Bette. She put her arm around her daughter's shoulders.

Bette crumpled into her mother's arms.

Marta led her trembling daughter into the house and closed the door with the heel of her shoe once they were over the threshold.

"That's the way of it then, I guess." James tugged

on his ear.

"Yah, I wish there was a different end to this." Peter shrugged.

"You best be off then, young man. I can help take care of things here. Good luck to you."

Ginny, love, please have me.

****

Nightfall had landed.

I 'spect Joseph will be peeved when I knock on his door at this hour, but I need to set things straight before another day begins. Peter tethered Star in the Dahlke paddock and strode past the chicken coop and barn. A kerosene lamp gave off an intimate glow in the front room.

Kathleen sat in the rocking chair with her head bent over her chest and her eyes closed.

He rapped on the window, causing it to rattle. He jumped and fell on his butt.

Kathleen shrieked.

Angel flailed her arms, kicked her bootie-clad feet, and spit out her mother's nipple.

The baby's tiny face twisted into the vision of a red-faced demon. "Damn," Peter cursed under his breath.

"Joseph!" Kathleen cried.

Baby Angel screamed.

Peter framed his face in the window and waved frantically. *Damn.*

Ginny lurched from behind the curtain partition. Her short hair stood around her head like a bent halo.

"What the hellfire?" Joseph yelled as he stepped behind Ginny. He stomped to the door.

The rasp of metal scraping metal ensued.

Joseph threw open the door. The tip of his shotgun leveled with Peter's chest. "Peter? What the hell?" He ran his hand over his face and the disheveled hair that stood perpendicular to his head and stepped back into the house.

Peter held up his hands. "Can I talk to you?"

Joseph stepped back, moored the gun, crossed the threshold, and closed the door. "Is everything okay with the Oberskis? Are you all right? What the hell?"

"I'll get right to it, then." Peter blew a big breath and ran his hands over his thighs. "Joseph, I am not in love with Bette Oberski. And Joseph, I am not marrying Bette Oberski," Peter blurted.

Joseph shook his head. "For God's sake, man, I could've shot you dead. Couldn't you have waited until daylight? Have you been sucking Martin's vodka? What the hell is wrong with you?" He ran a shaky hand over his hair. "I'll ask you again. Is everyone okay at the Oberskis'?"

"Well, I'd say everyone is pretty good, including Martin's extensive liquor cabinet. But I did cause a ruckus. Bette's all stirred up, and I think Marta would like to take a broom to my sorry ass."

"What the hell happened?"

"I told Bette what I told you."

"Oh. Guess that explains the scratches on your face." Joseph eased low to sit on the top porch step.

The door opened, and a coat sailed onto the porch floor.

Suckling mews and the crick of Kathleen's rocking chair sounded from the front room.

The door slammed shut.

"Thank you." Joseph grabbed the coat and

shrugged into it.

Peter pulled a cigarette from his pocket and offered it to Joseph.

"Sure." Joseph stretched to reach the smoke.

Peter pulled another cigarette from the pocket and then a box of blue diamond matches. He struck a match against the flint on the package, touched the flame to Joseph's cigarette, and then his own. Both men sat in silence and puffed smoke into the frosty air.

"Joseph, there's more." Peter sat on the top step, spread his legs, and hunched over his knees.

"I'm listening." Joseph set his elbows on his thighs.

"The day of the fire, I rode to Brockway Centre to see the new woolen mill."

Joseph rolled the cigarette between his fingers and gazed mutely at the sky. "Yah, I remember thinking that was a dumb idea, and I still do."

The men shared a chuckle.

"Well, I met the owner, Charles Andreae, and he offered me a job." Peter chewed his lower lip.

"Guess I can see why moving away from this place would be a notion you'd be having."

"So, here's the real reason I'm here tonight." Peter stood, inhaled, put his hands on his back pockets, and arched his back. "I've got to make it right with Ginny. Joseph, I know how much you and Kathleen depend on Ginny, especially with having Angel, but Joseph, I'd like your permission to ask Ginny to be my wife."

Joseph cleared his throat. "Well, friend, we've survived some confounding times." He extended his hand to Peter. "Brother."

"Yah, Brother." Peter grasped Joseph's hand. "If

she'll have me, that is."

Joseph blew a long breath. "That one is up to you, Peter, but you've got my blessing, you damn, crazy Pole." He dropped the cigarette on the ground and dragged the toe of his boot over it. "Ready?" Joseph edged to the door, pulled it ajar, and turned toward Peter.

"Yah, nervous." Peter rubbed his hands on his thighs.

"Is everything all right?" Kathleen called.

"Yes, everyone is good. Peter is waiting for Ginny." Joseph stood in the doorframe.

"Me?" Ginny squeaked. She fumbled with the ties on her wrapper as she struggled to stand.

Joseph nodded.

Peter waited, with his hands in his pockets and rocked on the balls of his feet.

Ginny stepped barefoot and blanket-shrouded onto the porch.

Joseph closed the door behind her.

"Ginny." Peter stood erect, his arms at his sides, shivering. "I need you to hear this." She kept her head lowered, as if she was submitting to an axe blow on the back of her neck. *Oh God, Ginny, what have I done to you?* "I don't love Bette. I am not marrying Bette, and I told her so." He kept his feet rooted, but he extended a hand and held it, palm up, in invitation.

A muscle contracted in her jaw.

The blanket fell from her shoulders, exposing her thin nightdress that did a poor job of concealing the shape and contour of Ginny's breasts, belly, and hips.

Peter leaned to pick it up and held the crumpled covering in his hands.

Ginny stretched her hand to his and flicked the tips of her fingers across the hardened tips of his.

Blood rushed to his extremities. He groaned. *Ginny.*

She retracted her hand and secured it behind her back.

A gust of wind rattled a pile of oak leaves and spun them around their feet.

Ginny shivered.

He handed her the blanket and watched her wrap it around herself. Peter drifted to the opposite end of the porch and turned abruptly on the heel of his boot. "Ginny, can you forgive me?"

"Forgive you?"

"For stealing your trust. For using you. I need to know before I ask you something."

"Yes, Peter, I forgive you."

She rose to her full height and righted her shoulders.

She stared with the piercing accuracy she had rallied the day they teamed together to piece a bawling ewe back together. "Ginny, do you love me?" he asked in a voice reserved for mouthing a prayer.

"Do I love you? What does it matter, Peter?"

What does it matter? Oh, God, Ginny, how do I begin to tell you? He cinched his arms around his abdomen in an attempt to quell the urge to retch. "Oh, Ginny, because I love you. I can't live without you. Ginny, will you marry me?" He bent on one knee and reached for her hand.

She knelt and twined her fingers in his. "Marry you? Oh, Peter, marry you and have your babies? And all that goes with that?"

"Yes, and all that goes with that, love." He pulled the blanket around them and embraced her. Every muscle in his body turned gelatinous. He drew a shaky breath, squeezed shut his eyes, and moved his lips over her ear. "You didn't give me your answer. Say yes, or I'll die."

She ran her fingers through his beard and kissed his lips. "Yes. Now, let's tell Joseph and Kathleen."

Peter kissed her forehead. "Yes." He drew her up by his hand, and together, they walked over the threshold of the puncheon-floored cabin.

Chapter 38

Sunshine poured through the frosted windows of the Nickles' cabin, kindled a flush of gratitude in a bride-to-be's heart, and triggered dashes of glimmer along a trending, cuirass silhouette of the sage-green jacket Ginny wore.

The tight-fitting bodice extended beyond her waistline, snugged her hips, and rustled as she smoothed it over her skirt. *Our wedding attire is one more miracle to celebrate today.* She gazed out the window and pressed a palm to her heart.

Last week, Ruta, Nadia, Harriett, and Kathleen had sifted through barrels sent by the Detroit Relief Society. Harriett opened a cask and found opera glasses, a beaded purse, appliqued leather gloves, a Scottish kilt, three elaborately embroidered, child-sized pinafores, five sets of practical woolen underwear, cotton sheets, and one green silk matching jacket and skirt. Ruta's barrel contained several pairs of men's boots and a man's suit, keen enough to wear to a Detroit Boat Club gala or a Parisville wedding.

****

Between the potted ferns in the Pawlowski parlor, Peter stood next to Ginny. Tears shimmered on his eyelashes.

A recovered Father Graca lifted his right hand and made the sign of the cross—the final act in blessing the

413

bride and groom with the sacred sacrament of matrimony.

The newly married groom gathered his bride to his chest and kissed her dewy cheek. "You are my air and my sun. I love you, my wife."

Ginny rose on her toes and tilted her head. "I love you, too, my husband."

He clasped her hands, swallowed, and choked.

She withdrew a lace handkerchief from her jacket pocket and daubed his face from below his eyes to the border of his beard.

"Everyone, let's eat." Ruta ushered the guests to the kitchen for a wedding luncheon of honey-smoked ham, *pierogis* with plum stuffing, sauerkraut, noodles studded with poppy seeds and raisins, beets with horseradish—per Henryk's suggestion—and a cake with real Belgian chocolate made to the specifications of the hostess's long-gone grandmother.

Vodka flowed freely. Toasts rambled unchecked and gained in bawdiness like a snowball gathering girth as it hitched a ride on an avalanche.

Joseph gripped Peter's shoulder. "The going is good now, Peter," he murmured. "This party will go on long before they notice you are gone. You know how the Poles celebrate."

"You're right, Joseph." Peter clapped him on the back. "We'll sneak out like a good newly married couple. Fewer tears that way, too." He watched Ginny turn misty-eyed as she looked around the room. He nodded to Leon and Linda and blew kisses to his nieces and nephews—the newest one nestled in his sister's arms. His heart swelled with love as he thought about their wedding gift.

Shortly before the ceremony, the Nowakowski family arrived with Bertie tethered behind their wagon.

As Linda alit, she handed the new baby to Leon and walked to the wagon's back. She loosened the rope attached to Bertie's bridle and held the reins to Peter. "This is the best solution, brother. You and Ginny need another horse. Bertie needs a new home. Please take him as a wedding present from Leon and me."

Peter took Linda in his arms. "Don't let sorrow drown the love you have to give. We have both earned the right to happiness." He clasped her shoulders, pulled away from his reverie, and reached for Ginny's hand.

She wove her fingers in his and put an arm around his waist.

He led his bride down the Pawlowskis' front porch steps.

Joseph and Henryk waited with Star and Bertie.

"Be off, you two," Joseph wrapped his arms around Ginny and kissed her on the top of her head.

"No dallying, so you get to Brockway Centre before dark." Henryk snapped his suspenders.

Peter squeezed Ginny's hand and brought it to his lips. *Home. We're going home, to forge a life together with our skilled hands and our hopeful hearts.*

****

Peter had delivered their possessions to their new home the week before. Their combined worldly goods amounted to an Isaac Merritt Sewing machine, assorted sewing tools, a blue tin with one hundred dollars, two woolen blankets gifted by the Pawlowskis, an heirloom quilt that had belonged to Ginny's mother, several sets of woolen socks, pants, and shirts from the charity baskets sent to the thumb area fire survivors, an assortment of kitchen paraphernalia from the wives of St. Mary's Parish, and a winter coat and two wool dresses sent from Ginny's friends in New York.

As she stepped into their new home, Ginny's heart swelled. Her thoughtful groom had set dishes in the cupboard, hung curtains in the windows, and made their bed, which caused her to blush. She gazed into Peter's eyes as he seated her at the kitchen table. She had no words but the ones only her eyes and arms could communicate.

"I bet you're hungry. Ruta packed a meal." Peter set a basket on the table. "You really should eat something. It's been a long day."

Ginny nodded. "I'll share a ham sandwich."

"I'll share my life with you, love." Peter kissed her hand.

"Well, in the meantime, would you like mustard on your dinner?"

He laughed. "No, just plain. But you could put butter on the bread. Be right back." He rose, took a few steps, opened a kitchen drawer, and rummaged through a mound of utensils. "Madam, a knife."

She drummed her fingertips on the table and giggled. "That's a button hook."

"Madam, we may have to make do. This is not Taraski's General Store." He extracted two slices of bread and a crock of butter from the basket. Then he plunged the end of the button hook into the butter and spread the creamy substance over the rye bread.

Ginny handed him two generous slices of ham.

Peter slapped together the sandwich, sawed it in two with the button hook, and handed her a half.

"Best ham sandwich I ever had." Ginny smiled and shoved a fallen morsel back into her mouth.

Peter gulped his dinner in five hasty bites and wiped his lips with a napkin his wife handed him.

Ginny pushed aside her plate and thrust back her chair. She raised her index finger to the crown of her head and wound spirals of hair around it. She crossed her legs and then uncrossed them.

Peter coughed. "Would you like some privacy, Mrs. Nickles?"

Ginny jerked her head. She folded her lips tightly to her teeth and studied the floor. She raised her chin and met his gaze. "No. Every moment I can be with you, I will be."

He groaned and lifted her hand and stroked the underside of her wrist. "Let that be how we live the rest of our lives."

She followed him to the bedroom that he had so carefully prepared. "Now, Mrs. Nickles." He brushed the soft fringes of hair from her temple. "We are a married couple." His thick hands fumbled as he worked buttons loose on her bodice.

Her steady dressmaker hands threaded one arm at a time from his jacket.

The smile she prayed for lit Peter's face. The beam that flashed through his eyes indicated muscle rigidity and decisive action. She shuddered.

Their clothing fell to the floor.

Peter carried her to their bed. Still smiling, he nestled beside her between the covers. He turned on his side and lowered his face over her, teasing her with kisses that lingered over eyelids, sucked the end of her nose, nibbled on her sensitive ears, and licked along her cheekbones.

She sighed and gathered his face in her hands, then maneuvered on top of him. She kissed his beet-red nipples, and she licked his hand as he lowered it on her short-cropped hair. "I wish…"

"Shhh…don't say it. I love you and your hair—whatever length. I'm looking forward to being here as your hair grows longer, and as it turns gray, and for the right of protecting every hair on your head for the rest of my life."

She laughed and exhaled warm air on his chest. "I don't remember that as part of our vows." Then, reaching her arms around his back, she feathered the corded scars. "Turn over." She kissed the tracks of raised skin. "I've wanted to do this since the day of sheep shearing. I saw you wash at Pawlowskis' well."

He flipped her over, lay atop her, and kissed her.

His kiss evoked a passion that surpassed all the dreams she had conjured in the lonely life she led before this moment.

"I've wanted to do this since the day you almost murdered some nuns."

His voice was a husky growl, and the vibrations rumbled through her ears and to her feminine sensors. Every remnant of loneliness, doubt, fear, and horror left her mind. Instead, wonderment, rapture, and soul-searing joy sluiced through her as she realized the literal meaning of "and the two shall become one."

Afterward, Ginny sighed and nestled her head in the hollow of his shoulder.

"Right where I want you. I love you, wife."

Moonlight splashed across them through a four-paned window. It illuminated a glittering black sky washed in watercolor splatters of Lake-Huron blue and North-star white.

Ginny pointed an index finger and traced the smattering of blinking stars. She carefully transferred a star at a time to the face of her beloved—a star for each eye, a star for his nose, and four stars for the forever smile that now belonged to her.

Epilogue

The fire that brought so much devastation to Michigan's thumb also brought new life to the area. When Casimir Urdzela said good-bye to his neighbors and headed to Chicago, the price of land rose. Now stripped and cleansed of roots and bramble, the ground held no barriers to plows and became more valuable to incoming farmers.

Three months following the fire in December, a farmer stumbled upon an eight-hundred square-foot sandstone flanking the Cass River. Depictions of birds, mammals, and stick figures holding arched bows etched the rock. The artifact was laid bare whilst the Thumb Fire of 1881 cleared the forage camouflage.

Geologists, geographers, archaeologists, journalists, anthropologists, and sightseers swarmed the area to marvel over the landmark findings that revealed previously unknown histories of Michigan's indigenous peoples. This artifact's discovery substantiated the blood memory Thomas experienced as he fished the Cass River. This spectacle is on Germain Road, eight miles west of Lake Huron. The irony of indigenous people leaving the area following the Great Thumb Fire of 1881, which brought to light their past, went unnoticed.

Father Graca oversaw the third, but not final, construction of St. Mary's Church. Almost one hundred years later, in 1974, the church burned and was rebuilt once again.

Black bears vanished from Michigan's thumb.

Kirtland warblers, partial to the new cone growth in jack pine trees promoted by the cleansing fires, thrived.

The American Red Cross, in its beginning stages after the Thumb Fire, flourishes today, with over six hundred local chapters and five hundred thousand volunteers across the United States. This independent organization prevents and alleviates human suffering, provides disaster relief, blood banks, and assistance to military families.

The C. Andreae and Sons Woolen Mill, later named the Yale Woolen Mill, was immune to the fire of 1881. However, in 1892, the wooden structure burned to the ground. Rebuilt in brick, the longest-lasting of Michigan's full-production woolen mills survived until 1963. Like hundreds of other domestic textile manufacturers, it fell prey to the competition of foreign markets, union wages, and environmental barriers.

A word about the author...

Carol Andreae-Nickles is a novelist living in Western Michigan. She earned a Master's Degree in Clothing and Textiles from Michigan State University and held faculty positions at both Utah and Michigan State Universities. She is a quilt artist and a professional Mrs. Claus.

https://www.carolnicklesauthor.com